A Midwinter's Tale

ANDREW M. GREELEY

A Midwinter's Tale

A TOM DOHERTY ASSOCIATES BOOK
New York

A MIDWINTER'S TALE

This book is printed on acid-free paper.

A Forge Book
Published by Tom Doherty Associates, Inc.
175 Fifth Avenue
New York, NY 10010

Forge® is a registered trademark of Tom Doherty Associates, Inc.

Design by Helene Wald Berinsky

Library of Congress Cataloging-in-Publication Data

Greeley, Andrew M.
    A midwinter's tale / Andrew M. Greeley.—1st ed.
      p. cm.
    "A Tom Doherty Associates book."
    ISBN 0-312-86571-6 (alk. paper)
    1. Irish Americans—Illinois—Chicago—Fiction. 2. Germany—
History—1945–1955—Fiction. I. Title.
PS3557.R358M5   1998   98-21183
813'.54—dc21   CIP

First Edition: October 1998

Printed in the United States of America

0 9 8 7 6 5 4 3 2 1

While Charles Cronin O'Malley did indeed graduate from "St. Ursula" in 1942, as I did, and while our contemporaries did win the city championship at Fenwick High School by beating Tilden, Charles and his family and friends exist only in the world I have created and not in the one God has created. And the conclusion of the Mount Carmel/Fenwick game in 1945 in my world has no similarity to the game in God's world. Everything else in this book is fictional. The story is autobiographical only in that Charles O'Malley and I have lived through the same historical events, he in my world and I in God's world.

We both also have come to believe that She is a comedienne.

The commander of the First Constabulary Regiment in Germany after the war was Col. (later General) Creighton Abrams, one of the most remarkable soldiers the United States produced in this century, much more able than many of the better-known commanders. Like General Meade in this story, he put together a relatively effective unit from unpromising material. However, General Meade is not based on General Abrams.

I am grateful to the late Marvin Rosner, MD, onetime major in the U.S. Army, for his recollections of those times and those places.

For Marilyn, who will remember the times and the people

A Midwinter's Tale

Prologue

Bavaria, August 1947

It was always cold the two years I was in Germany, even during the hot August of 1947. The bitter winter of my first year had permeated my body like a permanent infection. I shivered even in the bright summer sunlight. Germany after the war was like that.

One morning in August with the searing sun shining through the tall windows of the Renaissance palace that was the Constabulary HQ, a tall, skinny, grinning civilian, with an unnaturally red nose, came up to my desk. "You O'Malley, sport?"

"And if I am?" I felt the cold seep in after him.

His eyes were close together, his nose that of a battered hawk, his receding hairline an arrow pointed at my face.

"Clarke, FBI, sport." He flipped a card at me. "Your general said you were to work with me."

I picked up the phone and asked for General Meade.

"He's on some special search someone in Washington wants," the general informed me. "It's important to help him, but keep me informed every day. I don't like him."

"Yes, *sir*."

"See, sport?" Clarke lounged casually against my desk.

"What can I do for you, sir?"

"Well, sport, I got here a special request which the State Department has passed on to my boss. The Russians urgently want some Nazis that are wandering around loose, have a special case on them. And you, sport, are supposed to find them for me."

"I see." I tried desperately to keep my voice neutral. "What's the charge?"

"The Russkies say they're war criminals, whatever that means. I don't care. And you don't either. Just get them for me."

"I'll need some details."

The whole trouble with me, my sister Peggy once informed me, is that my mouth ran ahead of my brain. Her friend Rosie Clancy said that she had it wrong: my instincts ran ahead of my mouth, and that's why I would make a good precinct captain.

She was right on the last point. I have never failed to deliver my precinct for the organization.

"All I have is names and the report that they live above a bakery somewhere in the old section of town."

"Names?" I reached for a pencil with an icy hand.

"Gunther Wülfe, sport, and his wife, Magda, and two kids, girls it looks like." He flashed two square sheets of paper at me, pictures and fingerprints. All four of them in Nazi uniforms, the girls in Hitler Jugend garb. A very much younger and quite unrecognizable Magda. "I want them, sport, and I want them real bad, understand?"

"What will the Russkies do to them?" I asked.

"Shoot the guy probably." He shrugged his shoulders indifferently. "Rape the three women to death. Kids are probably old enough now to provide some fun for their troops."

"Oh."

"They're Nazis, sport." He shrugged again. "You seen Belsen?"

"Yeah." I tried to control my shaking body.

"Anything they get serves them right. You got it, sport?"

"Yeah," I said with no enthusiasm. "I got it."

I felt the pencil slip from my fingers as soon as the FBI agent sauntered away from my desk. I was shivering again, despite the bright sunlight. I had to save them, that I knew. But how—without ending up in Fort Leavenworth myself? Whoever in Washington wanted to turn the Wülfes over to the Russians must want them pretty badly to have sent the FBI drip all the way to Germany.

I had come a long way from Menard Avenue, had I not? Indeed, had I ever lived there?

—ಽ 1 ಽ—

When we lived on Menard Avenue, I used to lie half-awake listening to my parents' conversation after the Bing Crosby program or Amos and Andy.

So I heard their conversation about love between Rosemarie and me.

I slept on an old couch in the enclosed front porch of our small third-floor apartment. My brother, Mike (called Michael by everyone else in the family), five years younger, slept on another couch against the opposite wall after he had graduated from his crib. Thick, royal blue drapes, tattered and worn, were drawn to shut out the street-lights, and an old carpet protected our feet from the concrete floor. In the winter a wheezy electric heater, glowing like a rising sun, and several layers of blankets kept us warm. Dilapidated shades hung on the other side of the glass doors to the living room. The doors would not close tightly so it was easy to hear my parents, but difficult to stay awake and follow what they were saying.

My memories of those days, brought back now so that, remembered, they may exist once again and forever, are hazy and insubstantial. The different time periods in my first twelve years, so long in their duration at the time, are mingled in my recollections. The boundaries between sleep and half-sleep, that magic time when you are still awake to enjoy your dreams, are uncertain. What I actually heard, what I dreamed I heard, what I wanted to hear, what I created because of my later experiences—all are fused in an intricate puzzle over which has been spread a patina of nostalgia, a golden glow of reconstructed joy with an occasional sharp pain.

The conversation I am about to describe certainly happened. I can locate it in time—late summer of 1940: *Knute Rockne, All American*, with Pat O'Brien as the Rock and a kid named Reagan as George Gipp, the Fall of France, the Battle of Britain, the German-

American Bund, boogie-woogie, nylons, the early color movies (*God's Country and the Woman* was the first I saw), talk of a "third term" for Roosevelt, fifty-cent haircuts, and ten-cent beer.

I know the date because it was after our visit to the Clancys' home in Lake Geneva and my disgrace. I was a month short of my twelfth birthday. The worst of the Depression was over, but, as my parents would say, we had thought that before.

Although I recall lines of worry and exhaustion on both their faces, I do not remember anxious conversations about the Depression. Since I would later be obsessed by the Depression and our poverty, it is not likely that I would forget such discussions if they had taken place.

They would occasionally laugh about the day their "ship comes in," a common phrase in those days to anticipate in fantasy a prosperity that no one ever expected to see again.

Mostly their colloquies were interchanges between two good friends who shared many interests, including (though by no means exclusively) the four children for whom they were, surprisingly it seemed to them, responsible and St. Ursula parish, which was the matrix for their family life.

I recall the affectionate sound of their voices, the gentle outer surface of the masks they had adopted in their *commedia dell'arte*: my mother naive and shrewd, my father experienced and realistic. The tones were mere hints of character, and not always accurate revelations of the person behind the persona.

Nonetheless, I find myself on the edge of tears when I re-create, hopefully forever, those lost voices of gentle love.

I cannot recollect quarrels. Later my father would tell me that my mother's temper, once aroused, was a fearsome spectacle. Still later he would explain that I was unlikely ever to see it because she reserved such displays for her bedroom. Yet later he would hint that the reason was that in her personality one strong passion quickly changed to another.

Were these preludes to interludes of intense emotion when they went to their bedroom?

I must ask whether perhaps I came to be as part of one such episode. I know that science does not believe the emotional atmosphere of a conception affects the personality of the one conceived. Moreover it requires hours for sperm to penetrate egg after it has been sent on its frantic rush.

But if I am the result of such an episode of anger turned to violent tenderness, it would explain a hell of a lot.

We loved to listen to the radio after supper and hum along or sing with the music, such as Glenn Miller's "Imaginary Ballroom" and Carmen Miranda's "Begin the Beguine," which I still find myself humming occasionally.

Sometimes they were quiet after the radio was turned off and we children had all gone to bed, not very often. I was not an eavesdropper much less a voyeur. I listened to the voices because they were there to listen to. If perhaps the conversation was about me, what harm was there in knowing where you stood?

Right?

I remember the content of few of their talks, so I must have been the subject only rarely—hardly appropriate for the firstborn son. They did comment on Jane's "first period," which seemed to me, having only the slightest notion what it was, more appropriate for repugnance than for Mom's rejoicing. Often they talked about Peg's beauty and emerging talent on the violin.

"She is special," my father would say.

"And such a dear," my mother would add.

Fair enough. My little sister, Peg, was my favorite person in all the world, Wendy, I thought, to my Peter Pan. She became objectionable only in the company of the Clancy brat.

They did lament one night my failure on the flute.

"But he has a fine voice. I think he'll be a tenor, don't you, dear?"

"He'll be all right."

"And he's clever with his cute little camera, though I don't know what that's good for, do you?"

"He could become a world-famous photographic artist. There are such people, you know."

"Wouldn't that be cute?"

If I had been awake, I would have protested that I didn't want to be a world-famous picture taker. At the threshold of sleep, I think I was flattered.

On that pleasantly cool night in late August of 1940 when they talked of Rosie and me, I was so close to sleep that I almost chose to ignore their exchange even though it seemed to be about me.

Dad: "I don't think there's any chance for the poor little tyke. Her mother drinks and her father is . . . well, you know what he is."

Mom: "She and Peg are like two peas in a pod. They even managed to have their first periods the same week!"

Dad: "They'll probably have their first children on the same night."

Laughter from the two parents.

I look over that bit of dialogue and shake my head. Both little girls were going on ten. I must have remembered that exchange from a later overheard exchange.

You see how hard this "remembrance of things past" is?

Still, I have the major images in this part of the story right. My humiliation that day at Lake Geneva is imprinted on my memory in all its rich detail and will never be erased.

Nor am I likely to forget the first time I ever kissed a girl. Even if I was going on twelve and she was going on ten.

As I type those lines onto my word processor screen, I remember the joy of that moment. I tasted the sweetness of my awakening sexuality, surely; but, even more, I tasted the sweetness of the power of my tenderness to wipe away tears.

As I said to two psychiatrists, one my brother-in-law and one my son, in a late-evening conversation a couple of years ago, "There is no such thing as a latency period between infancy and puberty. A man always wants women, no matter how old he is. During what you guys call latency years, his desire for women is overwhelmed by his fear of them."

They admitted that my position was not unreasonable.

Mom: "She's such a darling child, not really like either of her parents, poor dears."

Dad: "I still can't believe Clarice married him."

Mom: "She wanted to have a child. She thought he'd be kinder than her father. Maybe he is. Remember what the Gypsy woman said: that Clarice would have a little girl who would do great things. Maybe we can help Rosemarie, even if we couldn't help her parents. And she so adores our little Chucky."

Dad: "They're children, April."

Mom: "Children love too. Our Chucky is a devilish little imp, but I think he is really fond of her. He pretends to tease her, but he really is very kind to her."

I think I wondered uneasily, seven-eighths asleep as I was, whether they knew about the final scene of that ugly day at Lake Geneva. I was pretty sure she would tell no one, not even Peg. It was our secret, wasn't it?

Well, we hadn't negotiated about it.

Of course, she told Peg. She told Peg *everything.*

Dad: "If he wasn't, Peg would sock him."

Mom: "I think Rosemarie is trying to adopt us."

Dad: "Not a wise choice, given our finances."

Mom: "Dear, it's not money the poor child is looking for."

Dad: "Well, April, what do we do about her?"

Mom: "We can't turn her away, can we?"

Dad: "I suppose not . . . and Chucky?"

Mom: "Shouldn't we let nature take its course and see what happens? Even now, when he's not being Peck's Bad Boy, they make a cute couple, don't you think?"

Dad (after a contemplative pause): "If we're the only ones who can help her, we certainly should do what we can. Maybe we can save her."

Mom: "Maybe, dear, she'll end up saving us."

Looking back later, I would have liked to think I was furious at their dialogue. How dare they make such decisions about a boy my age. Besides, I felt no emotion for Rosie Clancy other than distaste. She was a spoiled rich brat, the daughter of a wealthy man whom I despised, in great part because of his wealth.

If I had been able to face up to my real feelings in those days, I would have had to admit that Rosemarie was on my mind constantly even then. I pretended to dislike her, but in fact, she dazzled me. Her face, her body, her long black hair, her laughter, her quick wit, her obvious intelligence, had created fascination and fear—in roughly equal parts—in my soul. I think that as I fell asleep that night on Menard Avenue, I knew that somehow our destinies would be intertwined.

I may even have felt happy about that fate.

$$\underline{}\mskip\, 2 \,\mskip\underline{}$$

When I was in high school, I considered the possibility of a vocation to the priesthood because it seemed to me that living without a woman would not have been all that difficult. I chose not to join the Dominican order because my observations had led me to believe that the life of a priest, even in those days of the middle 1940s, was too complicated and disorderly for my meticulous and methodical personality.

I often wonder whether, in the final analysis, the priesthood might have been a wiser choice.

On my junior retreat at the ripe old age of sixteen, I wrote out my "life plan." Since I am an incorrigible paper saver, I still have it:

> I am convinced that I can best serve God and my fellow man by exercising the lay vocation. I will join the service after graduation because it is the obligation of a citizen to defend his country and to obtain veterans' benefits for my college education. When the war is over, I will attend a small Catholic college and major in accounting, a field well suited to my personality and character. I shall work at a part-time job during my college years to amass a certain amount of capital against hard times. After graduation I will go to work for a small and reliable firm of accountants, the kind of firm which is not likely to be engulfed when the Depression returns.
>
> Then I will pass the C.P.A. exam and settle down to a sober and industrious life. I will not smoke or drink or gamble. I will date only occasionally until I am ready to contemplate marriage. I will marry a quiet and loyal woman and ask that God bless us with a large family. We will live in a modest apartment in south Austin. Eventually, when we will have saved enough money, we will buy a convenient house in Oak Park from which I can walk

to Lake Street every morning and thus protect my wife and children from the risks of owning and driving an auto.

All our children will attend Catholic schools, hopefully Fenwick and Trinity.

I hope to lead a decent, sober, productive, and respectable life and to live to see my grandchildren and perhaps a great-grandchild or two.

As I look over that nicely thought-out and carefully expressed statement, I feel a profound admiration for the steady mind and clear eyes of the young man who wrote it. He was sensible and wise beyond his years.

My kids did go to Catholic schools, even to Fenwick and Trinity. I don't smoke; never did, thank God. I avoid gambling unless it is a sure thing, like betting on the Chicago Bulls. I take only a small sip of the creature now and then. And I did join the Army when I graduated from high school in 1946.

All my other resolutions went up in smoke.

In this memoir I will try to explain what happened, though I'm not sure I will be able to do that, even to myself.

I must make clear to the reader that I am not without faults that go a long way toward explaining my bizarre life.

I have a quick mouth, far too quick for my own good. I talk without thinking. Some find this fault charming. I, however, find it dangerous.

I have a bad habit of intervening in other people's problems, again without thinking. Rarely do I bother to wonder whether they might not want my help. In fact I tend to act on occasion like a romantic, a man on a horse with a lance jousting with the bad guys while protecting the good guys—and the good gals, of course. John Wayne in armor. Patently such fantasies are utterly incompatible with my basic identity as an accountant.

Women overwhelm me. For their part they find me "cute" and want to run my life. Rarely, in my perhaps obsessive fascination with them, am I able to resist their plans.

A woman of some importance in this story once remarked to me, "Chuck, you take everything away from a woman—her clothes, her defenses, her modesty, her secrets, her hiding places, her inhibitions, her shame, her will to resist you. She is naked in every sense of that word."

I doubted and still doubt that description.

"So then," I replied to her, "she takes charge of my life and runs it for me."

"Naturally," the woman replied, as though that conclusion followed from her previous remarks with unassailable logic.

Much of my professional career has been devoted to the celebration of women. However, and despite the comments cited above, they remain a mystery to me. Which is as it should be.

The recent article in the *New York Times Magazine* reported to the world that I look like Bob Newhart, a somewhat older contemporary on the West Side of Chicago. Should this comment be accurate—I am not the one to judge—then the similarity is appropriate: like the Newhart persona I am the kind of man to whom things happen, a man whose most sober and grave intentions are swept away by events.

My serious goals, in other words, were swept into comedy by the women in my life, usually in concert with one another.

I never had a chance.

When we were at Twin Lakes that summer, I did not want to visit the Clancy house at Lake Geneva. I resisted the lure of a ride in their big Packard convertible, the enticement of a spin on their Chris-Craft, and a run down the lake in their sailboat. I hated Mr. Clancy. He was, in my moderate judgment, rich and crooked. I lost my protest as I always did.

Rosie certainly had everything a girl could want, every material thing anyway; but she shared her possessions with others generously, compulsively.

"If she wants to give you her dolly, Peg," Mom would say cautiously, "you should accept the gift graciously."

I refused to accept anything from her, not even the model airplane that must have been bought especially for me.

I think I did take a ship model once.

Nor did she insist on her own way. She had strong ideas about what we ought to do next ("Ask Daddy to give us a ride in his speedboat"), but would almost always yield to Peg's suggestions and sometimes to mine.

Even at nine, my sister and my foster sister, as she would become, were young women with robust wills. Instead of fighting, they arrived at quick consensus—often against me. In time I would realize that of the two dominant personalities, Peg was the more dominant.

Later I came to understand that Peg's judgments were essential for Rosie, almost for her life itself.

I always protested, for the record, a visit from Rosie to Twin Lakes or a venture of ours to the Clancys' at Lake Geneva.

Until 1940 my objections were not too vigorous, however. I liked to ride in speedboats too.

In 1940 my objections were more forceful than usual. I really did not want to leave Twin Lakes, speedboat or not. I cannot remember the reason for my resistance. Perhaps something had happened the year before. Moreover it was definitely not fair that Jane and Michael would be dispensed from the trip to the Clancy cottage and I would be constrained to go.

"Rosie expects you, dear," Mom tried to cut short my protests.

"She's a spoiled brat," I insisted.

My memory of that day is vague, perhaps because I know that my behavior was somehow less than heroic.

It was a clear day, rather cool, and with brisk winds. The Battle of Britain had begun. The Republicans had nominated Wendel Wilkie for president, in part because Wilkie's campaign managers had filled the galleries with their own people. We did them one better in Chicago: an employee of the sewer department gained control of the public address system and began to chant "We want Roosevelt!" immediately after the president's message "releasing my delegates." Some of the early polls showed Wilkie winning, although no one in our cottage at Twin Lakes, including the only one who read the papers, thought that he had a chance of winning. None of us thought that the United States would get into the war, though we had fun mocking Roosevelt's accent when he said, "Ah hate wah!"

We didn't mock Winston Churchill's "blood, toil, tears, and sweat" and "we shall fight on the beaches, we shall fight on the landing grounds, we shall fight in the fields and in the streets, we shall fight in the hills; we shall never surrender."

Churchill came to power as the Germans were overrunning Holland, Belgium, France, Denmark, and Norway and driving the English Army out of Europe. Though the Brits would escape in an astonishing evacuation from the French port of Dunkirk, they were in no shape to fight an invasion. In August of 1940, the Germans began a campaign to destroy the Royal Air Force to prepare the way for an invasion. To everyone's surprise the RAF won the Battle of Britain and occasioned another Churchillian outburst: "Never in the field of human conflict was so much owed by so many to so few."

"The man is a fraud," my father said, "but he's got guts."

"They'll have to fight them with shovels," I observed. "They don't have any guns left."

I had laughed at *Road to Singapore* with Bob Hope and Bing Crosby and delighted at Dorothy Lamour in a sarong before we came to Twin Lakes and had been unamused by Chaplin's *The Great Dictator*.

"The man is not funny," Dad said, closing the book of pictures of the New York World's Fair he had been studying. "Not at all."

I knew he wanted to visit the fair. The papers were telling us that the Trylon and Perisphere—a pointed tower and a globe that were the symbols of the fair—also pointed to the future of architecture. He couldn't afford to bring the family to New York. And he would not go by himself.

"I'm not sure that architecture has a future," he said, laughing. "Anyway Twin Lakes is better than New York."

"So long as we don't have to visit Lake Geneva," I added.

No one listened to me.

So that morning we went to Lake Geneva. "I'd much rather see the Trylon and the Perisphere," I said brightly, "than Mr. and Mrs. Clancy."

"Hush, dear," Mom said in a tone that meant I had better keep my big mouth shut.

"*Mom,*" Peg demanded. "Don't let him embarrass Rosie!"

"She's a spoiled brat."

"You heard what your mother said," Dad remarked mildly as we entered Geneva town.

"Everyone is against me," I sighed, relishing the final word.

We skirted the south side of the lake, turned at Fontana, which was still mostly swamp and beach in those days, and drove up to the Clancy "cottage" on the north shore of the lake.

It was maybe fifteen times bigger than our cottage at Twin Lakes. My resentment increased.

Why were they rich and we poor? It wasn't fair. I didn't want money for myself. I wanted it for Mom and Dad.

And Peg.

Mrs. Clancy met us at the door. She was dressed in pink lounging pajamas and looked beautiful in a vague, uncertain way. She welcomed us much like a grand duchess would welcome poor but virtuous peasants. That metaphor reads back into the situation a later judgment. Then I felt more angry than humiliated, angry because somehow it seemed that she had insulted my parents. Especially my mother.

"I'll find Jim," she murmured, suppressing a yawn. "He's probably down by the boats. Margaret Mary, why don't you run along and find Rosie."

"Yes, ma'am." Peg dashed across the lawn at the only speed she knew in those days—all engines forward.

"Still a striking woman, isn't she?" Dad remarked while we waited at the door.

"I thought you'd noticed that," Mom chuckled. "She uses too much makeup and she doesn't have to."

"Meow," Dad imitated a cat.

Mom laughed again. "Only a very mild kitten, dear. She was my best friend once. I wish she still was."

"How can a woman like her stand to . . ."

"With a man like that? I don't know, but there are big ears around here." Mom nodded at me.

"Sleep in the same bed with a toad like Mr. Clancy," I finished the thought for them, beaming brightly, I'm sure.

"Chucky," they said together.

"Don't ever say that again," Mom warned.

"It's not nice," Dad agreed.

"It's true," I insisted.

I'm sure they both wondered whether I knew the full implications of the phrase "sleep in the same bed with."

I didn't, not really. But in the next exchange I worried them even more.

"There are some things, dear"—Mom patted my head—"that we don't say even if they're true."

"Maybe they have separate bedrooms. This house is big enough, isn't it? So is their house at Thomas and Menard. Should I try to find out?"

"*No!*" they both said together.

"Maybe," I said philosophically, "it's better for a husband and wife to have separate bedrooms—if their house is big enough, I mean."

"Maybe it is." Mom couldn't stop laughing now.

"It certainly is not," Dad insisted vigorously.

He was laughing too, sharing some joke that I didn't quite understand—although I wanted to in the worst way.

Further conversation on the subject of the sleeping patterns of the Clancys was halted by the appearance of Jim Clancy, wearing white flannels, a navy blue yachting blazer, and a captain's cap. He looked like a character from *Popeye*.

Or a fat, balding, ugly circus clown.

I'm sure I laughed.

He shook hands vigorously with Dad, kissed Mom on the cheek, and tried to ruffle my wire-brush hair.

I cannot say for certain whether Mom winced when his lips touched her. Kissing friends was less common then than it is now. I know I wanted to punch his fat belly for daring to kiss her. We were invited into the house "for a few moments. Then I'll give the kids the boat rides they're expecting. You *are* expecting a boat ride, aren't you, Chucky?"

"I don't care."

He patted my head. "Sure you care. You *like* boats."

I pulled my head away.

"He likes them," Mom said gently, "but he gets sick on streetcars sometimes. I think you looked a little green on the car ride over here, dear. Are you feeling all right?"

"I feel fine."

Would Mom and Dad like a drink? Maybe some sherry? Couldn't buy this brand here in America, but he knew someone in England. Great stuff. Costs an arm and leg, but worth it, don't you think?

But then what's money for, unless you enjoy it? Easy come, easy go, huh? Let me tell you, John, about a funny thing that happened at the exchange the other day.

I don't remember the story, except that it didn't seem very funny and that Mom and Dad didn't laugh much. Someone had tried to cheat Jim Clancy, and instead he cheated them.

Then he turned to me. "What's the matter with our Cubs this year?"

Whenever Mr. Clancy turned to sports, he became a different person. I couldn't hate him anymore. Instead I felt sorry for him. I understood that he wanted to be friends and didn't know how. As much as I disliked him, I had to help him to be friends for at least a few moments.

"The trades they made after the 1938 season ruined them," I

explained. "Dumb trades. They always make dumb trades. I don't think they'll ever win a pennant again. They won in '32, '35, and '38, and we won't win again ever."

I was wrong. They won, mostly by mistake, in 1945. Since then they have been on a fifty-year rebuilding program.

"How come?" He seemed really worried, almost as though his heart were breaking.

Jim Clancy was a little kid who had never grown up. I think I realized that even then. So I probably adopted the didactic tone I used with other kids when I explained the complexity of Chicago sports.

"Sounds like Bob Elson with a Ph.D.," Dad would often say.

Bob Elson was a perennial Chicago sports announcer who always managed to sound as if he were about to fall asleep.

I pointed out to Mr. Clancy the "front office" problems of the Cubs. I told him that his Lake Geneva neighbor Mr. Wrigley should make gum instead of trying to run a baseball team. I insisted that the Cubs would never hire adequate people to turn the team around because Mr. Wrigley felt he had to know more about baseball than anyone else since he had inherited the team from his father.

"And anyway"—I glared at my smiling father—"I'm a Sox fan."

"What about the Bears?" Mr. Clancy seemed about to cry.

"They should have won last year," I asserted. "They were unbeaten till the play-offs with Washington. Then they got overconfident. This year they're going to get even with the Redskins and everyone else. They have the best players, and no one has figured out how to stop the T formation. They may even," I admitted reluctantly, "beat the Cardinals."

That was in the time when the Cardinals were a Chicago team, long before they went off to St. Louis, for which God forgive them says I. And then to Phoenix, which is welcome to them.

"Gee, I hope you're right," he said wistfully.

"I'm right. Here, let me show you, Mr. Clancy." I grabbed a paper napkin from the table on which the expensive sherry bottle had been placed. "The quarterback—that's Sid Luckman from Columbia—takes the ball. The halfback goes in motion this way, the defense tries to cover him. Either the quarterback gives the ball to the fullback, who goes through here, or if they try to plug up the center, then he throws a pass to the halfback. You can't stop it."

"The quarterback is Jewish, isn't he?"

"Yeah, like Marshal Goldberg on the Cardinals. They're very smart people."

"They work hard, but you can't always trust them."

I saw my mother's lips tighten.

"You can't always trust the Irish either." I folded up the napkin.

Mom smiled proudly. Dad winked.

"Well, hey," Mr. Clancy pounded me on the shoulder, "let's go for a boat ride. Speedboat first, huh? Let's find the dames, they're probably afraid anyway, huh?"

"I don't think," I said reverently, "that those two hellions are afraid of anything."

"Chucky!" Mom did her best to be serious. "Such terrible language!"

"Well," I insisted stubbornly, "it's true."

Jim Clancy, even in those days, struck me as a strange, complicated little man. I despised him and still felt sorry for him. I didn't like the way he looked at Mom, though I couldn't say exactly what I didn't like about it. I didn't like his crass display of wealth. I didn't like the feel of his clublike hand on my head. Yet I also understood, dimly maybe, how sad and unhappy he was and tried to go along with his little game of being a kid just like me.

Only he was a mean kid.

His boat was a brand-new Higgins, an enormous twenty-two-foot speedboat with an eight-cylinder Chrysler inboard marine engine and three cockpits. Mom and Dad begged off and sat on the pier to watch us. Mrs. Clancy drifted to the pier, uncertainly, it seemed to me, followed by a black lady with a couple of trays of little sandwiches.

"Girls in the backseat, boys in the front seat," Mr. Clancy ordered.

Rosie frowned at that order, but jumped in the rear cockpit anyway—gracefully and noisily. Peg followed with a little bit more delicacy. Jim Clancy unraveled the bow line with considerable difficulty.

"Cast off the stern line, Rosie," he ordered.

"I already have," she replied.

He jammed the throttle into reverse and backed away from the pier with a vigor like that which, I imagined, the *Queen Mary* would have displayed.

Or like a teenager a few years later, peeling rubber in front of his girlfriend's house.

My head jerked back. I felt a touch of the motion sickness that had bothered me during the ride from Twin Lakes to Lake Geneva.

However, the small waves of Lake Geneva were no match for the two hundred and fifty horses inside the Chrysler. We roared from the Fontana end to the Geneva end of the lake and back in less than ten minutes.

I didn't have the nerve to turn around and see how the girls were reacting. I hung on for dear life and loved every second of it.

Weak stomach or, as I know now, weak inner ear or not, I reveled in the power of the engine, the rush of the wind, the boiling wake cutting out on either side, the sense that I was almost flying over the water.

The sailboat was the problem. Now I remembered why I didn't want to visit the Clancys at Lake Geneva. The last time I had barely escaped the sailboat with my dignity. I didn't want to risk it again.

Peg and Rosie jumped out of the Higgins, deftly secured the lines, and stood side by side, staring at me still in the front cockpit. I was healthy, mind you, but daunted by the prospect of the sailboat.

Maybe it would rain.

Alas, not a cloud in the sky.

Rosie extended a hand. She was wearing, I remember, a white blouse and light blue shorts.

I climbed out by myself.

"Great fun."

The two she-demons had the gall to giggle.

Mrs. Clancy had disappeared, for the day it later developed. My parents were sitting under a beach umbrella, towels around their shoulders. My mother looked pretty, I thought, in her imitation-sharkskin swimming suit—"old and out of fashion, I'm afraid, but I still fit in it."

"Had a swim while we were running over to Geneva," Jim Clancy shouted exuberantly. "Ready for a bite of lunch?"

He looked around for his wife.

"I'll get the stuff, Daddy." Rosemarie was already running toward the house. The pier shook under her thundering feet.

"I'll help." Peg raced after her.

"Don't forget the chocolate ice cream," I shouted after them.

I devoured three ham-and-cheese sandwiches and two slices of chocolate cake drenched in chocolate ice cream and covered with chocolate sauce.

"You'll be real fat someday if you keep eating like that." Rosemarie shook her long black hair.

I almost said, "Not as fat as your fat and ugly father," remembered my manners, laughed, and returned to my lecture about the Chicago Bruins, the Halas family's pro basketball franchise in those long-forgotten days.

As best as I can remember, I was against them on the general principle that their name and their owners if nothing else suggested a link with the Bears and the Cubs.

I considered asking for a third slice of chocolate cake. I had been told by someone that motion sickness was less likely if your stomach was full. On the other hand if it was too full, it might turn against me even without the motion of the sailboat.

Moreover, a cruel heaven had not only not sent rain; it had arranged for the wind to increase—"freshen up" as Mr. Clancy said.

At no point did it ever occur to me to say that I did not want to join them in the sailboat or that I would probably become ill on the sailboat. The thought of such reasonable responses did not even occur to me.

"Rosie"—Mr. Clancy stood up as if he were the skipper of the _Titanic_—"let's have a little run under sail. Why don't you load some ice cream bars on the boat. We can have more dessert on the way."

I had paid no particular attention to his intake of food during lunch, but it had certainly exceeded mine.

The sailboat was a small craft of a variety I haven't seen since after the war. She was made of wood (in those days, what else?), perhaps fourteen feet long, shallow draft, lightweight, little more than a skiff with a wooden mast and a sail. Something like a dory or perhaps an undersized lightning class. She was fast and agile and easy to steer.

Also easy to capsize.

We were instructed to put on swimming suits. I was embarrassed because, unlike my trim fellow crew members, I felt I was scrawny.

But I wasn't funny like Mr. Clancy in his red-and-white one-piece suit, which made even my charitable mother smile.

The sails were canvas and had to be packed and unpacked in precise fashion. Mr. Clancy barked orders to Rosemarie about rigging the sails. Usually, I noted, she had anticipated the orders. She seemed proud that she knew how to play the crew game, a full-fledged partner in her father's sailboat adventure.

At going on twelve you begin to notice the quality of relationships between your friends and their parents. Rosie liked her father, or so it seemed, and desperately wanted his approval for her skill with the boat. Yet some of the time she also seemed to detest him.

He did not notice either the skill or the look in her eyes that pleaded with him for a word of praise.

"Okay," he shouted, "Rose, you man the mainsheet and I'll take the tiller. Peg and Chuck, you sit athwart and duck your head whenever we turn so you don't get hit by the boom." He laughed, I thought maliciously, and patted the thick wood boom. "It's pretty hard on heads. And everyone put on life jackets."

He shoved us away from the pier, yelled, "Hoist the mains'il," and shoved the tiller around sharply.

We almost capsized on the spot. Only Rosie's quick movements with the sails kept us from going over.

Mr. Clancy, I now remembered from the previous summer's adventure, didn't know much about sailing. It had been a calm day last summer too.

My stomach was already queasy.

The first run across the lake and back was easy enough. I began to relax.

"You take the tiller, Rosie," he shouted. "Let's see how you can do in this wind."

Without a change of expression, she shifted into the helmsman's place in the stern.

Mr. Clancy opened the freezer box, helped himself to an ice cream bar, and offered one to Peg.

Peg never turned down free food.

He turned to me. "How about you, Chuck? Stomach okay?"

I was sure that he had leered at me.

"It's fine, but no thanks."

"He ate too much at lunch," Peg explained.

Rosie did quite well at the tiller, especially for a ten-year-old, better than her father I thought.

The boat had heeled over pretty far and was running with its edge only a few inches above the wake.

"This is really living!" Mr. Clancy exclaimed.

Peg calmly dispatched her ice cream bar. Rosie kept her eyes on the edge of the sail.

Chucky began to get sick. Alas, real sick.

As motion sickness sufferers know, the first feeling is a kind of generalized unease, then tenseness, then a foolish conviction that you are not sick, then the desire to die immediately a peaceful and a happy death. At the end of Rosie's run across the lake I had reached that point. Peg was watching me carefully, not sure whether to call the game on account of darkness.

"One more time across the lake and we'll be finished," Mr. Clancy sang out. "Let me take the helm, honey, I think the breeze is too much for you."

"Yes, Daddy." She clambered back to her station at the sheet, ready to release and draw in the sail when it was time to turn.

I almost made it on the first leg of the run. Only when Mr. Clancy shouted, "Ready about," and Rosie released the sail, did my lunch begin to demand its proper freedom.

"Hard alee!" he bellowed, and shoved the tiller.

Rosie pulled in the sail and I threw out my lunch.

"Chuck!" Peg's arm was around me immediately. "Are you all right?"

"Never been better," I said bravely as I retched again.

"Can't take the wind, eh, Chucky?" Mr. Clancy crowed.

I don't think he had intended to make me sick. But now that I was sick, he was enjoying it.

Rosie watched me grim faced.

By the time we had returned to the Clancy pier I had lost all my lunch. But my intestines were still protesting.

"Ready about!" Mr. Clancy bellowed in front of the pier.

"*No!*" Rosie screamed at him.

"Hard alee!"

Automatically Rosie hauled in the sheet. If she had tried to stop us, I suppose we would have capsized and I would have drowned.

A blessing it would have seemed.

The final run across and back was one long episode of nausea, much worse than the worst purgatorial images of the nuns at St. Ursula. This is what God must do to the damned that he particularly did not like. Peg's arm was my only link to the world of the living.

Finally, the sails were lowered and we drifted to the pier.

The worst was over. My stomach had, not unreasonably, given up on me. I was exhausted, drained, despairing—but over the worst.

"Here, Chucky, have one of these." Mr. Clancy shoved an ice cream bar under my nose. "It will help settle your stomach."

I was in hell and the devil was laughing at me.

I retched again, discovered some residue of breakfast deep in my gut, and covered myself, the ice cream bar, and Peg with my sickness.

Not, alas, Mr. Clancy.

That was when Rosie hit her father.

Sobbing hysterically, she beat his back with her tough little fists. "You did it, you did it, you did it," she wailed.

Then she leaped out of the boat and, still crying, ran up the walk to the house.

Peg started after her, hesitated, and then returned to me. She and Mom and Dad lifted me out of the boat and dragged me to a chaise lounge under a big oak tree. Peg covered me with a beach blanket.

"Just go to sleep, dear," Mom murmured. "You'll be fine after a nice little nap."

"I'll never eat chocolate again," I whimpered. "Never again."

Well, not till the next day.

Later, maybe an hour or so, I woke up. Peg was sitting on the grass next to me, watching me intently.

"You okay?"

"Is this Mount Calvary Cemetery?" I asked.

"You're okay," she sighed with relief. "Chucky, I felt *so* sorry for you."

"Where's everyone?"

"Mrs. Clancy is in her room." Peg wrinkled her nose. "Mr. Clancy left in his car. Mom and Dad went for a walk. Rosie's somewhere crying still. I leave her alone when she gets that way."

I didn't know that she got that way.

"I'm all right," I lied.

"I'll go look for Rosie, if you're sure you're all right."

"I *said* I was all right."

So poor Peg went in search of her other charge.

That was the first time that I can remember that I felt that I would very much like to kill Jim Clancy. I remembered that day vividly when I learned years later that he had been blown into thousands of pieces by a car bomb and I experienced not the slightest grief.

After a few moments I decided that maybe I ought to find out whether I would ever walk again. I stood up, wobbled slightly, and ambled uncertainly along the lakeshore into a stand of trees between the Clancy property and the house next door. I thought I might find Mom and Dad there, holding hands as they often did when they thought no one was looking.

Instead I found Rosie, leaning against a tree, still crying.

I felt sorry for her.

"It's okay, Rosie." I put my arm around her as Peg had put hers around me. "Don't cry. It wasn't your fault."

It seemed perfectly natural to put my arm around the poor little kid. So too it seemed perfectly natural for her to lean her head against my chest and begin sobbing again.

"It's all right, I'm not mad at you," I repeated, and held her until finally the sobs stopped and her heartbeat slowed.

It also seemed perfectly natural to kiss her then, first her cheek and then her lips—a light, childish touch of my lips against hers.

Not clumsy though. I was astonished that I was not clumsy at all.

Much later in my life a psychiatrist (not treating me, incidentally) would explain that I had learned from my father and had practiced in my own "very intense" relationship with my mother the art of being gentle with women. It would be hard for me, the shrink said, to behave spontaneously in any other way with a vulnerable woman.

"That makes you a very dangerous man."

"Who, me?"

"Women tend to be pushovers for men who know how to be tender at the right times."

I guess.

Anyway, Rosie turned crimson, beamed happily, and said, "Thank you, Chucky."

That was that.

Anyway, kissing a girl cures nausea. Well, it did that day.

We walked back to the house and found the rest of my family. Peg begged her to join us for dinner; after some hesitation, Rosie rushed up to her mother's room, obtained permission, and jumped in her mother's car for the chauffeured ride back to Twin Lakes.

"I think Chucky still looks a little peaked." Mom considered my face anxiously.

"Chucky is so nice when he's sick," Rosie chuckled. "Maybe he should be sick all the time."

She was still glowing and her eyes were filled with stars.

4

When I was growing up, the sobriety about which I wrote in my Fenwick retreat resolutions was not the result of the good example of my parents. They represented two decaying, not to say decadent, Chicago lace-curtain Irish families. They firmly believed that, if one had to slide down the social ladder, one ought to do it with style. Noisy style.

My mother was a Cronin, a niece of the Dr. Cronin who was killed in an Irish-nationalist fight during the 1880s. Her father was also a doctor, who lived in the Canaryville section of the South Side, a pillar of St. Gabriel's parish and a great friend, in his youth, of the legendary Father Maurice Dorney, the founder of the parish, a great friend of organized labor, and the man responsible for building a Burnham church in the shadow of the Yards.

"The smell of the Yards," she would say, laughing, "is what puts the color in our cheeks in Canaryville."

(The name, by the way, referred originally to swarms of noisy sparrows that settled each year just east of the Yards, and somewhat north of St. Gabriel's at Forty-fifth and Wallace. Only later did the term extend to the whole neighborhood and especially to the Irish who lived in it.)

"Canaryville," she would continue, groping around her littered worktable for her glasses, "is not to be confused with Back of the Yards, which is *west* of the Yards, or New City, which is *south* of the Yards, or Bridgeport, which is *north* of the Yards."

She would then find her glasses and examine the sock she was darning, astonished that the sock was gray and the thread brown.

"New City is German, Bridgeport has a lower class of Irish, and there are foreigners in Back of the Yards."

In 1940, when I imagine this paradigmatic scene taking place, my mother was thirty-four years old, tall, brown-haired, thin but not quite gaunt, with the cheekbones, jaw, and elegant manners and the slightly dotty approach to life one might have expected from an exiled White Russian countess, not that I would have known in those days what a White Russian countess was. Her habitual clothes were long skirts and sweaters whose colors never matched. She must have realized that the two-bedroom, third-floor apartment in the ten hundred block of North Menard was a big step down from the sprawling, Victorian, three-story home at 4502 Emerald (her father had purchased it from Gustavus Swift when the packinghouse barons migrated from the "Village of Lake" to Kenwood) in which she was raised in Canaryville. Nor could it be compared to the magnificent Doric-revival brick home on the park behind the Austin Town Hall to which she had brought Jane and me home from West Suburban Hospital, only a few blocks away.

Our flat was small and cramped. Before 1938, our ice was delivered through a hatch on the back porch. We kids hated the day our secondhand Serval refrigerator appeared because we knew we would miss the "iceman." He lugged blocks of ice up the stairs on his back and dumped them through the "ice door" into the "icebox" inside, a metal-lined wooden cabinet that anticipated the modern refrigerator. He always had a kind word and a joke for us, poor man, too old for such hard work but knowing no other way to earn his living.

For Mom the fridge was a welcome relief from some of the worries and strains of housework—an ironing board in the kitchen, walks up and down four flights of stairs to the basement to a primitive washer with a hand-operated "wringer" through whose rollers clothes were passed after they were washed, heavy clothes baskets to drag out into the concrete backyard, laundry hung by wooden clothespins on lines that had to be put up after each washing, hot-water heat in noisy radiators fed by a coal furnace that left a fine layer of dark dust on everything in the house.

We were better off than many. We had inside plumbing and our dark apartment was lit by enough electric lights (some fixed to the now unused gas jets) that one could read after dark. But Mom had never lifted a finger at housework until the "Crash."

I may have minded more than she did. I suppose my passion for money and order must have resulted from being very young but conscious enough when this dramatic change occurred in her life. As a little boy I must have been furious at what had happened to her. I wanted money so that I could restore her to those happy days in the house behind the Town Hall.

If the setbacks bothered her, she never let anyone else know about her discouragement. "Refinement," she told us often, "has nothing to do with how much money you have or where you live. It's part of your character."

Even in those days I wanted to marry a woman like my mother, only one who was better organized and less absentminded. A wife like April Mae Cronin but one who would keep the house neat as well as herself and her children.

The coal furnace in the basement had to be fed by hand, a task that the other members of our family routinely forgot. So it was quite possible that they would wake up on a near-zero morning shivering with the cold: no coal in the furnace.

And even worse, no coal in the coal room because we had forgotten to call the coal man (on our wall-mounted four-party-line phone).

When I was old enough to assume responsibility for a morning paper route, I would go first to the basement and shovel coal into the furnace. And if the coal supply was running low, I would make a note in my notebook (carried even then) to call the coal man later in the day.

"And Englewood?" My father would look up from his Shakespeare and sip on his glass of port.

Mother would make a gentle face of displeasure, skin tightening over her high cheekbones.

"Lace-curtain, people with pretensions."

Dad would howl with laughter and drain the port. "Which the Cronins were not."

"Well"—Mom would smile sweetly—"we did have some lace in our house, but no pretensions." The sweetness would acquire a sly tinge: "Not like the West Side Irish."

And they'd both laugh together, often ending with an affectionate kiss.

My mother's snobbery, like everything else about her, was amiable and kindly. *Foreigners* was a term applied to anyone who was not Irish, with the sometime exception of the Germans. (Protestants did not figure in the calculus because they were not important folks in the lives of the Chicago Irish at that time.) They were not bad people; you would never treat them unkindly and certainly never exclude them from your house. Given enough time, they would become as American as anyone else—meaning as American as we were. Indeed Mom found "foreigners" fascinating, puzzled as she was by the fact that anyone would choose to be a foreigner.

"They really are," she would assure us with a benign smile, "very nice people."

When I was in fourth grade, 1938, I came home from school one night during the week before Halloween and announced proudly, "We waxed that dirty kike Fineman's windows for him. He'll never get them clean. Serves the hebe right."

Later I would learn to my dismay that I had become a bigot at about the same time of *Kristallnacht*, the night of the first major Nazi anti-Semitic outburst in Germany.

"Don't ever say those words again in this house." My mother took off her glasses and stared at me. "I won't tolerate them, Charles Cronin O'Malley. I am not raising any bigots, do you understand?"

"I'm not a bigot," I pleaded, near tears because Mom never shouted at me.

"Yes, you are. Now you go right back to that little dry-goods store and apologize to Mr. Fineman and clean every last bit of wax off his window."

"Why?" I wailed.

"Because Jews are every bit as good as us, aren't they, Vangie?"

"A little better, maybe. They work harder." No help from my father, that was obvious.

"Jesus was Jewish." Mom was still angry at me.

"So was his mother," I said brightly.

"The Finemans are his relatives. Now go clean their window."

Mr. Fineman, a little man with a gray face and dark, dark brown eyes, accepted my apology graciously. "So"—he waved his hands— "boys will be boys. You're a good boy, you apologize. Why should you clean it up?"

"I didn't know those were bad words," I said honestly enough.

"You're a sweet child," said his plump little wife, "such cute red hair. You go home and tell your mother that I said so."

"Mom won't let me back in the house unless I clean the window." I was beginning to understand what we later called ethnic diversity. "You know what Irish mothers are like."

They both thought that remark was much funnier than I did. So they let me clean the windows.

So they gave me chocolate ice cream with chocolate sauce and chocolate cookies and a chocolate candy bar.

"Eat them," Mrs. Fineman said, "chocolate is good for you. It gives you energy."

"Yes, ma'am." I slurped up my reward. "May I wax your windows tomorrow?"

"Such a cute little boy. Isn't he a darling?"

"Your mother"—Mr. Fineman pointed his finger at me—"is the classiest lady in the neighborhood."

"Yes, sir," I agreed. "She says you're God's relatives."

They both laughed joyously at that.

"So we have clout?"

"You sure must."

I went back often to their store after that to volunteer to run errands for them. They wanted to pay me, but I would accept only one Hershey's bar.

Well, sometimes, maybe two.

Mom had attended St. Xavier's Academy and then Normal School (later Chicago Teachers College and still later Chicago State University) in Englewood, even though the position of a teacher (like that of a nurse) was a bit beneath her social level. But her justification for that loss of caste was that she wanted to be a music teacher, even if that meant sitting in classrooms at the three-year college with foreigners.

"They really enjoyed my harp." She would pause in her darning. "Sometimes"—another soft smile, suggesting enormous understanding and tolerance—"I think foreigners appreciate music and the arts more than we do."

"Especially your Polacks!" My father would fill up his port again.

"Dear, the *children!*"

"Please call them *Poles*, Daddy." My older sister, Jane, would frown with mock primness. "You don't want us children to pick up bad habits, do you?"

Then they'd all laugh.

Jane, going on fourteen, astonished and delighted by the womanly body that had suddenly become hers, knew the lines in our improvised family comedy. It was her role to feed them to the principal actors while I played straight man and Peg and Rosie Clancy watched from the box seats with wide eyes and ready laughter.

April Cronin was really not designed for this world. She was most content when her long, graceful fingers were moving across the strings of her beloved harp. She should have gone to the Chicago Conservatory as Margaret Mary, her younger daughter, would do after the Second War, playing the violin in that august institution on Saturday mornings even when she was a pregnant college student. But such a choice was even more beyond the ken of the Canaryville Irish after the First War as was attendance at the University of Chicago—a choice exercised by her contemporary James T. Farrell.

"Oh, I knew Mr. Farrell," she would tell us after playing the harp at the end of the day. "Not well. And I knew the poor boy on whom Studs Lonigan was based; his father repainted our house once."

"What I want to know"—Dad would lean back in his springless easy chair and examine Mom through the ruby colors of his port—"is whether you know the real Lucy Scanlan."

"Of course I did." She would pick out a cord on the harp that sounded like love or maybe an invitation to love. "She is a dear, sweet woman, a few years older than us. Even nicer than Mr. Farrell makes her in the book."

"Has she read the book?" my father would demand, turning the port glass in his fingers.

"Do you know, dear"—with a sigh Mom would put the harp in its sacred place against the "parlor" wall—"I've never had the courage to ask her? I guess I didn't want to spoil the story."

"Well"—he grinned like Mephistopheles, a puckish demon with egg-bald head and vast red eyebrows—"maybe, dear, we shouldn't be discussing a dirty book in the presence of the kids."

"It's *not* a dirty book—yes, just a tiny sip of port; oh, that's too much"—but she didn't pour it back into the chipped Waterford decanter—"not nearly so dirty as those terrible books you read by Mr. Joyce and M. Proust."

"Mother," Jane, bursting with her old wit and her new full-figured sexual energy, came in right on cue, "how do you know that the books are terrible, unless you've read them too?"

"Your mother"—Dad refilled his Waterford goblet (designed for claret, not port)—"particularly likes Molly Bloom's fade-out in Mr. Joyce's book."

"Vangie . . ." Mom blushed and shook her head with the despair a mother might display over a cute but mischievous boy child.

Dad's name was John the Evangelist O'Malley, John the Evangelist Mark Luke O'Malley—a three-of-a-kind label that for some reason discriminated against St. Matthew. Mom called him Vangie only occasionally and almost always with a blush. Dad was always faintly disconcerted when she used the nickname, but, mysteriously to me in those days, pleasurably so. In later years I would realize that it was a pet name in which there were strong overtones of sexual invitation.

Born in 1900, Dad was five years older than Mom, just old enough to be accepted as a volunteer (lying about his age) in the Army in the spring of 1918 after he had graduated from St. Ignatius College, as the good Jesuit high school was known in those days (with two extra years added on so that many young men went straight to law school or medical school after graduation). He was sent to Camp Leavenworth, Kansas, where in the autumn as the war in Europe ended, men would collapse and die on the parade ground every morning from the "plague of the Spanish lady" as the 1918 flu was called.

"I used to worry a lot, just like you do now, Chucky," he would say to me with his expansive grin, one hand resting on his rather large belly. "Then it was my turn to collapse on the parade ground, November twelfth, 1918, the day after the war ended. I remember thinking that it was a nice irony to die from a bug after the shooting was over."

"Why didn't you die, Daddy?" Jane, the most lighthearted and merry of the family, could be counted on to have her lines letter-perfect, even if she had to work at being properly serious on the subject of our father's escape from death.

Dad would laugh loudly, swallow another sip of sherry or port, and say, " 'Cause God didn't want your mother, who was then an innocent little freshman at the Academy, to go through life as a spinster."

Laughter from everyone but Chucky.

"You flatter yourself, dear," Mom would giggle. "I had lots of suitors."

Dad would wave his massive paw, dismissing them as inconsequential. "They were in no rush to carry me off the parade ground to the base hospital. They figured I was dead already and the hospital was overcrowded anyway. I remember one medical orderly saying to another, 'This kid is dead already.' I tried to explain to him that I wasn't, but, tell the truth, I thought I might be. I couldn't move, I couldn't talk, I felt like I was going to bed on Christmas Day for a long nap. Some people"—he would shrug his big shoulders—"made it and some didn't. That's when I made up my mind that my worrying days were over. Isn't that right, dear?"

Mom would smile affectionately. "You certainly haven't worried for more than five minutes since the morning you proposed to me."

More laughter.

"Will the Spanish lady ever come back?" I would ask somberly, ready even then to take the grim view.

"Oh, Chucky, you're so silly," Rosemarie Clancy, who was even then hanging around our house, would protest because I had spoiled the story. Rosie loved stories and I loved facts.

"Let's hope not, dear," Mom would say, also a bit disappointed in me. "And pray to God."

Dad left the Army in the spring of 1919, his red hair already vanishing from the top of his head. He enrolled in the Illinois National Guard and in Armor Institute, one of the forerunners of Illinois Institute of Technology. The National Guard was an excuse to ride in the Black Horse Troop during Chicago parades. Armor Institute was an excuse to be a painter. His father's family had come to Chicago before the Civil War and, unlike most Irish immigrants, had made common cause with "Mr. Lincoln"—as Grandpa O'Malley called him, much as if he were a next-door neighbor—and the Republican Party. Grandpa, once a Republican county commissioner, had become a federal judge, an old man with a white beard like Chief Justice Hughes, and a stern, almost Protestant, instinct for sobriety and decorum. He dismissed his son's inclination to scrawl cartoons as harmless and insisted that if he wanted to be "artistic," he ought to study architecture. Dad, like running water, followed the path of least resistance, and enrolled in the Institute. His mother, an immigrant Irish maid who had done a reasonably good job of educating herself after her marriage, surreptitiously encouraged her son to continue his painting.

As long as Dad had his paintbrush and Mom her harp, there were no insurmountable problems in the world. The cranky old Philco console that occupied a large part of our living room in the flat on the ten hundred block of Menard played all day long, normally blaring the current hit tunes such as "Jeepers Creepers," "September Song," and the memorable "Flat Foot Floogie (with the Floy Floy)." But I was the only one who heard the newscasts about the fall of Barcelona in the Spanish Civil War. (Like *The New World*, the Catholic paper in Chicago, I was, at the age of ten, a supporter of the Spanish Republic.)

The war between the right and left in Spain caused the deaths of half a million people, mostly civilians. Both Germany and Italy on the one hand and Russia on the other became involved, tried out tactics, and struggled for control of Spain. The left (the Spanish Republic) murdered priests and nuns by the thousands; the right (the Rebels or the Nationalists) bombed cities and killed civilians. The right won the war. Its leader, General Franco, cleverly stayed out of World War II, though his sympathies were certainly with Germany and Italy.

The rest of the family hardly noticed the deal with Hitler at Munich. In 1938, British prime minister Neville Chamberlain made a deal with Hitler at Munich that turned over substantial parts of Czechoslovakia to Germany in return for a guarantee from Hitler of "peace in our times." Hitler didn't keep his promise, and the Munich agreement has ever since been a symbol of the folly of appeasement.

The rest of the family was too busy singing and dancing, storytelling and drinking, painting and playing the harp, to pay much attention to the invasion of Poland, the German blitzkrieg into the Low Countries in the spring of 1940, the fall of Paris, the collapse of France. The day Paris fell—I heard a cop say to the local druggist, "It makes you wonder whether there is a God"—the Philco was

firmly turned off in the middle of H. V. Kaltenborn's funereal news-
cast so that the evening harp session could begin.

"Forget your silly old war," Rosie Clancy snapped at me.

In 1940, Rosie was a diminutive, black-haired banshee with a
pinched face, flashing eyes, and a furious temper—an angry Gypsy
princess from a musical film. Her family lived in the most elaborate
home on the block—the only two-story house on a street of bun-
galows and two-flats—a yellow-brick fortress with casements and
turrets from which, in my imagination, guns were trained on all of
us who walked by en route to St. Ursula's school. I suppose I should
add, in yet another effort at candor, that in my romantic dreams, I
was the brave knight who rescued the Princess Rosa Maria from the
evil warlock who had imprisoned her in a tower.

Rosie's mother drank, not the way my parents did, not several
drinks before and after supper every night, but all day, starting at
breakfast.

"The poor little thing," my mother would again sigh, "is going
to be a real beauty too, like her mother was. She'll break a lot of
hearts." When she was ten years old, you did not argue with the
Princess Rosa Maria, whom I thought of as a spoiled little brat, not
even when she interrupted Kaltenborn's obsequies for Paris.

The only times the Philco wasn't blaring during the daylight
hours was when one of its tubes blew out. Then it would remain
sullenly silent for days—until I pointed out that it wasn't working.

"Mustn't cut you off from Bob Elson and the White Sox," Dad
would mumble, searching among the bits of paper stuffed into his
pockets, some of them from many years before, for money with
which I could run off to Division Street to buy a new tube. He was
a Cubs fan and could not comprehend why I would support a team
that hadn't won since 1919.

After I began working my newspaper route, I bought the tubes
myself.

My parents' wedding must have seemed a match with great prospects indeed. The bride and groom were the handsome and gifted
offspring of two distinguished Chicago Irish families. Good history
was behind them and good promises were in front of them.

During the Depression and the war I don't think either of them
felt their prospects were at all blighted. Mom did her own washing

and ironing, mended our clothes on her pedal-operated Singer, and strove cautiously if without too much skill to make ends meet. The journey from the forty-five hundred block on Emerald to the ten hundred block on Menard was from genteel affluence to genteel poverty. Mom and Dad hardly noticed.

She always thought we lived in the eleven hundred block on Menard. If Augusta was ten hundred north, she would argue, then the houses north of it ought to be eleven hundreds.

That's the way it was on the South Side, anyway.

In 1940, Dad was a big, husky, bald man with a large belly that did not seem so much fat as strong. He looked like pictures I had seen of Irish rural horse-traders. Later, during the war, he would lose weight.

"Vanity," he would chuckle. "I don't want to look like Major Blimp."

"Colonel Blimp," I would correct him, to the amusement of everyone but Rosie Clancy.

"I think you look wonderful, Mr. O'Malley," she would thunder, "no matter what Chucky says. He's just angry because he's so short."

Still later Dad would grow a fierce red beard, which eventually turned white. Then he looked like the abbot of a Trappist monastery.

He had worked on the plans for the Chicago Century of Progress World's Fair (the fourth star in the city flag, if you hadn't realized it) and supervised repairs on the fair during the summers of 1933 and 1944. "Broke my heart when they tore it down," he would say, shaking his head sadly. "We beat that man Nice or whatever his name is to modern architecture."

Dad was not exactly a fan of the Bauhaus, to put it mildly, and despised Mies and all his works, except the Lake Shore Drive apartments: "Well, they look pretty, April dear, but you wouldn't want to live in them."

At the end of the fair he found himself out of work with four children in the midst of the Great Depression. All our grandparents were dead, their resources wiped out in the Crash, as the stock market collapse was called. The house by Town Hall was sold and we moved into our crowded, chilly flat on Menard.

Fortunately for Dad he had converted to the Democratic Party, secretly, to vote for Al Smith in 1928, and openly, after the death of his parents, in 1932 to vote for FDR, as he was always called at our house, and the repeal of the prohibition amendment.

"It wasn't economics, to tell the truth," he would chortle later, "nor the hope of a job, if you take my meaning. It was the drink, don't you see? It cost too much, even if I did meet your mother in a speakeasy in Walworth, Wisconsin."

"That's not true, darling," Mom would say, blushing. "You'll have the children thinking I was a loose young woman."

"Not loose enough, *then*." The emphasis on the last word would make Mom blush all the more. We would all laugh with them, though in 1940 only my precocious sister, Jane, understood.

And maybe the ever-present Rosie Clancy.

The Cronin Democratic connections and my father's newfound Democratic faith, plus some residual Republican clout (there was some in Cook County in those days) landed him a job as "assistant architect" of the Chicago Sanitary District. The District was a treasure-house in which Chicago's mayor after the murder of Anton Cermak in 1933, Edward J. "Sewer Pipe" Kelly, and many other Chicago politicians had become millionaires.

The Sanitary District (later the Sanitary District of Metropolitan Chicago, with its own rather grotesque Magnificent Mile high-rise right outside my window as I type these words, and still later the Metropolitan Water Reclamation District, with a fountain and a sundial at the mouth of the Chicago River) was locally hailed as one of the seven engineering wonders of the world. It was a wonder all right—it permanently reversed the flow of the Chicago River, solved Chicago's sewage disposal problems, ended floods, and made possible navigation from the Great Lakes to the Gulf of Mexico. Even more wonderfully, it made possible jobs and income for legions of party faithful, often with no discernible inclination to work. In its combination of operational efficiency and monumental corruption, the Sanitary District, I tell my own kids, is a quintessential Chicago institution: a sewage system that works!

The assistant architect had little work to do. No, that's not accurate: he had no work at all. Dad would show up at the District offices on North Wabash a couple of mornings a week and reshuffle plans for the future—including, if I might say with some pride, his design for the Deep Tunnel, which is still under construction all these years after. Then he would come home to his palette and easel and draw great, sweeping skyscrapers for the days "when our ship comes in."

When the ship did come in, when the myth degenerated into reality, no one was more surprised than Dad.

The salary of an assistant architect was not all that much—twenty-two hundred dollars a year (multiply it by twelve to get the mid-1980s value), but as my father would boisterously insist, "It's a hell of a lot better than nothing, isn't it, darling?" He would then wrap his arm around Mom's waist.

"It certainly is, darling," she would reply with an attempt at being prim. But she never did escape his grasp.

To have a job during the Depression was much better than not having one, especially since prices fell steadily in the middle 1930s. We should have been able to make ends meet with some frugality and prudence. But my parents were quite incapable of either. We bought good food and good drink—single-malt whiskey, the best Spanish sherry and port, the best cuts at Liska's meat market—and good books. We did not worry about clothes or bills or furniture for the flat. We were always clean as were the frequently altered and repaired clothes we wore (April Cronin would not let dirty children leave her house), but the apartment was invariably a chaotic mess, despite Mom's occasional burst of feverish ordering activity. The chaos in our home—newspapers, books (old and new; in 1940, Galsworthy juxtaposed with Eric Ambler, Richard Wright, and Upton Sinclair), magazines, laundry, unwashed dishes—seemed to me to represent the disorganization of all our life. With a little bit more planning, I thought, even in the later years of grammar school, we would not be in endless difficulty with bills, we would wear better clothes, and we would not be humiliated at the realization that we were poor.

I'm sure I was the only one who thought we were poor.

I was especially offended that we didn't have a car. I didn't expect us to be able to buy a new one. Only rich people like the Clancys could afford a new Packard every year. But there was no reason, I knew even then, why our ancient LaSalle, bought at the time of our parents' wedding, should have died in 1938, no reason except that my mother and father were quite incapable of maintaining a car.

Many of the old LaSalles (for the younger generation it was a GM car between the Olds and the Caddy on the prestige scale) lasted right through the war, but not the O'Malley car, which expired quietly of many afflictions, most notably the absence of an oil change for ten years.

It didn't matter, Mom and Dad agreed. No one used the car anyway. It was a nuisance and an unnecessary expense during "hard times." Dad took the Lake Street el to work; when Mom did substitute teaching at St. Ursula's grammar school, she had to walk only three blocks, "well, really only two."

"Two and three-quarters," I would add, but no one ever heard me when I added precision to a discussion.

"And the children won't be driving for at least ten years anyway. Our ship will certainly come in by then. We'll have money for a new car."

"Lots of them."

"Jane will be able to drive in five years," I observed.

No one paid any attention.

"It would be different," Mom would continue, with her extraordinary ability to rationalize every economic necessity, "if we had a garage. I always say that no one should have a car unless they have a garage to protect it during the winter."

"It would be nice to drive to Twin Lakes in summer," I pointed out.

The other three kids laughed at me, not meanly, because my siblings were incapable of meanness, but as though I were Fred Allen or Jack Benny on Sunday-night radio.

"The train is more fun," Dad would chortle, and pick me up and swing me in the air like a sack of new potatoes, which from his point of view might have been exactly what I was.

The four O'Malley children arrived quickly after our parents' marriage—Jane in 1927, Charles Cronin in 1928, Peg in 1932, and Michael in 1933. Mom was twenty-seven then when Michael was born. (Perversely, he was only called Michael, not Mike or Micky. Peg was always Peg, so it was hardly a nickname. Only Chucky was favored with a distortion of his actual name.) During the birth-control crisis in my own marriage, I wondered how Mom and Dad resolved the problem of avoiding more children in the dark days of the Great Depression. It is inconceivable to me that they did not sleep together. There were three bedrooms in the apartment, two occupied by children. And their affection was too physical—hugs, kisses, affectionate touches—not to seek consummation. Moreover, my memories of the muffled laughter from their room when they were "napping" on Saturday afternoons, or when we would come in from school on the days Dad would not go down to the District, leave little doubt about the passion between them.

Years later I figured out that they probably crept back into the blankets of their unmade bed three days a week as soon as we went off to school after lunch. (We came home every day for a "hot" lunch—it was as important as vaccination in my mother's health-protection efforts.) No wonder they were happy.

I supposed they solved the birth-control challenge the way many other Catholics did then and in the years after: they simply ignored what the priests told them. Before the Vatican Council, such inattention to Church authority was private, rarely discussed even between husband and wife; and my parents were marvelously skilled in ignoring or reasoning away obstacles to their rose-colored life.

I look at my snapshots taken at Twin Lakes in those years and marvel at how handsome Mom and Dad are and how complacent they are in their affection for one another. If ever there was a serene love match, theirs was it. I can't remember them bickering about anything; it was impossible to argue with Mom anyway. And I wonder, as I ponder the faded pictures, how they managed to produce someone so totally unlike themselves as their son Charles.

Money was rarely far from my mind. I resented those who were rich, or at least whom I perceived as rich. I hated those who owned summer homes when we had lost both of our homes—the Cronin house at Long Beach and the O'Malley "cottage" at Lake Geneva (purchased after the wedding, especially for their new grandchildren).

I was not greedy in my envy. I did not want great wealth, as my Fenwick retreat resolution proves. I wanted only a modestly good life, orderly and restrained. And precise. Moreover I was willing to work hard for such a life. I fully expected a life of long and demanding hours over double-entry ledgers to earn my Oak Park bungalow, six-cylinder Chevy, and well-organized wife.

That was long before I came to terms with the reality that my life was to be a comedy of errors. You cannot escape the persona you are given. Rather you must improvise around it, skillfully if you are fortunate, ineptly if you are not.

I have a shoe box jammed with Twin Lakes pictures. I bought my Kodak Brownie with my newspaper delivery money—profit earned on a job that worried my mother constantly because it was her fiction that my health was "delicate" (how else to explain the changeling in your midst?) and that I was literally endangering my life when I trudged forth with my yellow pushcart filled with the *Chicago Herald-Examiner* every morning.

The *Tribune* was not tolerated: recent converts or not to the FDR faith, Mom and Dad wanted no part of "the Colonel" as the Roosevelt-hating editor of the *Trib* was called. Indeed the only time serious attention was paid to the Philco was when Col. Robert R. McCormick used the musical-comedy setting *Chicago Theater of the Air*—on WGN, owned then as now by the *Trib*—to blast away at Roosevelt.

"Turn that damn fool off," my father would bellow.

I thought the Colonel was plausible enough. Had not FDR caused the 1937 recession, just when it looked as if the Depression might be over? Still, I turned him off. Obviously my life plan dictated that I would become a Republican, perhaps in time for the 1952 presidential election. But here too my plans went awry.

I used my newspaper money for film and for seats at the Rockne theater's Saturday-afternoon triple features—in 1940, for example, one "major" film like *Gaslight* or *Rebecca* or *Ninotchka* and two B films, often with Richard Arlen, so readily forgotten that I'm not sure they were ever made.

(In those days I could not understand the fuss over Garbo. Having watched her again on tape more recently, I have no trouble understanding the fuss.)

Tolerantly skeptical about my wasting time at the Rockne, the rest of my family viewed my addiction to the camera with good-natured amusement.

"It shows the way things are," I would insist, "not the way we would like them to be."

My argument was a criticism of Dad's increasingly surrealistic paintings. He did not, however, so perceive it.

"The camera," he would say, rubbing his hands appreciatively at the prospect of a serious argument—I was the only one in the house who could satisfy that need—"has its uses as an archival tool, but it cannot express the insight of the artist nearly as well as the paintbrush."

"I don't want to, uh, express any insight," I said, "I just want to catch things the way they are."

"But"—Dad would favor me with a huge grin—"the way things are at any given moment is not the way they are the next moment. The photographer is exercising choice in angle, perspective, light, timing. He is interpreting despite himself. For example, take this picture of Rosie: you've caught her here on the beach in a very sad instant. Normally she is a vivacious child, bubbling with energy. It is an interpretive exercise to select out just the right second in which a pretty little girl is also sad. That's art, inferior art compared to a canvas and paint I would contend, but art just the same. And, Chucky"—he would examine the picture critically—"not a bad portrait considering the limitation of your tools."

"It was the only time she'd stand still long enough for me to take a picture. My Brownie is too slow to take her picture most of the time. Now if I had a Leica . . ."

Of all the things I wanted in the world, a Leica was what I wanted most.

"It still is an insightful shot." Dad ignored my greed.

"Anyway," Rosie protested, "I'm not a sad person."

Yes, she was, but I wasn't going to argue. She was not only sad but an intolerable pest.

"Don't you think it is a lovely picture, Rosie?" Dad persisted.

"Yes," she said grudgingly. "Only it's not me . . . would you print a copy for my mom, Chucky, *please?*"

"Sure," I would agree, with no intention of ever doing it. I had better things to do in my crude little darkroom, which I had fixed up in the basement—with the landlord's permission—than print pictures of obnoxious pests.

The shoe box of pictures of Twin Lakes—where we rented a tiny cottage for a couple of weeks every summer—wrench at my heart. It is a truism that youth slips away too quickly, yet when it's your own youth, the experience of loss is absolutely unique.

I hated the bumpy Northwestern train ride to Lake Zurich and Crystal Lake and Richmond and finally to Genoa City, Wisconsin, where we would be picked up in a bus and ferried over to Twin Lakes, but loved those precious weeks of summer fun—heat, water, tiny beach, thick humidity, boats on the lake, hot dog and wiener roasts. We romanticize our memories of youth, but in my shoe box of pictures there is still plenty of summer romance. Our clothes are funny and the cottages and the lake are incredibly small, but my mother is beautiful and my father is handsome and everyone seems to be excited and happy.

One slips into the simmering wetlands of the past and finds them again warm and comfortable and sweet smelling, the true reality, while the steppes and the tundra of the present are mere illusion.

One wants to stay.

This one does anyhow.

I'm not in any of the pictures, since I was taking them. And most of the time I was not with the family anyway. Camera in hand, I spent much of my vacation exploring the lakeshore and the woods and the nearby farms—and daydreaming.

The snapshot of Rosie Clancy, in which my dad wanted to see so much meaning, was taken when I banished her from an exploration of birdhouses in the front yards on the lakeshore. Rosie spent most of her time during our two weeks at Twin Lakes visiting with us—chauffeured over every morning in her mother's Buick. Neither of my two tormentors could tolerate a long separation from one another. *Long* was defined as anything more than a day. The shoe box still holds, within a tight and now fragile rubber band, my yellowed series on birdhouses. Pretty undistinguished stuff.

The snap of Rosie has long since disappeared. I often wonder what she really looked like in that picture.

Do I make myself seem to be an unattractive boy? Perhaps I was in fact quite unappealing as a child. Or maybe I only thought of myself as unattractive because I fit so poorly into the atmosphere of our family life. My grammar school classmates did not seem to dislike me. Short and red-haired, I was in fact selected as the class jokester. My outrageous comments, unnoticed at the family hearth, seemed to amuse classmates and teachers alike. Strangely, I cannot remember any of the school jokes while I can remember the remarks, decent and indecent, at home.

When Paris fell and Rosie wondered what difference it made to anyone in America: "Your mother will have to buy her new clothes at Marshall Field's."

Rosie didn't get it; Mom and Dad both laughed in spite of themselves.

My delivery must have been special that day, because in retrospect it was a crude and cruel crack.

I justify it because I tried to convince myself that I hated Rosie and her money and Rosie's mother and her expensive clothes, jewelry, and perfumes. And Rosie's father and his new Packard every year.

Better to hate her than to succumb to the impulse to adore her.

Her mother's furs too. While my mother had to wear a cloth coat that antedated the Depression.

"If they are so rich, why can't they keep her in her own house some of the time?"

"Money doesn't produce a happy family, dear," Mom would reply, a touch wistfully.

"Why not?"

There was never any answer to that question.

While I was dissatisfied with the way our family lived, I cannot say I was unhappy. Neither, however, could I agree with Mom years later when our family fortunes had changed that "those days in the flat in the eleven hundred block on Menard were the happiest in our lives."

They were not, not by a long shot. Money doesn't necessarily spoil happiness. Poverty doesn't help it either. But Mom never could see the point in that position.

Oddly enough, my brother and sisters, far less conventional than I was, have had quite ordinary and respectable lives: Jane the wife of an MD and an active civic volunteer; Peg the wife of a lawyer and commodity broker, busy with her concerts and her role as first violinist in the Chicago Symphony and a tenured professor at the Conservatory; Michael a rather stereotypical post-Conciliar pastor.

("Father Michael," sighs my little priest, "speaks all the proper progressive dicta at all the proper times. I fear he finds my irreverence a trial, but I am"—he grins like the slightly kinky cherub that he is—"after all a monsignor!")

And Chucky, the family straight man, is the one whose life has been a comedy of errors.

Which, as Mom would say years after, just goes to show you.

What it just goes to show has always escaped me.

The blissful confusion on North Menard came to an end on December 7, 1941.

When the news of the Pearl Harbor attack came on December 7, 1941 ("a date which will live in infamy," FDR said), the Cardinals were ahead of the Bears, an upset that would have rocked the NFL (ten teams in two divisions) and knocked the Bears, who had previously lost only one game, to the Packers, 16–14, out of the two-team play-off.

I was loving it; my father being a Bear fan, it was necessary that I be a Cardinal fan: necessary for me to oppose and necessary for him to have someone with whom to argue.

In truth more the latter than the former.

An announcer cut into the game: Japanese planes were bombing Pearl Harbor. The *Oklahoma* was on fire. The Japanese special envoy and ambassador were meeting with Secretary of State Cordell Hull.

Then the game resumed; the Bears were ahead again: George "One Play" McAfee had scored the decisive touchdown.

Dad and I stared at one another silently. Some units of the Illinois National Guard had already been called up and were freezing in tents at Camp Forrest in Tennessee (named after Confederate general Nathan Bedford Forrest, who, depending on your source, said either, "Git thar fustest with the mostest" or "Because I was able to take a shortcut and ride very rapidly, I arrived first on the field of battle and with the most men"). Dad had promised Mom many times that he would resign from the 131st Cavalry, as the Black Horse Troop was officially called. "A forty-year-old cavalry captain would not be much use in modern mechanized war, as I myself am the first to admit."

But he always postponed the resignation until after "next year's parade." Michael, he reasoned, should be given one more chance to see his father ride down Michigan Avenue in shining armor on a big black horse. The Troop was supposed to be an elite cavalry unit of the Illinois National Guard. In fact, it was useless militarily but great at parades.

We had all enjoyed the spectacle; and now we were about to pay the price for it.

I was an eighth grader at St. Ursula's, and I read the papers every day—all of them: the *Trib*, the *Herald-Examiner*, the *American*, the *Daily News*, and Marshall Field's new left-wing *Sun*. I had switched my thirteen-year-old support from the isolationists of Col. Charles Lindbergh and America First to the "interventionists" of William Allen White and the Committee to Defend America by Aiding the Allies, mostly to give my father someone with whom to argue. To my dismay, that summer he had begun to agree with me. (I note in passing that in a neat historical irony the descendants of the latter became Vietnam "doves" while the political offspring of the isolationists were transmuted into "hawks.")

"It won't be just Camp Leavenworth this time," he sighed.

"Will it be a long war?"

"Probably. I suppose I could get out—too old, family, all that. I couldn't live with myself if I did that."

"Uh-huh."

"We'd better go tell your mother."

"Yes, we'd better."

Mom pretended to be brave. "Certainly you'll have to go, no question about it," she said, her eyes wet with tears. "You couldn't live with yourself if you didn't do your duty as a citizen."

My sisters and little brother wept fiercely, but Dad and Mom cheered them up with the falsehood that he would only be away a few months.

He left before Christmas. So desperate was the rush to get troops to the Pacific that there wasn't even Christmas leave. Dad's letters said that the rumor was that units of the Thirty-third Division would be sent to Australia in March and that he might have a short furlough before he left. He also insisted that he was in good health, despite the cold weather, had lost weight, and was as spry as kids twenty years younger.

We all kept a stiff upper lip. Mom began to teach full-time at St. Ursula's to "tide us over" until Dad's family allotment checks came through. The girls and Mike stopped crying and our harp concerts and songfests resumed the week before Christmas, with Peg working her soaring enchantments on the violin. I was the only eighth grader with a father in the service. That bestowed on me a certain status that I would quite happily have done without.

The pastor's sermon at midnight mass about our "brave boys in the service" bothered the hell out of me. It wasn't our boy; it was our father, who had no business running through obstacle courses and crawling under barbed wire while live ammunition crackled above his head. Nor was there any sense in him diving into foxholes while enemy artillery shells fell all around him.

I read the newspapers, you see. Thank God Mom and the kids didn't read them, or they would have fallen apart completely.

And what good would a forty-year-old horseman, without his lance, be in combat? An intelligence officer somewhere, maybe. But a combat commander? He'd be a threat to his own men.

Or so I argued. And so I told Fr. John Raven, the young priest at our parish. He didn't disagree.

The day after Christmas, as American troops fell back from Manila to the Bataan peninsula, I asked Mom why we didn't use our political connections to get Dad out of Camp Forrest and away from combat.

"He's not going to win the war in some jungle, is he?"

"Hush, darling, your father would never want to be known as a slacker."

"If you care so much, Mr. Smarty," Rosie snarled at me, "why don't you do something about it? You read the newspapers, you ought to know how to get him transferred."

"Why don't you mind your own business? He's not your father."

"I don't care. I'm still right."

"You are not."

Anyway, I thought about her suggestion and then on New Year's Eve did the sensible thing. After hearing on the news that the Japanese had refused to consider Manila an open city and that someone named Chester Nimitz had assumed command of the Pacific Fleet, I shut the Philco off, cutting short perhaps the hundredth rendition that day of "White Christmas."

I thought a few more minutes, put on my jacket, and slipped out of the apartment.

I walked five blocks in subzero weather to see our congressman, who was home for his Christmas vacation. I rang the doorbell at his quite ordinary bungalow at Mason and Hirsh in the north end of the parish and waited, shivering and scared.

"I want to see the congressman about my father, who is in the Black Horse Troop," I told his silver-haired wife.

"Dear, there's a cute little boy with red hair out here to talk to you about his father, who is in the Army."

The congressman was a tall, lean man with thin salt-and-pepper hair and a politician's easy smile.

The new *Sun* tucked under his arm, he walked to the door, shook hands with me gravely, and bowed me into their living room.

"I'm Charles Cronin O'Malley and my dad is John E. O'Malley and he almost died of the flu at Fort Leavenworth in 1918 and he's forty years old and has four children and is down at Camp Forrest and will probably go to New Guinea and there's no reason why he would be a good combat officer because he's a painter and an architect and he worked for the Sanitary District."

"Sure, your mother was a Cronin and your grandfather was a Republican judge and you've been good Democrats since 1928 because you hated Prohibition. . . . What's he doing down at Camp Forrest?"

"He used to like to ride in the parades and make us all laugh."

"Dear God in heaven . . ." The congressman sighed. "We're not in such trouble that we need idealistic dreamers . . ."

"Who doesn't even know how to fire a Garand rifle."

"You know what a Garand is?"

"Sure."

"How old are you."

"Almost fourteen."

"Hmn . . . you look three years younger. Okay, I'm sure we can work something out. You can tell your mother—"

"She'd be awful mad if she knew I did this. Please don't tell her."

"All right." He grinned. "It's our secret. Would you take off your coat and have some eggnog?"

"Thank you."

I was embarrassed and ashamed of my ill-fitting clothes and did not want the eggnog. But I took off my coat and drank two glasses. The congressman and I talked about the war.

"I think you should be the combat officer instead of your father," he said, smiling, when I put on my brown leather jacket with its dried-up imitation fur to leave.

"I would be better than my father," I said fervently.

We both laughed. I guess he knew Dad pretty well.

"You're in eighth grade, are you?"

"Yes, sir." I could be very respectful to adults when it was appropriate.

"Where are you going to high school?"

I hesitated. Dad wanted me to go to St. Ignatius, so naturally I couldn't go there. I wanted Fenwick because that was where everyone in my class was going. My mother, worried about high school tuition for four children, hoped I would go to St. Mel's, which cost only fifty dollars a year instead of the hundred and fifty at Fenwick and the hundred at Trinity, to which Jane was already riding off on the bus every morning, her head filled with daydreams about Navy fliers she might date someday.

"Fenwick," I answered truthfully enough, "if I can earn enough money for tuition."

"That's a good school," he said, beaming. "The Dominicans are fine priests. Excellent preparation for college. The best."

Exactly what Dad had said about the Jesuits.

"Yes, sir."

"You play any football? Too short?"

"Pretty short, sir, but I do play. Not first string much."

All perfectly true. They let me hold the ball for kickoffs as was the custom in the days before kicking tees. Not for points after, however, because I had a difficult time catching the pass from center.

"What position? Quarterback?"

"Yes, sir."

Again it was the absolute truth. Third-string quarterback. But hadn't I told him that I didn't play first string? Was it necessary to say that I was a kind of team mascot?

Not in the service of truth, surely. I had made no false claims, had I?

But that final snatch of conversation would change my life and point me down the path to follies that would not end.

I didn't tell anyone about my visit. Especially that miserable little spoiled brat, Rosie Clancy.

But when Dad came home at the end of February with a transfer to Fort Sheridan in his hand, Rosie tossed her long black hair defiantly, as if to say that she was responsible for what I had done. I worried that she would not keep her big, loud mouth shut. She did. Not that her unusual discretion earned her any credit from me, the spoiled little brat.

Well, actually I admired her caution, but I couldn't admit that then, could I?

Later, when we met in the corridor as I was heading for the only bathroom in the apartment, she winked and grinned at me. It is unthinkable that I did not grin back.

Dad was assigned to the Signal Corps training center at Fort Sheridan to design buildings for battlefield communication centers. I guess he was pretty good at it. "More fun than the Sanitary District," he told us.

The routine of our lives slipped back into familiar patterns. Dad commuted to Fort Sheridan on the el and the North Shore, clad in his tailor-made major's uniform. By summer when the marines were preparing to land on Guadalcanal, he was expected at the Fort only three days a week, so long as his designs were done correctly and on time, an easy enough task for him because he would usually do the next batch of work on the trains coming home. The harp sing-alongs (we didn't know the word then) continued as always.

We had a little more money. Dad's salary as a major and our family allotment and his living allowance for a dwelling off base and his PX privileges made our poverty a little more genteel. We wore better clothes and slept under warmer blankets. Some old furniture was replaced. Mom bought a new coat. I hosted a graduation party, against my wishes, when I graduated from St. Ursula—in the gym turned basement church since the long-awaited "new" church would not be started till after the war.

Actually we probably had more money than we realized because Mom continued to teach at St. Ursula's. The extra funds sat in checking accounts, not even earning the interest that, I observed, we would receive if we invested in war bonds.

I decided that my parents were actually comfortable in our Depression lifestyle (as we would call it now) and couldn't be bothered to find ways to spend their extra money during wartime when many of the things we might buy were unavailable.

Like a new Philco.

Or a car.

No matter how much money they had, their financial affairs would always be a mess. They would only regain their past affluence if there was so much money around that you couldn't help buying a couple of homes and a couple of cars and a couple of fur coats.

No one expected that kind of a ship would ever come in.

Which just goes to show you.

If Dad had left the National Guard a year or two before the war, he would have earned much more as an architect planning defense factories around the fringes of the city. Some of his friends did just that and ended the war with a head start.

But he was happy with his contribution to the "war effort," a contribution that was not very great, I suppose, but notably more constructive than being shot in the first day of combat in New Guinea, which would certainly have happened if our republic had sent him off to the jungles.

Mom probably made a bigger contribution in 1943 and 1944 when she worked at the Douglas plant at Orchard Field making B-24s—painting the tail assemblies to be precise. She believed the Rosie the Riveter propaganda and, looking attractive in worker's slacks and dark blue turban (essential for women at that time, even if they weren't working in defense factories), rode the Central bus to Foster Avenue and then out to Manheim Road to change for a third bus to the plant. The little kids—Peg and Michael—were at first unhappy that they had to eat lunch at school; but the job seemed to make Mom happier than ever, so they were quickly won over.

The long fingers that plucked the strings of the harp were now stained with camouflage paint, but the woman who moved the fingers was happier than she had been for many years. Not that she was ever particularly unhappy. But, to tell the truth, I think she was glad to get away from the kids and talk to adults, especially since Dad was not around the flat as much as he had been before the war.

So there was enough money and more than enough to pay my Fenwick tuition by the time I was a sophomore. There was enough to buy an old jalopy so Mom wouldn't have to ride the Central Avenue trolley bus too, a car that I could use in the evenings in the summer and on the weekends. But Mom claimed that she liked the bus ride and that the women in the babushkas who rode with her were "interesting." Some of them were "very well informed musically too."

So no car until 1944.

And no worry about the Fenwick tuition either because I had a scholarship. Theoretically it was an academic scholarship, and one to which my grades might have entitled me. In fact it was an athletic scholarship offered—nay, imposed—because of the congressman's conviction, on the basis of a single conversation, that I had the makings of a great quarterback, a conviction that I can say with no false humility was totally without factual foundation.

I was momentarily overjoyed to be told about my scholarship when I tried to give my fifteen dollars to the old Dominican who was collecting tuition on registration day.

"Can't take your money, O'Malley. You're down here as a scholarship student, young man."

The next day Coach Angelo Smith (always called Coach Angelo), the kind of colorfully outspoken coach out of whom legends are made, cornered me as I came out of class.

"I hear you have the makings of a great quarterback." He contemplated me the way a man might regard the Brooklyn Bridge just after he had purchased it.

"No, sir," I said with perfect sincerity. "Ask my classmates. They'll tell you."

"The congressman says you're smart and brave." He scratched his jaw, skepticism increasing.

"And clumsy, sir. Very clumsy."

I didn't add that I was also a physical coward and had played on the grammar school team only because my friends thought it was a joke to have a specialist in holding for kickoffs.

"If the congressman says you're a football player, then in this district you're a football player. For the next four years. Understand?"

"Yes, sir."

It was not worth a hundred and fifty dollars a year to suffer through the agonies of football practice for the next four years, to be taunted—as I perceived an absolutely certain event—by Peg and Rosie because I never started, indeed never played. Except on kickoffs.

I had not the slightest choice.

Fortunately my grammar school friends rallied round and I became the team joke again, the little redhead guy in the black Friars uniform who knew all the plays and held the ball on the kickoff.

I would like to say that just once I made a tackle that prevented a touchdown. In fact—until our senior game with Mount Carmel—the opportunity came only twice in my career, and both times I did not catch the streaking kickoff return man. I have no idea what I would have done if by some miracle I had caught him.

Already I was a figure of fun. Things had begun to happen to me. All because of a slight lack of precision in my conversation with the congressman.

The mask was already fitted to my face.

The congressman I'm sure had long since forgotten about me and could not have cared less whether I donned my black jersey every Sunday (when high school games were played in the Catholic League in the old days).

"You won't even win a letter," Rosie Clancy sneered.

"They'll give him one for endurance," Peg said, laughing.

"Maybe"—I could go along with the joke because I had to go along with it—"for survival."

Yet, my absurd career as a football nonplayer would make me a hero twice in my senior year, phenomena that would change my life and begin to make me part of a legend, a legend of which, I assume you will believe, I didn't want any part.

When the war was raging, my mother often took me to the Sorrowful Mother novena services. I was late getting there for the services one harsh winter night because of late football practice. So, I knelt down for a few moments of prayer. In those days, the churches were always open so that people who paid for them could pray in them, a profoundly radical idea as far as the clergy of the present are concerned.

In the darkened church, a woman was sobbing. I remember the date precisely—January 3, 1945. It was just after the Battle of the Bulge. I remember the cry and the nervous flicker of the red sanctuary light as though it too was startled by the sudden sound.

Another grieving woman who had lost a man she loved in the war! I thought.

It is hard for me to explain what it was like to be a teenager during World War II. I have no experience of what it was like to grow up when there was not a war, when you did not take it for granted that every month or so the parish would bury another one of its young men.

Did we talk about the war all the time? Perhaps more than teenagers talked about Vietnam. Perhaps less. We didn't have it in living color on TV every night. It was all far away. We read about it in the papers and followed the maps on the front page, if we read the papers, which most of us didn't. We heard Gabriel Heater on the radio at night begin often during the early days, "There's bad news tonight," so often that it became a joke. Then we heard, "There's good news tonight," more often. Kids my age thought it would be over before we would be drafted, but only because at fifteen, eighteen looks like forever.

We saved money perhaps for war bonds. You gave $18.75 to the government and it promised to give you back $25 in ten years, a rotten return on investment as it turned out. Fortunately, someone persuaded my parents to cash in all our war bonds in 1946. Who? I never asked. I knew it was Rosie, who must have heard it from her father.

We tended victory gardens, counted ration stamps (which was an unnecessary fraud on the American people because there were never food or gasoline shortages), and cheered at the great victories.

But unless we were fascinated by the war, we barely knew where Midway Island was—that tiny spot of land near which in five minutes the dive bombers (SBDs) from the *Enterprise* and the *Hornet* destroyed four Japanese carriers and ended all hope they might have had of winning the war.

It was said in the papers then that sixteen of the eighteen bombs dropped on the largest carrier were direct hits. It turned out later to be an exaggeration—five or six hits were enough with all the bombs and aviation gasoline on the deck.

As you can guess, I was one of those fascinated by the war, alas, I suppose, the way I would be fascinated by the pennant race. It was a great big game, more deadly than some but still not the horror that war really is.

Later when I watched the documentaries—Pearl Harbor, Ploesti, Schweinfurt, Anzio, Rapido River, Arnhem, Stalingrad, Kursk—and realized how ugly and evil and deadly war really is, I felt guilty about my adolescent insouciance in the face of death and destruction.

Yet, sometimes I would hear on the news that "only one of our planes is missing" and wonder about that one young man and those who loved him.

I sang the war songs—"The last time I saw Paris, its heart was young and gay," "There'll be blue birds over the white cliffs of Dover just you wait and see," "I left my heart at the stage door canteen."

I worried about the war and the people in it. I took the film *Casablanca* far more seriously than it was intended to be taken. How many women were there like Ingrid Bergman, I wondered, whose lives had been destroyed because there wasn't a Bogart around to save them? Or a Claude Rains to order the roundup of the "usual suspects"? (A phrase that became popular with us at Fenwick whenever anything went wrong. We also loved the great Bogart line "Not so fast, Louie!")

So I prayed.

My parents were wrong in thinking that my devotion was a sign that I wanted to be a priest. The decision on my junior retreat that I would choose accounting instead merely formalized an instinct I had always had about the priesthood.

I was devout because Mom was devout. If she did it, I wanted to do it. If she prayed through the Depression, I prayed through it too—for people who were less fortunate than we were.

She prayed for everyone—on both sides. So concerned was she about the Japanese and German boys who were being killed that I did not have the nerve to remind her that the B-24s she was painting were destined to kill Germans and Japanese. I'm sure, Pangloss that she was, she managed to harmonize her work and her prayers. She prayed that Dad would not be sent overseas, that Mike and I would not be drafted, that Jane's various boyfriends would not be killed or injured. She prayed for almost everyone.

Since she prayed, I prayed with her. She rose at five forty-five to walk over to St. Ursula to receive Communion before the six-o'clock mass and then walk to the Central bus (before we bought the jalopy) for her ride to work. I would accompany her to church, accept her kiss on the forehead, and then trudge through the snow (it always seemed to be snowing) back home to help Jane serve the breakfast that had been prepared the night before.

I was in church when the young woman began to cry because I went to the Sorrowful Mother novena.

"It always works, my dear," Mrs. Burns, the elderly woman below us on the second floor (with the patience of a saint to put up with our music), told my mother in the middle 1930s. "If you put your trust in Our Sorrowful Mother, she'll grant you anything you want. She'll even work miracles. Believe me, I know."

The devotion spread through the country in the middle 1930s, a religious response to the Depression. On cold winter Fridays, tens of thousands of people would stand patiently in line in front of Our Lady of Sorrows Church on Jackson Boulevard to gain entry to one of the fifteen services that were held there from early morning to late at night. Most of them had come on buses, many of them were not dressed to resist the winter cold, some of them barely had the money for the extra bus rides.

Novena Notes, the little magazine published by the Perpetual Novena, became the most influential Catholic paper in the nation. Its weekly report of favors granted, prayers heard, requests answered, cures accomplished, was eagerly devoured by the faithful.

I find in the vast pile of papers in my basement archives a yellowed little booklet with an unhappy young woman on the cover—"Novena in Honor of Our Sorrowful Mother."

Consider the prayer for the fifth station of the Sorrowful Mother (there were seven such, distinct from the fourteen stations of the traditional Via Dolorosa):

> O Mother of Sorrows, who wouldst not leave Calvary until thou hadst drunk the last drop of the chalice of thy woe, how great is my confusion of face, that I so often refuse to take up my cross and in all ways endeavor to avoid those slight sufferings which the Lord for my good is pleased to send upon me. Obtain for me, I pray thee, that I may see clearly the value of suffering, and may be enabled if not to cry with St. Francis Xavier, "More to suffer, my God! Ah, more!" at least to bear meekly all my crosses and trials.

All language I have since learned is symbolic, all religious language doubly symbolic. The rhetoric in that kind of prayer may have its uses, even if I doubt that many folks ever used the term "confusion of face" in their daily discourse. It was not my cup of tea then and still isn't, if only because I think God can understand straightforward idiomatic English.

So, Mom and I went to the novena at St. Ursula. I suppose I was the only teenage boy there. When altar boys failed to show up, I would go into the sacristy, dress in cassock and surplice, light the candles and the incense, and lead the priest around the seven stations with a cross.

John Raven assumed I'd be there when he made his appointment list.

"Isn't he devout?" they'd say. "That cute little redhead?"

John had it better. "Doesn't he love his mother?"

Sometimes he'd add, "With good reason."

I realized that visiting the church after the novena did not make up for failure to attend. I would have to begin my nine Fridays again. However, no harm would be done by saying some prayers.

So, there I was in the church, praying for someone I knew who had been killed in action.

And I heard the woman cry.

Should I do something? I wondered. Should not the ever resourceful Chuck O'Malley, age sixteen, who had saved his father from death in the jungles of New Guinea, find the woman and heal the pain that caused her tears?

And stumble on his face in the process?

She was, I told myself, probably a woman who had lost a husband or a lover in the war. Once before in my surreptitious visits to the basement gymnasium/church of St. Ursula, I had seen a woman mourning her husband. It turned out that he was missing in action and came home alive and well.

I had not said anything to her. In fact, feeling powerless and guilty, I had slunk out of the church and hurried home on my bicycle. But that time it was broad daylight. I had heard her sobs as I walked down the stairs to the church. This was somehow different. Night. Winter. Undulating red light. A sob heard in the darkness.

So I made the sign of the cross, indicating to the Deity that my prayers were over, rose from the kneeler, genuflected reverently, and began to prowl the church in search of the agonized woman.

What I would have said if I had talked to her escapes me even today.

Probably something extremely intelligent like "Can I help?"

A sixteen-year-old, redheaded punk helping a mourning woman? Absurd.

I picked my way down the main aisle. The weeping grew fainter. So, she was not in the back of the church.

I crept up the left side aisle. No, not here either. She must be over on the other side.

I crossed in front of the altar, remembering to genuflect again, lest God think I was becoming too familiar.

She was in the front of the far row of pews, right next to the confessional. I decided that it was best to approach her quietly from

behind. So I groped my way down the main aisle again and back up
the right side aisle. I stopped a few pews behind her. The sobbing
stopped, not because she had heard me, but because she seemed to
be cried out.

Now what was I supposed to do?

She blew her nose, sniffled, and then blew again.

A car came through the parking lot next to the church, its headlights casting two quick beams of light on the windows high above
us. In the brief flashes of light I saw the outline of her bent head,
long hair, and fragile body.

Rosie! My Rosemarie!

When, I wondered, did the first train leave for Kabul? Or Kath-
mandu?

Fearful that she would hear my thumping heart, I retreated back
down the aisle and vaulted up the stairs on tiptoe—a feat that seemed
possible then.

Only when I was out in the bitter-cold night air, crunching across
the playground toward Menard Avenue, did I begin to breathe more
easily.

I didn't stop to reflect about my spineless exit until I was safely
back in front of our Philco. She probably was home now. What could
I have done or said?

I know that I expressed the firm intent to murder Jim Clancy if
I ever had the opportunity—although I had no solid grounds to think
that he was the reason for his daughter's weeping.

I told no one about the incident. I tried to forget about it and
succeeded. Mostly.

In later years I often asked myself what would have happened if
I had quietly sat next to her and asked if I could help.

I might have fallen on my face.

Again.

One of my most memorable moments during 1945 was the Sunday the whole family, en masse, strode out of the ten-o'clock mass
at St. Ursula's.

Franklin Roosevelt had died at Warm Springs, Georgia, the previous Thursday. All who were alive at that time can tell you exactly
where they were when they learned of his death. I came home on a

warm, sunny April afternoon from a softball game in the St. Ursula schoolyard (they let me play right field because few balls were hit to right field). My mother was sitting in the kitchen, crying softly.

"What's wrong?" I asked anxiously.

"The president is dead!"

"Now we're stuck with Truman!"

"Hush, dear, he's a nice man too."

"He's no Roosevelt, Mom."

The family gathered together solemnly in the parlor after a silent supper to say the rosary for FDR.

"He beat the Depression, he won the war," Dad announced. "We all owe him a lot. This country will never forget him or what he did. He saved us, not once but twice. Thank God he lived to see victory in Europe."

A lot of Americans hated Roosevelt, but those who admired him thought he was the greatest president in history. I was the only one in the family who didn't weep through that rosary. But I felt as rotten as I ever had in my life.

The next Sunday at mass, Msgr. Joseph Meany celebrated the president's death.

Joseph Peter Meany was a tiny man, a shriveled gnome, not much over five feet three, thin, bald, and like my mother, nearsighted and too vain to wear glasses. He compensated for his height, so my father said, by communicating with mere mortals in a deep bass bellow.

Meany firmly believed, Dad also said, that within the boundaries of St. Ursula he was God.

At least.

"Everyone," Mom would sometimes protest with little conviction, "thinks he's done such a splendid job as pastor."

That observation was also true. Meany Meany, as we kids called him, was of that generation of Irish pastors who could have counted on the complete loyalty of a majority of his parishioners even if he had been caught fornicating with the mother superior on the high altar during the solemn mass of Easter Sunday.

"Sure," Dad would snort. "It was a brilliant financial decision not to build the new church in 1937 because he thought prices were going down even more. Now we won't have the church till after the war is over. If then."

My father had some interest in the topic. He had designed the long-awaited new church. For free. In the middle of the Great Depression.

Rarely did any parishioner who was not wealthy speak to the pastor. He inurned himself in his suite after mass each day (at the most a seventeen-minute exercise) and descended only for meals. He would talk to no one in the rectory offices. Rarely did he attend wakes or funerals or weddings, and never did he make a hospital visit. His curates had to make an appointment to talk to him, and sometimes they waited for weeks.

He kept, locked in a sacristy safe, a special bottle of wine to be used only at his masses, a much more tasty and expensive vintage than the wine assigned to the other priests. I speak as one who had sampled both, with more restraint, I hasten to add, than certain other altar boys (who depended on me to open the monsignor's safe).

Monsignor Meany was convinced that John Raven's name was James and called him that, as in "James, that car door ought not to be open. Take it off!"

So great was the power of the pastor's command that John Raven, as he later admitted, without any hesitation or reflection, drove the monsignor's sturdy old LaSalle straight into the offending door and continued serenely down Division Street as the door bounced a couple of times on the bricks before it halted at a stoplight.

"Serves the damn fool right!" the pastor crowed.

No one ever complained about damage to the car.

The other priests called Father Raven "Jim" at the meals that the monsignor attended.

The pastor thought that William McKinley was the last American president not to be tainted with Communist sympathies, took the biased news stories in the *Tribune* as Gospel truth, insisted that FDR was a Jew, opposed aid to "bloody England," became a fan of Father Coughlin when the "radio priest" turned anti-Semitic (the same time that my father made me stop selling Coughlin's paper, *Social Justice*, after mass on Sundays), and firmly believed that Roosevelt had conspired with the Japanese to launch the Pearl Harbor attack. Meany never spoke against the war, exactly; but whenever someone from the parish was killed in action, he would audibly mutter, "Another young man murdered by that Jew Roosevelt."

That he would easily have won reelection as pastor if such had been required pointed to the monsignor's extraordinary personal piety, as evidenced, people would say, for example, by his pilgrimage to Lourdes in the spring of 1939. They did not add that the monsignor shipped to France on the same boat that he favored with his presence both his LaSalle and his housekeeper. (I forget her real name, but we kids called her Mrs. Meany Meany.)

My father lamented that the monsignor got out of Europe before the war started in September. "Hitler probably would have given him an Iron Cross."

"Vangie!"

"With oak-leaf cluster!"

"They don't give oak leaves—" I began.

"Enough from both of you."

Wisely, we both lapsed into devout silence.

On the Sunday after the president's death, the monsignor scrambled over to the pulpit in our basement church after John Raven had read the Gospel and before John had begun his sermon.

Meany leaned against the podium and glared fiendishly at the congregation, a gargoyle from a French cathedral.

"All I have to say," he chuckled, "is that God certainly has been good to the United States of America!"

"I won't stand for this!" I said so loudly that the whole congregation heard me.

Was that my voice? I wondered.

A demon must have got inside me and ignited my grief at the loss of a president who meant so much to so many people and my permanent dislike of the monsignor.

What do I do now?

I rise up from my seat at the end of the pew and walk out, that's what I do!

I was halfway down the aisle before I thought to look back. Dad and Mom and Jane were right behind me, as were a couple of dozen other good West Side Irish Democrats. (Peg, Rosie, and Michael, still in grammar school, had gone to the children's mass at nine.)

Audible gasps filled the church. The monsignor had disappeared, apparently unaware of the diminutive anarchist and his Pied Piper march out of mass.

"I hope you never learn to make bombs, Chuck," my father said with a laugh.

"Someone had to say that, darling," the good April informed me. "I'm glad you did."

All of the rebels piled into cars and drove over to St. Egbert's for the eleven-fifteen mass.

The legend said that I led a revolt at St. Ursula. Peg, who was furious that she had missed the fun, was closer to the truth: "Your mouth is quicker than your brain, Chucky. Sometimes it knows what you should do better than you do."

It would not be the last time that happened.

When Msgr. Joseph Meany reached out from the tomb in the spring of 1945 to prevent Rosie from crowning the Virgin Mary, the monsignor's ghost encountered a grimly determined exorcist—my mother, April Cronin O'Malley.

April *Mae* Cronin O'Malley.

"Unlike the Mercy Sisters," my father would say, looking up from a blueprint or a drawing, "old Joe Meany was well named."

"Vangie!" My mother would protest the irreverence and uncharitableness and then laugh, thus honoring the obligations of respect for the pastor, love for her husband, and truth with deft economy of effort.

Meany expired consuming his third Scotch in celebration of the death of Franklin Roosevelt, two days after we walked out of the ten-o'clock mass. I had the good sense not to claim credit.

I hated the monsignor, mostly because he had, I thought, cheated my father out of payment for his work. I did not feel the smallest hint of grief when he went to meet his maker because of a heart attack.

"God knows the old man died happy," John Raven, the young priest, said to my mother, "but if they assign Joe and the president to the same section of purgatory, he'll ask for a transfer to hell."

"Where he belongs," I added piously.

"Chucky!" my mother protested. And then laughed.

"Like father, like son," Father Raven noted.

"Look at the way he treated gold-star families," I pressed the point. "He won't even come down from his office to tell them that they can't have a priest from outside the parish say the funeral mass. Instead he makes you do it. And he doesn't even show up for the wake or funeral unless it's a rich family!"

"Chucky!" The tone this time said I'd better shut up. Even at sixteen I had sense enough not to argue with such a tone in the voice of an Irish woman.

In Joseph Meany's religion, there was only one sin—"impurity." It was denounced with great vigor on every possible occasion—with, need I add, not the slightest indication of what it consisted.

Hence his stern injunction to Sister Mary Admirabilis ("Mary Admiral" to us kids and then "Mary War Admiral," after the Kentucky Derby winner) that only "a young woman who is a paragon of purity may crown the Blessed Mother. We must not permit Our Lady to be profaned by the touch of an immoral young woman."

"One with breasts," my older sister, Jane, snorted. "If Rosie didn't have boobs . . ."

"That's enough, young lady." Mom didn't laugh, but she kind of smiled, proud of Rosie's emerging figure as though she were her own daughter.

It was the middle of May, a week after VE day and the end of the war in Europe. Monsignor Meany was in his grave—and whatever realm of the hereafter to which the Divine Mercy had assigned him—and Msgr. Martin Francis "Mugsy" Branigan had replaced him. In his middle forties then, Mugsy was already a legend: shortstop for the White Sox in 1916, superintendent of Catholic schools, devastating golfer, ardent Notre Dame fan, genial, charming, witty.

The red-faced, silver-haired Mugsy had been assigned to St. Ursula with indecent haste.

"Old Joe is hardly cold in the ground," Dad commented as he toasted (in absentia) the new pastor. There was always something to toast when he came home after the long ride from Fort Sheridan. "I guess the cardinal knows that he has a problem out here."

So, Monsignor Mugsy was ensconced in the great two-storied room in the front of the second floor of the rectory, the part that was covered with white stone. But Mary War Admiral had not yet extended diplomatic recognition to him. In the school, the word of the late pastor was still law.

Even though, as John Raven remarked, there is no one deader than a dead priest.

So Mary War Admiral voided the nearly unanimous election by

the eighth grade, in solemn conclave assembled, of Rosemarie Helen Clancy as May queen because she was not the "kind of young woman who ought to be crowning the Holy Mother of God."

She then appointed my sister Peg as Rosie's replacement. Peg would have won on her own—she never lost an election that I can remember—but she had determined that her inseparable friend Rosie was going to crown Mary, and that, being her mother's daughter, was that.

When informed by Sister Mary War Admiral that she was to replace Rosie, Peg replied with characteristic quiet modesty, "I'd kill myself first!"

My mother's reaction was that (*a*) she would go over to the convent and "settle this problem" with Sister Mary Admirabilis and that (*b*) I would accompany her.

"I will not visit the parish," she insisted, "unless I am accompanied by a man from my family."

"I'm a short, red-haired high school junior," I pleaded.

"Your father's in Washington this week at some meeting with the War Department, young man, and you *will* come with me."

"You don't need a man to ride the Central bus with you up to the Douglas plant," I countered.

"That's different. Besides, you're as bad as your father. You're dying to get into a fight. Now go wash your face and comb your hair."

"My hair doesn't comb. Wire brush. Good for scraping paint. Bad for combing."

"*Try!*"

"Yes, ma'am. . . . Why can't Mr. Clancy protect his goofy daughter? Why do I have to do it?"

"Not another word, young man."

"I hate him!"

"I *said* . . ."

"Not another word." I exited quickly toward the bathroom and a hairbrush.

I kept my opinions on the May crowning to myself. Sister Mary War Admiral, I thought, might have a point. The word from Lake Delavan (alias Sin Lake) the previous summer was that for someone just entering eighth grade, Rosie Clancy was terribly "fast." Admittedly, "fast" in those days was pretty slow by contemporary standards.

At that time, she and Peg were slipping quickly and gracefully—and disturbingly as far as I was concerned—into womanhood. Standing together, whispering plots, schemes, tricks, and God knows what else, they seemed almost like twins—same height, same slim, fascinating shapes, same dancing eyes, same piquant, impish faces. Like Mom, Peg was brown-tinged—eyes, hair, skin—an elegant countess emerging from chrysalis. Rosie was more classically Irish, milky skin that colored quickly, jet black hair, scorching blue eyes.

Peg was the more consistent and careful of the two. She worked at her grades and her violin with somber determination. Her grace was languid and sinuous, a cougar slipping through the trees. She rarely charged into a situation—a snowball attack on an isolated boy (such as me)—without first checking for an escape hatch or an avenue of retreat. Rosie was more the rushing timber wolf, attacking with wild fury, mocking laughter shattering the air. If Peg was a countess in the making, Rosie was a bomb thrower or revolutionary or wild barroom dancer.

She might also have been, to give her fair credit, a musical-comedy singer; she had a clear, appealing voice, which, I was told to my disgust when I was constrained to sing with her at family celebrations, blended "beautifully with yours, Chucky Ducky."

I must give her due credit. If she and Peg tormented me by, for example, putting lingerie ads from *Life* in my religion textbook and stealing my football uniform the morning of a game, they also came to my aid when I was or was thought to be in trouble.

Once when I was in eighth grade, two of the more rowdy of my classmates made some comments that Dad was a "slacker" because he was stationed at Fort Sheridan. In fact, he was the oldest serviceman from the parish. Moreover, neither of their fathers were in the service.

Instead of pointing out these two truths I made some more generalized comments on their ancestry and on their probably sexual relationship with their mothers.

And thus found myself on my back in the schoolyard gravel being pounded, not skillfully perhaps but vigorously.

Even one of them would have outnumbered me.

Suddenly two tiny fifth-grade she-demons charged to my rescue, kicking, clawing, and screaming. My two assailants were then out-numbered—not counting me.

"Where did you guys learn those words?" I demanded.

"From listening to boys," Peg, breathless but triumphant, answered.

"Boys like you, Chucky Ducky," Rosie added, her face crimson with the light of battle.

They then, without my knowledge, went to the rectory and enlisted John Raven's support. The two rowdies were put to work sweeping the parish hall until, as Father Raven put it, "the day before the Last Judgment."

Rosie was or at least claimed to be brokenhearted at her demotion by the War Admiral, much to my surprise since I would scarcely have thought of her as devout. "I feel so sorry for Peg," she told me. "It's not fair to her."

"It's not fair to you," Peg snapped, "is it, Chucky?"

"My position on Sister Mary War Admiral," I observed, "is well-known."

"Stop talking to the girls," Mom intervened. "We must settle this silly business tonight."

So, we sallied forth into the gentle May night, an ill-matched pair of warriors if there ever were such.

"Now please don't try to be funny." Mom tried to sound severe, always a difficult task with her husband or her firstborn son.

"I'll be just like Dad."

"That's what I'm afraid of."

The war in Europe was over. Churchill's "long night of barbarism" in Europe had ended. Some men were being released from the service. Dad expected an early discharge. We were destroying Japanese cities with firebomb raids. They were wreaking havoc on our ships with their kamikaze attacks. We had lost twelve thousand men in the battle for Okinawa. Mom was worried that I would be drafted when I graduated next year and would have to fight in the invasion of Japan, despite my plans to be a jet pilot. (A legitimate worry as it turned out. If it had not been for the atomic bomb, I would surely have ended up in the infantry. They didn't need pilots.) The cruiser *Indianapolis* was about to sail for Tinian (and its own eventual de-

struction) with the first atomic bomb. Bing Crosby was singing that
he wanted to "ride to the ridge where the West commences and gaze
at the moon till I lose my senses," so long as we undertook not to
attempt to fence him in.

A battle over a May crowning surely did not compare to the
major events that were about to shape the new, more affluent, and
more dangerous world.

But it was our battle.

The O'Malleys were "active" Catholics as naturally as they
breathed the air or played their musical instruments. Mom had been
president of the altar guild. Dad was an usher, even in uniform. Jane
had been vice president of the High Club. I was sometime photographer in residence, and the always available altar boy to "take" sudden funerals, unexpected wartime weddings, periods of adoration
during Forty Hours, and six-o'clock mass on Sundays. When our
finances improved, we discussed together increasing our Sunday contribution.

We voted, over my objections, to quadruple the amount we gave.
Dad insisted that the Sunday gift be anonymous because he didn't
believe in the envelope system or the published list of contributions.

"Why give if we don't get credit?" I demanded, at least partially
serious.

"Chucky!" the other five responded in dismay.

Despite the anonymity of our gifts, we were still prominent members of the parish. Even Monsignor Meany almost came to our house
for supper one night. So Sister Mary War Admiral must have known
she was in for a fight.

I whistled, "Praise the Lord and pass the ammunition," as we
walked up the steps to the convent.

"Hush," Mom whispered; and then joined in with "All aboard,
we're not a-going fishin'."

"Praise the Lord and pass the ammunition and we'll all stay free,"
we sang in presentable harmony as the light turned on above the
convent steps.

"You're worse than your father," she informed me when she
managed to stop laughing.

There was a long delay before the door opened—it is an un-
written rule of the Catholic Church (as yet unrepealed) that no con-

vent or rectory door can be opened without a maddening wait being imposed on the one who has disturbed ecclesiastical peace by ringing the bell.

Sister Mary Admiral did not answer the door, of course. Mothers superior did not do that sort of thing. The nun who did answer, new since my days in grammar school, kept her eyes averted as she showed us into the parlor, furnished in the heavy green style of pre–World War I with three popes, looking appallingly feminine, watching us with pious simpers.

The nameless nun scurried back with a platter on which she had arrayed butter cookies, fudge, two small tumblers, and a pitcher of lemonade.

"Don't eat them all, Chucky," Mom warned me as we waited for the mother superior to descend upon us.

"I won't," I lied.

The convent cookies and fudge—reserved for visitors of special importance—were beyond reproach. I will confess, however, that I was the one responsible for the story that, when the lemonade had been sent to a chemist for analysis, he had reported with great regret that our poor horse was dying of incurable kidney disease.

"April dear, how wonderful to see you!" The War Admiral came in swinging. "You look wonderful. Painting airplanes certainly agrees with you." She hugged Mom. "And Charles . . . my how you've grown!"

I hadn't. But I did not reply because the last bit of fudge had followed the final cookie into my digestive tract.

The War Admiral hated my guts. She resented my endless presence with camera and flashbulb. She suspected, quite correctly, that I had coined her nickname. She also suspected, again correctly, that I had been responsible for pouring the curate's wine into the monsignor's wine bottle. Finally, she suspected, with monumental unfairness (and inaccuracy) that I had consumed most of the monsignor's wine and was thus responsible for the necessity of filling the bottle with lesser wine.

"You look wonderful too, Sister." Although Mom had blushed at the compliment, she was too cagey to be taken in by it. "My husband is at the War Department this week, so my son has come with me."

Actually Sister Mary Admirabilis looked terrible, as she always did. Like the late pastor, she was tiny and deceptively frail. Her eyes darted nervously and her fingers twisted back and forth, perhaps because she did not bring to the parlor the little handbell that she always carried while "on duty"—the kind of bell you used to ring on the counter of a hotel reception desk.

Most of the other nuns also carried little handbells, on which they pounded anxiously when the natives became restless.

War Admiral launched her campaign quickly, hook nose almost bouncing against jutting chin as she spit out her carefully prepared lines. "I'm so sorry about this little misunderstanding. Your precious Margaret Mary should be the one to crown the Blessed Mother. She is such a darling, so good and virtuous and popular. I often worry about her friendship with the Clancy child. I'm afraid that she's a bad influence. I hope you don't regret their friendship someday."

You praise the daughter, you hint at the danger of the friend, you stir up a little guilt—classic mother superior maneuvers. And how did my mother, soft, gentle, kindly April Cronin O'Malley, react?

April Mae Cronin O'Malley.

"Oh, Sister, I would be so unhappy if Peg did not graduate from St. Ursula next month, just as Jane and Chuck . . . uh, Charles here did."

Oh, boy.

"But there's no question of that . . ."

Mom ignored her. "The sisters out at Trinity did tell me that they'll accept her as a freshman with a music scholarship even if she doesn't graduate."

"But . . ."

"And though it would break my heart"—Mom seemed close to tears—"I'll have to withdraw her from St. Ursula if she is put in this impossible situation."

"She wouldn't come back to school anyway," I added helpfully, licking the last trace of fudge from my lips.

"Shush, darling," Mom murmured.

"Please yourself." The Admiral took off her velvet gloves. "If Margaret Mary does not choose to accept the honor to which she has been appointed, we simply won't have a May crowning."

"Please yourself, Sister." Mom smiled sadly. "My family will have no part of this unjust humiliation of Rosemarie."

I began to hum mentally, "Let's remember Pearl Harbor as we did the Alamo . . ." This was a preliminary scrimmage. Mom was touching a base before cornering Monsignor Mugsy.

"My dear"—the Admiral's voice was sweet and oily—"we really can't let the Clancy girl crown Our Blessed Lady. Her father is a criminal and her mother . . . Well, as I'm sure you know"—her voice sank to a whisper—"she drinks!"

"All the more reason to be charitable to Rosemarie."

"Like Jesus to Mary Magdalene," I added helpfully.

"Shush, darling."

"Monsignor Meany established very firm rules for this honor."

"Monsignor Meany is dead, God be good to him."

"Cold in his grave," I observed.

"His rules will remain in force as long as I am superior."

"Time for a change, I guess," I murmured.

"You give me no choice but to visit Monsignor Branigan."

"Please yourself."

The warm night had turned frigid.

"I shall."

"Don't say anything, dear," Mom said as we walked down Menard Avenue to the front door of the rectory. "Not a word."

"Who, me?"

After the routine wait for the bell to be answered, we were admitted to a tiny office littered with baptismal books. Monsignor Branigan, in black clerical suit, appeared almost at once, medium height, thick glasses, red face, and broad smile.

"April Cronin!" he exclaimed, embracing her; unheard of behavior from a priest in those days. "Greetings and salutations! You look more beautiful than ever!"

"April Mae Cronin," I observed.

They knew each other, did they? Sure they did. All South Side Irish knew one another.

Monsignor Mugsy was right. Without my having noticed it, she had, as she passed her fortieth birthday, become beautiful. The worry and the poverty of the Depression were over. She no longer had to send me to Liska's meat market to purchase twenty-eight cents of beef stew ground from which to make supper for six of us. Her husband was safe at Fort Sheridan. The war would soon be over. Her children were growing up. She was earning more money than she would have dreamed possible. She had put on enough weight so that curves had appeared under her gray suit. A distinguished countess now.

"Is this galoot yours?" He nodded at me.

"Sometimes she's not sure," I responded.

"Vangie, uh, John is in Washington," Mom explained.

"What grade are you in, son?"

"I'm a junior at Fenwick."

"Do you play football?"

"Quarterback."

"What string?"

"Fourth."

"I thought there were only three strings." Monsignor Mugsy and I were hitting it off just fine.

"For me they made an exception." I was not about to tell him that I was more mascot than player.

"Where are you going to college?"

"I've seen *Knute Rockne, All American*. Win one for the Gipper."

"Great," the monsignor exclaimed. "Now, April, what's on your mind?"

Mom told him.

"Dear God." He breathed out and reclined in his swivel chair. "How can we do things like this to people? Someday we're going to have to pay a terrible price."

"Mary Magdalene—" I began.

"Shush, darling."

"I hear that old man Clancy is something of a crook." The monsignor drummed his stubby fingers on the desk.

"A big crook," I said.

"But you two are willing to vouch for the poor little tyke?"

"Certainly." Mom nodded vigorously. "She's a lovely child."

"You bet," I perjured myself because I thought my life might depend on it.

"Well, that settles that . . . ah, Jack . . . don't try to sneak by. I suppose you know the O'Malleys?"

"I think so." John Raven, golf clubs on his shoulder, grinned. "The kid has a reputation for switching wine bottles; watch him."

"Calumny."

"I hear"—the pastor peered shrewdly over his thick bifocals—"we have some trouble with the May crowning. Why don't you talk to Sister, Jack, and . . ."

Father Raven leaned against the doorjamb. "The smallest first grader has more clout with the War Admiral than a curate has." He chuckled. "It's your fight, Mugsy."

"And your parish," I said.

Everyone ignored me.

The monsignor threw up his hands. "See what's happening to the Church, April? Curates won't do the pastor's dirty work for him anymore. Well, go home and tell Peggy—I know which one she is, she looks like you did when you crowned the Blessed Mother at St. Gabe's—that her friend will do the honors next week."

When we arrived back at our tiny apartment three blocks south of the rectory on Menard, Peg hugged me enthusiastically. "Oh, Chucky Ducky, you're wonderful."

Rosie, her face crimson, considered doing the same thing but wisely judged from the expression on my face not to try. Instead, tears in her vast eyes, she said, "Thank you."

Actually, it would have been wonderful if she had tried.

"It was all the good April," I replied modestly. "I just carried her bowling shoes."

Parish reaction to Monsignor Branigan's intervention was mostly positive. The Clancy kid was too pretty for her own good and a little fast besides. However, it was time someone put Sister Mary Admirabilis in her place.

Was there any complaint that April O'Malley had gone to the new pastor to overrule the mother superior?

Certainly not. If you are April O'Malley, by definition you can do no wrong.

The Sunday afternoon of the May crowning, in the basement gym that had been Meany Meany's bequest to the parish, the blue-and-white plaster statue (pseudo–Italian Renaissance ugly) of the Mother of Jesus was surrounded by a circle of six early-pubescent girls dressed as though they were a wedding party and one pint-sized, red-haired photographer clutching his new Argus C-3 and flash attachment.

The ceremony had begun with a "living rosary" in the gravel-coated schoolyard next to the church. The student body was arranged in the form of a rosary, six children in each bead. At the head of the cross stood the May crowning party, Rosie in a white bridal dress, her four attendants in baby blue, and two of the tiniest first-Communion tots in their veils carrying Rosie's train.

The recitation of the rosary moved from bead to bead, the kids in the bead saying the first part of the Pater or the Ave and the rest of the school responding, accompanied with not too much enthusiasm by parents who had come to the ceremony with about as much cheerfulness as that which marked their attendance at school music recitals.

I lurked on the fringes of the "living rosary" automatically reciting the prayers and capturing with my camera the most comic expressions I could find. It wasn't hard to discover funny faces, especially when a warning breeze stirred the humid air and the bright sky turned dull gray.

The voices of seventh and eighth graders hinted at the possibility of adolescent bass. The younger kids chanted in a singsong that might have been just right in a Tibetan monastery. The little kids piped like tiny squeaking birds.

The spectacle was silly, phony, artificial, and oddly, at the same time devout, impressive, and memorable.

As we moved from the "Fourth Glorious Mystery, the Assumption of Mary into Heaven" to the verses of the "Lourdes Hymn," which would introduce the "Fifth Glorious Mystery, the Crowning of Mary as Queen of Heaven," the first faint drops of rain fell on the crowded schoolyard. The voices of mothers gasped in protest.

It was decision time. John Raven drifted over to the War Admiral, nodded toward the sky, and then toward the church. Fingers caressing her handbell, she shook her head firmly. We would finish the rosary. God would not permit it to rain.

Father Raven raised an eyebrow at Mugsy, resplendent in the full choir robes of a domestic prelate, red cassock and lace surplice.

"Looks as pretty," my father had remarked of the robes, "as doctoral robes from Harvard."

Mugsy peered at the sky through his thick glasses, as if he really couldn't see that far, and nodded.

John Raven shrugged: you're the pastor, Pastor.

Mugsy stepped to the primitive public address microphone and said, "I think God wants us to go inside."

Obediently the altar boys in white cassock and red capes—cross bearer and two acolytes with candles long since extinguished by the stiffening wind—began to process toward the church. The girls in the crowning party fell in behind.

The War Admiral's bell rang out in protest. Several other bells responded. A couple of nuns rushed forward and pushed the kids in the first decade of the rosary into line behind the altar boys: the rosary would unlink itself into a straight processional line with the crowning party at the very end, the way it was supposed to be, instead of at the beginning.

In which position it was most likely to be drenched since the rain clouds were closing in on us.

I snapped a wonderful shot of the War Admiral twisting a little girl's shoulder back in line and another of her shoving Peg to a dead halt. My sister had challenged the ringing of the bells and begun to cut in front of the procession and dodge the raindrops, which were even now falling rapidly.

Irresistible force met immovable object.

The conundrum was resolved by the push of parents, not bound by the wishes of the mother superior, rushing for the church door— despite the outraged cries of the handbells.

Peg simply ducked around the War Admiral, snatched up into her arms one of the first-Communion tots, and followed by Rosie, who had seized the other tot, raced for the church door in the midst of a crowd of parents.

I still have the prints—on my desk as I write this story. Peg was not to be stopped.

God may not have been sufficiently afraid of the War Admiral to hold off the rain. But He (or She if you wish) was enough enchanted by Peg to stay the shower until the crowning party had pushed its way into the shelter of the church.

Peg reassembled her crew in the vestibule at the foot of the steps leading to the basement church, waited till everyone was inside, then led the crowning party solemnly down the aisle toward the altar.

The nuns were too busy pushing and shoving kids and glaring at parents in a doomed effort to restore the "ranks" to cope with a determined young woman who knew exactly what she intended to do.

Peg would have made a good mother superior in her own right.

Doubtless given a signal by John Raven, the organ struck up a chintzy version of Elgar's "Pomp and Circumstance," an exaggeration if there ever were one for this scene.

Only about half the schoolkids were soaking wet when they finally struggled into their pews. The War Admiral's determined efforts to restore order had deprived the kids of the "sense to come in out of the rain"!

If Sister says you stay out in the rain, then you stay out in the rain.

The nuns all miraculously produced umbrellas from the folds of their black robes and stayed dry if not cool.

By the time the Admiral and her aides could turn their attention to the crowning party, Peg had herded them safely to the front of the church. There they waited patiently under the protection of Monsignor Branigan and Father Raven—and naturally in the presence of your and my favorite redhead photojournalist.

I still laugh at the pictures of the nuns turning misfortune into calamity.

Monsignor nodded to the younger priest, who strolled over to the lectern that served as a pulpit and began, "To make up for the rain, we will have a very short sermon. My text seems appropriate for the circumstances: 'Man Proposes, God Disposes'—I almost said, 'Sister Proposes, God Disposes'!"

Laughter broke the tension in the congregation and drowned out the clanging handbells. We were no longer wet and angry, we were wet and giddy.

I could imagine Mom and Dad arguing whether Father Raven had gone "too far." Mom would giggle and lose the argument.

The air was thick with spring humidity, girlish perfume, and the scent of mums, always favored by the War Admiral because, as I had argued, they reminded her of funeral homes.

The crowning party fidgeted through the five-minute-and-thirty-second sermon. Eighth-grade girls were too young for such finery, some of them not physically mature enough to wear it, and all of them not emotionally mature enough.

Peg, however, looked like a youthful empress, albeit a self-satisfied one.

And Rosie?

She was shaking nervously and deadly pale.

And, yes, I'll have to admit it, gorgeous.

She kept glancing anxiously at me, as if I were supposed to provide reassurance.

I ignored her, naturally. Well, I did smile at her once. I might even have winked, because she grinned quickly and seemed to calm down.

The sanctuary of the "basement church" was in fact a stage. The statue of Mary had been moved for the event to the front of the stage on the right (or "epistle") side. A dubious stepladder, draped in white, leaned against the pedestal. Of all those in church, only the statue was not sweating.

After the sermon it was time for the congregation to belt out, "Bring flowers of the rarest"—"from garden and woodland and hill-side and dale" as I remember the lyrics. Rosie bounded up the shaky white ladder, still the rushing timber wolf. The ladder, next to my shoulder, trembled.

Anyone who attended such spring rituals in those days will remember that the congregation was required to sing two times, "O Mary, we crown thee with blossoms today, queen of the angels, queen of the May!" During the second refrain, much louder than the first (which itself was pretty loud), the ring of flowers was placed on the head of the statue.

I had been charged to take "a truly good picture, darling. For her parents, who won't be able to come." Given the state of flashbulb technology in those days, that meant I had one and one chance only.

Just as Rosie raised the circle of blossoms, I saw an absolutely perfect shot frozen in my viewfinder. I pushed the shutter button, the bulb exploded, the ladder swayed, and Rosemarie Helen Clancy fell off it.

On me.

I found myself, dazed and sore, on the sanctuary floor, buried in a swirl of bridal lace and disordered feminine limbs.

"Are you all right?" she demanded. "Did I hurt you?"

"I'm dead, you clumsy goof."

"It's all your fault," Peg snarled, pulling Rosie off me. "You exploded that flash thing deliberately."

Leo Kelly, a gentle and intelligent young man who was going off to Quigley to study for the priesthood (and who later disappeared in Vietnam), helped me as I struggled to my feet to be greeted by an explosion of laughter.

"Nice going, Chuck," he observed with a wicked grin.

What's so funny? I wondered as every handbell in every nunnish hand in the church clanged in dismay.

Then I felt the flowers on my head. Rosie had crowned not the Blessed Mother, but me!

Even the frightened little trainbearers were snickering.

I knew I had better rise to the occasion or I was dead in the neighborhood and at Fenwick High School.

Forever and ever.

Amen.

So I bowed deeply to the giggling Rosie, and with a single motion, swept the flowers off my wire-brush hair and into her hand. She bowed back.

She may have winked too, for which God forgive her.

These days Catholic congregations applaud in church on almost any occasion, even for that rare event, the good sermon. In those days applause in the sacred confines was unthinkable.

Nonetheless, led by Monsignor Branigan and Father Raven, the whole church applauded.

Except for the nuns, who were pounding frantically on their handbells.

Rosie looped the somewhat battered crown around her fingers and joined the applause.

Then someone, my mother I'm sure, began, "O Mary, we crown thee with blossoms today . . ."

Rosie darted up the ladder just in time to put the crown where it belonged. As she turned to descend, the ladder tottered again. I steadied it with my left hand and helped her down with my right.

She blushed and smiled at me.

And owned the whole world.

There was, God help me and the bell-pounding nuns, more applause.

Rosie raised her right hand shyly, acknowledging the acclaim.

The monsignor stepped to the lectern.

"I think we'd better quit when we're ahead."

More laughter.

"Father Raven, who has better eyes than I do," he continued, "tells me that the rain has stopped. So we'll skip benediction of the Blessed Sacrament and end the service now, with special congratulations to the May crowner and her, uh, agile court. First, we'll let you parents out of church, then our bright young altar boys will lead the schoolchildren out, then, Chucky, you can lead out the wedding party. It won't be necessary for the children to go to their classrooms. We want to get everyone home before the rains start again."

It was a total rout for the War Admiral. To dismiss the kids from church without requiring that they return to their classrooms was to undo the work of Creation and unleash the forces of chaos and disorder, indeed to invite the gates of hell to triumph against the Church.

The clanging handbells displayed a remarkable lack of spirit.

Afterward, back in our apartment, the sun shining brightly again, Mom insisted that I was the hero of the day. Peg did a complete turnaround, a tactic at which she excelled, and told everyone that "Rosie would have been badly hurt if Chucky hadn't caught her," a generous description of my role.

Dad, returned from Washington in time for the show, affirmed that at last St. Ursula had a real pastor.

"Joe Meany is now in his grave permanently."

"And War Admiral has been put out to stud."

I was old enough to know vaguely what that meant.

My prediction was accurate. The following year, Sister Angela Marie, even older it was said than the War Admiral, appeared at our parish and governed with happy laughter instead of a handbell.

In the midst of the festivities, I wondered whether in my eagerness to freeze what I had seen in my viewfinder I might have brushed against the ladder.

And what was the instant I froze on my Plus-X film?

That night, when the apartment had settled down, I crept off to my makeshift darkroom in the basement of our building. After developing the film and exposing the paper, I watched the magic instant come up in the print solution.

What I saw scared me: two shrewd young women, one of them recognizable as a marble statue only if you looked closely, making a deal, like a buyer and seller at the Maxwell Street flea market. Rosie was about to offer the crown in return for . . .

Well, it wasn't clear what she expected from the deal. But she expected something. No, she was confident she would get it.

I hung the picture to dry, thought about claiming that the film had been ruined, and then reluctantly decided that I wouldn't get away with it.

"You could call the picture," Mom would say, "the way *Time* magazine does, 'Rosemarie and friend.' "

None of them would see in the photo the deal being consummated. They would say that it was all in my imagination.

After the ceremony that afternoon, my friends from Fenwick had demanded to know did I "cop a feel" when "Clancy" was on top of me.

"Nothing to feel," I insisted with notable lack of both honesty and loyalty.

"What was she like?" they demanded with horny insistence.

"Heavy," I told them.

Now, as I watched a second print materialize in the solution, I admitted in a deep, untended, and secret subbasement of my brain that the sensation of Rosie's body on top of mine had been so sweet that, if the ever-vigilant Peg had not pulled us apart, I might have been content to remain there always.

To hell, I thought, with Jim Clancy.

When I was a senior at Fenwick High School, the year was as un-memorable, in any objective sense of that word, as my first three years at Fenwick. My acts of heroism, winning a championship, saving a life, were as unmemorable as any two events could possibly be—save perhaps as comedy.

However, as I have learned through the years, frequently to my dismay, what matters is not that which actually happened, but what people think and say has happened.

Thus, in the *New York Times* profile it is stated, authoritatively and without qualification, that in high school "O'Malley was a triple-threat quarterback who led his team to a city championship. Only a family tradition of military service prevented him from a possible all-American college career."

I have always firmly believed that if it is in the *New York Times*, it has to be not only true but officially true.

I worry that someday I will begin to believe this part of the legend.

I also worry that my teammates, who are not *New York Times* readers, will stumble on an old issue of the *Magazine* and find the profile.

Presumably they will laugh. Possibly, I tremble at the thought, they too will have come to believe that the myth is fact.

During summer practice, which began the day after the bombing of Nagasaki, I tried to reach an amicable settlement with Fenwick's football coach.

"With war over, Coach, you don't need me on the team anymore, do you?"

"Who will hold the kickoffs?" The congressman no longer mattered. Now Angelo loved the joke too.

"Some clumsy freshman?"

"Who will advise me on plays?" He laughed heartily and slammed me on the back with his formidable paw.

I was, as I have insisted, quite worthless on the field, but I did know all the plays, even calls that Angelo rarely used and forgot himself. Occasionally he would jokingly ask me what strategy I would use on a series of downs if I were coach.

"Pass on the first down, they won't expect it. You usually play conservative."

He would laugh and tell the quarterback to keep the ball on the ground.

Once, when we were way ahead of poor St. Ignatius, he followed my advice, purely for laughs, and scored an unnecessary but spectacular touchdown on a seventy-five-yard play. He looked at me quizzically as I trotted out on the field to hold the subsequent kickoff. "Too bad there isn't a body to go along with that brain."

"No, it isn't."

After that our occasional consultations were what Mom would have called "half-fun, full-earnest." He acted as though I were a good-luck charm, a role I was perfectly willing to accept. Not for me, or anyone else on the team as far as that goes, to suggest that I knew more about the strategy of Catholic League football, pretty elementary in those days, than the coach did.

They didn't laugh on Monday mornings when they had to pay off on my parlay-card bets. Mind you, I didn't gamble. I told myself that betting on college football games wasn't gambling because I always won.

I read all the pages of all the papers, you see, including the sports pages. I digested them like my Wheaties in the morning (Mom had given up on oatmeal and cream of wheat by then). I knew who was going to win.

Good think, no play. A strategist at a time when there was not a market for strategy.

We didn't think we were quite good enough to be champs and we probably weren't. But we were better than champs, we were magic. We could do no wrong. We laughed our way toward the play-offs.

We laughed, that is, until our game with Mount Carmel, always a power, and always a threat to Fenwick. If they beat us, the magic would be over and we would not make the play-offs. We were the better team, we told ourselves nervously, even if they outweighed us by ten pounds per man. But we were worried about the South Siders' hex on us.

The week before the game, the hex seemed to be working. We were swept by an epidemic of the flu. Our second-string quarterback was so sick he had to be brought from the practice field to Oak Park Hospital and put in an oxygen tent.

There were only two men between me and something more than holding kickoffs.

I considered feigning a fever, but decided that was hardly necessary. My classmate who was the starting quarterback was healthy and strong. And the sophomore who was his backup was one of the few players who wasn't smitten by the bug.

It was a raw, gray Sunday with occasional snow flurries in the air, just before Thanksgiving, and Hansen Park Stadium, beyond the Milwaukee railroad tracks above North Avenue (flying into O'Hare, you can still see them) was jammed with people despite the wind and the snow flurries.

The game suited the day—what they call today "basic football," Woody Hayes's "three yards and a cloud of dust," except the field was frozen and there was no dust.

The kind of game, I muttered to myself, that Carmel might just win. But we led 14–12 going into the fourth quarter—three kickoffs for me to hold, amid loud cheers from my family in the stands.

On our first possession in the fourth quarter, the Carmel linemen finally broke through our weary guards and center and smeared the quarterback on our fourteen-yard line. In the current parlance they rang his bell and then recovered the fumble. He was carried off the field on a stretcher. "Concussion," said the doctor called down from the stands.

Eight plays later Carmel scored on a sneak from the two, and after their conversion we were down 19–14.

One player, I thought, between me and glory; and I wanted no glory, thank you very much.

Our sophomore backup was sensational. He brought the team down the field quickly in a skillfully executed series of end sweeps with himself as the ball carrier. On a day like that with both teams tired, one more touchdown would keep us ahead.

He fumbled on Carmel's twenty-yard line and they recovered. The poor kid staggered to his feet, looked around once as though he were trying to figure out where he was, and collapsed.

"This young man has a fever," the doctor announced in astonishment. "His temperature is over a hundred and one at least."

As if to confirm the diagnosis, our poor soph vomited all over Angelo's shoes.

"Where's Chucky?" the coach demanded.

"Leaving the stadium," I said, not altogether facetiously.

"Grab him," he thundered as I tried to slip away to the locker room.

Carmel began to march back up the field inexorably. There were no field clocks in those days, so you had to depend on the timekeeper's watch and his reports during time-outs or between plays. Maybe five minutes were left in the game. With any luck, Carmel would keep the ball for the rest of the game. We'd lose, but I'd save my life.

All the Carmel linemen now looked at least eleven feet tall.

We held on fourth and one at our own forty and took over.

"I'm not going to tell you what to call, Chucky," the coach sighed. "It probably wouldn't do any good, but for the love of God, don't call your own number."

With commendable lack of enthusiasm, he waved me in.

"Never fear," I shouted back at him.

There was laughter from the Fenwick side of the field and an audible gasp from the Carmel fans. Did they really grow quarterbacks that small on the West Side?

Then the Fenwick crowd, led I was later told not by the regular cheerleaders (Fenwick males; Trinity females came much, much later) but by Peg and Rosie, burst into a thunderous ovation. "Chucky, Chucky, Chucky!" they chanted savagely. Like mourners at an African funeral.

If you are going to lose, why not make it high comedy. Or maybe they thought that the funny little redhead, everyone's favorite mascot, might work a miracle. Wasn't I, by the coach's own admission, the team's good-luck charm?

We had three minutes left, three whole minutes.

Almost without thinking about it I called the plays in the huddle and snapped out the signals in a voice that sounded unconscionably squeaky.

Maybe I should note here that we were playing the old Notre Dame box. Only the Bears and Stanford and a few other teams were using the T. Notre Dame itself was about to abandon the box in favor of Angelo Bertelli in the T.

I sent Vince Antonelli, the wingback, around end. Something that he hadn't done all season.

Fifteen yards and a first down.

I called him again, this time for a quick sideline pass to Joe Raftery, our end (no wide receivers in those days). Ten more yards and another first down. Two minutes to go on Carmel's thirty-five.

Raftery again on an end around. I thought for a moment he would break away and end my agony.

Alas, the Carmel safety stopped him with a shoestring tackle. But he made fifteen more yards. First and ten on the twenty.

We had spread them out. Okay, now, through the center. Antonelli over the middle to the fourteen. Then Pete Delvecchio on a reverse from Vince to the seven. First and goal. Time-out. A minute and twenty seconds left.

Chucky the magician.

I should note that my principal concern after calling the play and watching the snap from center was to get the hell out of the way of the befuddled and now angry Carmel linemen. Indeed, I was so far from the action that no one bothered to lay a hand on me.

My success was hardly going to my head. I was convinced that I was living in a nightmare and that soon the gorillas from Carmel would eat me alive.

The stadium was as silent as a cemetery, whether in astonishment or awe or fear I did not know. The Fenwick bench seemed to be paralyzed. Angelo, I learned later, couldn't bear to look at the field.

My luck then ran out, the magic deserted me, my number was up.

I called Vince around the near side, figuring they would hardly expect me to do that. It was a perfect call, only the pass from center was wide of the mark. I watched in fascinated horror as it spun in my direction and bounced dead in front of me. Fortunately Vince dashed over and fell on it before the Carmel monsters destroyed the ball and me.

In the huddle, no one complained that I didn't grab the ball. I was still magic. Second and fourteen. Okay. Vince, pass it to Joe in the end zone.

"I haven't passed to him all year."

"That's why you're passing now."

Perfect pass. Joe dropped it.

Third and fourteen.

"Sorry, Chuck."

Vince around the near side again. "Make the pass good," I barked at the center.

"Sure will, Chuck," he promised contritely.

Eight-yard gain. Fourth and six. Less than a minute.

Fool them real good. Another Antonelli pass. "Don't drop it, Joe!" I ordered.

"I won't," he said grimly as we broke the huddle.

Someone on Carmel had me figured out. A tackle and a guard came storming in. Vince had to hurry his throw. The big tackle, now twenty feet tall, leaped into the air and blocked the pass.

Then the whole world crunched down into slow motion. Slowly, lazily, teasingly, the ball arched in my direction, taunting me as it came. My father would later say that he was afraid it would bounce off my helmet. That was my thought precisely. To avoid that disgrace I put up my hands to ward it off. The blocked pass, losing most of what little momentum it had, nestled contentedly in my hands.

And ten million howling Mount Carmel monsters, all thirty feet tall, swarmed in my direction.

I did the only honest thing under the circumstances. I ran—fearfully—for my life. If I had been facing toward the other goal line, eighty-eight yards away, I would have run in that direction. I would not have gone very far because I was so slow. As it was, I paid no attention to where I was going but simply ran.

As it turns out, toward the goal line.

Not fast enough. As I approached the point where sideline and the goal line intersect, called appropriately enough in my case the coffin corner, not caring much which line of safety I crossed first, I was hit by the Burlington Zephyr roaring through Lisle, Illinois, at seven-thirty in the evening. Or so it seemed.

I felt my body rushing through space, my arms flung out in front of me, the ball slipping out of my fingers. Then the first aluminum, diesel streamliner tossed me aside and I fell to the ground with a deadly thud. The train, not sure that it had finished me off, returned to run over me again.

And then there was nothing at all.

As to what actually happened, I'll have to rely on folklore and the account in the next morning's *Herald-Examiner*.

SUB SAVES DAY FOR FRIARS

Reserve quarterback Chuck O'Malley carried the Fenwick Friars over the prostrate bodies of the Mount Carmel Caravan into the Catholic League play-offs today with a dramatic catch of a blocked pass from Vince Antonelli.

O'Malley, whose previous role in three years on the Fenwick team has been holding kickoff placement, came into the game after three other quarterbacks were sidelined by injury or illness. Trailing 19–14, O'Malley sparked the team to a dazzling last-minute drive from their own forty to the Mount Carmel six.

When the drive fizzled, O'Malley called the fourth-down play, made a leaping catch of Antonelli's blocked pass, and scampered toward the goal line. Mount Carmel safety Ed Murray rammed into the five-foot-six-inch sub at the one-yard line, but O'Malley, in a desperate leap, flew across the goal line, breaking the plane just as the ball slipped from his fingers.

He then held for the point-after-touchdown kick that gave the Friars a 21–19 lead. Fenwick kicked off from midfield because of an unnecessary-roughness call against Murray on the touchdown play.

Reserve O'Malley, to put icing on the cake, tackled Murray at the Carmel fifteen on the runback with such ferocity that the ball popped out of his hands. Joe Raftery fell on it to end the game.

"Chuck is magic," said Friar coach Angelo Smith. "He will never forget today, I'm sure of that."

That, as my children would say, is for sure.

How I managed to catch the pass from center for the PAT I will never know.

Chuck O'Malley, mountebank and clown.

And unwitting and unwilling and literally unconscious hero.

The image of my spiking poor Ed Murray is so implausible that I would be inclined to think that the reporter made it up if my overjoyed family did not insist that it had in fact happened just that way.

And incidentally I was five feet nine. Well, eight and a half anyway.

My first recollection after the game was being hugged simultaneously by my mother, Jane, Peg, and the insufferable, if glorious, Rosie Clancy.

"Let go." I shoved her away briskly.

Unfazed, she screeched, "Chucky Ducky is a hero! He won the game!"

"What?"

"Dear, you scored the winning touchdown." Mom was beaming. "We always knew you were an athlete."

"There's been a terrible mistake."

I have repeatedly been assured by all present that those were my very words.

Well, Fenwick went on, as everyone knows, to beat Tilden at Soldier Field and win city. The other three quarterbacks recovered and I returned to my regular kickoff role.

But my unintended and unintentional feat was never to be forgotten. After we won the Kelly Bowl (as the game was called after the aforementioned Mayor Ed "Sewer Pipe" Kelly), Angelo told the press, "We knew we were a team of destiny all season. After the way Magic Chuck O'Malley beat Carmel for us, we knew we couldn't lose."

Yeah?

There was some talk of a football scholarship at Notre Dame, a joke, one more part of a joke that had run for four years and ought to have died a decent death when I was a freshman.

But the legend lives. And my daimon cackles.

I'm sure that if I had not been blocked into the end zone—and

Ed Murray hit me at the wrong angle or I would have soared across the sideline and halfway up the stands of Hansen Park Stadium—I would not have been forced to go to the senior prom, I would not have been hailed as a hero a second time that year, and my life would have been very different.

The second incident, by the way, was even more ridiculous and had consequences that are far more serious.

When Vince Antonelli expressed an opinion about my sister Peg in 1946, just before graduation from Fenwick, I was astonished.

"She's really cute," Vince said, leaning over my shoulder as I tried desperately to memorize Greek vocabulary for the final exam.

Greek was my weak subject, the only threat to my A average. Why Greek? It was 1946, remember, and the Catholic high schools were convinced that the classics would help you succeed in college. They did not mean what the English meant, namely that you learned enough to be able to read the classics and profit from their content. Rather, in our part of the world, the classics were extolled because they developed your intellectual discipline and your memory power.

"Jane?" I asked absently.

She was cute indeed, a pretty face, sweet rather than beautiful, the rounded curves of a classic full figure that the tight corsets and drab fashions of the "wartime" world could not hide. Jane had a returned F4U marine pilot on the line, a premed student named Ted McCormack. Doubtless, he had stared dreamily at a picture of Jane in a swimsuit between flights. Now poor Ted, the pilot, could look at nothing else when he was in the room with her. Lucky Ted.

And lucky Jane.

"Margaret."

"You mean Peg." I still didn't look up.

"Yeah, I guess."

"*Peg!*" I was startled and lost my place in the Greek lexicon. "Peg, cute!"

"Real cute." He nodded solemnly.

"Jeez, I hadn't noticed." I returned to my Greek.

"Do you mind if I invite her to the senior prom?"

"Peg?" Looking up in bewilderment from my book was becoming a serious distraction from my last-minute "plugging."

"Yeah."

"Suit yourself."

If he wanted to rob the cradle, that was his business.

"Good. I've already asked her."

"Fine. Marry her if you want."

"That might not be a bad idea."

I gave up on the Greek. I'd get an A anyway. I looked up at my massive wingback. The poor dummy was in love.

With my little sister, Peg. How odd of him.

"Isn't she a little young?"

"She's awful cute." He blushed happily.

"I guess. Well, I hope you both have a good time. Where is it? The Knickerbocker?"

"Yeah. I hear it's real nice."

"So they say."

"Will you double with us?"

Glory be to God, as Mom would have commented.

"I don't date, Vince. You know that."

"Yeah . . . but . . ."

"You don't date either. What's the matter with you?"

"This is our senior prom."

"So?"

"It happens only once in your life."

"How fortunate."

"I really want to go."

"Fine. There's a dozen guys who will double with you."

"But Peg says your mother won't let her go unless you come along."

"My mom, April Mae Cronin O'Malley, said that?"

And a herd of cattle just jumped over the moon.

I began to smell a rat and I knew its name too.

"I suppose you and Peg have chosen a date for me too."

"Well . . ."

"Let me guess—Rosemarie Helen Clancy?"

"Well . . ."

"You can sit here in this classroom and ask me till Judgment Day to go to the prom with that obnoxious little bitch and I'll still say no. She has no morals."

And she sobs in the darkened church at night. And nurses me tenderly when I am sick. And I would like to hold her in my arms. And sometimes I daydream about taking off her clothes.

Ambivalence? Fear? Stubbornness? Why did I make such a big deal of not going to the prom with her, especially since it was, after all, not a bad idea?

I'm not sure why it became a matter of principle with me. Who knows what goes on in the head and the heart of a seventeen-year-old? Maybe it was merely anger that I was being manipulated by "the monstrous regiment of women," as John Knox called them. Looking back on the prom, I am not proud of myself, even though I emerged again as a phony hero.

Also to be candid once again—and don't expect candor all the time in this memoir—I was frightened at the prospect of the U.S. Army claiming me before the month of June was over.

The test that morning was easier than I thought it would be. As I finished the last part of it, I realized that I was close to being trapped. Peg probably reciprocated Vince's crush. But it was un-thinkable for her to venture anywhere without the dragon lady in tow. Or vice versa. So, we had to get a date for her too. Why poor little Chucky Ducky?

Because (a) he was a hero and (b) if Peg could persuade Mom that it was a good idea, there would be no peace in the family until he had agreed. Thus the Bitch (a capital letter was already being added in my mind) would not have to worry about overcoming her Delavan reputation for being "fast."

They had already trapped me.

Well, I wouldn't go quietly.

Our family meals were even more chaotic than in the past. Dad was overwhelmed with work and seemed to be flourishing. He la-mented the "good old days when I could paint all day long," but bent over blueprints while the paint boxes dried up, he looked like a harassed and bemused Merlin.

Curiously enough, Dad was only a fair painter, too much man-nered impressionism, I would say now. You simply couldn't make Twin Lakes look like the place where Monet hung out, no matter how much of a romantic you were. But he was a fine architect, prob-ably a great one. He did not recognize in 1946 what was obvious to me: that buildings, not canvas, were his métier. Mom continued to "help out at the office" and glowed with pride at her husband's return to his profession. She must have thought how much it was like those few years they had together before the Depression blighted both their dreams. They were getting a second chance, which neither had expected.

And what a second chance!

"We've been lucky, dear," she would sigh. "Unbelievably lucky."

"You said a mouthful."

That week Mom was also looking for "something with a little more room"—a larger apartment, perhaps in one of the rather elegant and expensive buildings over on Austin Boulevard.

I considered my sister Peg carefully. Without my noticing it, she had turned into a young April Cronin: tall, elegant, with delicate, graceful, classic curves and a hauntingly lovely face. Not as voluptuous as Jane and not as bubbly either, but lithe and cool and supremely self-possessed.

Whom was she like? Teresa Wright? No. Donna Reed? No. Cathy O'Donnell? Heavens no. Jeanne Crain? Blasphemy to suggest it. Nope, Peg was not cut from the same cloth as the wholesome actresses of the time. Ava Gardner? Well, maybe.

A wholesome Ava Gardner? Maybe.

Not too wholesome, however.

Anyway, she indeed was on her way to being the real beauty that Mom had predicted for the noxious Rosie. Small wonder that poor old Vince was smitten.

Not that her inseparable coconspirator at that age in life was hard to look at. In point of fact in those days, Rosie was unbearably beautiful, a slender girl with a subtly carved body and a pale, alluring face of the sort you normally saw only on covers of women's magazines. Even if you hated her nasty tongue and her loud mouth and her foul temper, you couldn't quite stop your imagination from undressing her. Not that my imagination, despite Dad's books of paintings, had any clear idea what might lurk underneath the blouse and/or sweater and skirt, which were the uniform for fourteen-year-olds in those days.

"Did Vince talk to you today?" Peg cocked one of her shrewd little eyes at me.

"Yes."

"Are you going to the prom?"

Not very subtle, that.

"That's a ridiculous question."

"Then you will take Rosie!" Peg clapped her hands gleefully.

"Not if that fat little dope was the last woman in the world. Anyway, I don't date."

"She's not fat," Peg stormed.

"She will be just like her drunken mother and her disgusting little father. . . . 'Let me tell you,' " I mimicked Jim Clancy, complete with the wave of the jeweled fingers, " 'how I made my last million. You see, there were these widows and orphans and I—' "

"She's not fat," Dad remonstrated with me. "Not at all. She looks like her grandmother McArdle, who was one of the great beauties of the turn of the century."

"It's not the turn of the century." I reached for the potato dish. "These are good, Mom."

"We're going to her house at Lake Geneva the day after." Peg was close to tears. "It will be fun."

"Fine. I'm sure you can find someone else to take her." I dug into the potatoes. "Someone who doesn't know about her cheap escapades at Delavan. Me, I'm afraid that I might catch something from her."

A little strong, I'll admit.

No, stupid, rude, intolerable. Like I say, I was seventeen and scared stiff about the Army, which would carry me off to Fort Benning, Georgia, a couple of weeks after graduation. I'd never been separated from my family before and now truly did not want to leave them.

Jane (laughing as always): "You're a little brat, Chucky, you know that?"

Peg: "Mom, make him stop!"

Mike: "I think she's the most beautiful girl in the neighborhood."

Me: "If you're going to be a priest, you shouldn't notice that."

Mom: "Chucky, I'm surprised at you."

Me (defensively): "Why me?"

Peg: " 'Cause she likes you, stupid."

Me: "She is too spoiled to like anyone but herself, a selfish little bitch!"

Omnes: "Chucky!"

We didn't use that kind of language, not around the fair April, not even if you were Dad.

Me: "I don't care. I don't like her. I wouldn't walk to the drugstore with her."

Jane (trying unsuccessfully to be angry): "You don't deserve a date that pretty."

Peg: "You're stuck-up, that's all. You think you're too good for anyone."

Mom: "She really is a sweet little child."

Me: "You're all conspiring against me!"

"You were safer"—Dad rubbed his bald pate—"when Ed Murray was charging after you."

"Don't I know it!"

Mom played music from "The Desert Song" after supper. Sigmund Romberg was supposed to do me in. Rosie did not show up to do homework with Peg that evening, apparently having been warned off.

I had won the battle, but not the war?

On the contrary, I had struck out.

"You will take that poor little child to the prom, won't you?" Mom demanded as I tried to sneak off to my darkroom in the basement.

"I'll have to fix up my darkroom in the new apartment building," I pleaded. "Maybe they won't even let me have a corner of the basement."

Her fingers, steel strong from the harp, descended on my shoulder. I was a wicked little boy running away from home.

"Then we won't rent the apartment. You didn't answer my question."

"April Mae Cronin O'Malley"—I was imitating my father—"you'd try the patience of a saint."

"You know how far that gets your father." The fingers tightened.

"I don't like her."

"She's a nice little girl."

"I don't want to."

"But you will, won't you?"

A will of steel to match her fingers? Sure.

"All right."

"You'll have a good time."

"Do I have to?"

"Have a good time?" The vise had not yet released me poor shoulder.

"Yeah?"

"Certainly not, but she's such a sweet little tyke, I know you will."

"Wanna bet?"

She sighed and let me go.

It will be argued that my behavior was typical of an adolescent male who discovered that the obnoxious pest whom he had known since first grade had suddenly become an attractive young woman. Secretly, it will be said, I had always kind of liked her and now was both fascinated and disturbed by her. Deep down, it will be contended, I knew that her Delavan reputation was mostly exaggerated: she was only marginally "faster" than any Trinity freshman of her generation.

My sisters and my mother, with my father's amused acquiescence, were only forcing me to do what I wanted to do. Indeed I was delighted with the prospect of dancing with this troubling young woman.

Yeah?

I'm prepared in the interests of candor to admit the partial truth of that charge. The chemicals of young manhood were roaring through my bloodstream. I clung to my orderly plans and sensible goals as best I could, but my unruly emotions were threatening to get in the way. Ten years—my target for beginning to think about marriage—was a long time.

And Rosie was as physically appealing as any girl I had ever known, despite the frowns of anger and hatred and contempt that often distorted her delicate, fine-boned features.

I despised her parents and disliked her dagger tongue and hair-trigger temper. No, I'll be more precise. I was afraid of her scathing intelligence, which, when combined with her undeniable sexual magnetism, made her a dangerous girl.

So, I was ambivalent—attracted and scared.

What seventeen-year-old, even in the infinitely more sophisticated world of the present, could admit to those emotions?

Anyway, I rented the cheapest summer formal I could find, sent her an insultingly inexpensive corsage of wilted orchids, and embarked on the prom adventure grimly determined that neither of us would enjoy ourselves.

And she and Vince had to come to our place to pick up Peg and me. We had both packed small bags to take with us to Lake Geneva after the prom. Mrs. Antonelli would join Mrs. Clancy as a chaperone, a precaution on which the good April had insisted.

I turned off the news as they came into the apartment: there was a new Japanese government, the English were disarming two hundred thousand Polish troops who had served with them during the war. Truman was taking over the coal mines.

"Aren't you afraid you'll catch cold in that dress?"

It was a peach-colored affair with thin straps, a deeply plunging neckline, hardly any back to speak of, showing her flawlessly smooth complexion—a lot of it. She looked as if she were about twenty-five.

"Did you steal your suit from a corpse on Maxwell Street?"

Even Mom raised an eyebrow at her dress, an eyebrow that said that she would never dress a fourteen-year-old that way, but then Clarice Clancy was never known for her impeccable taste, now, was she?

"You will be the most lovely young woman at the prom, dear."

Rosie blushed happily at the compliment. "Not as pretty as Peggy, Mrs. O'Malley. She looks just like you."

When Rosie blushed, I had noticed before, the color began at her throat and then rose to her face. Now I observed that it also spread in the general direction of her breasts.

Where was that desert island?

Mom's turn to blush. Clever little wench.

"Take good care of my Chucky, he looks cute, doesn't he? If only he would comb that awful hair of his."

"Oh, he can take care of himself, Mrs. O'Malley." She flicked her long black hair contemptuously and tilted up her chin. "Unless he sees Ed Murray running after him."

"I think someone else"—Dad's eyes twinkled—"may knock him out tonight."

"Shall we go?" I asked. "Maybe we can arrive at the Knicker-bocker before the last dance."

"What do you care? You don't know how to dance anyway. Why don't you bring your camera and take pictures of the girls? That's safer than talking to them, isn't it?"

My family laughed uneasily. Rosie's tendency to overkill always troubled them.

"More fun than some girls anyway."

Peg and Vince made such a handsome couple that I felt inferior even before we left our apartment.

So we walked down the narrow stairs of the two-flat and out into the soft warmth of the June night, Vince and Peg hand in hand, Rosie and I as far away from each other as we could possibly be.

And she was very, very beautiful.

And my heart was beating very, very rapidly.

Vince was driving his father's car, a resilient 1939 Mercury. Rosie and I sat in the backseat—I didn't hold the door for her—as close to the opposite doors as possible. One could have put the whole Black Horse Troop between us. We said not a word all the way to the hotel. I sighed loudly when she lit her first cigarette. Her glance of contempt would have withered a pine forest.

I ditched her as soon as we hit the dance floor.

It is still the custom, I believe, for young men who are, for one reason or another, pressured into such social situations before they have enough self-confidence to cope with them to find solace and courage in what the Irish with charming indirection call the Crea-ture. Hence by the end of any given senior prom and despite stern laws to the contrary, at least half the young men have, to quote the Irish again, too much of the drink taken.

I didn't drink, but I found a crowd that had already killed much of the pain of the evening.

"Who's the dame you brought, Chucky? Boy, does she have a cute set of tits."

"Friend of my sister."

"Yeah. Does she put out?"

"So I am told."

"Shit, this should be a good night for you."

"I doubt it."

"Where's she from? I've never seen her around. Great little ass too."

"Really?"

"Yeah. Where did you say she was from?"

"Elmhurst."

"Senior?"

"Would a football hero like me date anyone younger?"

"Great, great tits. Boy, would I like to get a feel of them."

"Naturally."

"Do they feel as good as they look?"

"So-so."

Lies?

Certainly.

I danced with her twice. The first time she embarrassed me into it.

"Find another date, hero?" She captured my hands and dragged me toward the floor.

"You seem to be doing all right."

She shrugged her mostly bare shoulders and twisted her lips in an expression of revulsion. "You think you're the only boy at the dance, but you're not."

It was, I will admit, not unpleasurable to hold her in my arms, at the farthest distance possible and still be said to be dancing.

"God damn it, Chucky, will you relax. I am not a football to be held while someone kicks it."

"For kickoffs only."

"You are an incredibly lousy dancer." Her dark blue eyes sparkled with amusement.

"Not very good at placements either. Anyway, your skin feels like a football's skin."

It certainly did not. Rather it felt like thick cream.

My face was burning. So, in truth, was the rest of me. The orchestra was playing "Tenderly," a song that expressed my sentiments at the moment perfectly.

She laughed like an experienced temptress. "Do you like me this way?"

"What way?"

"In a formal dress."

"You mean virtually naked to the waist?"

"If you want to describe it that way." She raised an eyebrow at my crudity. Most girls her age would have cried or yelled at me or both.

"No worse than any other way."

"And don't stay so far away." She drew close, very close. "I won't rape you."

Her head on my shoulder—she must have been wearing shoes with low heels—her breasts against my chest, she would not have had to rape me. Her waist felt incredibly slim. Her heart seemed to be beating in unison with mine. I found myself floating on a wondrous cotton-candy cloud.

"Don't struggle," she continued. "You're mine for another minute or two. Let me lead you."

"I thought that's what you were doing." I tightened my grip around her. Why not enjoy it?

She smelled of spring flowers and, alas, of whiskey. Drinking already.

"That's much better. You might grow up someday to be a really good date."

Then she smiled up at me, a warm, generous smile that turned her face into a radiant oval of invitation. It was the first of many surprises in that prom.

Surprises, always surprises.

"Don't wait," I gulped, and drew her as close to me as I could.

"I won't," she sighed contentedly.

My leering and half-drunk friend had spoken only the truth: wonderful tits indeed, round, firm hints of glory.

I was in trouble.

So, I escaped from the dance floor as quickly as I could.

And came back for the last dance, the moth to the candlelight, the lemming to the sea, the fly to the spider's parlor, Studs Lonigan to the arms of Lucy Scanlan. This time the orchestra was playing "Doing What Comes Natur'lly," which was indeed what I was doing.

"I thought you'd gone home."

"I almost did."

She leaned into my tight embrace, already dizzy from too much drink. "You don't seem afraid of me this time around."

"I wasn't afraid of Ed Murray the second time."

"Do I get knocked out?"

"Only if you try to fight."

She raised her head from my shoulder and looked up. "Really?"

"Course not. I was joking."

Mostly.

"There are times, Chucky, when . . ."

"When, what?"

"When I think you're something a little better than an insect."

"Don't bet on it."

And that was the end of the last dance and of our romantic love dialogue. Indeed, it was virtually the last conversation until the next day.

My verdict on the Charles Cronin O'Malley of that night?

What a jerk!

~ 10 ~

When the final dance was over that night, we adjourned to the Chez
Paree on Sinclair Court, behind Michigan Avenue. The decision was
made by the usual mysterious process by which mobs make their
decisions—citywide mobs in this case because there must have been
six or seven other proms that night. The club was filled with young
women on heels that were too high for them and dresses that were
either too tight or too revealing, and young men, many still sober,
who looked awkward and uncomfortable in rented summer formals
that were generally speaking designed for men with wider shoulders.

The Chez must have warned its usual patrons to stay away, because adolescents were almost the only patrons that night. I suspect
that they also curtailed the review featuring the Chez Paree adora-
bles, wisely suspecting that the inebriated adolescent males might be
moved to catcalls by the sight of too much womanly flesh.

The shoulders and chests of their dates didn't count.

There was no prospect of drinking at this ritual because no male
at a school prom could persuade the house that he was twenty-one.
Some of the girls were eighteen and hence legal (in a curious reversal
of male chauvinism that marked the State of Illinois in those confusing days), but the waiters were not taking any chances of having
the club's dram-shop insurance revoked if they were proven to
have served dram, or anything else, to a young woman who later
piled up her daddy's car somewhere in northern Illinois or southern
Wisconsin.

They also kept a wary eye for flasks, though they would have
needed a guard at every table to prevent the extracurricular tippling.

Ours was a Catholic school prom, so naturally the intoxication
rates were high. The North Side Protestants from Kelly and the
South Side Calvinists from Chicago Christian Reformed looked on

us with consternation and dismay, as though we were creatures from another planet.

"You're not from Fenwick, are you?" demanded a stern-visaged young woman whose white blond hair labeled her as probably Dutch Reform.

"With red hair and a face like mine, where else would I be from?"

"But you're not drunk!"

"I don't drink," I replied virtuously. She was not altogether unattractive if you like icy blondes, which I have been known to.

"But I thought Irish Catholics *had* to drink on their prom nights."

"Only a venial sin not to," I said, escaping from her before our theological discussion became more serious.

The management knew it would not be a night when it made money. They only hoped to sell enough steaks to keep the losses down. I suspect they also prayed that the natives did not destroy the premises.

Vince and I concentrated on devouring our steaks and most of the steaks of our dates. Peg dreamily watched Vince's every move. My date chain-smoked and, when she was not flitting from table to table, offered her friends a swallow at the "Glenlivet" in her "hand-tooled Florentine-leather" flask, which she had secreted in her large purse.

It seemed to have no bottom.

Ugh.

In the interludes when she deigned to sit with us, she blew smoke in my direction.

"You don't like girls to smoke, do you, Chucky Ducky? You're so old-fashioned you smell."

"Not of cigarette smoke," I replied, turning away.

She leaned over and, when I turned around, exhaled in my face. I was too busy coughing and snorting to fully enjoy the brief view of her breasts that this exercise provided me. Spectacular I told myself, but not worth the smoke.

"Rosemarie!" Peg exclaimed.

"Sorry," Rosie said without much conviction, "but he is such a stuck-up little sawed-off pig."

"I know, but you shouldn't sink to his level."

That's what I call sisterly support.

Vince found it all amusing. But then Peg could have read the stock market report that night and he would have laughed at her.

I slept fitfully during the ride to Lake Geneva. Rosie continued to sip from her flask and ridiculed most of the other girls at the prom. She had a sharp eye for the frailties of others and especially their poor taste in clothes. It was a nasty, mean-spirited harangue, delivered as though her existence depended on belittling others.

"That girl with Delvecchio, you'd think she'd have sense enough not to wear red. A fat person like her looks terrible in red. Why does he date her anyway?"

"Shut up, Rose," Peg snapped at her. "We've heard enough."

Never had I heard Peg draw the line on her friend. Apparently it was normal procedure. Rosie did shut up. She devoted the rest of the ride to sipping on her flask. Small sips, to tell the truth. Vince, who drank but apparently not on a date with Peg, drove carefully. When we arrived at the sprawling, old, late-nineteenth-century Clancy "cottage" ("Took it away from a Protestant trader who couldn't meet his margin calls, poor dummy!"), I sought an empty room as far away from the singing and drinking as I could get, pulled off my ill-fitting formal, and fell into bed.

I had glanced into the parlor for one quick look around. It was not exactly a revel appropriate for the fall of the Roman Empire. Or even for *The Great Gatsby*—some drinking, some hugging, some groping, not much else. Not even the "bundling" of which Puritan New England was tolerant, although some couples were approaching that amusement. From a long distance.

Mom would not have approved, though I would have been surprised if the same kind of behavior didn't happen in her day too. Or any day since we evolved into creatures who couldn't get sex off their minds.

But Mom wasn't there. And neither was Mrs. Clancy, who was the technical chaperone. She had already vanished into an alcoholic haze in the master bedroom, also far away.

Peg and Vince were wandering about outside looking at the stars. What else was there for me to do but sleep?

What indeed?

There is a prom custom of watching the sun come up with your date, a custom that survives even to this day, though it was deemed irrelevant by many in the late sixties and the early seventies.

I seemed to have missed it that day. When I woke up, the sun was, if not high in the sky, at least obviously present. Eight o'clock according to my new-graduation-present Bulova. I struggled into the slacks and sweater that I had been instructed to bring for the frolics of the day and began the search for food. I encountered Vince in the kitchen in the same virtuous activity. Peg was asleep, he informed me while he gobbled down coffee cake and doughnuts, but she was furious at me for abandoning "poor Rosie."

"I didn't want to date poor Rosie in the first place."

"She's a nice girl, Chucky, really she is. You just never give her a chance."

"The voice is the voice of Vince, but the words are the words of Margaret Mary O'Malley."

He grinned sheepishly, poor lout. "I guess you're right, but I agree with her."

"Naturally."

I swallowed a modest breakfast, half a bottle of grapefruit juice and four doughnuts, dug my camera out of the old World War I duffel bag Dad had brought home from Fort Leavenworth, and went out to record the appearance of spring at Lake Geneva—still insisting to myself that my goals were archival, not interpretive.

I was glad I had brought the sweater. The sky was clear, the sun bright, the deep blue waters of the melted glacier inviting, but the weather had changed overnight and the day was as cold as early April. I touched the surface of the lake with my hand . . . ugh. No swimming in that for Charles C. O'Malley today.

The water temperature was probably about fifty-five, a remedy for concupiscence as one of our retreat masters would have said. I found little to demand the attention of my Argus. I stumbled back to the vast gray house, wondering if there might be a possibility of striking a deal that would prevent a report to the good April of my behavior.

The house I noted needed a fresh coat of paint. Moreover, with its gables and turrets and battlements, it looked as if it might be haunted—perhaps by the ghosts of the Protestants from whom Jim Clancy had swindled it.

As I pushed open the heavy oak door—which needed a coat of varnish—I saw out of the corner of my eye a splash of color on the windblown surface of the lake that did not belong there. It was the same peach color as Rosie's prom dress.

I paused. That blur ought not to be there.

It was probably an illusion, a trick of the sun on the water. My conscious self prepared to dismiss it. Then my superego—or some such—forced the image from the periphery of my consciousness to the center. I turned around and raced toward the pier as instinctively as I had raced out of the church eighteen months before.

Sometimes we don't get to choose our improvisations.

Sure enough, there was the prom dress, maybe thirty feet off the end of the pier, mostly underwater with a frail hand rising tentatively above the surface.

Looking back on the event, I note with some surprise that I had the presence of mind to kick off my shoes and lay the Argus on the pier before I jumped in.

I lacked, however, the presence of mind to consider two facts: I was a rotten swimmer and I had no idea what I would do when I got to the waterlogged prom gown with a perhaps dead young woman inside it.

The water was so cold I thought I would die too—it was like jumping out of a warm shower into a meat freezer.

Somehow I managed to plow my way out to her, though my plowing seemed to consume an eternity or two. I grabbed the pathetically small hand just as it sank in abject resignation beneath the surface of the lake.

I pulled with all my limited strength. Rosie ascended to the surface and I slipped under. Gagging and gasping, I shoved my head up again. She was choking too, just barely, as though her last breath was expiring, but still alive.

And mean.

She had enough life left to kick and tug and pull and drag me under.

Now what did I do? Given half a chance she would drown us both.

In the movies the hero swats the heroine when she is hysterical. Moreover I remembered from my swimming course at Fenwick that at times a lifeguard must "immobilize" the person he is saving.

So I immobilized her with a solid blow to her pretty little jaw. It worked—too well, because now I had an unconscious girl on my hands in a huge, water-soaked prom dress that would, if I didn't think of a remedy quickly, pull us both under the icy water.

I must report that despite my antipathy toward the young woman, I took no pleasure in socking her. Nor was there any joy in ripping off her dress, an activity that, under other circumstances, might have had its rewards.

The remedy worked more or less; stripped of her dress and slip, Rosie Clancy was a buoyant child (in a massive, white, strapless corset) who could easily be dragged to the pier.

Especially since after maybe five feet of trying to draw her through the water, I discovered I was standing on the muddy bottom, the frigid water barely up to my chest. Perhaps she had been in no danger at all. Perhaps the water where I had grabbed her was not over her head. Perhaps my absurd gesture—my teeth were chattering now—had been unnecessary.

Typical.

One can drown in a bathtub. And if one has had too much to drink and is weighed down by a prom dress, one can all too easily drown in five feet of water.

Later no one would accept my contention that she was in no danger. Humankind must have its heroes.

I had to figure a way to lift my unconscious burden out of the water to the pier. Slim five feet five inches of girl-becoming-woman that she was, she must still have weighed a hundred pounds, substantially more than I could lift even at my best, which by then I wasn't.

So I pushed and shoved and pulled and yanked and finally landed her like a beached Moby Dick, this season's great white whale of Lake Geneva.

She woke up just as I put all my weight into a final shove, waved her hand as if taking a bow, and knocked my camera into the lake.

I was too tired and too cold to care.

The next problem was to pull myself up on the pier. I tried three times and after each effort fell back into the water. Had I saved the foolish little girl's life only to lose my own?

Walk up to the shore?

Chew gum and think?

I made it, barely, on the fourth try, just in time for a horde of promsters to appear and watch the proceedings with astonishment.

I was lying on the pier, fully clad, quaking and inhaling desperately. Rosie, in her erratically attached armored undergarment, was vomiting and crying hysterically.

Peg broke the stunned silence. "Chucky saved her life!"

"She ruined my camera while I was doing it."

A churlish comment?

Yeah, but she did ruin it. Maybe if it were summer, I could have salvaged my beloved Argus from the muck at the bottom of Geneva, but not in the middle of winter—which is what, shivering uncontrollably on the pier and gasping for breath, I was convinced that it was.

I thought that I should throw her back in as a trade with the lake for my camera.

I wasn't the only person who had brought a camera to the after-prom celebration. I heard shutters clicking as I struggled to my knees. Probably none of them had enough sense of composition to frame the shot right.

"She's suffering from shock and exposure." Peg took charge as was her wont. "One of you idiots get blankets for her. And call a doctor." And to me: "Why didn't you pull her up onto the shore?"

An excellent question and one to which I had no answer.

"Weeds," I muttered incoherently. On the spur of the moment it was not a bad excuse.

I tried to stand up and stride off the pier the way Buck Jones would have done in the old western films. Or more recently John Wayne. Instead, I fell on my face, assuming a position not unlike that I had occupied in Hansen Park Stadium after Ed Murray had crunched me.

They laughed.

Hero as fall guy.

They wrapped me in blankets too.

Rosie refused to be taken to a hospital or to see a doctor. She did not want to worry her mother. So she was bundled in blankets and fed with hot chocolate and eventually, it was reported to me by Peg, helped into a hot bath and a warm bed.

I crawled back to my room, hung my clothes by the heat register, a great improvement on our noisy radiators at home, and collapsed into the bed.

"Are you all right, Chucky? We've been looking for you."

I rolled over, opened my eyes, and peered at my sister and the unfamiliar room. "Sure I'm all right."

The only questions are Where am I? and Why am I here?

"She was drunk of course." Peg watched me somberly.

"Naturally."

"And she fell off the pier, she didn't jump in."

"Fell off the pier?" The idea that she had jumped in seemed absurd. Why would anyone do that?

"At least she claims she fell in. I'm not sure she's telling the truth."

"Why would anyone jump in Lake Geneva in this kind of weather in a prom dress?"

"I don't think she knows herself." Peg sat on the side of my bed, more interested in her own problem than in her heroic brother. "I hope she doesn't do it again."

"At least not before I have another camera for her to ruin."

"You *are* all right." She hugged me fiercely. "I'm so proud of you. You were so brave. That little bitch isn't worth risking your life."

"I can't call her that."

"That's different." She hugged me again.

"If you don't mind, I think I'll go back to sleep."

"Okay. Vinny and I will drive you home whenever you want. Take your time."

I had every intention of doing so.

When I woke up again, I reached for my wrist. The Bulova wasn't there. I had not put it on. So it had not suffered the same fate as my camera.

It was on the table next to the bed. Four o'clock. Enough sleep. If my lungs would stop aching, everything would be fine.

As I walked to the bathroom, I amended my evaluation. If I could also walk without wobbling, everything would be fine.

My clothes were dry, so I put them back on. My wrinkled shirt and my unshaven face made me look like the kind of person who would routinely be routed to the back door of the Clancy "cottage."

An Irish tinker the sight of whom would make you wish you had hidden your silver.

I wandered through the house. Either the others had left for home or were amusing themselves somewhere else. I found Rosie in the two-story living room, curled up in front of the fireplace, smoking and reading a book. She was wearing a white sweater and matching slacks and was wrapped in a red blanket that might be authentic Navajo.

When she saw me, standing in the door, she put the book aside, snuffed out her cigarette, and straightened up, the blanket hanging like a royal cloak from her shoulders. "Are you all right?" we both asked together.

"Sure, fine," we responded in unison, and then laughed. Weakly.

The book, I noted with disapproval, was *Brideshead Revisited*. Why was a mere girl reading a serious book?

I sat uneasily on the edge of a chair in which one could have sunk almost as readily as into the lake. The room had been created out of an original parlor and an upstairs bedroom or two. Strong oak arches soared to the ceiling. The wall was paneled in knotty pine. An enormous picture window looked out on the bright waters of the lake.

An idealized painting of Mrs. Clancy hung on the wall opposite the fireplace. She was probably an attractive woman for a few years long ago. Before she started to drink. They'd say the same thing about Rosie someday.

"Sorry about your camera."

"Sorry about your prom dress. And slip."

"They found the dress." She brightened. "It drifted ashore."

"Cameras don't drift."

"I know. I'll buy you a new one."

"You will *not*."

She winced as though I had hit her.

"You're sure you're all right?" again we spoke simultaneously. Neither of us laughed this time.

"Prom dresses tear pretty easily." I tried to sound lighthearted. "Slips too."

"I'm sure"—she flushed—"you've had lots of experience."

"I try to rip off a dress—and a slip too—whenever I go to a prom. I haven't any experience with corsets yet." My tongue took over on its own. "I need practice in ripping off corsets."

She giggled and seemed to relax.

I charged on, "You really do look lovely in a corset, Rosemarie. Though I can't imagine why someone as beautiful as you would have to wear one. I'm sure you'd look even more beautiful without it. But, like I say, I have no experience in that area yet."

What in the hell had got into me? I couldn't possibly have said those absurd things.

Rosemarie flushed deeply and then began to laugh. We both laughed together.

"Chucky, when you choose to be, you're the sweetest boy in the world!"

"I think you may have said that before." My face was burning.

"You knew exactly what to say to make me laugh. God knows I needed to laugh. . . . You wouldn't have dared to pull off my corset."

"Never can tell what I might do with an unconscious body of a lovely young woman floating on the lake."

More laughter.

Ought not she be offended by my risqué remarks?

For a moment I was again the knight in shining armor who had saved the Princess Rosa Maria and even made her laugh.

Forget that my remarks were stupid.

She stopped laughing and smiled wanly. "They say you saved my life, Chucky."

"I don't think so. You were pretty close to the shore."

She sighed. "At first I was terrified. The water was so cold. Then, well, I kind of knew I was going to die and it seemed peaceful and I wasn't afraid anymore. Why hang on to life anyway?"

I listened silently. Who was this girl? What furies tormented her? I wished I could disappear like an invisible man. I did not want to hear her bare her soul.

"Then when I knew it would only be another minute or two, I sort of changed my mind and wanted another chance. I tried to pray, but I knew God would not listen to me. Then you were there. I'm sorry you had to hit me."

"It was kind of fun."

"Really?"

"No."

"Thank you for saving my life, Chuck," she said solemnly. "I'll never forget what you did. I promise I'll never do anything like that again."

"You really look terrible," I blustered to cover my embarrassment. "I mean, as far as a pretty girl like you can look terrible. You should see a doctor."

"I'm all right."

Then my mouth took over again. "I have an idea."

"Really?"

"Yeah . . . we didn't dance much last night. Why don't we do one more."

"Wonderful!" she exclaimed happily.

She jumped to her feet, turned on the phonograph, which just happened to have "Tenderly" ready to play, and gathered me into her arms. We stayed a respectful distance from one another.

And so we danced, like longtime lovers, easily, happily, without comment or conflict.

We kissed each other gently a couple of times. I'm not sure what would have happened if Peg had not stuck her head through the door.

"Chuck!" she screamed. "What are you doing!"

"Dancing," I said.

"Being the sweetest boy in the world," Rosemarie added, a smile in her voice.

"You healed her," Peg whispered in my ear when we finally arrived back at Menard Avenue. "You made her feel that she was worth something. She was smiling and laughing like nothing had happened. Chuck, that was wonderful!"

"Naturally," I said urbanely.

The secret of prom day at Lake Geneva did not survive the next twenty-four hours.

ATHLETE SAVES DATE'S LIFE AT LAKE GENEVA

Charles "Magic Chuck" O'Malley, the reserve quarterback who led Fenwick's football team into the Kelly Bowl last year, proved on Friday that he could be a hero off the football field as well as on it. At a picnic after the Fenwick Senior Prom, he plunged into the icy waters of Lake Geneva to save the life of his prom date, Rosemarie Clancy, 15. Rosemarie had stumbled off the pier in her prom dress and, according to witnesses, would have drowned if it had not been for O'Malley's quick-thinking bravery.

Rosemarie is the daughter of the well-known commodities trader James P. Clancy. O'Malley's father, Lt. Col. John E. O'Malley, is an architect and former commander of the Black Horse Troop of the Illinois National Guard.

Mom and Dad (who never commanded the Troop, by the way) stared at the story as though they did not really believe it.

"The poor child doesn't have much on, does she?"

"It was kind of fun pulling off her clothes," I said modestly. "It would have been more fun if I were not freezing to death and I knew what to do about a corset."

"Chucky!" Mom protested, but not enough to stop her from laughing.

"I don't know what's happening to you, Brother." Jane looked at me as if she had discovered a new species of amusing elf.

"She was drunk, Mom." Peg was somehow defending me. "It was the first time she ever drank *that* much. She'd be dead if it weren't for Chucky."

"Pulling off the slip," I sailed on merrily, "was the most fun. You can't drag a victim to shore with all those clothes."

"Not another word, young man!"

"I can basically sympathize with his position." My dad looked up from the comics.

"Vangie! Shame on you! She's too young even to think that way!" Mom was still trying to suppress her own laughter.

"Not that young," I said wisely.

And then everyone laughed.

"Anyway, darling," Mom said, striving to regain propriety, "we're all very proud of you."

At supper the next night, an envelope was on my plate. Expensive parchment stationery. From James P. Clancy, Esq.

I opened it with nervous fingers while the other five watched me intently.

Inside there was a check. No note, only a check.

"Five thousand dollars," I said.

Multiply it by ten in 1946. My college education. Graduate school too, if I wanted.

"Five thousand," I muttered through tight teeth. If he were in the room, I told myself, I would tear Jim Clancy's head off. The bastard! He was responsible for his kid's problems.

I looked around the table: every face expressionless.

I tore the check in two, put it back in the envelope, and scrawled Clancy's name and address.

"She's either worth a lot more than that or she isn't worth anything."

"What do you mean, Chuck?" My father cleared his throat.

"If she were my daughter"—my fists clenched and unclenched—"she'd be worth either a million dollars or an honest 'thank you.' Nothing in between."

They applauded.

"What's the matter with him?" I demanded. "Why is he so evil?"

"He's not *really* evil, dear," Mom said. "He means well. His mother spoiled him."

"He never really grew up," Dad added.

"That's no excuse," I added.

"Poor Rosie," Peg sighed.

"I don't intend to grow up either," I announced, "but I won't ever be a cruel bastard!"

There were no reproofs for my bad language. Instead, my mother and my two sisters hugged me, affection that I pretended not to like.

There was one more surprise before I left for Fort Benning.

It appeared at the door of our apartment just as I was leaving with a backdrop of five sets of watery eyes, a small package, wrapped carefully in white gift paper.

I opened it slowly. A new, postwar Kodak 35mm camera.

No note or card. Not that there had to be one.

"Rosie," Peg breathed softly.

"I won't tear it in half," I said, a catch in my voice.

Of all the surprises during those years, that was the one that would most change my life.

I insisted that I would ride up to the Fort Sheridan induction center on the North Shore line by myself. After bidding everyone good-bye with a brave Chucky wisecrack, I walked over to Austin Boulevard, took the bus to Lake Street, and rode the el downtown. I got off at Randolph and Wabash and waited for the North Shore train that traveled around the Loop before heading north again. I thought about calling Rosemarie to thank her for the gift and to bid her farewell. Why had she not come over to our place for the session of tears? I had not asked and Peg had not said.

What difference did it make? That part of my life was over, was it not?

Still I tried a call from the public phone on the el platform. The line was busy. Probably she was talking to Peg.

Was there a lump in my throat as I rode up to Fort Sheridan and my new life?

I can't quite remember.

~ 11 ~

"Just exactly what do you think you're doing, young man?" a woman's voice demanded.

"Studying accounting," I replied politely.

Then I looked up to behold the goddess Maeve looking down upon me with thunder in her dark blue eyes.

I'm not sure that I knew who Maeve was in those days. However, the woman towering over me looked like a goddess. Even if she wasn't, she wore captain's bars, which meant trouble for the poor little orphan redhead. I wasn't an orphan of course, but I felt like one.

I struggled out of my chair and endeavored to stand at attention, something I was not good at. About all I had learned in basic training was how to talk military. I knew nothing about how to be military.

In my clumsy effort to look like a soldier, I knocked my stack of accounting books off my desk. I tried to pick them up off the floor and dropped them. The captain, her eyes threatening at least court-martial and probably immediate execution, retrieved them for me and stacked them neatly on the desk.

"You have a name surely?"

"Yes, Captain, ma'am," I said, wondering if it was too late to salute. "O'Malley, Corp. Charles Cronin, Army of the United States, serial number oh nine—"

"You are not yet a prisoner of war, Corporal," she interrupted me. "You only look like one."

"Yes, ma'am, Captain, ma'am. I only arrived an hour ago from Nürnberg, ma'am."

She was real old by my standards; that is to say, twenty-four or twenty-five. She was also paralyzingly attractive, maybe six feet tall, willowy in a flawlessly fitted uniform, pale complexion, a halo of curly, black hair, and those dangerous, dangerous eyes. There was also I noted, a slight twitch in her lovely lips, a hint that maybe, just maybe, she found me amusing.

"I'm not interested in your excuses," she said implacably. "I'm Capt. Polly Nettleton. I seem to be the senior officer present."

She spoke English with a foreign accent. Boston.

"Yes, ma'am, Captain, ma'am."

"Have you been assigned to this unit, Corporal?"

"If this is the First Constabulary Regiment, Captain, ma'am, then I have been assigned here as a clerk typist."

"Clerk typist?" she said with a sneer, all trace of the latent smile vanishing.

"Yes, ma'am. I asked one of the other men where the new clerk typist worked. He pointed out this desk."

I noted that the others in the room—the grand ballroom of the *Residenz* of the prince bishop of Bamberg—were watching with interest. How would the ridiculous little punk cope with Captain Polly?

"You have orders?" she asked crisply.

"Yes, ma'am."

"Did not they teach you at Fort Benning that you were supposed to present your orders to the senior officer present?"

"No, ma'am."

"They didn't teach you much of anything, Corporal, did they?"

"No, ma'am."

"I see. . . . What do they call you?"

Her lips were twitching again. Ah, there was still hope.

"Chuck, Captain, ma'am."

"All right, Chucky, do you think that as a matter of military formality you might present your orders to me so we can make you part of this outfit, find quarters for you, issue you a proper uniform, and maybe even put you to work?"

"Yes, ma'am."

"Where then are your orders?"

That was a good question.

"They're around here somewhere, Captain, ma'am." I searched frantically in my trousers, my Ike jacket, and my wallet for them.

No orders.

"Do you think this might be what you're looking for, Chucky?"

She reached into my *Principles of Accounting* and removed the pertinent bureaucratic document. It was dog-eared, crumpled, and dirty. She held it between her thumb and forefinger as if it might contain dangerous bacteria.

"Yes, ma'am."

"I take it that upon presentation of these orders you are reporting for duty?"

"I think so . . . er, yes, ma'am, Captain, ma'am."

"Good. . . . Can you type?"

"Yes, ma'am. My MOS [military occupational specialty] is clerk typist."

"I can see that. . . . My question was whether you can type."

Of course I could type. Hadn't I typed half the term papers of my Fenwick graduation class? Perfectly.

"Try me, Captain Polly, ma'am."

A snicker floated around the room. The good captain smiled, the kind of Irish womanly smile that made the sun flee in shame because its light suddenly had become dim, a smile like that of the good April Mae Cronin O'Malley.

"All right, Corporal Chucky. We'll do just that. Here is a sheaf of letters that Gen. Radford Meade, our commanding officer, dictated this morning. They are all directed to Gen. Lucius Clay. Am I wrong in assuming you have heard of the military governor of Germany?"

"No, ma'am . . . yes, ma'am. I mean, Captain, ma'am, that you are not wrong. I have heard of General Clay."

"Good! These letters must be typed perfectly by twelve hundred hours. That's noon, Corporal. You have two hours to do your work. If the letters are not flawless, we may just send you up to the border of the Russian zone for the rest of what promises to be a very cold winter."

"Yes, ma'am."

I amused her. That was good. Another Coach Angelo. One who smiled like my mother.

A half hour later I strolled up to her desk, which was in front of an ornate oak doorway, behind which there was either the prince bishop or the commanding officer of the First Constabulary Regiment (there was no Second Regiment, by the way).

"Captain Polly, ma'am . . . ," I said timidly as I handed her the stack of letters.

She considered me skeptically.

"They had better be perfect."

"Infallible," I replied with my best Chucky Ducky grin.

She glanced over the papers quickly, then read each of them carefully.

"Catholic high school, I suppose?" She looked up at me, her totally radiant smile almost breaking my heart.

"Yes, ma'am. Fenwick in Chicago. Well, Oak Park to be precise."

"Dominicans. . . . What are you doing out here at the end of the earth?"

"Earning money to attend Notre Dame," I said candidly.

She smiled again. "My husband went to Notre Dame."

"A fortunate man on many counts."

She threw back her head and laughed, the rich, happy laugh of a woman who loved her husband so much that any reference to him, even by a miserable little runt of a corporal, made her even happier.

All the others in the ballroom laughed too.

"I'm not sure we need another glib mick here in Bamberg," she said. "However, you certainly can type."

At that moment the great oak doors swung open and two officers emerged, one with the eagle of a full colonel and the other with the twin stars of a major general.

No one in the room seemed to change his or her manner in the presence of the two officers.

"General Meade," Captain Polly observed, "this child is our new clerk typist, Corp. Charles Cronin O'Malley. Despite all our expectations, he actually can type. Quickly and skillfully."

"Sirs," I said, snapping to attention, or what passed for attention in my case, and saluting clumsily.

General Meade, a man of medium height, iron gray hair, vast eyebrows, and a ramrod-stiff back, considered my efforts with a critical eye. He handed them over to the colonel.

"What do you think, Dick?"

The colonel perused them with the same frowning skepticism.

"Flawless," he murmured.

"Perfect," the CO agreed.

"A miracle," Captain Polly agreed.

"Infallible," I added to the litany.

General Meade smiled a frosty but tolerant smile.

"Another smart-mouth mick, Polly?"

"It would seem so, General."

"First clerk typist this year who can type. Remarkable."

"What else can you do?" Col. Dick McQueen, as I would later learn was his name, demanded.

"Not much, sir. I can do shorthand. I take pictures and develop them. I sing with almost any excuse. I've been known to hold the ball for a point-after-touchdown kick. Don't count on me to know anything about firing a gun."

"I think we've heard of your football exploits," Colonel McQueen observed. "Quite impressive."

Wrong story, wrong image. But I wasn't going to argue.

"Shall we keep him, Polly?" the general asked.

"Till someone better comes along."

Thus did the poor little orphan from the West Side of Chicago find a home away from home. It was not one that made me any less homesick. But at least they were ready to keep the funnylike clown off the streets through the winter.

In a few weeks, I owned the HQ staff. It took only some wit and a few political skills for me to shape up the outfit. Practically no one noticed, neither military nor civilian (mostly German), neither man nor woman. Indeed they seemed delighted to have me around, especially since I effectively covered their mistakes and protected them from Captain Polly's dark moods.

We were the Constabulary, a command of some ten thousand carefully selected American troops—a substitute for a national police force—who were supposed to maintain order in occupied West Germany and in particular hunt out the remnants of Nazi fanatics who had promised to continue guerrilla warfare after the surrender a year and a half before.

The most powerful military establishment in history had demobilized itself promptly after the end of the war with Japan. Our leaders had two choices: they could try to fight the massive demand to go home at once and risk mutiny and shattering defeat in the next election; or they could acquiesce with as much grace as they could

and commit the occupation of Germany and Japan to a mostly volunteer army of kids and malcontents.

People like me.

The situation was pretty bad, as you will doubtless perceive from
the fact that, seven months out of Fenwick High School, I was a
sergeant in command of two picked squads of our allegedly best unit.
Somehow my press clippings had caught up with Maj. Gen. Radford
Meade, who commanded the Constabulary, and he decided that, as
matter of absolute faith, I was a "first-rate" soldier.

I was in effect a desk sarge in a third-rate state police force.
"Magic Chuck" guarding the O.K. Corral when there weren't any
Clantons around and without any idea of what he would do if the
Clantons showed up, especially since on our side we had no one
remotely like Wyatt Earp or Doc Holliday.

Fortunately for all concerned, there was not that much to do.
Genocidists or not, the Germans were a law-abiding people. There
were a few criminal gangs to hunt down, mostly on the fringes of
the black market (remember Orson Welles as Harry Lime in Graham Greene's film *The Third Man*?). If the gangs were too big for
the military police to chase, we were called in with our blue berets
and white jeeps and automatic weapons. Occasionally we were assigned to round up refugees who were wanted for war crimes in our
or allied sectors. And once or twice, we were supposed to search for
werewolves, the legendary Nazi diehards.

They made me a sergeant after a couple of weeks, much to my
surprise.

We were not exactly elite troops, but we were better than the
rest of Seventh Army; that is to say, we were a little less likely to be
selling on the black market, buying women with cigarettes and nylons, and worrying about our venereal diseases. If the Russians had
pushed across the boundary line, only about thirty miles north of
our headquarters in Bamberg, a quaint medieval city untouched by
war for a thousand years (because the prince bishops wouldn't let
the burghers build walls so they had to negotiate with invaders instead of resisting them), we wouldn't have been able to hold them
up for more than thirty minutes.

But they were not likely to do that because we still had our monopoly on the atomic bomb.

My only complaint about the HQ was that Captain Polly reminded me not only of the good April, but also of Rosemarie.

She wasn't my girl, I tried to argue, I didn't want her as my girl.
I had somehow forgotten, I tried to explain to God, how crazy she
was. Sure she was beautiful and bright and passionate and fragile,
but she was also wild and unpredictable and already she drank too
much. It was her father's fault indeed, but there was not much I
could do about it, was there?

The Deity did not venture an opinion on my faint heart.

All I wanted, I tried to explain to God, was letters from home. I
was homesick from the day I left Menard Avenue—the family had
not yet moved into our new apartment on Austin Boulevard—and
never got over it. Never even improved. The twenty months ahead
of me stretched out like an eternity. I felt that the Army would be
my life for the rest of my life. I'd not been away from my family in
my life and had no idea till I lost them, temporarily I kept telling
myself, how much they meant to me.

I was so lonely I even wrote that last sentence in one of the letters
to my mother. It was the letter in which I told her about my photographic efforts at the *Hauptbahnhof.*

The worst part of living in this town is the scenes enacted
every day at the railway station. Most of the GIs are out in the
encampment on the edge of the city, across the Rhine-Danube
Canal (unlike we lucky few who are in the hotels and the homes
near the HQ of the Constabulary). At the end of the day, I climb
into my white jeep (yep, I have my own jeep and I've learned
how to drive, mostly by trial and error) and pick my way through
the Germans on their bicycles out to the encampment with mes-
sages from HQ.

Am I a good driver?

I haven't knocked anyone off a bicycle yet!

Anyway, I drive to the station at the time of the arrival of the
train from Leipzig every afternoon. It's the route for soldiers
returning from prison camps in Russia.

Our wartime ally, good old Uncle Joe Stalin, for reasons of
his own has decided to send home some, maybe all, of the surviving German POWs. They dribble in groups of five or ten or

maybe fifteen every day. Scores of women, young, middle-aged, old, wait patiently every day for the train. Some days all of them straggle away in the gloom—the days are mostly night in this part of the world in winter and the sun doesn't shine much during the day either—shivering in their thin coats, their heads bent, their shoulders bowed.

Then some days, a husband or a son or a lover appears. Every woman in the station celebrates the good fortune of the woman whose man has returned.

You wonder how they'll put together their lives after so much suffering, especially since many of them are missing an arm or a leg.

A scene from the *Inferno* I sometimes think.

Yes, Dad, I am reading it, you'd be surprised how literate a guy can become when there's nothing else to do and he can't take the smell of photographic chemicals any longer and has seen *It's a Wonderful Life* for the sixth time.

Then, other times, at the station, I marvel at the power of human hope.

I take pictures when there is enough light. They don't try to stop me, partly because I'm an American and can do anything I please, partly because they're too tired to resist, and partly, I like to think, because they somehow see I'm on their side.

The side of those who hope.

Yes, I did write that last line.

All of Europe and Germany especially were in deep economic trouble in the winter of 1946. England was paralyzed by blizzards, shortages, and unemployment. Food rations were smaller than during the war. Berliners, with characteristic efficiency, dug thousands of graves in the autumn before the ground froze, for those who would die of starvation during the winter. More than nineteen thousand people in that city were treated for frostbite during the winter. Signs appeared saying, "Blessed are the dead, for their hands do not freeze."

Things were not quite so bad in Bamberg that year. Few starved to death or froze to death, only those who were already old or sick. Yet, almost everyone was hungry and cold. Nothing had prepared me for the physical and moral degradation of the Germans in 1946. I had grown up in the Depression. I had seen vets selling apples. I had helped my mother in our parish's soup kitchen on West Madison Street. I had seen bread lines. I had seen the bleak despair on the faces of neighborhood children when they were ejected from their apartments and sat forlornly on the family furniture that had been summarily thrown on the front lawn. I had recoiled with horror at the Negro (as we called them then) slums along the Lake Street elevated on the way to the Loop. Yet, nothing prepared me for Germany the year after the war. For the first month I could not eat, the only time in my life that I experienced such a problem.

I tried to persuade my GI friends who were working in the small-time black market—those who were sending home a couple of thousand dollars a month—that they were cheating these sick, dispirited, shivering people. They didn't see it that way, or if they did, they weren't troubled.

"Hell, Sarge, everyone's doing it."

"It's no skin off my ass."

"They lost the war, didn't they?"

"You seen the concentration camps? They don't deserve our pity."

"Their own are robbing them, why shouldn't we do it?"

"They owe me two years of my life. I'm getting mine back."

The Bambergers, their faces pinched, their eyes averted in shame, listlessly shuffled down the streets in tattered old clothes, shoes with newspapers for soles, thin blankets clutched tightly around their shoulders for coats. Some of them were as thin and worn as the survivors of the concentration camps in the newsreels I had seen. Many of them died of pneumonia or influenza complicated by exposure and malnutrition. Some lived in freight cars that had been damaged in the air raids on the railway yards, burning pieces of their crude homes to stay warm. Others huddled under the bridges in lean-tos made of *Wehrmacht* greatcoats. They were the Nazi enemy, but I could not harden my heart against them, particularly against the kids.

I gave most of my monthly supply of cigarettes, nylons, and chocolate bars to kids. The Depression, I often thought, was the Garden of Paradise compared to Germany in the winter of 1946.

Corruption permeated the Army of Occupation, as I would later learn from history books it permeated all armies of occupation everywhere. A GI I lived with sent home eighty thousand dollars to his parents after six months in Bamberg. In 1947 dollars. It was routine for some soldiers to send home ten thousand dollars a month. They'd make out a postal money order for eleven thousand dollars, one thousand of which was a tip to the postal clerk for winking at the transaction.

Everyone was doing it, they would argue. So it couldn't be wrong. We could buy a gallon of gas for ten cents and sell it for twenty dollars. A carton of cigarettes (we could buy one every week at the PK) was worth fifteen dollars on the black market. We paid the elderly woman who straightened up our room in the old Messerschmitt House two packs of cigarettes a week. She took care of ten rooms. Not a bad profit. She was our slave maybe, but a well-paid slave.

As were the women and girls whom we made our sexual playthings—slaves they were for all practical purposes, but we paid them well and sometimes even took good care of them.

I didn't smoke, but I bought my carton a week and gave packs to people who seemed to need help. I also stashed them away in a locker at the *Residenz*, against a rainy day, as my mom would have said. I didn't deal, however, in the black market, not the minor one that most of the other GIs played in or the big-time one that ran so efficiently that it reminded me of the Chicago mob. No matter how corrupt everyone else was, I told myself after I'd been in Bamberg for a month that I was a good Catholic, the product of twelve years of Catholic education, eight years at St. Ursula, four years at Fenwick (from which I had graduated a lifetime ago, that is six months ago). I would not become a crook, not even if everyone else around me did.

Before my term in Germany was over, I had violated far more serious laws of both God and country.

"We corrupt everything we touch in this country," I had exploded to Col. Dick McQueen, the chief of staff of our outfit. "Especially their women. Our guys claim that for a pair of nylons, a chocolate bar, and six packs of cigarettes, they can have any Bamberger woman they want."

"They exaggerate."

McQueen was a tall, handsome man with thick blond hair, fair skin, and a vast smile. He was the most competent officer of our unit, much smarter than General Meade. He owned a Medal of Honor that he never wore. The only decoration he did wear was the badge of the combat infantryman. He seemed to me to represent the integrity and ability that West Point was supposed to inculcate in its officers. If there were more men like him in Bamberg, I told myself, there would be a lot less corruption. Like General Meade, whom he would replace the next year, he had taken a shine to me.

"Not all that much."

"I don't like it either, Chuck. I don't know what we can do about it. The GIs are lonely and hungry and have the nylons and the chocolate bars, and the women want to live. Don't underestimate these people. They're going to bounce back. You can see their determination in the hatred in their eyes."

"If they were buying my sisters with nylons and cigarettes, I'd hate them."

"It's this way after every war when one side is completely vanquished, Chuck. We're corrupt but not as corrupt as most armies of occupation."

At first, I hadn't noticed the hatred. The Bambergers seemed eerily docile to me. Maybe that was the flip side of hatred. They did bounce back all right. Hatred was perhaps less the explanation than habits of hard work. They also exploited their own, just as my buddy had said. Their great postwar artists, such as the novelist Heinrich Böll and the filmmaker Werner Fassbinder, thundered against the corruption and greed of the German "economic miracle" and rightly so. Yet, it was not all corruption and greed. Survival was a powerful motive. So too I thought was determination to overcome shame and humiliation.

And guilt. A few of the Germans—not many—I came to know before I went home were ready to admit that their country had done terrible things.

"We kick them into the gutter and stomp on them," I said to Colonel McQueen at the end of that discussion. "And now we're starting to pick them up, dust them off, and give them another chance. Why?"

"Because we're Americans, Chuck." His eyes had a faraway look in them. "Because some of us can see ourselves in the same situation but for the grace of God." His face became grim. "Because we can imagine our women having to do the same kinds of things to stay alive."

"We're helping them so they can fight off the Russkies for us, aren't we?"

"We'd do the same thing if the Russkies all became Boston Irish Catholics tomorrow like John Nettleton."

Colonel Nettleton was the husband of Capt. Polly Nettleton, General Meade's assistant.

"God forbid!"

"It's good to have people like you around here, Chuck, people who worry about morality. We should have more."

"I have the impression that here at HQ one of me is almost too many."

We both laughed, but uneasily. Colonel McQueen had said exactly what I had hoped he would say, and my conscience was calmed for the moment. Yet, he had seemed anxious through the whole difficult conversation. Later I would wonder if his nervousness was that of a man who knew he was violating his own principles.

My ambivalence about Germany is as strong today as it was in the winter of 1947, when Dean Acheson in the State Department was preparing the drafts of the Truman Doctrine and the Marshal Plan, which would save the economies of Europe and launch the German "economic miracle."

Germany would play an important part in my ongoing comedy of errors, and not always a benign one either.

— 12 —

"O'Malley," said Major Carpenter, his Southern drawl turning clipped in anxiety. "You take one of your squads down there and y'all see what's going on with those werewolves."

"Yes, sir," I said briskly, trying to hide that I was as scared as he was.

I mean, werewolves are supposed to be scary, aren't they?

So I waved the other seven men out of our two jeeps, barked, "Follow me," and led them down the snow-covered hill to the edge of the clearing in which our target stood—a run-down, old farmhouse in the foothills of the Bohemian Alps.

It had started the day before when Gen. Radford Meade had stopped by my clerk typist's desk, a sheaf of newspaper clippings in his hand.

"What do they call you, Red?"

"Chuck, sir." I had risen to my feet with considerable lack of grace as I told him for the tenth time what people called me.

"Sit down, Chuck." He had rested his rear end on the side of my desk.

"Yes, sir."

"You know what werewolves are?"

"Of course, sir. A werewolf is a legendary character in German folklore, a human by day and a wolf by night, or at least on nights when the full moon is shining. A kind of Teutonic Dracula."

He had grinned. "You believe in them?"

I hesitated. "No, sir, I don't. But as my mother would say, there are a lot of things that happen in this world that we don't understand."

"A wise woman, your mother . . . but this time the question is about an underground Nazi guerrilla movement that intends to continue the war. Ever hear of them?"

"I read about them in *Time*, sir. But I've never met any of them."

"Precisely. The poor Krauts have enough to worry about trying to keep alive and persuading us that they were never Nazis and hated Hitler. But Mr. Luce of Time Incorporated takes the werewolves seriously. He has sent out one of his best photographers to take pictures of the Constabulary capturing some of them."

"I see, sir."

"They've even got a locale, over in the Bohemian Alps."

"Close to the Russkies?"

"You bet. We have no evidence of any guerrilla activity in our area. But Major Carpenter of CID has information about this nest of werewolves."

The general made a slight face to indicate his distaste for Major Carpenter, a spit-and-polish soldier with paratroop wings and looks but, as I knew and the general did not, no record of combat.

"I see, sir."

"So the major will be in charge of the raid, if you can call it that. We'll send along two squads of our men because it's our jurisdiction. I want you to be in charge of our lads, Chuck. Keep an eye on both the man from *Life* and the major."

"Me, sir?"

Fear had erupted in my loins and permeated my whole body, not a shiver this time or a chill, but bitter cold as if from a fierce arctic wind.

"Yeah. I like what I read about you in the papers, Chuck." He had waved the sheaf at me. "You seem to know what you are doing, unlike most of the misfits we have out here."

"Yes, sir. Those stories are exaggerated, sir."

"I don't believe it." He had laughed.

Polly Nettleton, the one who really ran the Constabulary if anyone did, frowned later when I brought a stack of memos up to her.

"Be careful, Chucky. It could be dangerous out there."

"I'll wear my long underwear, ma'am."

"I don't mean the cold."

"Why me?"

"Because after McQueen and me," she said with her wondrous Irish smile, "you're the smartest person in this outfit."

"Shows how bad things are."

So there I was in the Bohemian Forest with two squads of our comic-opera soldiery, assigned to do battle with a Nazi guerrilla army that we were pretty sure did not exist.

Even now, I remember the sour taste of terror. I had been numb with fear during the long, bitter-cold ride in our rickety jeep. Now I was so scared that I could hardly climb out of the jeep in response to the major's orders.

It's natural to be afraid, I had told myself, when you are going into combat for the first time. Except this wasn't combat, was it?

Well, it could be, couldn't it?

I said the Act of Contrition twenty times during our ride up the foothills.

Or was it the grace before meals?

And, good Catholic that I was, I had examined my conscience in preparation for death almost as many times.

If the werewolves were good soldiers, they would hear us coming. If they had as many weapons as they were supposed to have, they could cut us down in about three seconds.

We were the good guys, however. It was easy to tell because we wore the white hats—well, actually, blue hats, but we drove in white jeeps. As to the werewolves, how could anyone with a name like that be anything but bad guys?

The only sin for which I could not plead excusing cause or at least extenuating circumstances was my treatment of Rosie, or Rosemarie as I now called her more politely. Faced as I was with what my fevered imagination considered the prospect of almost certain death, I figured I ought to apologize to her for all my nastiness.

I would write her a letter:

Dear Rosemarie,

Maybe I've grown up a little here in Germany, not much, but perhaps just a little. So I want to apologize to you for all the times I was rude or sarcastic to you. Maybe you know that it was just a silly little game that both of us played, but I was the one that kept the game going, and I'm sorry. I hope we can be friends when I return.

I also want to thank you, however belatedly, for your won-

derful gift before I left for the Army. I use it every day and think
of you whenever I click the shutter.

Love,
Chuck

In my head, I hesitated about the second-last word of the letter.
It would certainly guarantee a reply after she and Peg had discussed
its implications, and I was so lonely and so sexually hungry that I
desperately wanted mail from a beautiful young woman, even my
sometimes despised foster sister.

As we inched down the hill toward the farmhouse, slipping and
sliding on the snow, we looked like comic-opera soldiers, in paratroop boots although we were not paratroops, yellow scarves, blue
berets (or helmets), blue cords on our shoulders, .45-caliber pistols
on our wide, white belts, everything but the Sam Browne straps over
our shoulders.

The fancy uniforms were supposed to impress the Germans.
Maybe they did, though at the time most Germans were in no position not to be impressed by the occupying armies.

Mostly we rode around the country in our white jeeps and looked
as efficient and as competent as we could.

I can't remember what I thought as we drew near the farmhouse.
But I'm sure the letter to Rosie was in the back of my head and
maybe her image close to the front of the same head. I probably
decided that I would not tell her that her mixture of beauty, passion,
and intelligence overwhelmed me, though even then I kind of half
knew that was the truth. Nor would I write that while one part of
me resented that my family had destined us for one another, another
part of me was both delighted and terrified by that prospect.

Nor would I say how much I disliked her father. I disliked him
mostly out of envy. He was rich and we were poor.

The word *love* would be enough and more than enough when I
finally transferred the letter from my head to paper when we got
back to Bamberg.

If we got back to Bamberg.

Thus, I must have persuaded myself I had made my peace with
both Rosemarie and my Maker, though given who and what I am,

I'm sure I cautioned the latter that the word *love* was still open to discussion.

As I had cheerfully told my "men," all of whom were my age or even younger, we should not worry much about the Russkies. There was no reason to think that their occupation armies, even their elite troops, were better than we were.

The frightened *Life* photographer was hiding behind one of our jeeps on the rim of the little wooded hill where the rest of our command cowered as I led my squad toward the farmhouse where the alleged Nazis were waiting.

"Want to come with us?" I asked him as I flicked the safety off my machine pistol, John Wayne riding to battle.

I had fired the pistol exactly twice in practice and was by no means certain that it would either work or stay in my hands if I had to squeeze the trigger.

The photographer shook his head with an effort at nonchalance. "I'll let you guys make sure that there's something to photograph."

Right.

If I were killed in action, General Meade would have shaken his head sadly and said, "He was a damn fine soldier."

All I wanted to be was a damn fine accountant.

Well, we didn't have to put up with TV cameramen in those days.

My skepticism about the werewolves was based on a few months of watching the Germans struggle back from defeat. It seemed to me that whatever their faults, they were not about to risk either their lives or a chance for an improvement in their living conditions in the name of a lost cause.

Especially since, to hear the citizens of Bamberg, no one was or ever had been a Nazi. Bamberg had not been bombed because it had very little industry. Through the years the burghers were too busy fighting with the prince bishop to build up much industry. In ages past they had learned how to live with invaders. They bought off the Hussites back in the fifteenth century. During the Thirty Years' War they were Catholics or Lutherans depending on which army was in town. So they could get along with us if they had to, and they had to.

But they didn't much like us, even if we were preferable to the

Russians, who had preceded us and had terrorized the city and raped every woman they could find in the months before we replaced them. When I had tiptoed into the concert hall (on Dominican Street and in the old Dominican church, which was then a concert hall), I had been favored with a number of dirty looks. What is this barbarian doing here? Surely he cannot appreciate the Bamberg Symphony playing and singing Beethoven's Ninth?

I had given them dirty looks back and sat down to enjoy the music. It had been well enough done, heaven knows, but not much joy was displayed in the choral movement. Admittedly the Bambergers did not just then have much to be joyous about, but I suspected they wouldn't have smiled during Schiller's verses even in the best of times.

Dirty looks are one thing, I reassured myself as I led my seven-man team across the clearing toward the farmhouse, armed revolt is quite another.

Snow was beginning to fall again from dark clouds scudding, it seemed, almost above our fingertips. I wondered how warm it was inside the house.

I waved my arm in a signal to my men the way I had seen officers do in the war movies. They fanned out around the house the way they had seen soldiers fan out in the war movies. I wondered if any of them besides me had fired an automatic weapon even once.

"Kelly, Crawford," I whispered hoarsely above the wind, "cover me."

"Huh?" Kelly yelled. "What'd you say, Sarge?"

"I said cover me," I shouted back.

Neither of us was quite sure what that meant.

I took a deep breath, murmured a prayer, decided absolutely that I would add *love* to my letter to Rosemarie, and kicked the battered old door of the farmhouse open.

Rather, to be precise about it, I tried to kick the door open. It didn't budge. I kicked it again. And yet again.

You see it in a movie and you laugh till you cry.

Finally the door swung open and an elderly German woman said, "*Ja? . . . Mein Gott!*"

I shoved her aside and pushed my way into the front room of the old house. An old man, a middle-aged couple, and a boy about four-teen crowded up against the wall by a weakly burning fireplace, hands reaching for heaven.

What else do you do when comic-opera soldiers crash in on a cold winter day?

"Search it," I ordered my men. "Every inch . . . and put the safe-ties back on your weapons."

Only one man did so. The others had forgotten to release them in the first place.

My quintet of prisoners hardly seemed a threat to the United States of America. Rather they looked hungry, threadbare, tired, and scared stiff, exactly the way most Germans looked when the Con-stabulary paid them a visit.

If this was the best the neo-Nazis could do, they weren't much of a problem.

"No one else, Sarge," Kelly shouted happily.

"Crawford?"

"Empty, Sarge."

"Great."

I stepped outside into what was now a blizzard and signaled Ma-jor Carpenter and the rest of our "combat team," which was hardly a team and certainly wasn't ready for combat, and the *Life* photo man.

They came running down the hill pell-mell, like Pickett's charge at Gettysburg.

What if it was a trap, I thought, with a real-life werewolf holding a gun at my head.

"How many men, Sergeant?" Sam Houston Carpenter waved his gun dangerously.

"Three, sir, including an old man and a boy."

Carpenter, who, as I knew, had fought the war from a desk in Grosvenor Square (Der Eisenhower Platz it was also called) in Lon-don, seemed more relieved than disappointed.

"Have you found the weapons?"

"We're searching, sir."

The *Life* man, now heroic, brushed the two of us aside and charged into the house, camera clicking wildly.

With all the film he was using he ought to come up with a few shots in which by accident the light and composition were presentable.

I followed him in, unlimbering Rosie's Kodak, as I perhaps perversely called it in my mind, and carefully snapped a few shots of my prisoners. *Life* was looking for fanatical neo-Nazis. I saw only five terrified human beings.

"Can't find any weapons, Sarge," Kelly reported to me, not the major, a violation of military courtesy that the major hardly noticed.

"Oh, damn," *Life* moaned, "there have to be weapons. I came a long way in the cold to get pictures of weapons."

Did he want us to fake a weapons cache? Maybe.

"Another false alarm," Major Carpenter sighed. "Keep on searching, Sergeant. We have to find something."

I pondered making a deal with the Germans. Tell me where the guns are and I'll see that you get off. But they were going to get off anyway, even if there were guns.

I prowled around one of the crude, simple bedrooms. No running water, poor devils. I moved the small homemade wooden bedstead. Underneath it a trapdoor.

"Kelly, open this trapdoor."

"Sure, Sarge."

Good military response, right?

Underneath the trap was a tiny, bitter-cold cellar, maybe a four-foot cube. Unwrapping tattered, old *Wehrmacht* gray blankets, I discovered a half dozen rifles and a couple of boxes of ammunition, maybe two hundred rounds.

Jeez, why didn't we bring the Second Armored Division?

"Huh, Sarge?"

Had I said it aloud?

"Never mind, Crawford. . . . Major Carpenter, we've found the weapons and ammo, sir."

So the *Life* man got his pictures, Major Carpenter would probably get a promotion, and the Constabulary got its werewolves. Don't the Mounties always get their man?

And I caught a few good shots in my project, sanity protecting, of documenting what it was like to be defeated in a war.

"Well, son," the general asked me the next day, "what do you think of our werewolves?" I had reported to him in his steamy quarters in the Concordia, a fabulous eighteenth-century burgher's home on the banks of the Regens down the street from our HQ on the *Domplatz*. There was enough heat in the house for the whole shivering city of Bamberg.

"They claim that the weapons were left there in 1945 by a retreating SS unit and that they never touched them. They were afraid to turn them in because they didn't want to be accused of being werewolves."

"What do you think, Sarge?"

"None of the weapons were operational, sir. And the ammo is worthless."

"Precisely."

"And *Life* has its pictures."

The general smiled at me. "You catch on quickly, son."

"But what about those poor farmers? They have no record of being Nazis."

"They're warmer in our custody than back on their farm."

"That's for sure."

"And better fed."

"So when *Life* leaves, we keep them around for a while and then drop the charges for lack of evidence?"

"That's the humane thing to do," he sighed as he rose from his easy chair and tossed another log on the fire, "isn't it?"

The general doubtless missed his wife and family, but he lived like a Renaissance prince, except with running water and central heating. Being a ranking officer in an army of occupation was by no means all bad.

"Yes, sir."

"Then I guess we'll do something pretty much like that, huh?"

"Yes, sir."

By then, we were probably, for all our corruption, the most humane conquerors in history. We'd seen the pictures of the concentration camps; some of us, myself included, had visited Belsen. But, despite my arguments with Dr. Jack Berman in the darkroom, Americans find it hard to believe in collective guilt. Cold and hungry kids are cold and hungry kids, no matter what their country might have done in a war.

The farmers with the guns in their cellar were poor and frightened peasants, regardless of Belsen. Had they voted for the Nazis in 1933? Probably not. Their part of the world, the far northeastern fringe of Bavaria, usually voted for the Center Party, a mostly Catholic, mildly liberal group. Yet, they were part of a culture and a country that had done unspeakable things to millions of innocent people.

Jack Berman, a psychiatrist at the local Army hospital with whom I argued philosophy in the dim red light of the darkroom next to the post exchange (in the basement of the *Residenz*), thought that all Germans were guilty. I was clever enough to say that not all Jews were guilty for the death of Jesus, only a handful who had died long ago (a line I had picked up from a Dominican at Fenwick). Berman laughed and replied, "You Irish are always quicker with words than we are. We are, however, talking about different kinds of guilt."

"So the people we picked up in the Bohemian Forest?"

"They are guilty of course, but what purpose is served by imprisoning them on charges which would never stand up back in the States?"

"So we must try to be just and fair and humane all at the same time. We come to the same conclusion but by different roads?"

"Mine is better," he said with a laugh as my pictures of the women at the railroad emerged in the solution.

"I'd rather be judged by mine."

"Wouldn't we all."

"God is mercy," I insisted, using the words of the Fenwick Dominican.

I expected him to answer that God was just.

Instead, he said, "So we must all hope."

We had at least provided the editors of *Life* with the pictures they wanted.

Including a picture of me standing triumphantly over a half dozen unworkable *Wehrmacht* rifles, with the dangerous werewolves up against the wall behind me. On the cover of the magazine. If that was the best shot our madly clicking photojournalist had produced, he hadn't done very well.

A hero, right? In that fancy getup I should be singing a Rossini aria, I told myself with disgust when I saw the picture.

The family were delighted. "Rosie thought you looked real cute in your scarf," Peg wrote to me.

Great for Rosie. She was Rosie again.

Yes, I had drafted a letter to her. I still have it; that's why I was able to quote it verbatim.

But I didn't mail it.

Did I know then how much I really loved her?

Yeah, I knew. I didn't admit it to myself, but I knew.

— 13 —

I lost my virginity to a Nazi. And received a Leica from her. It was a momentous exchange.

I was seduced. By a girl who was fighting desperately for her life. But there was more to it, I still believe, than just seduction.

It was another surprise, another error in my comedy of errors. But it didn't seem like comedy then.

The affair—I know of no other word—began the week after we had "liquidated the werewolf cell" (*Life*'s phrase, not mine) in the Bohemian Alps. I was driving back from Nürnberg late at night in my white jeep, shivering from the cold, against which the jeep's canvas top was little protection, and peering through the erratic windshield wipers as I drove in a small blizzard on the autobahn.

The trip had been long because a heavy convoy, using both lanes of the autobahn, had slowed my ride down to Nürnberg. Oddly, they had turned off the road and disappeared into the forests about halfway to Nürnberg.

I worried about that convoy. I worried that I had seen John Nettleton with some dubious-looking characters in the shadows outside the headquarters at Nürnberg. I worried about the "shipment" I was bringing back to General Meade. I didn't want to become involved in any of the Army's generalized corruption.

I was late and so I was tempted to hurry on the way home. I told myself that I had to be careful. We'd been losing men all over the European Theater in accidents on the autobahns. I was sober. But I was tired and discouraged and lonely, and that didn't help.

I was a perfect target, an accident waiting to happen, a young man looking for love, or something like love, without even knowing it.

As veterans of any military service in the last century will tell you, the greatest enemy is boredom. Occupation duty did not involve combat dangers, but the boredom was almost as bad. There was literally nothing to do. I could finish the work of my "clerk typist" specialty each morning in about an hour. I would draw patrol duty once a month at the most. An occasional errand for the general down to Nürnberg (to pick up a case of bourbon he was not about to trust to ordinary channels) became a welcome relief from the monotony, if it also troubled me about his possible connection to the black market. In Bamberg I was taking courses from the University of Maryland extension so I could have enough credits to enter Notre Dame as a sophomore. I spent a lot of time in the base darkroom. And still there was nothing to do much of the time.

Except daydream.

I cursed myself every day for the stupidity of my stubborn determination to earn my college education by two years of service. They were two wasted years. Maybe I could earn one of them back by taking enough classes. Possibly, if I worked at it, a year and a half.

I don't want to suggest that everyone in the Seventh Army was drunk every night or gambling away their paychecks or buying girls in exchange for chocolate bars and nylons or profiteering on the black market. There were some who, like me, did their work, played their basketball, and counted the days and the hours till they went home.

But the atmosphere in Bamberg in those days reeked of depravity and corruption (with the sentimental strains of "I'll Dance at Your Wedding" providing an ironic counterpoint to the depravity). I was so sickened by the way we were degrading ourselves and those whom we had conquered that, instead of seeking friends whose values were something like mine, I became, for the first time in my life, a loner. I withdrew to my darkroom in the USO (and continued my philosophical arguments with Dr. Berman), and to my tiny cell at the Vinehaus Messerschmitt (when it was built in 1832, it was a home in the country and not so long ago the country home of Willy Messerschmitt, the pilot and airplane designer, though they didn't talk about him in Bamberg in 1946). I curled up with my class books about English literature and art history and even photography (yes, there was a class in that).

And my daydreams.

I turned off the autobahn and limped carefully through the snow to Bamberg. The city was so far east that it was subject not to the weather produced by the Gulf Stream but to the weather of the Eurasian landmass. In other words Russian weather instead of English or Irish weather. That meant hot summers and bitter winters.

The Regens River was frozen, the slanted tile roofs and the platzs covered with snow. Under a half-moon, ducking in and out of the clouds, the city glistened like a magic imperial capital in a fairy tale. The streets were deserted, even near our housing. What revelry occurred in this kind of weather took place indoors.

I crossed the river and drove carefully down the Untersandstrasse and by the *Dom*, the strange cathedral whose front was Romanesque and back Gothic. My destination was not HQ in the *Residenz* (where most of the lights were already out) but the general's quarters down the river in the Concordia. An MP patrol stopped me at the intersection of the Judenstrasse (a ghetto street, in the days when there were Jews in Bamberg) in the oldest section of the town, where the streets, if not the buildings, had been shaped in the Middle Ages. "Sorry, Sarge," the corporal in charge said cheerfully in a cracker dialect so thick that I could hardly understand him, "but we've got word that there are black-market folks coming through with medical supplies. Mind if we check your cargo?"

"Suspect even the Constabs?"

"My grandmother if she's out on a night like this. What you got?" He swept his flashlight around my jeep. It paused on the carton on the seat next to me. "What you got there, Sarge?"

"Bourbon for my general."

"No kidding?"

It dawned on me that this cheerful MP had the flap on his .45 open. He half-suspected me. Brave soldier that I was, I felt my stomach turn anxiously.

"Take a look."

"Wow! That's Old Fitz!"

"Couldn't prove it by me. About whiskey I don't know much."

"Good stuff, a long way from the bluegrass country," he sighed. "Sure your general couldn't spare a bottle?"

I pointed at Gen. Radford Meade's name on the carton. "I don't know. You want to come along and ask him?"

"I value my ass too much for that. Okay, Sarge, thanks for being cooperative. The last group through here were shitheads."

"Not ours?"

"Naw. Never seen them before. Which doesn't prove anything."

He waved me on.

I thanked God that He had not put me in the world with the mind and heart of a black-market operator.

At the next corner, right behind the Oberpfarrkirche—the big Romanesque parish church—I slowed for a slippery spot and skidded anyway. The jeep bounced over the curb and settled peacefully, like a Saint Bernard ready to rest for the night after a difficult, all-day trek in the Alps. The motor died, telling me that it too was ready to call it a day.

I was about to start the ignition when I heard a muffled scream from a distance. A woman's scream.

Hand on the key, I listened. If there was no repeat, I would mind my own business and drive on to the Vinehaus.

I heard in my brain Rosie's sobs in the dark church. This time, I gritted my teeth; I would not panic.

There was another and more terrible scream. Someone was hurting a woman, hurting her badly, down a flight of steps and in a twisted alley on the left, across the street from where I had stopped.

What happened next is of the same order of folly as catching the blocked pass in Hansen Park or plunging into Lake Geneva. Exit Charles Cronin O'Malley, enter daimon on horseback and with a lance.

I grabbed my automatic weapon and my flash, jumped out of the jeep, and raced toward the screams, now even more plaintive. I turned a dogleg corner, shone my light on the thick, old walls, and saw in a boarded-up doorway three GIs tormenting a civilian who, from her screams, was obviously a woman.

Dear God, they must need sex bad if they'd rape on a night like this.

Or perhaps only entertainment.

"Halt!" I shouted. "Constabulary!"

One of them shone a flash back at me, saw my automatic weapon and blue beret, and shouted, "Let's get the hell out of here!"

They took off down the street, their boots clattering on the cobblestones, despite the cover of new snow.

I should have taken off too. I had saved her, had I not? Wasn't that enough?

"Fräulein?" I turned my light on the heap of rags slumped on the ground at the doorway.

Her face was incredibly young, fifteen or sixteen at most, a pretty face framed in long, pale blond hair, the kind of face that should have been beaming next to a date at a weekend dance. Now it was dirty, bruised, and wet with tears.

I helped her up. They had torn most of her clothes. They now hung from her thin shoulders in shreds. Her breasts were dirty and red where they had abused her, but she was alive and not hurt too badly. I took off my jacket and draped it around her quivering torso.

"What are you doing here?" I tried my terrible German.

"I speak English," she sobbed.

"Good. I'll take you home."

Give a lonely male a battered woman to take care of and he thinks he's the king of the universe.

"No, please, please. I am all right."

"You haven't answered my questions."

"*Polizei?*" she asked dubiously.

"I'm not here to make an arrest, fräulein."

She stifled her sobs. "Out to the square, then down two streets, Obersandstrasse off Kasernstrasse, but you need not . . ."

"Not all Americans are rapists, fräulein."

"I know that," she said in a tone appropriate for admonishing a little boy. But she leaned against my arm, trustfully I thought, as I led her back to the jeep.

"And my second question?"

"I don't remember it." She was still quaking, as though the cold and her terror would shake her poor little body apart.

"What are you doing here at this time of a bitter-cold winter night?"

"They promised me medicine for my sister if I paid them." The words tumbled from chattering teeth. "I gave them the money, but they wouldn't give me the medicine. Instead they tried . . . but you came. *Danke*, Herr Yankee. You saved me."

"What's wrong with your sister?"

Note how masterfully the young hero speaks his lines, the young knight in shining armor on his white horse. Well, in Constabulary finery and on white jeep.

"Pneumonia. We need, what is it you call it . . . ?"

"Penicillin?"

"*Ja.* Otherwise she will die."

It sounded implausible. "That drug is available on an emergency basis for civilians in this city at the American hospital."

We were back at the jeep. I opened the door for her.

"Not for us."

"Why not?" I pushed her elbow toward the door of the jeep.

"We have false papers. If they are examined, we would be found out. We . . . are not legal."

"Why are you illegal?" I shoved her harder toward the door.

She cowered against the side of the jeep. "If you had not come, they would have tortured me more and then raped me. Then perhaps they would have killed me."

"Perhaps," I admitted. "Probably."

"You saved my life."

An old trick of mine, fräulein. I salvage pretty girls once every year or so, just for the hell of it, if you know what I mean.

"You could say that."

"I can trust you?"

"I think so. I mean, you don't seem to be a criminal that I should turn in. I'll help you if I can. Now, why don't you have real papers?"

"We are worse than criminals, Herr Yankee. My mother and my sister and I are Nazis."

"No one has ever admitted to being a Nazi to me before in this city," I said to the shivering young woman. "Don't tell me you're a war criminal?"

"I am." She was shaking again.

"Nonsense." I lifted her into the jeep. "Get inside. We'll turn on the heat to warm you up, you can rearrange your clothes, and you can tell me the whole story. Then we'll look at your sister and see if we can help her."

"Why do you do this?"

Fair question. Because it makes me feel like a knight in armor, I suppose. Or Scaramouch back from the Spanish main. Or the *Rei-ter*—the ideal medieval German knight—over in the *Dom*.

"Because I object to women being attacked at night in a city for which my country is responsible."

Ah, noble sentiments, were they not?

I walked around to the other side of the jeep, climbed in next to her, and turned on the ignition.

Her breathing was still uneven, half-gasp, half-sob. I turned the heat up to high. I considered putting my arm around her and thought better of it.

Eventually she calmed down, tried to restore her blouse and skirt, and considered me cautiously.

"I must trust you."

"I think I can get medicine for your sister."

Her story came in gulps. Her father had been a Nazi official in Dresden; her mother was a party member too. He had charge of the utilities in the city. He had to join the party. He was not an enthusiastic Nazi, but when she had asked him what had happened to two Jewish girls who had been friends of hers in school, he replied that it was good that the Jews would leave Germany and not interfere with its racial purity. She had wept because she loved the two girls so much.

She herself had belonged to the Jugend. She was seventeen, her sister thirteen. Her father was not an important man in the government. He did not approve of everything Hitler did but lacked the courage to quit. When the Russians came, he fled on foot from the town with his wife and daughters to protect them from Russian rape. They hid in the woods and the fields and struggled toward the advancing American Army. They were caught in an air raid on the road south. Her father was killed. She and her mother and sister managed to straggle across the American lines before the armistice was signed. At first they had hidden in Coburg, living as best they could from garbage cans. Then the Americans began to hunt for them because the Russians wanted her family for war crimes.

"A woman and two children?"

"They did not know my father was dead. We had many enemies in Dresden who had become Communists when the Russians came. They wanted my mother too. We came to Bamberg after the Americans replaced the Russians here. We had some friends from before the war. We work at the Bambergerhof where American civilians stay. When we have enough money, we will buy new papers, then we will go to Stuttgart where we have good friends. . . . But now they took all our money . . ." She started to cry again.

"You were in Dresden during the raids?"

"Yes," she said softly. "So many died. So many of my friends. Sometimes I wish I had died. We cursed the pilots. But now I know that we started the war. It was perhaps what we deserved."

The raid on Dresden occurred the last month of the war. The city had not been attacked previously because, like Bamberg, it lacked military or industrial targets. It was a jewel of a city, filled with the great architecture and art for which the Elector Augustus the Strong (also king of Poland) had been responsible. Stalin wanted it destroyed and Churchill went along, gladly it seemed. A few nights of incendiary bombs and the resultant firestorms obliterated the city and burned at least thirty-five thousand people to death. Just to keep good old Uncle Joe happy.

Never once in the months we knew one another did she use the Dresden raid as proof that the Allies were as much murderers as the Nazis had been. Yet there was no excuse for what Winston Churchill and the RAF had done to that harmless and defenseless city. Murder is murder, even if it is small-scale murder—compared to Hiroshima or Buchenwald.

The young woman worked right across the Schönleinsplatz from my Vinehaus. How convenient.

"What is your name?" I extended my arm around her shoulder.

"I am Trudi," her tears turned to sniffles, "my mother is Magda, my sister is Erika."

"Your father?"

"Gunther . . . Gunther Strauss." She was watching me closely, trying to read my reactions.

"Is that your real name or the name you use now?"

She leaned over the gearshift and examined my eyes, searching for clues to my character. I stared back. Her eyes were more green than blue, worried, anxious eyes, a rabbit trapped by a dog.

"Our real name"—she turned away from me—"is Wülfe."

"What did you see in my eyes?"

"Kindness." She spoke with a catch in her voice that might have been a sob.

"There's a chocolate bar in the pocket of my jacket. Go on, eat it, there's more where it came from. Now let's have a look at your sister."

I did not necessarily believe the whole story. Right after the war we had shipped back to the Russians whatever refugees they wanted and we could find. A charge that they were war criminals was enough. Then we learned that they routinely shot without trial everyone we sent them, women too if they survived weeks of gang rape. Moreover their requests were often grudge lists put together by local Communists (frequently ex-Nazis). So, we had become much less cooperative. But if you'd had a narrow escape or two during the first year after the war, maybe you'd be cautious. There was indeed a thriving business in preparing artificial papers. Our intelligence men at Constabulary headquarters knew it was going on and even how to get them, but by then our relationship with the Russkies had deteriorated so badly that we didn't much care about some hunted folks acquiring a new identity. Also, Stuttgart was in the French zone, and they were even less disposed to turn refugees over to the Russians.

So the story was not implausible; but the Wülfes, if that really was their name, seemed like pretty small potatoes to be on anyone's hit list.

Maybe they didn't know that they were small fry.

All of this analysis came long after the fact. That night, with the heater making my jeep toasty warm, I was exhilarated by the feeling of total power over a pretty and gutsy girl. Whatever her parents might have done, I told myself, she was only fifteen when the war ended. She deserved a chance for a life of her own.

Had millions of other young women lost the same chance? Sure, but turning her over to the Russians would not bring a single one of them back to life, would it?

Much later when I shared my dilemma with Dr. Berman, he agreed.

And she was so pretty and so badly frightened. And I had saved her. I could hardly have been raised in the house of Vangie and April O'Malley and not have some romanticism rub off on me, could I?

The Wülfes lived in a single chilly room over a bakery (with a Madonna statue decorating the outside wall) on the Untersandstrasse, a cramped and twisted little street one block above the river. The room smelled of stale bread and sour milk, but was starkly neat. Frau Strauss embraced her daughter when we entered. They sobbed an exchange in German too rapid for me to understand.

Magda looked like Trudi's grandmother instead of her mother, a woman who had once probably been handsome and elegant, now wasted and broken. Nor was there any doubt that the kid, younger even than Peg, who was tossing restless on the only bed in the room, had pneumonia.

"I think I can find some medicine for her in the morning. Who were the men who took your money and tried to assault you?"

"I cannot tell." Trudi began to cry again.

"Why not?" I snapped.

"Because . . . because they will try to kill me again."

"Look, Trudi." I gripped her shoulders, underneath my jacket, with demanding hands. "I'm willing to help you because I think you are a brave girl and because you have the right to a life of your own. But only if you tell me the truth."

Clark Gable? Or maybe Jimmy Stewart?

Or Stewart Granger as Scaramouch?

Can I help it if I had seen all the movies and therefore knew how men who were both heroes and gentlemen were supposed to act? Or that my father had the manners and style of those same heroic gentlemen?

She squared her shoulders, as I suspect she had done during the Hitler Jugend parades. "Very well. I will always tell you the truth."

Far too big a promise for her to keep even if she meant it then.

She gave me the names of the men; they were orderlies at the base hospital. Were they the black-market operators for whom my cracker corporal had been searching?

"I'll be back before noon."

"Your coat," she said as she slipped it from her shoulders, holding together the tattered front of her dress. "Thank you, Herr Yankee." Her appreciative smile melted me completely, butter in a frying pan. "I will never forget your bravery or your goodness."

"Bravery?"

My heart pounded as should the heart of the knight in shining armor who has just rescued a fair damsel. I knew that my reckless charge down that alley, armed with a flashlight and a weapon with the safety on (yes, I forgot to release it), was not bravery, but folly. What if the three men had been part of a dangerous gang that didn't panic at the sight of a blue beret or had their own automatic weapons that they were prepared to use?

Folly or comedy?

Probably a little bit of both.

My next stop was at the Concordia where General Meade lived. My orders were to deliver the Old Fitz no matter how late. I figured that 2 A.M. wasn't too late.

Shivering in the bitter cold, I leaned on the doorbell for five minutes before someone opened it—my old comrade-in-arms Maj. Sam Houston Carpenter.

Sam was every inch a spit-and-polish, hell-for-leather soldier. Over six feet two, rangy, slim-waisted and slim-hipped, with slicked-back black hair, cut short, and a Clark Gable–like face (until you looked closely at the weak jaw and slightly shifty eyes). His uniform was tailor-made and fitted him perfectly. He wore highly polished paratroop boots (which I would not have thought possible), the Eighty-second Airborne shoulder patch, and the only decoration on his chest were paratroop wings—as if that were the only medal that mattered. He was the kind of hero-soldier, one would have thought, that would be ideal in a film or an ad for the volunteer army or maybe West Point—the ring he wore was surely a West Point ring, was it not? Even his cologne, of which he tended to use a little too much, oozed masculinity.

"What in hell are you doing here, you fucking worthless little shit?"

Sam Houston had more than a little of the drink taken.

"I have a delivery for General Meade," I said, lifting the carton from the sidewalk. "Personal."

"Gimme," he said, reaching for the precious carton. "I'll give it to him."

I backed off. "Sorry, sir. My orders are to deliver this to General Meade personally."

"I said I'd take it," he insisted, swaying slightly as he tried to pursue me down the steps.

"Who is it, Sam?" Colonel McQueen appeared at the doorway.

"This little shitface won't give me a box for the general."

"My orders, sir," I said firmly, "are to deliver this material personally to General Meade."

Colonel McQueen nodded his head. "All right, son, why don't you come and deliver it to him personally."

He reached out and grabbed Sam Houston's arm because that worthy was about to plunge into a snowdrift.

Colonel McQueen ushered me into a drawing room with a thick, soft carpet and elaborate tapestries on the walls. In the middle of the room, under a single lamp, a poker game was taking place. The fourth player was a large, rawboned Irish pirate with black hair that plunged almost to his eyebrows and with a heavy scowl on his face. Doubtless Lt. Col. John Nettleton, Captain Polly's husband. He didn't seem pleased to see me. The other three men, I saw immediately, were woozy with the drink. John Nettleton was stone sober.

Dangerous man.

Guess which one of them was winning.

"With respect, sir," I said to General Meade, "the delivery from Nürnberg."

"Wonderful!" the general exclaimed heartily. "We were just running out of the last shipment. . . . You're entitled to a bottle for bringing it in on a cold night like this."

"Thank you, sir," I said, saluting vaguely after I had placed the carton of booze on the floor next to General Meade. "With respect, sir, I don't drink."

"More power to you, son," General Meade said. "More power to you."

"There's two of us micks who don't drink in this city," John Nettleton said softly.

"Sir," I said, trying to figure out this dangerous-looking giant.

"How was the ride, Chuck?" Colonel McQueen asked casually. "Any trouble?"

The four of them were now sitting around the poker table, looking not at their cards but at me. An atmosphere of tension, even suspicion, had suddenly descended upon them.

"Nothing much, sir. A group of MPs stopped me on the way into town. Hunting for black-market personnel, they told me. One of them went so far as to suggest, felicitously I'm sure, that I might want to provide them with one of the, ah, units in that carton. I observed that they would do well to consult you first, General, sir."

They laughed uneasily.

"My men," Major Carpenter insisted.

"Sir."

"Had they found anyone?" Colonel McQueen asked lightly.

"They said they had stopped one other group, but found nothing on them, sir."

"I told you, Sam"—McQueen turned to the major—"that nothing would happen tonight. Another worthless tip."

"It came from my best source," Carpenter protested.

"Another leak, maybe," Nettleton observed.

There was something wrong in the chemistry at that table. I wanted out.

"If that is all, sir?" I said to General Meade.

"Oh, yes, Chucky, that's all. Thank you very much. Return to your quarters and get a good night's sleep. You've earned it."

Come to think of it, I had.

"I'll show you out." Colonel Nettleton rose from his chair.

"That's not necessary, sir."

"Yes, it is."

In the long, ornate corridor whose delicately carved molding was obvious even in the dim light, he said, "You're the genius that works for my Mary Elizabeth?"

"Not a genius, Colonel, sir. . . . You mean Captain Polly, sir?"

He laughed proudly. "What do you think of her, Chuck?"

"She's an extremely capable officer, Colonel, sir. And the most beautiful woman in Bamberg, indeed arguably the most beautiful this side of the Rhine."

"I think so too," the colonel agreed. "Take good care of her for me."

A strange comment.

"Sir, with respect, I think Captain Polly can take care of herself."

"None of us can take care of ourselves," he said ominously. "We all need help. Especially in a weird place like this. . . . Be careful on that ice."

"Yes, sir."

There was something odd about that poker game, I told myself. But as I cautiously drove down the ice-covered streets of Bamberg along the frozen Regens River, I could hardly think about the black market. The memory of Trudi's pliant body in my arms exorcised all suspicion of high-level corruption.

14

The next morning, I phoned the CID and gave them the names of the men at the hospital. Information received, I told them; ask me no questions and I'll tell you no lies.

I also stacked up on chocolate bars and cartons of cigarettes at the PX in the basement of the *Residenz*, next to the darkroom in which I often worked.

Then, no one being at Captain Polly's desk, I entered the general's inner sanctum with a copy of the receipt I had signed for the Old Fitz in Nürnberg.

Captain Polly was there, apparently dressing after she had used the general's shower, a right conceded to her after her morning bike ride when he was not around.

I gulped as she put on her shirt.

"You should knock before you enter, Chucky," she said, quite unperturbed by my appearance.

"Yes, ma'am," I said with another gulp.

"And you shouldn't stare at a woman while she's dressing." She buttoned up her shirt without any show of haste.

"Can't help it, ma'am."

"You met my guy last night?" she continued as she stuffed the shirt inside her skirt.

"Yes, ma'am, Captain Mary Beth."

"What did you think?"

"I think if there was a woman like you waiting for me at home, I wouldn't be wasting my time playing poker, ma'am."

She shrugged indifferently. "Depends on whether the woman will wait for you."

"Yes, ma'am."

"John and I were almost killed by a V-1 on a street in London before D day three years ago. We both decided that life was too uncertain to take chances. So, we were married the next morning. He was pretty sure he'd die in the invasion. Tank commanders didn't live very long. We wanted to conceive a kid while there was still time." She smile ruefully. "No kid, alas, but he made it without a scratch."

"Thanks be to God, ma'am."

"He was a great tank commander, but what he's really good at is intelligence. What you'd expect from a Boston politician, I suppose. . . . Sometimes he needs to sniff around . . ."

Was that an explanation for the poker game? At what and at whom was John Nettleton sniffing?

"I imagine he wins at those games, ma'am."

"Of course. He gives the money to the Red Cross. His family is very rich . . ."

"Ah?"

"I'm not sure they'll like me. I'm from South Boston, my dad is a cop."

"With respect, ma'am, they can't help liking you."

"That's what he says." She laughed, happy again. "All you Irish men stick together."

"We have to, ma'am."

"Now let's get you some work to distract your imagination from me in a bra."

"I don't want to be distracted, ma'am."

She laughed again, content with herself. "Next time knock."

"Yes, ma'am."

Before I started typing I wondered what that interlude had been about. Did Captain Polly need my reassurance that no Irish family in the world could reject her?

Who the hell was I?

A kid from a rich Irish family in Chicago?

What the hell!

Suddenly the dull weeks in Bamberg had become fraught with interesting and disturbing possibilities. I told myself that the black market was not my concern, nor official corruption. Nor John Nettleton's "sniffing around."

I should focus on Trudi. She was more than enough. Only much later did I understand the obvious hints at the poker party.

When I had finished my own work, in forty minutes, I walked down to the small dispensary on the floor beneath mine and asked the medic in charge of our headquarters unit for some penicillin for a friend. He raised an eyebrow, but I was so straight that he didn't even ask who the friend was or whether she was pretty. He also instructed me on the use of a syringe. I would not have thought of asking.

The storm had blown over. It was still cold but the skies were clear and blue, a rare enough phenomenon in Bamberg in the winter. In the back of my head I realized that the photography of such a glittering winter wonderland would be spectacular. I had other things on my mind, not excluding the impossible shot of Captain Polly in her underwear.

But mostly I was thinking of the statue of the Rider in the *Dom*, the perfect medieval knight.

I did reflect as I climbed up the narrow stairs next to the bakery that the blue in the sky could well be called a cruel blue.

Poor little Erika was much worse than the night before, her face on fire with fever, her body twitching with ugly spasms, her high-pitched voice squealing hysterically. If the medicine did not work, she might not last the night.

Trudi was holding the sick kid's hand, pleading with her sister not to die. Mama was at work. Too many women were waiting for jobs at the Bambergerhof. The two of them dared not miss work at the same time.

So, we injected Fleming's wonder drug into the suffering child's rear end, without much skill, to tell the truth. I promised I would be back after work and assured Trudi that there was nothing more to worry about.

She hugged me briefly as I left.

"I do not know your name."

"Charles O'Malley."

"Karl O'Malley?" She laughed. "What a funny name. Irish, no?"

"Irish American." It was the first time I had seen her laugh. The lines of tension and fear were erased from her face, and she was a pretty girl who might have danced with me at her prom if I went to proms and if I danced.

Well, I had gone to one prom, but I didn't want to think about that just now.

And "Karl" was a lot better than "Chucky Ducky."

I felt as if I were only a few steps beneath the Lord Jesus. And far ahead of the damn knight in the *Dom*.

I was not sure, however, that Erika would be alive that evening when I returned on my way to my accounting class.

I had never seen how quickly penicillin could do its wondrous work. The little girl was sleeping peacefully, now a junior edition of Trudi, though not as pretty.

Frau Strauss was in charge and Trudi at work on the night shift. I was thanked in high-speed German.

The third night I encountered my friend Capt. Jack Berman in the darkroom.

"Guilt like Germany's can never be expiated," he said, renewing our argument.

Jack's voice, like the rest of him, was gentle. A short, dark, handsome man with soft brown eyes, he generated the calm reassurance that you'd expect in a psychiatrist, even though his military service was in effect merely his residency.

"Never?"

"Never."

"Everyone's equally guilty?"

"Of course not. Some more than others."

"You treat German patients."

"Some of the women who were raped by the Russians. That is my work."

"They're not guilty?"

"They're guilty but they are my patients."

"Again we end up in the same place in practice if not in theory."

"Perhaps."

"You think you can be effective with such women."

"Of course."

"They haven't got what they deserved?"

"Who am I to judge?"

For an Irish Catholic from Chicago this Talmudic (as I would later call it) argument was too confusing. I couldn't make up my mind whether we were on the same wavelength or not.

That night I proposed a new case.

"Suppose you found out that a young woman whose family had

been Nazis and herself a member of the Jugend was dying of pneumonia and could not obtain any penicillin lest her family be arrested. Would you steal some to save her life?"

He did not hesitate a second. "Of course. It would be my duty."

"But she's a Nazi."

"So?"

"She's guilty of the holocaust."

"Who am I to judge whether she should live or die?"

"You do judge that she should live, don't you?"

He paused. "You argue like a rabbi, Chuck."

He stirred the fluid in which one of his architectural shots—of the baroque Jesuit church—was developing.

"So?"

"It would not be right for her to die because I refused to acknowledge our common humanity."

"Even if you might get in trouble with the Army?"

"That should not make any difference, should it?"

"I guess not."

He probably guessed that it was not merely a rabbinical case. However, he said nothing about that.

On the desk as I type this chapter in my comedy of errors is my famous photograph of Trudi. The picture, taken several weeks after I worked my miracle for Erika, prevents me from romanticizing either Trudi or myself. She is certainly pretty, not beautiful like my sister Peg or her despised buddy, but appealing, a wan and pale girl with uneasy eyes and tense mouth. The fascination of the picture, however, is not in her attractiveness but in the mixture of fear, determination, and hope that permeates her thin face and youthful body. The title, "Hitler Youth Two Years Later," adds to the uncertainty. Ought you admire this sad young woman or feel sorry for her or maybe even dislike and fear her?

As a critic wrote, "The ambiguity of this photograph haunts and troubles. Is it a parable of perversity or a comment on the power of hope? O'Malley sternly refuses to spare us the uneasy implications of our attraction and revulsion."

I've been asked often to explain the picture, which I can't do. I've also been called on to defend it, which seems to be an illegitimate demand.

"By what possible standard of morality," I am quoted in the *New York Times Magazine* profile, "can we deny to this young woman the right to hope? Is not hope, after all, a biological necessity?"

When I am asked whether I love or hate the young woman, I always say I have no justification for hating anyone.

In truth I loved her then and love her now, but my love, like all love, is problematic and equivocal. My unease, even today, is more with myself than with her.

The next day, the sergeant who was my counterpart at CID phoned to say that the three orderlies had been picked up and that they had "spilled the beans" about a big black-market operation in stolen American drugs.

"What will they get?"

"A few months in the disciplinary barracks, maybe a general discharge."

We were not hard on our own in those days. But down in Nürnberg we were prosecuting others as war criminals.

After class that night, I sat in my room in the Vinehaus and stared at the starry sky through the slanted little window above my head. The sounds of "South America Take It Away" on the armed forces network was coming through the walls from other rooms. My elementary-accounting text on my lap, I pondered the fact that the world underneath those stars was far more complex a place than the world of double-entry ledgers.

The other two noncoms quartered with me were out at one of their drinking haunts where they were every night. I was lonely, confused, far from home.

Perhaps I should visit the room above the bakery on the Untersandstrasse again and see if Erika was continuing to recover. Would they know how to reach me if they needed more medicine? I had tried to explain to Frau Strauss how she could find me. But had she understood my pidgin German?

Had I not done enough for them? Should I not disengage from them? Or at least leave the next step, if any, to them?

I closed the text, stood up from my desk, reached for my jacket, and changed my mind. No, damn it, I did not want to become more involved.

And the next night too I resisted the temptation, which had now acquired explicitly sexual overtones. The gratitude and admiration in Trudi's eyes left little doubt that she would give herself to me. My virginity, a burden whose heaviness I had not noticed until I had put my arms around her in the jeep, would finally be given up.

Was it not time, anyway?

It was raining that night. Warmth had begun to slip across the Eurasian landmass from the Gulf Stream, bringing torrents of rain as a false promise of a still distant spring. The beat of the raindrops on the tiny window out of which I looked from my room in the Vinehaus at the Schönleinsplatz seemed a melody of foolish loneliness, an absurd and melancholy cry of despair.

I was homesick, desperately lonely, and depressed. The rest of the cosmos was racing by, unaware of me, not caring about me, utterly indifferent to my fate. I felt like a kid lost on a wide and desolate beach, a rainstorm moving in over the water, who hasn't seen another human for hours and fears that he will be alone for the rest of his life.

I put on my jacket and left the room.

In the lobby of the Vinehaus I wondered whether I should pick up a couple of cartons of cigarettes and a dozen packs of nylons from our supply in the back of the Vinehaus (probably liberated by my colleagues from the PX), pure gold for my impoverished friends. I decided that such a gift might be too obvious; it might impose on Trudi an obligation I did not want to impose.

I wanted her to love me for myself, not for my tobacco. Besides, Trudi might not be in the tiny apartment. Or she might not be alone.

I walked through the rain across the town, hunkered in my jacket, down the Langstrasse, across the bridge through the arches of the *Rathaus* (without looking at St. Cunnegunda, who might remind me again of Mom), and into the Kasernstrasse. Somehow, my pilgrimage seemed more justified if it was uncomfortable.

The Untersandstrasse was deserted. And bitter cold. Even the crowned Madonna, above the shop, holding a feisty little crowned kid, seemed cold.

"*Ja?*" Trudi's voice. Sleepy.

"Karl."

Wrapped in a blanket, she opened the door and let me in. No one else in the room.

"I am so glad you came. We wanted to tell you that Erika was well, but we did not want to embarrass you."

She had been sleeping, in her underwear to judge by the straps peeking above the blanket.

"I would not have been embarrassed. Where is Erika?"

Trudi huddled on the little bed, under the light of the single bulb hanging from the ceiling. "She is at work. She insisted. She feels so much better. All of us"—Trudi waved her hand to encompass the room and the three women who lived in it—"are grateful to you."

"The men who took your money have been arrested. They were part of a gang. They probably had the medicine you needed, but they saw no point in giving it to you when they could have both the penicillin and your money."

"Do they know that I . . . ?" She frowned anxiously.

"No. And they will be sent home. You need not fear them."

"Do sit down." She gestured again with the barest hint of Middle European hauteur—a well-bred woman impatient with the rough manners of an *Ausländer*—toward a battered old lounge that would not have made it into the O'Malley family living room during the Depression.

"Thank you."

The rain was pounding on the slate roof above us even more mournfully than it had on my window at the Vinehaus Messerschmitt. The room was damp and chilly; the smell of bread from the store below teased me with its sweetness. I wanted her as badly as I had ever wanted anything in my short life. In a distant corner of my brain I thought, quite abstractly, that the bigger they come the harder they fall.

"You have been very good to us. I will always remember how I knew I was about to suffer terribly and then die, slowly and painfully," she raced on. "I thought how foolish all our walking and working and worrying had been. It would have been better that the Russians had killed me. I tried to pray, but God does not listen to Nazis. Then I heard your voice . . ."

"Maybe God did listen to you."

"*Ja.*"

She read the desire in my eyes. How could she not have read it?

She walked slowly to the couch, sat next to me, and folded her blanket around me.

"You don't have to do this, Trudi." I wrapped my arms around her warm body. "I know you're grateful."

She began to kiss me, slowly, gently, lovingly. "I want to do it, Karl, I want to do it so very much."

Enchanted by sweetness and wonder, I forgot who I was and where I came from and abandoned everything in which I ever believed.

—⁊ *15* ⁊—

The next day a letter from home reminded me of a life that I now wanted to forget. I had awakened immensely proud of myself. I had given pleasure to a woman and received it from her. I was now a man. What more could one ask?

What I did not want was a puzzling letter from the good April, especially not one about Rosemarie. My mother's letter was obscure. The good April was often obscure. The problem was separating the ordinarily obscure from the deliberately obscure. Even today, I know the two lines by heart:

> Poor Rosie has been so upset ever since her mother's death.
> It would be so sweet if you wrote her a nice sympathy note.

The letter assumed that I knew all about Clarice Clancy's death. It was strange, I reflected, given my mother's reverence for the details of wakes and funerals, that she had not recounted any of the facts about Rosemarie's mother's death. Clarice was a young woman. However unhappy her marriage had been and however much she might have failed as a mother, the death of a woman who was not yet forty years old was a terrible tragedy. The good April should have spilt tears on her letter to me.

It was a momentary question. I was preoccupied with Trudi. I figured one of Mom's letters had not made it and that was the one with the tears and the details.

I did write a note to Rosemarie, however. That very day. Despite Trudi. It was a most uncharacteristic act of humanity on my part. Refusing to reflect on what I was saying, I sat down at my typewriter and banged out a letter.

Dear Rosemarie,

I received a letter today from the good April alluding to the tragedy of your mother's death. I don't know how long ago this happened—perhaps an earlier letter was lost in the APO. So, if this note is late, I apologize.

The thought of losing a parent is pure terror. I have had that thought and fear often enough to have some remote idea of how much pain you must feel. I know nothing I can say will diminish that pain, but I wish at least to say that I am sorry for your loss and your pain.

I know that your mother loved you deeply, that indeed you were the most important part of her life. I know too how proud she was of the prediction of that Gypsy woman long ago at Twin Lakes that she would have a daughter who would be a great woman.

You're already that, Rosemarie, and you'll become even more that as the years go on. And your mother will look down from heaven proudly because she brought you into the world.

The rest of us will say that we are proud to have known both of you.

God bless,
Chuck

PS. I apologize for being a complete heel and not thanking you for your wonderful going-away present. I use it almost every day. When I come home, I'll have lots of pictures to show you.

Then I dismissed Rosemarie from my mind. Trudi was now the love of my life, the only love I would ever have. Naturally, the "little Clancy tyke" would not stay where she was put.

A month or maybe six weeks later, she pushed her way back into the forefront of my consciousness.

I read Rosemarie's response in the beer garden in the park next to the Schloss Geyersworth on a warm early-spring evening while I was waiting for Trudi and another night of magical romping. I was drinking coffee, a concession of the Germans to the peculiarity of

American tastes, eating sausage, listening to a band playing polka music, savoring the soft night breezes.

"Dear Chuck," the letter began, "I figured if I started out 'Dear Chucky Ducky,' you'd tear this up and throw it away in your silly old beer garden where you're probably reading it."

I stirred uneasily. How did she know about the beer garden?

Leave it to Rosemarie to make a good guess.

I had picked up my mail as I left the office long after it had closed and jammed the letters into my pocket. I had finished studying for my exam in German lit the next night and, feeling hunger pangs, decided that my mouth was watering for a sausage. I treated myself to a stiff shot of self-pity, consumed two monumental sausages, and then remembered my mail. I read Mom's letter first—filled with bright and cheery family gossip—and then pulled the second one out of my pocket. The envelope edged in red and blue had no return address. My name and APO number were written in a clear and elegant hand, a woman's probably. I was sure I'd never seen the handwriting before.

My fingers trembled as I neatly slit the envelope. I always neatly slit envelopes. I quickly glanced at the signature at the bottom of the final crisp page: "Fondly, RHC."

RHC? Who the hell?

Only after the Chucky Ducky comment did I know who my correspondent was. The rest of my body joined my fingers in trembling. I imagined I heard birds singing and violin music instead of the vulgar tuba.

She had written after all.

Dear Chuck,

I figured if I started out "Dear Chucky Ducky," you'd tear this up and throw it away in your silly old beer garden where you're probably reading it. I've torn up about a million and a half previous versions. In fact, I've done nothing this week except work on drafts of this letter.

And read Trollope. That's not a woman of ill-fame but an English novelist who wrote the longest stories in the history of the human race.

I won't say that this is the best of the drafts. It is merely the last. I said to myself when I sat down to write it that no matter how bad it is, it's going in the mail.

With that heartrending preliminary, you obviously wonder what important message I have to deliver.

Funny thing! I can't quite remember!

Oh, I know!

I want to thank you for your very sensitive letter of sympathy last month. It was typical of the kindness and sensitivity which lurks just beneath the surface of your comedian mask.

I had never heard about the Gypsy's prediction before. I am torn between hoping it was accurate and hoping that it wasn't.

I did love my mother very much and I know she loved me. For reasons you know as well as I do, we were not able to love each other enough. Her death was a terrible shock. I mean I never knew someone who died before and it made me realize that I'm going to die someday too, probably having wasted my life and the talents God gave me. And He did give me talents, Chuck, I don't know why, but He did.

The one hope I have is that growing up with the crazy O'Malleys and with a foster brother like you who is more than just a brother will give me a long-shot chance in life.

My face is warm as I write these words. I don't want this to be a love letter. Only a letter in which I say thanks and tell you, as a kind of foster sister, how proud I am of you.

I'd better stop now.

God bless.

Fondly,
RHC

Oh, boy!

She had enclosed two clippings that only increased the mystery of Clarice's death.

The first clipping was a standard death notice:

CLANCY (Powers), Clarice Marie. Beloved wife of James Patrick,
Mother of Rosemarie, Daughter of the late Helen (McArdle) and Jo-

seph Powers, MD. Suddenly. Visitation Wednesday and Thursday at Conroy's Funeral Home, 420 North Austin. Funeral mass at 9:30 Friday to St. Ursula's. Internment at Mount Carmel Cemetery. Please omit flowers.

The second was a news story:

WOMAN'S DEATH RULED AN ACCIDENT

The Cook County coroner's office ruled late yesterday that the death of Clarice Powers Clancy, 40, last Tuesday was an accident. Mrs. Clancy, wife of investor James Clancy, died as a result of injuries incurred in a fall at her home at 1005 North Menard. Assistant Coroner Joel Stone said that Mrs. Clancy apparently tripped on the hem of her dressing gown and fell down the steps, hitting her head on the concrete floor of the basement. Death resulted from a fractured skull and brain injuries. "There is no evidence of any foul play," Mr. Stone said.

Police are known to have questioned Mr. Clancy and the couple's daughter, Rosemarie Helen Clancy, 16. Rosemarie, a student at Trinity High School in River Forest, and a friend discovered Mrs. Clancy's body.

"It was a tragic and unnecessary accident," Stone told the *Tribune.*

Then Trudi, glorious in a new spring dress I had bought for her, arrived. I put Rosemarie's envelope in the pocket of my jacket and concentrated on Trudi's beauty and my plans for the evening.

Yet later I went back to my quarters—the other noncoms were never in at night these days—and composed a heedless and impassioned reply to Rosemarie.

Dear Rosemarie,

It was good to receive your letter. I can walk around HQ with it sticking out of my pocket and thus proudly proclaim to my buddies that I too receive mail from a girl at home—even if it took me almost a year to find one who would write to me.

I do know who Anthony Trollope is, Rosemarie, my love. I

am not a total idiot. I have even read part of one of his books. I'm sure I'm behind you on the subject, as I suspect I am on everything else.

Which ought to humiliate me but doesn't. Rather, I'm proud of my foster sister, who is smart as well as beautiful.

I don't know whether I've changed much this year away from home. I kind of doubt it. I'm the sort of character who doesn't change. But your letter was written by a young woman who is almost a stranger, more intelligent than the girl I fished out of Lake Geneva, more thoughtful, and I'm sure much more beautiful.

I can hardly wait to meet her again. Or maybe meet her for the first time.

All my love,
Chuck

The next week she replied, this time by U.S. airmail.

Dear Chucky,

You are SO sweet. Thank you.

I have to rush off to Trinity and have another fight with the nuns. I'll write in a couple of days.

Love,
Rosie

As our correspondence continued, I compartmentalized Rosemarie from my life in Bamberg. It was dishonest and irrational, but I've always been good at sealing up the various contradictions in my life.

Later letters, sent back and forth about once a week or once every ten days, were less passionate than the initial exchanges. We mostly talked about literature and life. As I read over them today, I realize that I sound pompous and she sounds intelligent.

Despite the frenzied passion with Trudi that glorious spring, whenever a letter from Rosemarie arrived, I left Trudi behind for a brief interlude and entered my Rosemarie compartment. It was a warm and wonderful cocoon from the West Side of Chicago.

Dear Chuck,

I've been reading James T. Farrell lately, mostly because the nuns said it was dirty and condemned by the Church. I called Father Raven and he said it was not condemned and that I'd learn a lot about the Irish if I read it. As you remember, the good April knew both the real Studs Lonigan and the real Lucy Scanlan, so I've had a couple of long talks with her about them.

Father Raven was right. I did learn a lot about the Irish. Poor Studs, Lucy was the one chance at grace in his life and he blew it. I cried at the end.

But wasn't the story of their eighth-grade love beautiful? I cried then too.

NOW, you're not another Studs as you said a couple of times. Not at all. If anything you're just the opposite. You're magic, Chuck, pure magic. Peg and I have been trying to tell you that for years and you won't listen to us.

I know what you mean when you say you're cold all the time: you're homesick for your family and neighborhood. You're in a strange place with strange people, both the Germans and the other Americans. You want to be home where you know more or less what people are going to do. Don't ever talk about your life being almost over. I forbid it. You're not in the winter of your life. Now is your springtime.

It may not be my springtime. I don't know about me, but I know about you.

I wish I could visit you in Bamberg. Wouldn't that surprise all your friends there if a shanty-Irish kid from the West Side sauntered in? You make the city sound so fascinating I'd love to see it myself. Well, maybe someday.

By the way, I'm not Lucy either and we definitely are not Studs and Lucy.

Write soon.

Love,
Rosie

I read the letter three times. For a moment I was no longer in my cubbyhole with the tiny skylight on the third floor of the Vinehaus Messerschmitt (a servant's room I was convinced). I was home.

Then I became a little uneasy. She wouldn't really come over, would she? It would complicate my life immensely. Rosemarie was the girl at home I got letters from, not a physically present love. Besides, she was too young and too vulnerable to take care of herself in this city.

I thought about that. Perhaps not. Perhaps she could take care of herself better than I could. I'd ignore that part of the letter in my reply. I'm sure with the slightest hint from me, she'd be on her way to Midway Airport, bound for Rhine-Main and the three-hour train ride from Frankfurt to Bamberg. Rosemarie would indeed create quite a stir if she sauntered into Bamberg. I thought about that with a pleased smile on my face. But it could not happen. Everything would go wrong if she showed up.

Just the same, I did not do my homework. Instead I fell asleep and dreamed pleasant dreams. I don't remember them now, but I presume they were about my very own Lucy Scanlan.

I was playing a double game. As spring came, I was exploring the outer reaches of passion with one woman and writing love letters to another. The letters to Rosemarie were technically not love letters, but in one part of my tightly compartmentalized mind I knew that she would take them to be love letters. Rosemarie was home. Trudi was the present. I could not face the deceit in that pretense. I am still ashamed of it today.

I had every intention of bringing Trudi home to America with me as my wife. No other behavior was honorable. She and Rosemarie would become great friends, right?

There was not a chance in hell of that, someone whispered in my ear. You ought to know better.

I pretended that I didn't.

Naturally, I told neither of them about the other.

Nor did I tell anyone that I had kind of become Captain Polly's Friar Lawrence (or maybe Friar Tuck), a confidant to whom she confided her worries about how her husband's family would react to her and about her inability to become pregnant.

The few people who know about that bizarre interlude in my

life essay on occasion a defense. I don't give either woman, they argue, credit for any intelligence. Trudi, with her relentless self-critical realism, did not agree that she would go to America with me. Unlike many other German young women who wanted a GI to get them out of Germany, Trudi never mentioned that possibility to me and was silent when I talked enthusiastically about her life in America and how much my family would love her. Her dreams did not exceed traveling with her family to Stuttgart. Did she know that our extravagant love affair would be short-lived? Had she seen too much of life to expect any more? Did she understand that I was a callow young man, quite incapable of any long-term promises?

I don't know.

And Rosemarie? Was she not smart enough to see through me as though I were plate glass? Did she not realize that I was not much more than a little boy who did not yet know who he was or what he was going to do with his life?

At eighteen, going on nineteen, in Bamberg, did I not attribute to each relationship more than was in either?

I remember one warm day in high spring when Trudi and I made love on a blanket in a patch of grass under an old wooden bridge across a small stream that would shortly join the Regens. After we had finished, we snuggled together and giggled about our spectacular efforts at abandonment.

"Trudi," I said sleepily, "I want to be with you for the rest of your life."

"Let us talk only about now, Karl. God will take care of our future."

"I want to bring you home," I insisted.

"What is home?"

"Where I live."

"Would they like it if you brought home a Nazi?"

"They wouldn't have to know about what you did as a child. Even if they did, it wouldn't make a difference, they'd love you so much."

She did not reply.

"Did you ever hurt anyone?" I asked cautiously.

"Throw stones through the windows of a Jewish family? Or turn a hiding Jew over to the Gestapo? Oh, no, Karl, I never did anything like that. I didn't know till the last year of the war what was really happening. I couldn't do anything about it. But I don't think that is an excuse."

"You were no worse than the rest of the kids of your generation."

"And no better.... I'm sorry, Karl, to be talking about this. Eventually I will get it straightened out in my own head. Meanwhile, life must go on, must it not?"

She pressed her naked body against mine, an invitation to yet more love in the springtime.

Trudi was an intelligent woman as well as a fabulous lover.

Much more intelligent than I was. And certainly a much more fabulous lover.

— 16 —

Besides Trudi and Captain Polly, there was Brigitta.

Brigitta Richter was the strangest of my Don Quixote adventures in Germany. Even now I find it difficult to describe the relationship and her. I had intervened in her life with little justification, transformed it with little thought about what might happen to her, and become a mix of confidant, confessor, and guardian angel to her—for all of which roles I was supremely unqualified.

What had she become for me? I'm not sure. Not a lover exactly, but a friend who was willing to trust more of herself intimately to me than anyone else I had ever known or would know for many years to come. In a way she gave more of herself to me than Trudi would or could. And in possessing what she gave me, I found both terror and delight. And mystery—strange, frightening, delectable mystery. Brigitta was a light, delicate fruitcake, and as I say that, I can feel the taste of her on my tongue.

It was late afternoon in early November, before we raided the werewolves, when the weather had begun to turn cold and the skies were gray every day, except this one when the sky was a glorious blue dress, hiding all signs of suffering. Bamberg was a lovely city, untouched by the war, save for a few bombs over by the railway yards. It was not yet late in the day. The sun was still high in the sky, giving the thirteenth-century city on the left bank and the eighteenth-and nineteenth-century city on the right bank the look of a collection of picture postcards. The hunger and the cold were the same here as in other cities, but there were no ruins from the bombing raids as there were in such devastated cities as Frankfurt and Mannheim and Munich.

The Emperor Henry II, variously called the Holy or the Pious, had sketched out the design for Bamberg based on his conviction that it would be the new Rome, the capital of the Holy Roman

Empire. He had planned that the city on the left bank of the Regens would be built in the form of a cross created by the Carmelite church, the Benedictine church, the Dominican church, and the *Dom.* The left bank was filled with churches and statues, some of them on the fronts of ordinary homes and shops—most of them built long after Henry's time—so the piety had lasted for a while.

I often speculated that the world would have been a different and interesting place if St. Henry's dream had been achieved. One of the reasons it was not is that he and his wife, St. Cunnegunda, had no children, allegedly as legend has it because they abstained from sex. I kind of doubt that. Those Germanic royals always thought of dynasty.

The Bamberg he had planned was a fragile piece of china, beautiful and so easy to break. If the Russkies, who were only twenty-two miles north, chose to come crashing down on us, the china would be permanently shattered this time, and the lovely and corrupt summer idyll that most Americans were enjoying here would turn into a nightmare.

I decided to make one of my periodic visits to the *Bahnhof* to photograph the possible return of prisoners from Leipzig. By the time I pulled up by the station, low gray clouds had raced across the sky. No one got off the train. The shabbily dressed men and women who were waiting, heads bowed against the fierce wind blowing in off the steppes, walked away disconsolately, their shoulders stooped in discouragement. Hope once again frustrated.

A woman who had caught my eye before that seemed especially discouraged. She wore a patched and faded brown cloth coat, flat shoes stuffed with newspaper, and a babushka scarf. She was tall, thin, haggard, and yet somehow graceful. Nearly starving, I supposed, and weary, yet doggedly faithful. She was old and not particularly attractive, probably in her late forties, but once she must have been beautiful. What made me lift my camera to catch her face was the mix of sadness and unconquerable hope I saw there. If her man was still alive, he was fortunate indeed.

For a moment I captured her face in my 100mm lens and clicked. I still have the picture in a frame on my desk, one of my two best shots from Bamberg. I can see now what the eighteen-year-old kid did not see—vivid, ethereal, and haunting beauty, loveliness not far away from the tomb. I smile at the woman and once more taste the fruit (raspberry, I think) tart.

I have the second picture somewhere too, the one in which her face becomes knotted in fury and she is charging toward me.

"Bastard!" she screamed, shaking her fist at me. "Why must you damn Americans always exploit our misery!"

Even more surprising than her fury was her English—a perfect Chicago accent (the only proper accent for an American, I have always contended).

"I was going to call the picture 'Fidelity,' " I said, backing away from her fist. "If you want, I'll take the roll out and destroy it."

Her shoulders sank even lower and rage ebbed from her body. She turned her head away from me, like that of a novice who has been properly reprimanded by a wise mother superior. "It is perhaps a good title," she murmured softly. "No, don't destroy the film. Perhaps the photograph will help someone else someday."

"Perhaps it is also a compliment."

She lifted her head and looked at me with the lightest blue eyes I have ever seen, a touch of morning after a dark winter night.

"Perhaps."

"University of Chicago?"

She was startled. "How could you know that?" she asked anxiously.

"Pure Chicago accent. Like my own."

She smiled ever so slightly. "Of course. Kurt, my husband, and I were graduate students there before the war. We thought about staying in America but waited till it was too late. We were deported as enemy aliens. Kurt was drafted. He was a panzer commander. Disappeared three years ago at the battle of Kursk. I know he is still alive."

She clenched her fists in determination. A single tear appeared on each cheek.

"I know it. I know it." She began to cough fitfully.

What do you say to that?

What I said was stupid: "Biggest tank battle in history."

She nodded and reached in her dilapidated purse for a handkerchief, spotlessly clean at that. I noted two things: her clothes, however mangy they were now, were the sort that were chic and expensive five years ago, and she was much younger than I had thought, early thirties at the most.

"Kurt"—she stopped sniffling, but continued to cling to the handkerchief—"thought the war was stupid from the beginning. He said it was arrogant of us to think we could do what Napoleon could not do when he invaded Russia. He said the best way to fight Communism was to restore the historical traditions of German democracy."

They were intellectuals all right. I wondered what their democratic principles were.

"We were of the Center Party."

"Windthorst and that bunch."

She almost jumped in surprise. "How does one as young as you are know so much about German history?"

"I figure, you're in a country, you ought to learn something about it."

She giggled. "You do talk like a Chicagoan."

"Well, Frau . . ."

"Richter, Brigitta Richter."

"Sgt. Charles Cronin O'Malley, First Constabulary Regiment, Army of the United States."

I did not salute but almost did.

She bowed her head politely. Convent-school girl, I bet.

"Let me ask you a thoroughly Chicago question: Do you need a job?"

How the Organization would have loved that!

"I will not accept help from Americans!" she screamed at me. "We are not your slaves!"

I did what Chicago pols do when they hear something to which they do not want to respond. I ignored it.

"Can you type?"

"Of course," she snorted.

"We need more translators at the Constab. Your American is better than any of our bunch."

That was not altogether true. We didn't need more translators, but we always needed a couple of good ones, quick, efficient, and reliable.

"I will not take another woman's job away from her!" she said, shoulders erect, head high, breasts temporarily thrust forward. The effect was spoiled somewhat by a fit of coughing.

She did sound like a democrat.

"We don't fire people," I replied, truthfully enough. "Come on, Brigie, I'll give you a drive home in the jeep."

"No!"

"Don't be ridiculous. Do I look like a rapist?"

She hesitated. "No, you look like a funny little Irish kid."

"Than which there is no one more harmless. Come on."

We walked toward the jeep. I helped her in.

"You will really try to find me employment?" She looked at me again with those sunrise eyes, a suspicious examination.

"I didn't say 'try.' "

"Why would you do this for me?"

A perfectly good question to which there was no obvious answer—then or now. Chucky as Lancelot du Lac. Or maybe Galahad. Or the Black Knight. Or maybe *Der Rieter* over in the *Dom*. Or maybe *Der Rosenkavalier*. Hell, we did need a good translator.

"We Chicagoans need to stick together."

She lived on the left bank, in an apartment around the corner from the *Pfarrkirche* (parish church), not all that far from the *Domplatz*. A badly run-down neighborhood. What other kind of neighborhood would she live in?

"It is not a parish like those in Chicago," she said, "not like Holy Cross or St. Thomas the Apostle. Kurt says that your American parishes are peasant communes set down in a large city."

"Fair enough."

"Kurt says that you have solved the problem of anonymity in urban life."

"This Kurt I will have to meet," I said as we crossed the Rhine-Main–Danube Canal, which runs parallel to the Regens and about a half a kilometer northeast of it—the Regens empties into the Main a few miles downstream from Bamberg.

"Please God, you will."

I found out more about her. She lived with her two children—Heinrich and Cunnegunda (I'm not kidding!)—and her mother, Regina Klein. She worked two mornings a week in a shop on the Grünerstrasse, the down-at-the-heels market street near the Jesuit church. She and Kurt had grown up together in Bamberg and had married at the age of nineteen in 1936 (so she was only thirty). They had both earned their Ph.D.'s at Chicago. She had studied American history. Kurt was a sociologist. Jews were good people. What Hitler had done to them was diabolic. Many of their friends had died in the plot against Hitler. If Kurt had not been captured at Kursk, he might have been tortured and killed too. The Gestapo came to question her, but after a day of interrogation, they decided to leave her alone because her husband was a panzer commander missing in action. She and her mother and children had colds all the time. They were always hungry. She was not sure they could live through the winter, especially if it was as bad as the last one. She had little hope. But a little was better than none at all.

All the while she coughed, sometimes only a hack, sometimes a long spasm.

"What do I call you?" she asked shyly as I pulled up at the street corner near her apartment—the street itself was too narrow for anything but a bike.

"Sgt. Charles C. O'Malley, First Constabulary."

"Silly! Should it be Charles?"

"It should be, but no one ever calls me that. I'd think you were talking to someone else. 'Chuck' will do fine."

I jumped out of the jeep, opened the door on the other side, and helped her down.

"Your mother did well with you, Chuck."

"That's what she always says. . . . Now, tomorrow at noon I'll pick you up. We might as well walk over to the *Residenz*. I'll have a job lined up for you."

"What do you want for this?" she asked bluntly.

"Your kids are American citizens, Brigie. Native Chicagoans. Potential voters for the Cook County regular Democratic organization. I can't let them freeze to death this winter."

She nodded, not knowing whether to believe a word of it, and turned and walked down the lane to a very old building.

Since she still didn't really trust me or believe me, I deemed it wise not to accompany her.

The next morning I drifted over to Polly Nettleton's desk. I didn't quite have the clout then I would have after we routed the werewolves, but Polly already thought I was cute. Instead of donning the sergeant mask, I put on the precinct-captain one.

"Polly, I need a favor."

"Name it, you got it." She laughed. She understood the Irish political game as well as I did.

"We need a really good translator here, I mean one who is quick and efficient and speaks perfect English."

"Do we?" She raised a thick black eyebrow.

"Don't we?"

"If you say so. . . . How good is he?"

"She has a University of Chicago Ph.D. in American history. Talks as good as I do."

"That's not very good."

"Doesn't talk funny like you Bostonians. Her husband, panzer captain, disappeared at Kursk. She and the two kids are probably starving to death. Center Party type."

"Where did you meet her, Chucky?"

"I was taking pictures over at the *Bahnhof* of women waiting for their men. Fidelity."

Polly was jotting notes. "A *special* friend, Chucky?"

"Hey, Polly, she's older even than you are!"

"Yeah, I couldn't imagine you with your own fräulein."

Much less my own frau.

"Okay." Polly was uncharacteristically somber. "Bring her in. We'll see how good she is."

John Nettleton had been a tank commander too, I reminded myself. Good omen.

I arrived at the parish church promptly at noon. Still wary of me, Brigie was already walking down the lane. Her family was not to get a look at me just yet.

She was wearing what were clearly her best clothes, a somewhat newer cloth coat, pumps with moderately high heels, polished so they glowed, delicately carved silver earrings, and a small and outmoded hat. The coat was open because the landmass was teasing us with warmer weather. Beneath it she was wearing a severe brown suit, carefully pressed. Very professional and a bit pathetic. Her hair, which I now saw for the first time, was the palest of pale blond, cut short.

"Good morning, Charles," she said formally.

"Good morning, Frau Doctor."

Without cracking a smile, she told me that the title was not proper because her husband was a doctor. Then she explained that a woman who was married to a man with a doctorate and also had her own degree should be called *Frau Doktor Doktor*, but that in her case either would do.

She was a kraut all right.

"But you, Chuck, should call me Brig or Brigie like you did yesterday."

Not a trace of a smile.

"As we'd say in Chicago, Brig, the fix is in. Captain Nettleton agrees that we are in desperate need of a good translator."

"I have never translated, Chuck," she said nervously.

"You do it all the time when you talk English. Nothing to it. For the people we have it's hard work. For you it will be a breeze."

Inside the *Residenz* she lost not only her nerve but a bit of her class.

"I shouldn't do this."

"Yes, you should," I insisted, taking her arm and shoving her up the vast staircase with the bronze rails down which the prince bishop had once ambled.

I figured she had reason to be anxious. Her children's lives might well depend on the job.

In the ballroom that had become our bull pen, she froze up even more. Head and shoulders bowed, purse clutched protectively in front of her, she looked like a woman you might see in an old photo of Ellis Island.

"Captain Nettleton," I began, sergeant once more.

"Yes, Chucky?" She looked up at the two of us, and her eyes, suddenly filled with pain, riveted on Brig. She stood up slowly.

"May I present Dr. Brigitta Richter. Dr. Richter, this is Capt. Mary Elizabeth Anne Nettleton, alias Polly Nettleton, of the Army of the United States. She doesn't talk English very well because she's from Boston, but otherwise she's all right."

Neither woman laughed. I cannot explain the parapsychological dynamics by which women of our species communicate volumes of information in such brief interludes. I understand only the outcomes.

Polly extended her hand. "How do you do, Dr. Richter. Don't pay any attention to Sergeant O'Malley. He's only an inexperienced kid from Chicago."

Ouch. We could do without all that truth.

"It is my pleasure, Captain." Brigie bowed politely and exchanged the handshake. "But he is not a bad kid, only an angel with a dirty face."

They both chuckled, completing the mysterious exchange by which they had decided that they were kindred spirits.

"My face is clean!"

"You wish to translate for us, Doctor?"

Brig had recovered all her class. "I have not had much experience . . ."

"Yet you speak excellent English, especially given that you learned it in Chicago. . . . Tell you what, Doctor, why don't you sit down at the typewriter over at that empty desk and translate this dispatch into English and this one into German."

She handed Brig two one-page papers.

Brig bowed again and turned toward the desk.

"Let me take your coat."

"Of course; thank you, Captain."

Polly hung the coat on a hanger and put it on the coatrack near her desk. Brig sat down and began to type immediately.

Sergeant O'Malley did nothing. What's more, he said nothing, a most unusual event for him.

"Dear God, Chucky," Polly whispered next to me.

"Precisely."

"She thinks her life and her children's lives depend on this."

"Oh, yes, and not without reason."

"She types fast too. Classy woman."

"Yep."

"In every way."

"Right as always, Captain."

Brig pulled the first typescript out of the typewriter, put another sheet of paper in, and turned to the second dispatch.

Within five minutes, she was back with the two papers, proud of her work no matter what anyone else's verdict might be.

Polly stood up to receive them. She glanced down at the English translation. Put it aside and compared the German translation with one that had previously been prepared. She looked at me and rolled her eyes.

"Sit down, Brigitta, please. I can't judge the German, but the English is more elegant than the one I have here."

"Freer, perhaps. . . . Captain, I do not want to take someone's work away from them."

"My name is Polly, and you won't, and sit down."

I was not asked to sit down. In fact, I sensed that I would soon be given the brush-off. Yet, I stayed to see exactly how these two would work things out.

"Why didn't you come to us before? We need someone like you around here."

"I did not want to beg from my conquerors."

"We're not conquerors, Brigitta."

"It is true . . . Polly"—she hesitated over the name—"that you protect us from far worse. Yet . . ."

"Look, suppose I beg you to take the job?"

"That won't be necessary, Polly. I will be honored to work for you."

"With me. . . . Did you want something, Sergeant O'Malley?"

"No, ma'am." I saluted sharply and walked away with as much military dignity as I could muster. Witches.

Thus began the rehabilitation of Brigitta Richter. There was little work for me to do in the project, other than to bring toys at Christmas to the two Richter kids, pale, waiflike, shy children with their mother's hair and eyes. They did, however, permit me to identify with them against all the grown-ups. For the first time in my life—though God knows not the last—I had become Uncle Chuck. They in turn became Hank and Connie.

I was barred from all other efforts on Polly's premise that as a man I had no sense in these matters—a proposition that was unarguable. Nonetheless, tears pouring down her face, Brig thanked me with a light peck on the cheek and an apology for how rude she had been that day at the *Bahnhof.*

"I would have crawled on my knees and begged for the job if it had not been for my terrible pride."

"Self-respect."

Polly Nettleton took care of medicine, clothes, food, new furniture, and lights. In a few weeks, certainly by Christmas, Brig was hardly recognizable as the woman I had photographed at the *Bahnhof*. Her face filled out, her figure rediscovered its appropriate shape, her hair became glossy, she dressed tastefully and even smiled and laughed, and her natural beauty bloomed again.

Hers was an unusual and utterly unconventional beauty: a slim figure with curves that were more hinted at than defined, a long and slender face that seemed to be carved out of flawless ivory by a delicate tool, white-blond hair that clung to her head like a halo, and a natural grace of posture and movement that suggested a mystical ballet. In fact, Brigie often reminded me of the sculpture of a saint in the *Dom*, an ethereal, mysterious, numinous visitor from another world.

A man could not look at her for long without wanting to embrace her and undress her and revel in her uncanny appeal.

So, in our sex-starved and affluent Army of Occupation, many men tried to do all of these things, without success. Brig was a chaste and prudent matron of the sort the Scripture celebrates. Moreover, every afternoon she walked up—and later biked up—to the *Bahnhof* to wait for her husband.

She would talk to men (almost always officers of course) and attend dinners or concerts with them. But it stopped there. No kissing, no embracing, and no hint of the possibility of anything else.

It frustrated the hell out of a lot of guys and served them right. Their conquests had been too easy and they had become too clumsy.

And darling Chucky was always there to listen and offer limited and occasional advice.

I have no idea why she would pick someone a dozen years younger for her father confessor.

The most persistent and by far the smoothest of her suitors was my old friend Maj. Sam Houston Carpenter of the CID, cordially despised by all right-thinking Constabs. He was smooth, charming, attentive, and at first unthreatening. He did manage a few kisses and embraces, about which Brig would later have many guilty feelings.

"I am married," she said to me. "I should not kiss other men."

"Depends upon the kiss."

"Neither modest nor passionate."

"Risky."

"I know."

I personally thought that for all his gracious allure and his pretense to be unthreatening, Sam Carpenter was about as safe as a water moccasin. I was not quite so blunt with her, but when asked, I said frankly I wouldn't trust him with a used ticket to a Cubs doubleheader.

"You don't understand Sam," she said again.

When a woman says that you don't understand a man, it's a sign that she's falling for him (and vice versa I guess). Sam worried the hell out of me. I had come to believe that Kurt was dead, but why not go after some presentable single man, preferably Irish and Catholic and rich (or let one such come after you), rather than a married cracker.

I worried.

Had I given Brigitta a new chance on a life that would end up a horror?

Playing God again.

I never figured out how to cope with, much less understand, Brig's affection for me. It was clearly not an invitation.

So I had said, my face isn't dirty.

She had laughed.

Those women all found you sexually attractive, my current bedmate informs me.

Nonsense. I was a pint-sized, red-haired, freckle-faced loudmouth. Cute maybe, but not a sex object.

You still are all of those things, maybe even cuter with the white in your hair and that adorable beard, she says, laughing, and draws me close. And you are still sexually attractive.

To you.

She leads my hands to her breasts. To every damn woman that looks at you. I hate them all. I even hate that Brigitta for daring to look lustfully at you even if it was almost a half century ago.

She would never have gone to bed with me.

Maybe not. But I'm sure she enjoyed thinking about it. Particularly that night. No doubt she was grateful that you didn't proposition her but also a little sorry.

I never know whether to believe her when she makes such assertions because they are usually a prelude to passionate actions that give me little time at the moment to ponder what she has said.

— 17 —

In early August, Special Agent Clarke showed up and demanded that I help him find Trudi and her family. I knew I had to stop him from turning those three women over to Russian rapists, but I had no idea how I was going to do it. Lancelot at bay.

At noon I walked over to the *Dom*, the glorious, if confused, cathedral that was the center of the "Bishop's Town" on the left bank of the Regens River. I had not engaged in much dialogue with the Almighty for several months because I was technically in the state of mortal sin and had stopped going to mass on Sunday, religious negligence that shocked me when I bothered to think about it.

An old priest, clad in a tattered and soiled cassock, spit out a furious curse in German at Mary's portal to the *Dom*. Perhaps he had a point. The American occupation army had thoroughly corrupted Bamberg—prostitution, drugs, black markets, smuggling. On other occasions I would have replied to him with a quote about Christians loving one another and the observation that, while we Irish had converted this area to Christianity, we clearly had not done a very good job.

But I didn't want to make Himself any more unhappy with me than he already was.

The *Dom* is a subtle mix of Romanesque and Gothic, built by the Emperor Henry the Pius at the beginning of the eleventh century and redone by Bishop Otto in the thirteenth. It was cool and dark inside and I started to shiver again. I stared up at the most famous of the wonderful medieval sculptures, *Der Reiter von Bamberg*—the Rider of Bamberg. He was supposed to represent all the admirable qualities of German knighthood, such as these might have been.

If I were like you, I observed, I might be able to pull this off. You're tall and powerful and graceful with long, blond hair and a strong face and complete self-possession. I'm a runty, freckle-faced redhead, clumsy and cowardly and maybe a little sneaky. All I have is quick wit, an even quicker tongue, sometimes dangerously quick, and a surplus of phony Irish charm. Did you have to save any women back there in the thirteenth century?

The Rider did not deign to answer.

So I turned to Himself.

"I know You're upset with me," I began, hoping that my phony Irish charm might be acceptable in heaven, "and I don't blame You. But if Fr. John Raven is right, You still care about me. So maybe You'll listen to me. I didn't ask for any of this. It's not my fault that Gen. Radford Meade thinks I'm his ace troubleshooter, is it? That's based on bad information about my past. It's not my fault I saved Trudi from those black-market GIs who were trying to kill her, is it? It's not my fault that I have to save her and her mother and sister from being turned over to the Russians, is it?"

I paused, waiting for a response and well aware that I was whining and had left out some important details.

"You don't want me to turn those poor women over to the Russkies for gang rape, do You? Okay. They were Nazis. But a lot of women around here were Nazis too. We are not about to send them to the Russkies, are we?"

No, leave them here in Bamberg where we Americans can rape them.

"So I bought all the American propaganda during the war. All Germans are guilty, especially those who were Nazis. But where does collective guilt get you? Can I betray these women? Yet what will my family think if I'm caught and end up doing time in Fort Leavenworth?"

I really shivered at the picture of my mother and father and my brother and sisters visiting me in prison.

"I'm not expecting any miracles," I continued. "Just a little bit of help in getting them away from that FBI jerk."

Silence.

"I'm sure You can arrange that. I know I can't deal with You, but just the same I'll start going to mass again, maybe even every day like I did when I was in high school."

Two years ago when I was fourth-string quarterback on the Fenwick football team, a team that had only three strings, that's when all my troubles started. It seemed like a century ago.

"So I hope You can see Your way clear to lending a hand." I made the sign of the cross, rose, genuflected, and slipped out of the church into the brilliant sunlight. At the Mary portal I looked up at St. Elizabeth, the prophet who praised the Christ child at the time of His presentation in the temple. She looked just like my mother, the good April, determined, handsome, shrewd, compassionate.

I shivered again as I thought how I had let Mom down. I had arrived in Bamberg serenely confident that I would not be corrupted by the temptations of an army of occupation. I was a good Catholic with twelve years of Catholic schools, yet I had quickly fallen from grace. Not the way other GIs had fallen from grace perhaps. But still I was living in a state of mortal sin and was now prepared to violate my oath of office to my country.

I look back at that eighteen-year-old kid with the wire-brush, red hair and the small, pinched face, walking across the *Domplatz* to the *Residenz*, and shake my head in dismay. He was only a kid yet he thought he was responsible to wheel and deal, charm and deceive, so that he might save everyone in Bamberg who needed help.

Back at the *Neue Residenz* I approached Capt. Polly Nettleton.

"Staff Sergeant O'Malley, ma'am"—I saluted with as much competence as I could muster—"requesting an interview with General Meade."

I wasn't sure that she and her husband were not tied up with the black market, a pervasive presence in the Army of Occupation. What had he been doing in Nürnberg the night the previous winter when I had my first encounter with the black market, an encounter that led to my fall from grace? How had he got back to General Meade's poker game before I arrived?

Of course, I had been rescuing a fair damsel at the same time.

"Hi, Chucky." Polly grinned at me. "The general said you would show up and that I should send you right in. Are you coming to our party tomorrow night? My husband delights in you."

"Colonel Nettleton thinks I'm the only other mick in town, ma'am. And regulations strictly forbid fraternization between officers and enlisted men."

"We'll see you then on Thursday?"

"Only if Major Carpenter isn't there, ma'am."

She turned up her cute little nose. "My husband doesn't particularly like rednecks who pretend that they went to West Point."

"Admirable taste on his part, ma'am."

"You will escort Brigitta, won't you, Chucky darling?"

Peg asking me to escort Rosemarie to a prom.

"She's a bit old for me, Captain Polly, isn't she?"

"But she trusts you. . . . Besides, I bet you haven't had a date since you came to Bamberg."

I've had plenty of them, but I won't tell you about them.

"She has agreed?"

"She suggested it. . . . We were going to invite you anyway."

What was I getting into now? Tread carefully, Chucky Ducky, you have enough problems as it is.

"I'll look forward to my first date in Bamberg," I said. Better me than Sam Houston Carpenter.

"Staff Sergeant O'Malley reporting, general, sir," I said when I had entered the general's office.

"Sit down, Chucky." The general waved at a chair in which I suspected more than one courtesan to the prince bishops of the past had reclined. "I suppose you want to talk about the, uh,"—he glanced at the papers on his desk—"the Wülfe case."

"Yes sir, sir."

He put on his thick glasses and glanced at the papers. "I don't particularly like it, Chucky," he sighed. "I never like turning people, especially women, over to the Russkies, especially when the charges are so vague."

"Yes, sir."

"We do what we're told to do, but we don't have to be perfect, do we?"

"Yes, sir . . . I mean, no, sir."

"There's no real charge against the man. He was apparently a minor city official in Dresden. Waterworks or something like that. Never did anything to anyone. Probably joined the party to further his career, huh?"

"Yes, sir. Like joining the Republicans."

In my world, to join the Republicans was not quite as bad as joining the Nazis, but it was certainly not the moral thing to do. "Party of selfishness and greed," my father would say.

"I suppose so." General Meade looked at me sharply, trying to figure out what I meant. "Anyway, there's no particular war crime mentioned in the document sent me. The Russkies want them and that's that."

"Yes, sir."

"And I don't like that FBI man with the red nose. Someone probably sent him out here to get him the hell away from Washington."

"Yes, sir."

"So the whole thing looks smelly to me. That's why I assigned you to the case. Keep an eye on it all and let me know if you think this is one of the times we should be less than perfect."

"Yes, sir. Less than perfect, sir."

I knew exactly what he meant. He was giving me a chance to use my own judgment without promising to back me up if something went wrong. Not much there. But something.

"Like we did that time we raided the werewolves out in the Bohemian Alps, huh?"

"Yes, sir."

I agonized through the day, wondering what I would do if we were unable to fend off Special Agent Clarke.

There was a letter waiting for me in my room. From Rosemarie. By U.S. airmail. She disdained APO mail because it required a week. Pan Am was flying New York to the reopened Rhine-Main airport at Frankfurt every day, so airmail from Chicago arrived by train in Bamberg within four days. Time, to Rosie, was important.

"Are you sure it's all right if I fly over to spend a weekend with you in Bamberg?"

18

I woke up from my dream with a start. It was still bright outside. But here that didn't mean a thing. I had something to do tonight. Class? Not again! No, there was a party at Polly's at nine. I had a date with Brigie. I fumbled around for my watch. Eight o'clock. Still time. I stumbled out of bed and headed down the corridor for the shower—which I had to myself.

I picked Brigie up on time (show the krauts they have no monopoly on punctuality). She was waiting for me at the corner of the upper parish church (at the foot of the Kaulberg, the first hill east of the *Dom*), dressed in a sleeveless summer dress, aquamarine with a deep V neck, and the common currency of the occupation, nylons. Now that she had recovered her youth and her health and her flawless cream complexion (on which there was almost no makeup), she was even more vividly an image of mystery—haunting, tragic, sad yet hopeful. My estimate was that she wore only the minimum necessary under the dress, though be it noted in those days the minimum necessary was substantially more than it is now. Her smile when I got out of the jeep would break the heart of a man much stronger than I.

"So, Chuck, we continue to play the game of who can be more Teutonic in punctuality?"

I helped her up into the jeep. "And since I'm Irish and have a bit of the devil in me, I like to cut it closer than you . . . and you are absolutely gorgeous tonight."

"Thank you." She blushed deeply. "It is good to hear someone say that."

"Like a model in an American fashion magazine."

You cannot, I would later understand, ever compliment a woman too much on her appearance.

She blushed even more deeply, the flush extending down to the tops of her small, high breasts, a tiny part of which peeked out of her dress. What fun a man might have with them!

"Irish blarney," she chuckled.

"Then I won't say you smell nice too."

She turned serious. "Chanel. When I buy things like that at your PX, I think the GIs believe I am someone's mistress."

"Well, you're not." I turned on the ignition and fiddled with the choke. "And they'd also think the someone had incredibly good taste."

"Sam will not be at the party?" she said as I valiantly but un-skillfully backed the jeep down the street to turn it around.

"I don't think so, though Polly doesn't clear her invitation lists with me."

"Your friends don't like him, do they?"

With considerable help from both God and my guardian angel, I finally had the jeep pointed in the right direction.

"They're your friends too, Brig."

"Of course. But they do not understand him."

"You might want to consider the possibility that they understand him better than you do."

I had donned my mask of the wise old man of the world—a role I played pretty well, though I could not imagine why this ethereal medieval countess would take me seriously in it.

"You're being mean, Chucky," she sniffed.

"No, I'm telling the truth. You might also want to consider the possibility that your friends understand his kind of person better than you do. He's charming and gracious and utterly unreliable."

"He wants to marry me."

"Don't believe him." I drove across the bridge downriver from the Altesrathaus—which glowed in the sunlight like a daffy ship moored at a dock. "He's a married man with political ambitions in a Southern state, which ambitions would be ruined by a divorce and even more thoroughly ruined if he comes home with a foreign bride, much less a mystically lovely German bride."

"You're being very harsh."

I turned into the Grünerstrasse, a street that, unlike most Bamberg streets, was a little wider than Menard Avenue. I drove more confidently, distracted nonetheless by the lovely and sweet-smelling person next to me.

Thank God she was not crying.

"I'll be harsher. This town is a sexual marketplace. A lot of men without women, a smaller number of women without men. So the men acquire the women as prostitutes, concubines, mistresses, maybe even as potential wives. Since they're in short supply, the women hold out for the highest-priced role they can get. It's pure economics. And in this sexual marketplace, you are a very expensive prize. Don't settle for anything less than the maximum price, preferably guaranteed before the altar in the *Uberepfarrkirche.*"

Preferably some nice, rich, Irish Catholic bachelor.

She did not blow up as I was almost sure she would.

"I understand what you are saying, Chuck," she said thoughtfully. "But am I truly an expensive prize?"

A reasonable response; but after all she was a smart woman, a graduate of what we Chicagoans call *The* University. She could grasp an argument put together on the fly from my Econ 101 class.

"Bank on it. Haven't you noticed the way men look at you with longing? Check it out at the party tonight."

"Yes . . . ," she said hesitantly. "Since I've recovered my health and vitality."

"So," I said as two MPs waved us to a stop next to the broad Maximilliansplatz, "if you really want a man, don't settle for someone who will certainly not marry you, who in fact will not be able to marry you, would not be able to marry you even if he wanted."

The poor woman had been so beaten down by the events of the last five years that she had not been able to value herself enough to realize what the possibilities were. Self-respect, I began to comprehend, doesn't return just with physical health and attractiveness.

The larger MP, built like a nightclub bouncer, swaggered over to the jeep, evaluated Brig with a single lascivious glance, and snarled at me in pure Brooklynese, "Hey, punk, what you doing with a Constab jeep?"

I struggled into my Ike jacket that was on the backseat with its blue and white flummery and my sergeant's stripes. I flipped open my ID and barked out, "Staff Sgt. Charles C. O'Malley, Headquarters Company, First Constabulary Regiment, Corporal."

I kind of made the last word a sneer.

"I see. . . . What are you doing with a fräulein in your jeep?"

"Frau, Corporal." I held up her left hand with its thin wedding band. "Wife of a friend of mine. I'd ask you to show a little more respect."

He touched the tip of his helmet liner politely. "No disrespect intended, ma'am. . . . I still need to know where you're going, Sarge."

"Frau Richter is a translator at Constabulary HQ." Without looking at her I extended my hand for her ID. "I have been asked to chauffeur her to a party in honor of Gen. Radford Meade. You can accompany us if you want General Meade's confirmation of my bona fides."

Her ID appeared in my hand almost at once. She knew the game too.

"That won't be necessary." The big man grinned. "Sorry to bother you, Sarge." He gave the two IDs back to me.

"Not at all, Corporal. You got a job to do. I don't blame you for feeling that they're growing staff sergeants kind of young and puny these days. It's a market phenomenon. Supply and demand you know. They take what they can get."

I heard Brig stifling her laughter.

"Yes, sir." The MP laughed, though he didn't quite get what I had meant. "Have a nice time at the party tonight. You too, ma'am."

"We'll try," I said.

"Thank you very much, Corporal," Brig added, turning on all her charm.

"Not at all, ma'am." He touched his helmet again.

"You're outrageous, Chucky," she said, laughing. "You frightened that poor man, then you charm him."

"See what I mean?" I tried to be serious again. "Did not that man look at you first lustfully then respectfully as though you were a much sought after prize?"

"Yes," she said curtly. "They all do . . . but, darling Chuck, I am so lonely."

She was still not crying. Still her soft expression of loneliness tore at my heart. Actually she was also sexually hungry, another result of her returned health. It was not the time for me to let up.

"You still go to the *Bahnhof* every afternoon to wait for the train from Leipzig?"

"Of course!" she snapped.

"Why?" I drove across the Rhine-Main–Danube Canal, which shimmered blue and gold beneath the bridge.

"Because my Kurt is still alive!"

"And yet you could think of going to bed with Sam Carpenter?"

"I . . . It's two different parts of my life, I suppose."

"Hell, woman"—I pounded the steering wheel—"you're smart enough to know that you can't compartmentalize your life. The next time he turns on his charm and tries to seduce you, just think about how guilty you will feel afterwards."

Yeah, I did warn her about compartmentalization of life, me of all people.

As John Raven often said, your problem, Chucky, is not merely that you are so good with words. You have a precocious understanding of human nature, other than your own.

How else would a square like me survive in the O'Malley clan, I would reply.

"You talk like my father," she said sadly.

"I'm not your father, Brig. I'm an Irish Catholic punk from the West Side with only a high school education. But what I'm saying is true and you know it is true."

"My father was a very good and wise man."

I parked the jeep at the end of a line of cars behind the Nettletons' canal-front apartment—jeeps, staff cars, an occasional old Mercedes roadster, the kind the Gestapo used to favor in the war movies.

No, that's not true; I have never properly parked a car, because I never learned how to do it. Hence my family argues that rather than parking I merely abandon a car.

Brig kissed my cheek softly as I took the keys out of the ignition. "Thank you, Chucky. You're magic."

"I doubt it," I stammered. "But, if you kiss me like that, you can call me anything you want."

"Silly." She laughed.

To hide my embarrassment, I scuttled around to the other side of the jeep to help her down and was rewarded as she bent over with a much more extensive view of her exquisite little breasts.

When I recovered from the wallop of that sight, I remembered what I had intended to ask her before I was forced to play father confessor to her.

"By the way, Brig," I said as we walked down the street to the entrance of the Nettleton apartment, "do you know where I can buy some new identity papers in this town?"

She thought about it. "For a good cause, I'm sure."

"Naturally."

"On the Grünerstrasse, at the corner of the Jesuitenstrasse, in the shadow of Martinkirche . . . we passed it tonight."

"I know where the Jesuit church is."

"There's a small camera-supply store—for those who can't shop at the PX, I suppose. The owner is a former aerial photographer for the Luftwaffe. He is very good at that sort of thing."

"You know this town pretty well."

"Tell him that Brigitta sent you. We went to primary school together before the war. You can trust him."

It sounded like a story my father would tell about how you got into a speakeasy during prohibition.

"Fine."

"You're not planning to do something dangerous and be a hero again, I hope?"

"Not me, Brig. I'm not your hero type."

"Not at all." She kissed me again, this time leaning slightly against me and thus touching my chest with one of those adorable breasts.

"Chucky always comes with the most beautiful date." Polly Nettleton pecked at my cheek in a manner that, after my recent experiences, seemed perfunctory. "Brig, you are simply gorgeous tonight! Come in, both of you! We'll be ready for Chucky's songs in a few minutes."

"Not till I'm fed."

"Sit down in that chair. Here's your Coke, all iced up for you, and some Hershey's semisweet chocolate."

"Is there a shortage of it at the PX?"

"I have a dozen more tucked away in the fridge so they won't melt in this heat."

"No peanuts?"

"Of course there's peanuts. Here's a big bowl."

Paradise. I sank into my chair contentedly, only to be rousted out of it by John Nettleton, who wanted to introduce me, and more particularly Brigitta, to the other guests, perhaps thirty men and women.

Polly was wearing an off-the-shoulder floral-print dress that left no question about her full and sturdy charms. She was also wearing the same scent as Brig, presumably the result of a joint visit to the PX. The two of them were becoming as thick as Rosie and Peg. Her husband's eyes were usually dancing, his lips twitching, his expression changing, especially when he saw the opportunity to say something outrageous.

They could not be involved with the black market, could they? Yet the luxury in which they lived suggested a good deal more money than their combined salaries. In those days in Bamberg, no one asked where anybody's money came from.

"Colonel Nettleton," I said to him, "with all respect, sir, you look like an IRA gunman, maybe in *Odd Man Out*."

"My wife will tell you I'm a lot more handsome than James Mason, which shows how prejudiced a wife can be, doesn't it? But I'm sure there are terrorists and criminals and crooked politicians in our past, though my country-club Irish parents would stoutly deny it."

"Country-club, is it, sir?"

"It is. And if it weren't for this war, I'd never met herself, who is clearly an undesirable Southie. Which just goes to show you, doesn't it? And, Chuck O'Malley, if you call me 'Colonel, sir' once more, you might be needing dental attention."

"Yes, sir."

The colonel had found a kindred spirit. I didn't ask him what his encounter with the deliciously voluptuous, but socially undesirable, Mary Elizabeth Anne in London just went to show me. I knew.

I sighed loudly, as the good April often did under similar circumstances, an Irish sigh that can be interpreted scores of different ways and almost means several things at the same time.

The quick, affectionate glances between them and the brief touches reminded me of my parents. They would always be in love. I envied John Nettleton, not merely because he could sleep every night with such an appealing woman, but because I had little confidence that I would marry as happily.

"There's a lot of tit on display tonight, is there not?" I said to him in my phony Irish brogue.

"What's the point of hot weather if not to justify that? And wasn't I thinking that we could do with a little more without its being gravely sinful?" he responded in an equally phony brogue.

"Maybe even a lot more!"

Polly arrived, reproved us for our dirty laughter, dragged John away to meet newly arrived guests, and instructed me, go eat your chocolate bars and don't bother my husband with your fixations.

"Fair play to you, woman of the house," I replied, and the two went off laughing.

I made myself invisible in a chair for a while, munched three Hershey's bars, and devastated the supply of Coke and peanuts. All great empires probably had parties like this in the homes of their consuls and centurions—beautiful, underdressed women and handsome men, intelligent conversation, good food and wine, a teasing summer breeze, their equivalent of big-band music and dancing, a view of something like the now black canal, laced with rippling gold stripes, beneath us, and in the distance the churches and palaces of the bishop's city sparkling pink and purple and silver, like a drawing of a magical city in an expensive child's storybook.

And no questions asked about the money to pay for the parties.

But few such empires probably had parties so carefully designed to the South Boston standards of the hostess. Ideologues, fighters, boors, climbers, and drunks were banned. You didn't have to be an intellectual, but you had to be intelligent, witty, and relaxed. Formality was absolutely forbidden to both Americans and Germans. One did not say "sir" or "Herr Hauptman" in the Nettleton apartment. By exception, we were permitted to call General Meade "general." The men all wore sports clothes, but most had discarded their jackets.

For Chucky O'Malley most of these rules were waived. For example I wore a neatly pressed khaki shirt and trousers, without a tie or Constabulary folderol. Well, as neatly pressed as anything of mine ever is. I also called everyone "sir" whenever possible—in defiance of mine hostess's wishes—and called her "Polly, ma'am."

While there were more men than women at such parties (the wives of most of the Americans, including the general's, were still at home, and only those who had married their wife abroad were together), no woman was permitted to come unless she was accompanied by a man (hence my responsibility to squire the mystical Brigitta) and she did not leave with someone else. Married men whose wives were home were permitted to bring a date so long as they didn't become amorous at the party.

I am not running a house of assignation, the woman of the house insisted firmly. Sam Carpenter, a married man, had practically raped right here in the apartment a young woman who had come as his date. He was placed under solemn interdict. So, while sexuality permeated the apartment, the purposes of the party were not frustrated by attempts at seduction.

The buffet and wine were tasteful and expensive, the best you could get and quite possibly purchased from the black market, and the furniture in the large apartment was refined without being extravagant. There were no servants. Southies don't do servants. As conquerors, this bunch was pretty refined. No one fed to the lions or thrown off the balcony into the canal.

I glanced around at the two couples who were dancing on the balcony to Harry James music on the phonograph and at the rest of the group engaged in conversational murmurs—Brig and the general arguing about whether Longstreet was responsible for losing the battle on the second day at Gettysburg. Very civilized group, good-looking, cultivated, intelligent, witty, low-key.

Where did Charles C. O'Malley fit in?

He was the joker of course, the clown, the fool, the buffoon, the court jester, possibly a bit of a good-luck charm—and before the night was over also a bit of a Meistersinger.

John Raven had a different analysis when I went through my general confession to him after I was back home. Chuck, he would say, you were there because Captain Polly loved you and counted on you to be the life of the party.

She loved her husband.

There are, as you of all people well know, many different kinds of love in the world.

"You're in the Constabulary, son?" the middle-aged man who was sitting next to me asked, tweedy, pipe smoking, and New England. Probably Harvard too.

"Yes, sir. I'm the hired bard. I sing."

He looked at me to make sure I was kidding. "One of our men is working with you now, Rednose Clarke."

"Indeed, sir." I was listening carefully.

"Strange man. One of the best before the war. Had some problems. But he turns out to be very good at collecting people the Russians want. Seems kind of indifferent, but is relentless. Hasn't lost one search."

My heart sank toward the canal. "Kind of an official bounty hunter, huh?"

My companion raised his carefully manicured eyebrows. "You could call him that, I suppose. But these people are war criminals, you know."

"Can't let them wander around then." I sighed the good April's sigh again. "What happens to him if he loses one search?"

"He'll end up permanently as an agent-in-charge in some place like Pocatello, Idaho."

"Poor man."

"I wouldn't want to be there."

I prayed fervently on the spot that Rednose Clarke had been lucky and that his luck was running out. In the back of my head, a plan was taking shape. We'd need a little luck, I admitted, but more in getting the papers quickly than anything else. Slipping out of Bamberg after dark and driving the autobahn to Stuttgart at full speed ought to be easy. I had, however, never driven at full speed (no limits) on the autobahn even in daylight hours, and my driving abilities were minimal. Well, we'd have to chance it.

I was about to ask more questions about Rednose when my hostess approached. "Chucky, would you ever sing some of your songs for us, the party needs a little lift."

"Yes, madame," I said obediently.

"Folks," she interrupted the murmuring, "we are fortunate indeed to have with us tonight Staff Sgt. Charles C. O'Malley, the

John McCormack of the Constabulary and *der Meistersinger von Bamberg*. He will sing a few numbers from his wide repertory of international songs."

"I was afraid you'd never ask, Captain Polly, ma'am. The songs are all international all right, so long as you don't mind Irish songs."

She sat the piano to accompany me. She has lovely shoulders, I thought as I looked down at her. No, I wouldn't mind someone like her in bed with me for the rest of my life. I should be so lucky.

Now I'm not a McCormack by light-years, but I do sing on key, have what the good April called a nice tenor voice, and possess a large repertoire of Irish songs. I also know how the Irish songs should be sung—first melancholy, then sad, then triumphant, like the way McCormack did "The Kerry Dance." I also don't sing Irish American kitsch such as "When Irish Eyes Are Smiling," save as an encore and then only under pressure.

"If I have to compete with Harry James's trumpet I'll lose, Captain Polly, ma'am."

Captain Polly ordered her husband to turn off the phonograph, and I began the traditional plea of Percy French that one Paddy Reilly come back to Ballyjamesduff. Two more songs—so long ago now I don't remember what they were and I had other things to do at the end of the night than record them in the journal I was keeping. Then an encore of two songs—"Smiling Eyes" of course and then, because a demon lurks within my soul, "Clancy Lowered the Boom." I even prefaced the latter with the comment that the Clancy I knew was a woman. Since the song has one of the most melodic choruses that anyone has ever heard, I had everyone singing by the end.

I would tell Rosemarie in the next letter.

"Wonderful, Chucky darling." Captain Polly bussed me with more than her initial peck. "You're absolutely magic."

Third woman in a day. Try for four?

See what I mean? John Raven would say.

"My agent will see you about a fee, Captain Polly, ma'am."

She kissed me again and then directed us to find some more steak and wine for ourselves and come back. She was easing us into a meeting of the committee of the whole, when the best conversation would be expected.

"Is that Clancy a young woman?" mine hostess demanded as I brought back a plate for Brigie.

"Younger than springtime and older than the mountains."

"She sounds interesting. . . . Chucky, you can't eat all that caviar at one time!"

"Wanna bet?"

I had put aside my chocolates for other things. Once I had disposed of the caviar—which I had eaten only once at home—I could return to the semisweet chocolate.

Such goodies might have come from the black market, but they were also available at the PX in these postwar times.

The first subject of general conversation was the usual one: What might the Russkies be up to?

There were some fairly brilliant strategic analyses, ranging from that they would wait till they had an atom bomb so that they might come roaring down from Erfurt and Leipzig before the next morning. Or maybe on Sunday morning. The consensus seemed to be that we would be swept away in a few hours, but that the Allied armies would hold them at the Rhine. Maybe. A civilian analyst from G-2 suggested that there was no sign of their getting ready to move, but they were tricky people.

"What do you think, Chuck?" the general asked, knowing that I never joined in such conversations till pressed to do so.

"I figure that they are at least as incompetent as we are, maybe a little more so because we gave up horses and mules long before they did. On that basis, I figure that all their equipment would break down halfway between here and the border and that their infantry would be too drunk, too fat, and too sick from syphilis to get any more than five miles further. It might be the first war like the 1945 World Series between Detroit and the Cubs: neither side could possibly win."

There was some laughter, a lot of it hollow. General Meade, who was sitting on one side of my date while I was on the other, leaned over and said in a low voice, "I think you're probably right, son."

"No one wants another war," Brigitta sighed. "Not even the Russians."

Then the conversation turned to the black market. The received wisdom seemed to be that it was terrible and no one could stop it and that, if you rounded up the present gang, another would take its place. General Meade lamented that it was pervasive and yet elusive. Every time we get a tip about an exchange, it dries up before our patrols can get out there. They're pretty clever. We'll get them eventually, but we've put in a lot of time so far and come up empty-handed.

I felt that most of the dismay in the room was artificial, like a group of Chicago politicians of that era decrying graft.

"We're getting more and more of it out here," John Nettleton added. "It's like someone is taking over from all the small-time operators. Like prohibition in Chicago. What's your considered opinion as a native Chicagoan?"

He was talking to me because I was the only Chicago native in the room. I didn't have an opinion, much less a considered one, but I made up a spontaneous and unrehearsed opinion as I talked and found that, after I had stopped, I believed what I had said.

"Look," I said, after swallowing quickly my mouthful of caviar, "we have messed up a lot in this Army of Occupation. We're sluggish, sex-crazy, and corrupt. *But,* as armies of occupation go, we are a hell of a lot better than most. We're not here for reparations, we're not here to punish, we're here, glory be to God, to facilitate the rebirth of authentic democracy in Germany and protect this new democracy from our friends across the border. Has an occupying army ever in history tried to do so much for the folks it has conquered? We pour in money to rehabilitate their industries and give them back their jobs; individual and groups of GIs spend a lot of time with kids, old people, the sick, the poor, trying to help them, even in some cases to get them back to church—the damn American do-good impulse again. Sure some of us exploit the locals, but more of us feel sorry for them and try to help them. Not enough perhaps, but, I tell you, folks, this is an unique conquering army and precisely because it's American. I took Econ 101 last semester so I'm an expert on supply and demand. We put these black-market bastards out of business, sure there'll be others, but damn it, we have to put them out of business just the same because they're spoiling what we're trying to do!"

It was not bad for talk on the fly, especially since I had never believed any of it before. But now I believed and resolved that after I took care of the Wülfe problem, I'd really go after those bastards.

There was enthusiastic but, I thought, not quite sincere applause, and we then turned to a new subject, the similarities between depression novels in the United States and in Germany. I almost fell asleep.

Dick McQueen, in a light blue sports jacket, drifted over to me, an exquisite silver-haired German "countess" on his arm.

"As always, Chuck," he said, after introducing the "countess" (who for all I know may have been real), "you said it perfectly. I don't suppose I could talk you into West Point instead of Notre Dame?"

I kissed the countess's hand (first time I'd ever done anything like that) and thanked her for her kind words about my vocal ability.

"No thank you, Colonel, sir. I'm afraid I don't have that vocation."

"You probably wouldn't fit. Funny thing is that those who fit lose battles and maybe wars, and those who don't fit turn up winners."

"I think Doktor Richter would not think that so odd. Joshua Lawrence Chamberlin of the Twentieth Maine, who held the Little Round Top the second day at Gettysburg, she tells me, didn't fit at all."

"And didn't go to West Point either."

"Bowdoin College, if the *Frau Doktor* is to be believed."

"The Army really isn't a good life," McQueen went on, his handsome face in a deep frown. "For some of us like General Meade and myself there is solid reason to believe in our eventual success. Others are simply not going to make it."

"Like Major Carpenter."

McQueen smiled briefly. "Perhaps. . . . In any case, for men who see this future pretty clearly, an Army of Occupation provides them with an opportunity to insure their future and take their revenge against a system which they think has been unfair. I'm not defending them, just trying to explain their mentality."

"Yes, sir," I said, thinking that even for men like him and the general the rewards at the top would be fleeting and not all that great.

I kissed the countess's hand again. This time Captain Polly caught the act and rolled her eyes in feigned dismay.

We were then told to get our dessert and coffee.

I collected three plates of chocolate ice cream and a large mug of tea.

"Would I like this Clancy person?" Polly demanded as I tried to slip by her with my horde of ice cream.

"I dunno. My mother and sisters like her, so I suppose you might."

Polly beamed contentedly. They're all matchmakers, I tell you. All of them.

Brigitta watched with amusement as I disposed of the ice cream. I was searching for the man who had confided in me about Rednose Clarke but could not find him. Had he slipped out after delivering his message? Had I been set up? Were there plots within plots? Was I truly an innocent abroad? Should I even be here having fun while three women's lives were at stake?

Oh, well, eat, drink, and be merry for tomorrow . . . I didn't like that one.

Mom would have said, sufficient to the day is the evil thereof.

Both of them I would later learn were quotes from the Scripture. Which just goes to show you.

Anyway it was a pretty classy party for a poor shanty-Irish kid from the West Side whose eyes were popping all night, not only at the bare arms and partially bare breasts, but at the experience of what money can do for a warm evening in the summertime a long way from home.

"Shall I get the horses for your chariot, ma'am?"

Brig glanced at her watch. "Oh, my, is it that late? We must work tomorrow. Yes, we'd better go."

Yes, there was work to be done tomorrow.

There were the usual prolonged farewells and expressions of gratitude for the party.

"Cool, Polly," I said, figuring she deserved a compliment. "Not many people could pull this off."

"Why, thank you, Chuck." She kissed my lips. "I'm glad you liked it."

I managed to walk down the steps from the third floor under my own power, just barely. Let me see, that was five kisses in one night. Not bad for a rank amateur.

We drove back to the left bank in silence, each of us with our own thoughts of tomorrow and the many tomorrows after that.

"What do you think about their reaction to my black-market sermon?" I asked suddenly.

"You spoke very well, Chuck," she said cautiously, as if weighing her words. "I think you were the only one in the room who worries about it. To use the economic model you advanced about me earlier in the evening, there is a demand from Germans who are making money one way or another and a supply which Americans possess."

"By stealing it from the government of the United States of America."

"You Americans have so much. You waste so much. I think most of the black-market material would be wasted anyway."

"Penicillin?"

"Does anyone suffer?"

"The people who don't have the money to buy it from the black market."

"They would not be able to buy it anyway, Chuck—unless like me they work for the Americans. . . . Don't misunderstand me. I think it is wrong, but you seem almost, forgive me, obsessed by it."

"Maybe you're right. . . . I wonder whether I'm the only one in the *Residenz* who is not involved."

"I am not either and would not be. But why do you worry what others might do?"

"Our friends?"

"Can you not let them follow their own consciences? Are you their parish priest?"

Silence from the parish priest.

"I guess not."

What did it matter if my friends and colleagues and superior officers were making a few extra dollars? No one was getting hurt, was he?

Besides, I should have as guilty a conscience as any of them. I did sometimes, but that would not prevent me from making love with Trudi before the night was over.

"Nonetheless, everything you said tonight was true, but I think none of them could admit it. Not even the general."

We were silent for the rest of the ride. Did she know who was connected and who was not? She wouldn't miss much. But neither was she likely to report any of those who had saved her. I better drop the whole conversation.

"Thank you, Chuck," she said as I helped her down from the jeep. "It was a wonderful night. I'll never forget it."

This time I glimpsed not only her breasts but the deep-cut, pink bra that ingeniously held them in place.

"I don't think I ever will either," I agreed.

"And thank you for being a father to me when I needed one."

I had nothing to say to that. Then she kissed me on the lips as Polly had, somewhat more vigorously but still safely on the side of modesty.

Six in one evening.

"Good night, Chuck."

"I'm not sure I'm capable of reply."

"His name is Albrecht."

"Who?"

"The man in the photo store on the Grünerstrasse."

"Oh, yeah," I murmured. "Thanks."

"And do be careful."

"Sure . . . good night, Brigitta."

I watched her slim hips as she walked to her apartment and entered.

I should go home and get a good night's sleep to prepare for the risks of the next day. But as I sat there in the jeep, on fire from the sensual delights of the night, I thought of Trudi. A perfect end to the evening. And she was expecting me, wasn't she?

I pounded the jeep's front wheel. Had I not warned Brig about the dangers of compartmentalization?

Why had I not brought Trudi to the party? All right, it would be risky with Rednose Clarke looking for her. But why not previous parties?

Was I ashamed of her? She would not have fit in. She was too young, too intense, too inexperienced. She might be intelligent—I thought she was—but she was not as quick and articulate as the others at Polly's parties. She would have been embarrassed if I had thrust her into that environment. Did I really think she could fit into my world back home?

Yet soon I would lose Trudi, if only for a while. And she *was* expecting me, was she not?

I remembered again that bitter-cold night in the jeep and the warmth that would later come from that encounter, more warmth than I had ever known.

Trudi was wearing a thin nightgown, but this time she was wide-awake.

"I so hoped you would come." She hugged me. "I knew you would come. Was it a nice party?"

I brusquely pushed off the nightgown, and our play began. I had learned a few of the arts of love from her, how to be hungry and gentle at the same time.

"Oh, Karl," she groaned, "you are such a wonderful lover! You're magic!"

Although I was rapidly climbing the mountain of sexual arousal, I was enough of an O'Malley to note that this was the fourth time in twenty-four hours that this charge had been made against me. And I wasn't a wonderful lover, but perhaps I was better than anyone else in her life.

"You are especially passionate tonight," she sighed when our first romp was over.

I was a horny young man who had been aroused by the sexual atmosphere at Polly's party and whose bloodstream was drenched with hormones. I wanted, needed, a woman. This one was more than available. Was that all there was to it?

When I left her, sleeping peacefully, after several more romps, feeling guilty as I always did when I walked under the crowned Madonna and her kid, I told myself that I really did love her. I would save her and her family from the Russkies. I would bring her home to America with me, no matter what the obstacles might be.

Back at the Vinehaus Messerschmitt, there was no sign of my roommates—there usually wasn't—but I was too keyed up by the events of the night and especially my interlude with Trudi to sleep. I sat at the small table that served as my desk, filled in a few notes of my journal like "Kissed by three women and called magic by four. What the hell!"

Then I tried to outline my plan to get the Wülfes to Stuttgart, but the caviar-and-chocolate combination was creating unrest in my stomach and I was bemused from the sexual delights of the evening. I scrawled meaningless notes, and then eventually, just as the first streak of dawn appeared through my tiny window, I rested my head on my arms and slept with the sense of Trudi's body on top of mine. In my dreams, however, I remembered another girl's body. The dream became a lascivious reenactment of my performance at the St. Ursula May crowning in 1945.

I woke up from my lewd dream about the May crowning with Trudi and Rosemarie still confused in my mind. I felt terrible guilt and shame about what I had done in the dream to Rosemarie in church. To make it more difficult for me to distinguish between dream and reality, I was desperately ill: the caviar was having its revenge. I dashed madly for the jakes down the hall from my room and barely made it in time. As my poor stomach violently revolted against the indignities I had heaped upon it, my mind played punning games about Shakespeare's line about caviar to the general.

When I had contributed all I could to the Bamberg sanitation system, I staggered back to my room. The sense of health and well-being that follows such attacks cleared my head, and as I dressed, I saw the entire plan for saving the Wülfes, which had been forming itself in my mind. I considered it in detail. Yes, it should work. Unless some things went terribly wrong and unless I made some stupid mistakes.

Alas, Murphy's Law, as we have come to call it, was working overtime. Things would go wrong, even on that day; and I would make stupid mistakes, beginning on that day—including one that was monumentally stupid. For all of that, however, I can at least say today that my plan was an ingenious fantasy.

The first thing I had to do was to hunt up Agent Clarke and establish some facts about him to pass on to General Meade. Then I would have to stop by Albrecht's place in the Grünerstrasse and negotiate for the kind of papers that would get the Wülfes into the French zone and provide them with safe identities once they got to Stuttgart.

—ε19ε—

That morning I was late for work, not that anyone punched clocks when they went to work in the Army of Occupation. Captain Nettleton would notice—she noticed everything—but wouldn't mention it. If she did, I would claim that I was poisoned at her party.

I had sifted through pictures of Trudi, Erika, and Magda, searching for excellent likenesses so no one could question that the women bearing the papers were indeed the same ones depicted on them. I guessed at height and weight numbers and chose a name for them. I did not put on my Constabulary Ike jacket with all its opéra comique decorations because I did not want to alarm the good Albrecht.

I crossed the street and entered the Bambergerhof. Unless I missed by guess, Rednose would already be drinking. Sure enough, I found him in the bar of the Bambergerhof, a glass of gin in his hand.

"No point working all day, is there, sport?" he drawled. "Have one?"

"I don't drink, sir."

"No kidding? Can't really be Irish then, can we? What can I do for you?" He emptied the gin glass and signaled for another.

"I need those documents, sir, to pursue our search."

"What documents?" He smiled blissfully over his revitalized drink.

"The fingerprints and the descriptions, sir. And the photographs you showed me. My team needs to know for whom we are pursuing our search."

"For *whom*, huh? An educated cop, eh, sport?"

"The Constabulary is not a police unit, sir. Our role is to maintain order, not necessarily to prosecute. Would it be possible for me to copy those documents?"

"Don't carry them around with me, sport. Up in my room. I'll bring copies for you tomorrow morning, okeydokey?"

"Yes, sir. What time tomorrow morning, sir?"

"You are an eager one, aren't you? I'm not planning on working real hard in this operation. Let's say two-thirty, huh, sport?"

"Fourteen hundred thirty hours, sir?"

"Have it your way, sport."

I slipped out of the bar, hoping I would encounter none of the Wülfes in the lobby. It would not be safe for me to be seen with them in the Bambergerhof.

The documents in his room, limited working hours—both fit my emerging strategy neatly.

The next stop was the Grünerstrasse. In the shadow of Martinkirche there was a tiny hole-in-the-wall shop with a few dusty film cartons in the front window. I thought it would not hurt to renew negotiations with the One who purportedly lurked in the Martinkirche, so I sneaked in for a quick prayer.

I often argue that all European Jesuit churches look alike—cavernous, baroque, rococo; they are, I would say, beautiful if overwhelming art and generate as much sense of the sacred as did Hansen Park or the late, lamented Chicago Stadium. In fact, they are all different from one another, each striving to be more baroque than the others. Despite my complaint that they produced awe and amusement instead of prayer, I have to admit that they are impressive. Inside the Martinkirche that day I didn't need a sacred setting for prayer. I fervently prayed that the One in Charge would bless and protect my plan. While there was no explicit answer, I walked out into the August sunlight feeling that Himself was not uninterested in helping us.

I pushed open the door of the photo shop; a bell tinkled in the rear. The shop was musty and dusty and its merchandise was pathetic, a few secondhand Leicas and accessories, a couple of old Kodaks, and four piles of film, Agfachrome and Kodak.

Albrecht emerged from the back, a cup of coffee in one hand and the stub of a sausage in the other. He was almost a stereotype of the Nazi pilot we saw in movies during the war—blond, tall, lean, handsome, with smoldering eyes and a hard face. You expected him to be wearing the Iron Cross. In fact he was wearing an apron, suggesting he had been working in a lab in the back.

In the old Rockne theater, I used to cheer when the likes of him were killed. Now in Bamberg I realized many of the wives and sweethearts of men like Albrecht were mourning their deaths.

"Morgen," he said with a smile that wiped out the Luftwaffe stereotype.

He finished off the sausage.

"Morgen," I said. "I'd like to buy four rolls of Agfachrome."

He rolled his eyes and pursed his lips, an expression I would see several more times that morning. "It can't be better than the Kodak you can buy in your PX. And it costs more."

"It has much richer and warmer colors. Shots in a beautiful city like this deserve as warm colors as possible."

"Ja . . . so perhaps we Germans make some things better than you Yankees?" It was said humorously with a second rolling of the eyes and pursing of the lips as he drained his coffee cup.

"I am not a Yankee. I am an Irish Catholic from Chicago. And, yeah, a few things better like the Tiger tank and the eighty-eight-millimeter artillery piece and the Me 262."

"So"—he repeated his favorite facial expression—"you know about *that?"*

"There's nothing much to do here so I read books and the *New York Times.*"

"So you know something about us?"

"I'm living in Messerschmitt's house. . . . It's a good thing you folks didn't have more 262s at the end of the war. The outcome might have been different."

"Nein, we would have lost anyhow and the Russians might still be here instead of you. Much worse."

He reached behind the counter and pulled out a print, carefully mounted on a frame, of the first jet to be used in combat, one that had scared the living daylights out of the bomber crews in our Eighth Air Force. It was a marvelous color shot, taken against a background of clear blue sky, from the side and below the plane and displaying its sleek elegance. The Me 262 was a strange cross between the prop fighter aircraft of the past and the jet fighters of the future. Its fuselage was much like that of the Focke-Wulf fighters that the Luftwaffe had introduced during the war. Slung beneath its swept-back wings, however, there were two powerful-looking jet engines. It was not much different in appearance from the jets we were developing, but it would be another year before we had anything to match it (four years after the krauts had put the 262 in the sky)—the F-86 Saber, one of the most successful planes in the history of military aviation.

I examined the print carefully, noting the details of the plane and the skill of the photographer.

"Agfachrome?"

"Of course."

"Brilliant! . . . Your work?"

"*Ja.*"

"Wonderful. Is it for sale?"

"Of course, ten American dollars."

"It's worth more."

"Twenty?" He really rolled his eyes this time.

"Done."

"Good."

"You were in JG-7?" It was the name of the group that developed and flew the 262.

"*Ja,* for a time."

"Ever go up in the two-seat version?"

He nodded. "Real fast. Scary."

"Our 47s and 51s finally devised tactics to deal with them."

"*Ja,* they stacked up in the skies and caught them before they could fly through the stacks. Shot down twenty in one day. Then raided our airfields." He held up his hand in a gesture of surrender. "That was the end."

"Another thing, Albrecht. I need some papers for three women . . . Brigitta sent me."

"*Ja, ja,*" he said cautiously. "You have brought pictures and other information?"

I reached in my shirt pocket and produced the three snaps, which I placed on his decrepit counter.

"*Ja, ja,* lovely, lovely."

"They are indeed."

"Your work?"

"Yeah."

"You have talent."

"Maybe."

"Germans, *nein?*"

"Yes."

"In trouble?"

"Possibly."

"Why do you help them?"

"I'm impressed by the guy on the horse over in the *Dom.*"

"Der Reiter?" He frowned, not quite getting the allusion at first. Then, he threw back his head and laughed. *"Sehr gut,* Irish, *sehr gut.* . . . You know Brigitta, eh?"

"Yes."

His facial expression almost became a caricature of itself at the name of the fabled Brig. "Wonderful woman. Her husband was a great man. Too bad."

"She believes he's still alive."

"Better perhaps that he be dead than starving in a Russian camp."

"Perhaps."

"Ja, for these three, two hundred dollars. Three days. You pay when I give them to you."

It was a bargain.

"Fine."

The bell tinkled.

Suddenly, with an incredibly swift movement, he swept the three pictures into his apron. "It costs twenty-five dollars," he said smoothly, "for the Agfachrome and the print."

I was about to grab for the photos when I noted out of the corner of my eyes that two GIs had entered the shop, two of Carpenter's gumshoes. Damn, why had I not been watching for someone?

I gave him a twenty and a five; he had given me a discount on the film. At that point I wasn't about to argue. He wrapped the print carefully in old newspapers. I thought he might slip my snaps inside, but he did not. The two goofs were pretending to pay no attention.

Albrecht handed me the print. I put the film in my pocket.

"Danke," he said easily.

"Bitte," I responded, trying to keep my voice from cracking.

I walked out of the shop leisurely, as if I had every reason in the world to be confident. But my stomach was tight as a knot, I was afraid I'd be sick again, and my legs were shuddering.

First mistake.

But what were the CID gumshoes doing in the store? If they thought I was up to something, why didn't they arrest the two of us and seize the evidence? And why were they tailing me? Were they working with Special Agent Clarke? And what if Albrecht was in league with them? What if he had grabbed the snapshots with the intent of turning them over to the gumshoes?

But if that was his plan, why not just leave the snaps on his counter?

All the way back across the Regens to the *Domplatz* and the *Residenz*, I reviewed scenarios that might explain what had happened and how I might respond. Nothing made sense. I would have to make spur-of-the-moment decisions. Or what if nothing happened? Might it be that they—whoever they were—would wait till we were on our way to Nürnberg and Stuttgart and then capture me in the act of fleeing with wanted Nazis?

I wished I were home with all the crazy O'Malleys. But, since I wasn't, I had no choice but to continue with my plan, come what may. After all, they wouldn't keep me in Fort Leavenworth for the rest of my life.

I crossed the town-hall bridge to the Bishop's City, on the way asking St. Cunnegunda to help me. Even if I didn't believe she was a virgin wife, I still believed she was a saint. Having separated temporarily to create an island, the river roared together in waterfalls beneath the bridge. Then the water swirled around the toy town hall, which as always was spectacular. With so much beauty in the world, how could there be so much evil? In the *Domplatz*, I pondered the Alte Hofaltung, the old medieval seat of government, some of it built out of wood. How much good and evil had those walls witnessed? Who was I to think that I had any more right to miraculous protection than those who had once lived there?

So, I decided that the only thing to do was to go on with the plan. Die with your boots. Hail, Caesar, those about to die salute you!

I wandered into our office as serenely as if it were eight-thirty instead of eleven-thirty.

"Captain Nettleton, ma'am. Sgt. Charles C. O'Malley requests a few brief words with General Meade, ma'am."

"Chuck"—she grinned at me—"you look like you have a hang-over!"

"I was at a party last night in the house of the Borgias. They poisoned me."

She guffawed. "Too much caviar!"

"Yes, ma'am. If you say so, ma'am."

She continued to laugh. "Might you be able to tell me what you wish to discuss with himself?"

"I might."

"So?"

"Special Agent Clarke of the FBI."

"Pig," she snapped. "Okay, I'll tell himself."

It was, I conceded, a grand party, despite my poisoning.

A moment later she was back and nodded me into the inner sanctum.

"Chucky," General Meade began, "you look like hell!"

"Sir, I was poisoned last night!"

He thought that was hilarious. "You know, I can't wait to get out of this place. It's an impossible job for a career officer, but I'll miss Polly's parties."

"They won't be here too long either, sir."

"I guess that's right. Well, nostalgia for what used to be is part of the fun of life."

"Especially if you're Irish, sir."

"So I'm told." He smiled thoughtfully. "Now, what's this about Special Agent Clarke?"

"I thought I should report, sir, that he's very difficult to work with. I reported to him this morning at the Bambergerhof at ten hundred hours and requested the documents on the Wülfe case that he possesses—pictures, descriptions, fingerprints. He responded, sir, that they were up in his room and he was not willing at that time to return to his room to retrieve them. He stated that he would deliver them here tomorrow at fourteen-thirty, sir."

General Meade's brow furrowed in displeasure. "You found him in the dining room, son?"

"No, sir."

"In the bar?"

"Uh, yes, sir."

"He was drinking?"

"Gin, sir."

"Drinking or drunk?"

"I'm unable to make a judgment on that, sir. However in the brief time I was present with him, sir, he emptied two glasses of gin."

"I thought so." The general pounded his baroque oak desk with his fist. "I order you, Sergeant O'Malley, off this case until he begins to cooperate."

"Yes, sir."

I want to make it clear that General Meade was a distinguished soldier, a commander of an armored brigade in Patton's Third Army with a deserved reputation for tactical brilliance. He would not under other circumstances permit himself to be so adroitly taken in by a punk sergeant. But his present command was boring. He had been appointed CO of the Constabulary out here, Polly had told me, so the Luce publications could reassure their readers that a tough, smart, battle-hardened veteran was responsible for defeating the werewolves.

"There was a guy from the Bureau at Polly's party last night," he said.

"I trust he was not poisoned like I was, sir?"

"He was uninvited. Showed up at the door claiming to be an old friend of mine who was in Bamberg for just a few days and wanted to pay his respects. I guess I met him once or twice, but he had to introduce himself to me."

"Indeed, sir."

"Wanted to talk to me about Agent Clarke. Seemed to be a good man who went sour a few years back and turned to the drink. Very good at the job he does."

"Bounty hunter, sir."

"Good description. . . . Anyway, he said the director, old J. Edgar, wanted him protected and helped and would consider it a favor to him if we did everything we could to facilitate the search for these . . . Damn it, what are their names anyway?"

"Wülfe, sir. The Gunther Wülfe family."

"Yes, of course."

"I had a conversation with him too, sir; he didn't mention the director to me."

"What do you think his message was, son?"

"Put up with Rednose Clarke, as I think your old friend called him, no matter how much of a drunk he is and no matter how difficult he is to work with."

"Sounds exactly right to me." The general leaned back against his vast, thronelike chair and clasped his hands behind his head. "What do you think we should do?"

"I'm inclined, sir, to believe that we should certainly give the impression of accepting the director's advice."

"And?" He glared at me, unhappy that I seemed to be going along with J. Edgar.

"And keep a careful record of his behavior so that when and if he goofs up, we can say we tried."

"Ever read Machiavelli, Chuck?" The general leaned forward, elbows resting on his desk.

"No, sir. Didn't he play shortstop for the St. Louis Browns?"

Actually, the Florentine pol was on my reading list for the next semester. But I understood then what General Meade had meant. I later read *Il principe* with some interest, but he taught me little that I didn't already know.

"Well, we'll follow your plan. But we'll keep the pace slow until he becomes more cooperative and shows some signs of urgency."

"Great tactics, General, sir."

He beamed at my compliment, perhaps forgetting that they were my tactics.

Good, there was no hurry about Agent Clarke. We had perhaps a day or two more of grace. Yet, unless I misjudged the man, he was capable, like a rattlesnake, of swinging into action just when you least expected it—with only a few warning shakes from his rattle.

As I left the general's office, Captain Polly handed me four pages of rough draft. "Do you think, Chucky, you could squeeze into your convalescent time a little work?"

"Me, work?"

"Do your typewriter magic on these things for us."

"Yes, ma'am. Right away, ma'am. I must give some instructions downstairs for the general, ma'am, and then I'll get right to work."

"Don't work too hard!"

"No, ma'am."

I found three of our guys sitting around in the bull pen that used to be the entrance lobby—half a football field long. They were killing time, which was most of what the Army of Occupation did.

"Hiyah, Sarge."

"Hi, guys. . . . Hey, guys, I don't want to disturb your work. There is a guy we're kind of looking for. Name's Gunther Wülfe. Some kind of Nazi from Dresden. FBI wants him. When you feel like some fresh air, would you mind going around town to see if you can find him."

"Sure, Sarge. What's he look like?"

"Would the Bureau tell a mere sergeant—"

"Staff sergeant."

"Right. Would they tell me what he looks like?"

"How are we supposed to find him?"

"Ask around for him."

"Yeah, Sarge, you bet. How long are we supposed to look?"

"Until you find him. Or until the general calls off the search."

"We got you, Sarge."

They got it all right. They were supposed to go through the motions of a search for a while. Typical Army order of which they had heard many others in their careers: look like you're doing something when in fact you're doing nothing.

Tomorrow, if Agent Clarke showed up at fourteen-thirty, I'd give them more details about what Trudi's father looked like. They would never find him because he was dead. I could say that there were a wife and two daughters but they weren't the ones the Bureau was really after.

All bases covered.

I went back up to my typewriter. I glanced around our office. Brig, who had been hard at work when I showed up, was gone. I glanced at my watch. Probably off to the *Bahnhof.* Doubtless she had shown up at eight-thirty that morning, despite the party last night. She always showed up at eight-thirty—the only hardworking person in our office, probably in the whole building.

I sat at my typewriter and began to grind out the stuff Polly wanted.

A cracker voice bellowed, "O'Malley, what the hell are you up to?"

My heart and stomach dropped through the floor and my mouth went instantly dry.

Maj. Sam Houston Carpenter.

There were some misleading aspects of his image, which I dug up by getting a peek at his records and had not yet passed on to General Meade. His ring was from Texas A&M, not the Point, though it had been subtly altered to give the impression of being a Point ring. He had been an officer in the reserves in his state and had served after being called up at the time of Pearl Harbor. Son of an old political family and a lawyer, he had ambitions for the state-house and beyond. Yet, when his outfit was sent overseas to New Guinea, he remained behind. He was transferred to Europe in 1943 when London seemed to be a reasonably safe place. Somehow he had managed to get himself assigned to the supply unit of the Screaming Eagles—as the Eighty-second is called—but he never once parachuted out of a plane. When, two days after D day, the supply unit brought in equipment for ground war to what was left of the Eighty-second, Sam had remained behind in London, for reasons unexplained.

There was no explanation for why he did not return to cracker land after the war. Perhaps he volunteered for the Army of Occupation rather than ending up in the planned invasion of Japan.

That was, I thought, our Sam: a fraud through and through, not a smart fraud, not clever enough, it seemed to me, to be in the black market, but a threat to every woman in Bamberg he wanted and a real pain in the ass to the rest of us.

I didn't like him much, you see. I had not turned his record over to the general because I was waiting for just the right time to do so.

"Pardon me, sir?" I looked up at Carpenter as if he were a lamentable distraction to my work. He leaned over and jerked me to my feet. "Stand at attention in the presence of an officer, you fucking son of a bitch!"

I looked for Captain Polly, but she was nowhere to be seen. Mommy, where are you when I really need you?

"Are you physically assaulting me, sir?"

A couple of other Constabs were still in the office, watching in astonishment.

"I'll assault you, you shit-faced fucker."

But he let go of me because he knew that I was just nasty enough to bring charges against him. I stood at something that might remotely have resembled attention. I was never good at that sort of thing, but I was particularly slovenly that day to show my contempt for him—and to perhaps trick him into saying more than he wanted.

"Is there some problem, sir?"

"You're the problem, you disgraceful excuse for a soldier."

"Perhaps I should go to A & M, when I go home, sir, and learn what a real soldier is."

His face twisted with anger, he pulled back his fist to hit me, then controlled himself.

"Don't try to smart-ass me, you yellow-livered punk."

"Yes, sir."

That was an original and creative insult, wasn't it?

"So what do you think you're up to?"

"I'm typing some material at Captain Nettleton's request, sir."

"That's not what I mean," he snarled.

Did he have the pictures or did he not?

"Sir, at the risk of repeating myself, what seems to be the problem?"

"We're keeping an eye on you, O'Malley, a close eye on you."

A threatening revelation. Why were they keeping an eye on me? Because I was General Meade's favorite? Or because I didn't like his pursuit of Brigitta?

Strange.

"Yes, sir."

"We saw you going into that camera shop this morning, don't deny it."

"I was unaware that the store was off-limits, sir."

"You deny you were there?"

"I can hardly deny that, sir. Two of your agents entered the shop while I was there."

"Damn right. I said we were keeping a close eye on you. What were you doing in that shop?"

"Sir, unless you furnish me some explanation for this encounter, I will respectfully decline to tell you."

"Do you know what that place is?" he exploded.

"A camera shop, I believe."

"The guy is a forger. He makes false papers."

"I had not been aware of that, sir."

Until last night.

"We know about him but we're leaving him alone till we can use him to haul in a really big fish."

I took that to mean until they had enough evidence to convict him.

"Am I a really big fish, sir? I wouldn't have thought so."

I was enjoying this too much. I had better be careful.

"What have we got here?" He grabbed for my print of the Me 262 and tore the newspaper off it.

"Don't damage it, sir," I said in an ice-cold voice. "It's an expensive print."

He was more careful. "What the fuck is this, O'Malley? A fucking kraut plane? They're our enemies!"

"I don't think that's the proper term anymore, sir. . . . The plane is a Messerschmitt 262, the first jet ever to be used in combat. It was developed at the same time as our XP-59, but they went into production with it and we didn't."

If he was going for my print, he didn't have the papers. I relaxed a little, but he was still dangerous. Why was I being hounded by his gumshoes? Or had they just come into Albrecht's store by chance?

"It's fucking disloyal to have something like that."

"If you believe so, sir, you should bring charges against me."

"Why did you buy this?"

"I'm not sure that's a proper question, sir, but I happen to be a photographer and that's an excellent print. In ten years as perhaps the only color picture remaining of the Messerschmitt it will be a collector's item."

"What else did you buy?"

"Sir, I will answer your question under protest, if only to terminate this discussion quickly. As your agents doubtless told you, I purchased this print and four rolls of Agfachrome film."

I poured the rolls out of the paper bag in which they had nestled on my desk and dumped them on my blotter.

"American film not good enough for you?"

"Kodachrome is excellent, sir. But under some circumstances, such as those prevailing at the present, Agfachrome gives somewhat warmer colors."

"Hot shit!"

"Yes, sir. Will there be anything else, sir?"

"Yeah," he growled. "You just be goddamn careful. I intend to nail your ass to the highest flagpole in Bavaria."

"Yes, sir. I'll inform General Meade, sir."

He strode away in a precise military gait, doubtless practiced many times.

I sank into my chair, drained and sick to my stomach. Well, at least I didn't have to run to the jakes. Absently, I rewrapped the print and returned the film to the bag.

He probably did not have the pictures. Still, maybe he did and was holding back on them for his own purposes. Should I assume that he had them or that he did not have them? Perhaps he would pass them on to Agent Clarke, with whom he might be in cahoots. Where were the pictures now? But would Clarke recognize them when he compared them with his photo? Would he not wonder where Gunther Wülfe was? Clarke was not so dumb as not to suspect a connection.

Did Albrecht still have them? Would I dare go over there and talk to him again? Maybe Brig could, but that would put her in jeopardy. I had other pictures. Perhaps the best strategy would be to wait a day or two, make sure the clumsy gumshoes were not in sight, and then sneak over in the early morning to Albrecht's. Obviously he lived in the back of the store.

Or maybe I should give up on that source and find another counterfeiter. Where? I'd have to ask Brig. I couldn't ask her today. That would make her suspicious of what I was doing. She would want to be involved because of her sense of loyalty. We could be running out of time. Yet I did not want to endanger Brig. I'd wait till tomorrow to ask her.

I walked up to Captain Polly's desk. No sign of her. I laid the drafts and my retyped version on her desk. Should I go in and complain to the general about Sam Houston Carpenter? I put my hand on the door to knock and then thought better of it. Radford Meade, who detested Carpenter, would be furious. But he was no fool. A slight little doubt about me would remain in his head. Might I have been looking for forged papers after all? The doubt wouldn't mean much now, but other and later events could make it dangerous for me.

I had an accounting exam that night, for which I had already studied and in which I would surely gain my usual A. Even if I had not studied, I also would get an A. The stuff was disgustingly easy. American Fiction 101 was a lot harder and more interesting. So, I was going to be an accountant.

Trudi was still at work. What should I do?

I had better reply to Rosemarie. I had a hunch my letters to her were even more important to her than hers were to me—and the latter were pretty damn important. So I put a sheet of paper, a carbon, and another sheet in my machine and began.

Dear Rosemarie,

I'd love to see you here in Bamberg. I could tell everyone that you were my girlfriend, and while that wouldn't exactly be true, it would earn me a lot of admiration and envy. But let's postpone the visit for a few weeks. We have some sticky projects going on around here that will keep me busy for the next couple of weeks. I wouldn't have much time for you till we've wrapped up these matters. After that, it would be wonderful. I'd love to show you off, if you don't mind being shown off.

Last night, Captain Polly, whom I have written about before, had another of her parties. It was great fun, but I must confess I have a hangover this morning. Since I don't drink, I concluded that Captain Polly had poisoned me. But she insists that anyone who eats four semisweet chocolate bars, a quarter pound of caviar, and three dishes of Italian chocolate ice cream deserves to get sick.

I don't really believe that it was that much caviar—to which I could easily become addicted. I believe it was beluga too, which I gather is the best. The Russkie soldiers, out to make a dishonest ruble, smuggle it over the border and sell it to us. I don't know whether that's where the Nettletons got it. Out here we think our black markets are bad—though we're not able to do much about it. But everyone figures that we don't break any laws— except Russian laws and they don't count. Besides, maybe it's a way to help some Russkies to become capitalist.

Anyway the party was great fun.

I then described at great length the party, leaving out the man from the Bureau but leaving in the attractions of the women who were there.

It will not surprise you to be told that I was asked to sing, accompanied by the beauteous Captain Polly. I did three authentic songs (two Percy French and "The Kerry Dance") and was then constrained to sing "When Irish Eyes Are Smiling." My Bostonian friends think that's real Irish culture.

Then for the pure hell of it, I sang "Clancy Lowered the Boom" and had them all singing the choruses. I believe I mentioned to Captain Polly that the Clancy I knew was of the opposite sex.

Captain Polly, who doesn't miss much, demanded to know what age this Clancy woman was. I told her, older than the mountains and younger than springtime. I hope you like that as a quick reply. I thought it was pretty good myself. Then when I was leaving, she pried again into the identity of this Clancy person. Would I like her? she demanded.

To which I replied with full honesty that I supposed so because my mother and sister Peg like her. That did not settle the matter, as you might imagine. The next thing will be that she will want to see your picture. I'll have to dig deep in my archives and find if I have brought any with me.

Well, I have an exam in Advanced Accounting tonight, a subject I don't particularly enjoy, but I think I'll get an A. So I have to run. My best to all my friends.

Love,
Chuck

There was one lie in the letter. Or, since I don't normally lie, a bit of an exaggeration. Lies are sinful. There were a number of pictures of Rosie in the archives. But the one I had put on my desk (in an elegant silver frame I had purchased in Bamberg) was a prom-night picture of Rosemarie in her first prom dress. Let Miss Captain Nosy make what she wanted of it!

— 20 —

Just as I sealed the letter to Rosemarie and told myself that Rosie was a nice kid and I'd always love her as a sister, Brigitta entered our offices and walked over to my desk. Back from the *Bahnhof*. She looked especially discouraged, even worried.

"Anything wrong?" I asked lightly.

Solemnly she opened her purse and put a dirty, much used #10 manila envelope on my desk.

"From Herr Albrecht. He knew I would be out at the *Bahnhof*, waiting for the train. He said to give it to you and tell you he was sorry, but he could not take care of the matter at this time. He added that he was very, very sorry and you were a nice man."

I touched the envelope. Small objects inside. Pictures.

"Did he show you what was inside?"

"Of course not. I'm sure they're pictures, however. What else would they be?"

"He's a good man, a very good man."

"I know."

"He realizes he should not make any more false documents."

"Oh, yes. Not till there are new men in your CID."

"Is there a Frau Albrecht lurking in the back of the store?"

"She was killed in the raid on Dresden."

"I see."

So perhaps he was a good man for Brig if her husband did not return. How long would she wait?

"His work is excellent," I said, unwrapping the shot of the Me 262. "Color, composition, everything."

"What are you getting into, Chuck?" she demanded. "It must be dangerous."

"Not really, thanks to Albrecht's loyalty to a man who gave him twice what he asked for when he bought this picture."

"You trying to get someone out of the American zone?"

"Something like that."

"Can you tell me about it?"

For a moment I was tempted. Then I knew better. "I don't think so, Brigie. It would put you at unnecessary risk."

"I see. . . . Do they deserve to be saved?"

"Oh, yes. I wouldn't be trying to get them the papers unless they did."

She nodded. "I trust you, Chucky."

"Good. Can you find me another person who does this kind of work?"

"I have thought of it. He is expensive."

"That does not matter."

"And very good."

"Fine. Where is he?"

"*Nein*, I cannot tell you that until I see him and ask if he will do it for you. Perhaps I will know tomorrow. Do not rush me, Chucky. This must be done carefully."

"I won't challenge that."

"Are these people Germans?"

"Yes."

"Good." She rose to leave. "I must go home and cook supper. Do you wish to join us?"

"Love to, but I have my Advanced Accounting exam tonight."

"I forgot."

"Anything at the *Bahnhof* today?"

"One of the men from my husband's regiment. He has not seen Kurt since before the battle of Kursk."

"Doesn't necessarily prove anything."

"I know. I believe he's still alive. But, somehow, I am less sure."

Poor dear woman.

I picked up the envelope of photos and the envelope with my letter to Rosie and walked over to the exam. I made sure that none of the CID gumshoes were trailing me. My plan was still on track, more or less, but I could not figure out why Carpenter's men would want to follow me. Maybe it was just an unlucky chance. Maybe they were staking out Albrecht's place when I happened by.

But I was still uneasy about Carpenter. What was he up to? Why

did he hate me so fiercely? Because I had a role in the law enforce-
ment business that he wanted? Because I was Frau Richter's confidant and an obstacle to his possession of her? Maybe either or both,
but it still didn't make much sense.

The exam was a breeze. When I had finished—first one naturally—I put the paper on the teacher's desk and walked out of the
room. At seven o'clock the sun was still high in the sky, and because
of the humidity, the world was bathed in mellow gold.

I walked across the Regens to Untersandstrasse and found Trudi,
home from work and clad only in her panties. She was embarrassed
but also delighted by my gasp of wonderment.

"Let's go take some pictures while the sun is up."

"*Ja*, Karl"—she snuggled in my arms—"we take pictures when
it is light and save the dark for other things."

She put on sandals, a blouse with three buttons open, and a skirt,
and we left the house.

I loved her so much when I was with her that I could not imagine
ever giving her up. In those moments, even when we were not engaged in our sexual games, she was beautiful, fascinating, witty, intelligent. The perfect woman.

I take out the dry and cracked prints of the shots I made of her
in 1947 and find that she has the same impact on me now as then.
She *is* beautiful and mysterious. Only a child perhaps, but a child
who has known the tragedies and sorrows of life. Nor can I believe
that the glow in her eyes when she looks at me is bogus. She loved
me too. She must have known that she didn't have to seduce me to
earn my help.

Maybe she was lonely too—and frightened and fragile—and
wanted a little bit of warmth in her life.

So that evening, giggling and laughing all the way, we walked
through the streets of Bamberg, she with her treasured Leica ("My
father gave it to me for my eleventh birthday," she would say sadly)
and I with my prized Kodak. Sometimes we would change cameras
and I would make shots of her and she of me. As I look at prints of
that skinny, eighteen-year-old punk, I shake my head in astonishment. What could she have seen in me? Other than documents that
would make her and her family free?

When we had run out of film, we went over to the island upriver from the town hall and my favorite beer garden in the park in front of the Schloss Geyersworth. Against the background of the nineteenth-century *Schloss* gleaming in the pink and rose light of the setting sun, a small band was playing Strauss waltzes, GIs and their girls were dancing, and waiters were dashing around with trays filled with beer steins and plates of sausage, a frolicsome, *Oktoberfest* atmosphere. Had there been a war? No one seemed to remember. Young men and women were having fun on a Friday night. Neither the past nor the future mattered much.

"It is beautiful, is it not?" Trudi asked me, her hand on mine. "Time stands still."

"Time never stands still Trudi, but sometimes it is necessary to pretend."

We were in no hurry to eat. So we danced while we were waiting for a waiter. I was not much of a dancer despite the praise of the women with whom I had danced. Trudi joined the chorus. "Karl, you dance so well!"

"Not all that well, but thanks, Trud." I drew her even closer.

Her breasts now so familiar but yet always a surprise were clearly visible under the loose blouse and the open buttons. She was so, so beautiful. I was almost overcome with love. Not desire, though that was present too, but love. Or so I thought.

Mind you, our dance was relatively chaste compared to most of those in the beer garden. Many of the GIs were as close to sexual intercourse with their dates as one could be while still wearing clothes. Soon they will go home to America, I thought, and leave the girls behind without a thought about them and perhaps only the faintest memories. I would be different from the rest of them. Did the girls realize this? Probably, but they could hope it might be different, could they not?

We went back to our table and a waiter appeared. I ordered a beer for Trudi and "mineral water" for myself and four large sausages.

"I can eat only one," she protested mildly.

"I know. The three are for me."

"But you'll get sick!"

"Not me. I have an iron stomach."

While we were waiting for our food and drink, I put my hand

under her skirt and caressed the inside of her solid thigh. She stiffened and bit her lip.

"You drive me out of my mind, Karl."

"That's the general idea. I'll stop if you want me to."

"*Nein*, please don't stop."

Then the sausages came and I had to cease my amusements and devote myself to eating.

"Good," Trudi said as she munched on her sausage.

"Very good," I replied, banishing thoughts of caviar from my head.

Halfway through the second sausage, I saw Special Agent Clarke on the other side of the garden, at a table by himself, swilling down beer at a rapid rate.

"Excuse me, Trud. I have a little politicking to do."

I sauntered across the garden, ducking waiters and dancing couples.

"My respects, sir," I said to Agent Clarke.

"Hi, sport," he mumbled. "Nice dish you have with you."

"Thank you, sir. She is a very intelligent young woman."

"More than just intelligent, I'd say." He winked. "Is she any good in bed?"

"I am not able to offer a judgment on that, sir."

"How's your search coming?" he asked with sudden sharpness.

"My team is searching in the town, sir. But it is difficult without the photo and the descriptions which are still in your possession."

"Yeah, that's right," he sighed. "I did promise them for tomorrow, didn't I?"

"Yes, sir, at fourteen-thirty."

"Right, but tomorrow is Saturday, isn't it, sport?"

"Yes, sir."

"You guys work on Saturday?"

"Yes, sir. Till noon."

But not many of us showed and practically none of us worked.

"Silly waste of time. . . . Well, I can't imagine being up that early. Monday be all right?"

"That's up to you, sir. But it will delay the search."

"I'm in no rush, sport. See you Monday."

"Yes, sir."

"Enjoy your dame."

"Thank you, sir."

Most people round the *Residenz* knew that the beer garden on the Geyerworthstrasse was one of my hangouts, my only hangout as a point of fact. Agent Clarke could have found that out, from Carpenter, maybe, and come to check on me. Did he see any resemblance between Trudi and the girl in the picture? Was his lackadaisical manner merely a trick to deceive me?

I'd have to take my chances that he was as dumb as he seemed to be.

"Who is that man?" Trudi asked when I had settled down again at her table and began to finish off my second sausage.

"An American civilian government guy I have to work with. I thought it might be wise not to appear to be ignoring him."

"You are so clever, Karl." She laid her hand on mine.

"Not really. Just careful." I switched the third sausage to my other hand and found her thigh again.

She caught her breath and then sighed contentedly. "He looks evil . . . and dangerous."

"He drinks a lot. He may not be all that dangerous."

Or then again, he may. Why would Agent Clarke come over to the island for his beer when he could get his gin at the Bambergerhof? To enjoy the lovely evening and watch the young folk at play? Somehow that didn't seem much like Agent Clarke.

"He is the man who stays at the Bambergerhof, is he not?"

"Yeah, and it's a good idea for you folks to keep away from him, but he's not worth worrying about. . . . Want another beer?"

"Of course."

I ordered the beer and the mineral water. Then she guided me to the dancing area and leaned against me as though she were giving herself completely over to me in trust and faith, a gesture of generosity and surrender rather than mere sexual invitation.

Damn it, she did love me!

The full moon had risen in the eastern sky, orange and huge. A harvest moon, Mom would have called it.

We drank our beer and mineral water at a leisurely pace, and I continued to amuse myself with her thighs, now both of them.

When she had finished her second beer, I asked her if she wanted a third.

"Karl, I want only to go home and make love with you. Now. I want to run home and give myself to you."

"Then let's go home now."

Under the full moon we rushed back to her apartment. We didn't exactly run, but we walked fast.

"Oh, Karl, my love, hurry!"

We were barely inside the building when she stripped off her blouse and skirt and handed them to me as we walked up the rickety stairs. As she opened the door of the apartment, she discarded her panties and threw them inside ahead of her. Then she began an assault on my clothes.

It was a violent night of sexual games, our best night yet. Trudi needed passion and I provided it for her in every method I knew. Sex, I had discovered, was as important for women as for men but in a different way. I filed that insight for future reference.

"Tomorrow," she said when it was time for me to leave, "I will be with my mother and Erika all day. Then on Sunday we go to church together."

"Good. I'll see you on Monday."

"You will go to church too?"

"I suppose so."

"Good."

It might indeed be a good idea. Since I was trying to get back in the good graces of the One in Charge and since I thought we might need His help desperately, I figured it couldn't hurt.

Theoretically, we worked at Constabulary HQ on Saturday morning—and men were always on call in case of an emergency. There were few emergencies because Germans are, as I have said, a law-abiding people—until a demon takes over in their society and they turn crazy and kill millions of people, all the while, however, being obedient to what they take as the law, their laws of course.

My Saturday routine was to drop in for a few minutes to see if there was anything doing and then sneak out, which is more than what most of the officers would do. However today I went to work early with the hope that Brigitta might have news for me.

That Saturday as I walked into the *Residenz*, I met General Meade walking out. Off for a game of golf, no doubt.

"Anything on the FBI case, son?" he asked, barely stopping for an answer.

"Agent Clarke thinks he might be able to get the documents over to me by Monday afternoon."

"Idiot," he barked as he went out the door.

It was one more brick in the wall I was building around Agent Clarke, or perhaps around myself for protection against Agent Clarke.

"Brigie," I said to that worthy, the only person to be seen in the huge office, "hard at work?"

She did not look up from her typewriter. "I am German, not American, so I must work when I am told to work."

She was wearing her usual "uniform" of white blouse and dark skirt, this time summer-weight blue. The jacket of the suit was draped neatly over the chair next to her desk.

"Do you think anyone would fire you if you didn't show up to-day? Hell, Brigie, no one would know the difference. Who, besides me, could report whether you were here or not here?"

She stopped typing. "I am supposed to work on Saturday morning," she said stubbornly.

Jawohl, I thought.

"Tell you what: next Friday afternoon ask Captain Polly if she needs you on Saturday. She'll seem surprised but will tell you no. Then ask her the next Saturday and she'll say, if you're needed on any Saturday morning, she'll let you know. Do you want to bet against that scenario?"

Brigitta looked up at me, a faint smile on her lovely face. "I am so grateful that I do not want to take advantage of you Americans. But you are right of course. I should have figured it out for myself."

"Yeah, well, you can always ask me."

"I know, Chucky, I know."

I thought she was going to weep and wondered what the hell I would do in response to that.

"So, did you find out anything about new papers?"

"Yes, there is someone who will do it. But he is strange. You will bring him the pictures and the money—five hundred American dollars. He will make the papers for you. When they are finished, he will tell me and I will tell you. He will not tell you his name and he does not want to know yours. Is that too much money?"

"No." If need be, I could always borrow some money from my family for college. I didn't want to, but I could.

"The arrangements are all right?"

"I'll live with them. . . . How long will it take?"

"He would not tell me. He is a fine artist with etchings. He had a good reputation before the war, but then no one wanted etchings. He made reichsmarks. Some say he had been making them long before the war. The Nazis always suspected him, but they could prove nothing. It is also said he made reichsmarks for them too."

"I presume he is making American dollars now."

"I would be surprised if he wasn't. The challenge would be too much to resist. Probably he makes only a few, enough to provide him with money."

"And his friends?"

"He has no friends. . . . You are to knock on his door, then go in. It is always open. You tell him Brigitta sent you and give him the pictures. Then you leave. No joking, Chucky, and no buying anything like the picture you bought from Max Albrecht. This is a very serious business."

"Sounds like it."

"You will ask him how long. He will exaggerate, but do not push him or question him. He knows it's urgent. Maybe towards the end of next week."

I glanced at her calendar. Thursday was the fourteenth, Friday, the fifteenth—Mary's Day in Harvest time. The old Celtic feast of Lugnasad.

"Where can I find him?"

"You know where the Evangelical church is?"

"Sure, down the street from your parish church."

"You walk past it and turn right. There is tiny lane leading into a square of very old buildings. In the far corner of the square on the left, right at the corner, there is basement apartment. You can recognize it because there are always black shades on the window."

"All right, when is this eccentric genius at home?"

"He's home all the time. You will not interfere with his, ah, minting American dollars?"

"None of my business—not till too many of his products turn up. And I don't know his name, do I?"

She smiled thinly. "No, you don't."

"Okay. Why don't you show me the place when you go home?"

"I have much work to do."

"Did Captain Nettleton say she wanted it first thing Monday morning?"

"No . . ."

"Then she doesn't. She'd be horrified if she knew you were working on a lovely Saturday like this and with your two kids at home wanting to go on a picnic."

She hesitated. "Are you *sure* it will be all right?"

"Positive." I picked up her jacket and put it on her. She reached for her purse, jammed a number of things into it—lipstick, tissues, pen, and suchlike, slipped the papers into a desk drawer, and admired for a moment her empty desktop.

"Very neat, *Frau Doktor Doktor,*" I said, dragging her toward the stairs. "Now let's go. Connie and Hank are expecting a picnic."

"They bothered me all last night about a picnic," she admitted.

We strolled across the *Domplatz* and down the narrow streets to the parish church. I stopped at a small toy shop to buy a couple of things for her kids.

"You should not do that," she insisted. "You will spoil them."

"I should bring them back?"

She smiled. "No, of course not."

"You certainly know your way around this town. I ask for someone who might forge papers for me and you think of two almost at once."

"It is my neighborhood." She shrugged. "I should know it well."

"Well enough to have any leads on the black market?"

"I could not tell you if I did know. I cannot betray my friends."

"And if they were not your friends and they were hurting innocent children by stealing penicillin and charging prices their parents could not afford?"

"Then I might. But actually I know nothing. I try not to listen. My position is a difficult one."

"All we would expect from you at Constabulary HQ is that you tell us when Germans are being hurt."

"I will always do that."

The trouble with being a person with her kind of conscience, especially if you're Catholic, is that you end up having a lot of tough moral choices to make—and afraid to follow your instincts when they're all you have, which is most of the time.

We went beyond the *Pfarrkirche* and worked our way through the narrow lanes that created a maze of medieval streets, almost a labyrinth. In trying to explore during my early days in Bamberg, I became thoroughly lost and wandered by the same buildings several times till I asked one of the locals how to get to the *Domplatz*. I made it on the second try.

This area had once been the clerical quarters for the staff of the parish church and their aides. There must have been a lot of both. Then we passed the Evangelical (Lutheran) church and entered an even smaller, tighter web of old buildings. The area was the dingiest and most run-down part of the Bishop's City, the closest thing to a slum that Bamberg possessed.

As we walked, Brig chatted happily about her childhood and her family and her children. Then she fell silent.

"It will get better, Brig. This is just a transition. In a year or two at the most the American, British, and French zones will merge into a new country."

"It will be fine when Kurt comes home," she replied, her jaw set in grim determination.

What if anything would shake that faith?

Finally we turned a couple of corners, walked down a few lanes, and emerged into a tiny, dirty square with benches on which some elderly people sat. Despite the warm weather, no one else was in the square. The only occupants were pieces of paper floating occasionally in the summer breeze, like minor lost souls.

"Over there in the corner." She pointed. "You can just barely see the stairs going to his shop."

"Got it."

"Good luck."

"I'm going to walk you back home."

"That will not be necessary. It is safe here in the neighborhood."

"Regardless. I can find my way back."

During our half-hour stroll from the _Domplatz_, I had been on the watch for gumshoes. No one in sight—unless they were a lot better than the agents who worked for Sam Houston Carpenter. I found my way out of the maze with only one correction from Brig.

When we arrived at her apartment, I gave her the bag of toys.

"You must come in for tea."

"Thanks but no thanks. The kids want to get out into the country and so do you. Besides, I have work to do."

"Be very careful."

"Always; you know me."

"That's why I worry."

She looked as if she might kiss me, but then, good, prudent frau that she was, she decided not to do it in public.

"You really have quite a harem, don't you, sport? That one is a really classy babe."

"Agent Clarke," I said. "Good morning, sir."

He was standing at the head of Brigitta's street, just in front of the _Pfarrkirche_. Where had he come from and what was he doing here? I had paid little attention to possible tails since we left the square where the engraver's shop was.

"Yeah, how come you're so lucky?"

He was wearing a white shirt, without a tie, trousers with suspenders, and a Panama straw hat. He looked exactly like what he was, an American detective who had drunk too much for a long time, a character from a Raymond Chandler novel.

"She's a colleague at the _Residenz_, sir. I accompanied her home because I had some toys to give her children."

"Well, you weren't all over her, like you were that kid last night."

He smelled of gin already.

"Yes, sir."

"Figured I should get a view of this city before I leave. Pretty sloppy, dirty old place, huh? Too bad we didn't bomb out all this mess like we did in Frankfurt, isn't it?"

I let that go.

"How's the search coming?"

"My team continues its investigation, sir, but . . ."

"I know, I know, you need the documents I got. Take it easy. I promised them sometime Monday and I'm a man of my word."

"Yes, sir."

"I'll be shoving off. I'm getting thirsty and that bar at the hotel isn't all bad. Cool too."

"Yes, sir. Enjoy your excursion."

"That'll be pretty hard in this dump of a town. See you, sport. Keep on enjoying your women while you're young enough to have fun."

What the hell!

Was Rednose Clarke much smarter than he appeared to be? Was he wearing a mask to fool me? What kind of game was he playing? Why did he keep turning up at places where I was? He couldn't possibly be the stupid drunk that he pretended to be, could he?

Or maybe he was a good agent gone sour. In that case he was dangerous only because he had remnants of intelligence and instinct that could start to work at almost any time.

That was the best interpretation. The worst was that he was part of some massive plot involving Sam Houston Carpenter to do me in. But why me? Why use a sixteen-inch gun to swat a fly, albeit a pesky fly?

If they knew where the Wülfes were, why not sweep in and arrest them? Why dangle all of us on a string for a week or so? What more could they possibly hope to learn?

Maybe they were all just dumb. I had learned even then that the American government was permeated by incompetent people—as I would later learn so were all other governments. In fact, we were better than most.

So, hoping that the "stupid" explanation was the right one, I ambled back to the tiny, dingy square where the great counterfeiter lived. I made only a couple of bad turns and found the square on the second, well, the third, try. Before entering the square I checked out the lane behind me. No one. Then the square. Only paper, noisy pigeons, and a few old folks sitting on the benches under the sun.

I looked around cautiously when I arrived at the far right corner of the square. Still no one watching. I hoped I wasn't being trailed by real pros. But then, where would the Army of Occupation find any pros?

I hesitated before descending the dark and filthy steps to the foreboding shop. Somewhere I had read a story, I think by Charles Williams, about someone entering a shop like that and ending up in another world. I didn't want to go to another world just yet, not until I had cleared some of the decks in this world.

So I squared my shoulders, strode down the creepy stairs, and pounded on the decaying oak door.

"*Ja?*" said a strange, musical voice.

I pushed the door open and went into the strangest room I have ever seen in all my life. It was filled with a kind of misty blue light, though it was not clear whence the light came. A sweet, not unpleasant smell permeated the place, a lot like the smell of the model-airplane glue I had used when I was a kid, only more appealing. The room was filled with presses, plates, bottles, retorts, discarded copper squares, and piled everywhere, stacks of paper. A smiling, bald, little man, looking like one of Santa's elves and wearing a huge white apron, stood in the center of the room behind a large, white table that might have been a surgical operating table.

Where, I wondered, were Dante and Beatrice?

"*Ja, ja?*" the elf said, rubbing his hands together enthusiastically.

A closer look suggested that he was not a merry old elf at all. His eyes were stone cold, like hard, polished sapphires. I had better follow Brigie's suggestions to the letter.

"*Guten Tag.*"

"*Ja.*" He nodded, a brisk seemingly amiable nod, and rubbed his hands together.

I put the three pictures together on the operating table.

"*Ja.*" He picked them up. "*Ja, ja!*"

I waited.

"Four hundred dollars."

Another discount.

I counted out four hundred-dollar bills—I had been carrying five hundred around for the last couple of days, in case I would need it suddenly to buy papers. I'd have to get more from the bank on Monday. So I'd get a part-time job when I went to Notre Dame.

"*Ja,*" he said, examining my pictures, like a kid with new toys.

He shrugged. "Week, maybe."

No choice. I hoped Brig was right about his delivering ahead of schedule.

"*Danke schön,*" I said.

"*Ja.*" He nodded again, continuing to study the pictures.

I left the room and climbed up the stairs back to the planet Earth. I glanced around the square. No one, save the pigeons and the old-timers on the bench. Carefully watching the people behind me, I walked back across the Regens to my room at the Vinehaus Messer-schmitt.

On the way back I thought about my friends the Nettletons. They were the only ones I knew smart enough to carry out the black-market caper. Apparently he had a lot of money and was already a member of the family law firm back in Boston. They were charming and gracious and generous to me. *But,* truly clever criminals would also know how to be nice people. John could organize an extensive black-market ring with the same skill with which he would organize a political campaign at home in the Bay State. And you couldn't have a better intelligence operative than your wife in the Constabulary commanding general's office. They entertained tastefully but lav-ishly. Where did all the money come from?

Moreover John was smart enough, if he set his mind to it, to ferret out the black-market operation. It was not his job, of course. But it was his wife's job more or less. Why didn't he help her?

Perhaps because he truly believed that another ring would follow this one and found my argument for going against this one naive and innocent. However, he had nodded grimly at my oration the other night. Still that didn't prove anything.

Or the general. He was a gifted and able man who could have earned a lot more money in private industry. Yet he chose to stay in the military and accept two more years of separation from his wife and family. Could not such a man persuade himself in the moral atmosphere of the time that a little extra money was the equivalent of what my father would have called "honest graft"?

My father spoke ironically when he said those words, implying that all graft could become honest when someone was willing to cut corners—as even devout and virtuous and upright men might do on occasion.

I remembered the case of Old Fitz and wondered.

Brigie was right. The black market was becoming an obsession.

Well, it would have to wait till I got back from Stuttgart, hopefully on Friday.

I felt a little guilty about my suspicions. After all, these people were my friends. Would I really turn them in if I found them out? Then I thought of Trudi being assaulted in a dark alley on a cold winter night by some of the black-market people. Yeah, I'd turn them in.

I struggled to find solid proof that my friends were not involved. I couldn't think of any. All my evidence was circumstantial. Mere speculation. But I had to be sure there was nothing more than circumstances.

In my room at the Vinehaus, I outlined my plan in full detail as I now saw it. Hopefully next Thursday night, the eve of Mary's Day in Harvest, we would make the run to Nürnberg. I considered the plan carefully. A few twists and turns might not be necessary. Too cute by half, maybe. But each of them had a good reason behind it.

I still had a few days to think through the plan. I tore up notes. Nothing to do. I turned to American fiction and that obnoxious snob Sinclair Lewis. Then I went over to the *Residenz* and down into the basement darkroom next to the PX. Naturally Dr. Berman was already there.

"Who's worse morally," I began, "a German child who was born in 1940 or an American GI who trades in medicine on the black market?"

He chuckled as he carefully removed a roll of film from the developing tank. "You become more Jewish every day, Chuck. Now you charge in with your Talmudic questions. If you were still Irish, you would waste a half hour in preliminaries."

"Fair play to you. But when with the Talmudists, do what they do."

He laughed again. "You're still Irish after all. The German is more guilty but the American more morally reprehensible."

So we argued and had a grand time arguing. Only in the middle of the argument did I realize there was little difference between trading in medicine or Old Fitz and in trading in forged identity documents.

"Would you trade on the black market?" I asked him.

"Not usually, of course. Yet in a good cause, I might and indeed I have."

"Everyone thinks his own cause is good."

"Naturally."

I didn't ask him what his good cause might be. Was I not after all trading in forgeries for a good cause?

Yet my stubborn idealism said that, apart perhaps from the occasional good cause, Americans should not do those things.

They shouldn't sleep with defenseless eighteen-year-old girls either.

I wondered if he knew who the bosses were in the local blackmarket outfit. He was a smart man. Probably he did. I didn't ask him because I didn't want to know.

The next morning I went to the noon mass at the *Pfarrkirche*, although the Martinkirche was much closer to the Vinehaus. I met Brigie and her family going in. The kids, like good little kraut kids, thanked me politely for my gifts, as did Frau Klein, Brigitta's mother. A nice, decent German family going to church on Sunday as they had all through the Hitler years.

I wasn't being fair. Bamberg had voted for the Center Party, not the Nazis. And Brig and her husband were involved with the group that had tried to kill Hitler. If there was any hope for the future of German democracy, it would be in people like them. How would I have behaved if there were a Nazi-like government in America?

During mass, I spotted Trudi and her family on the other side of the aisle. They also looked pious and devout. Well, who was I to claim anymore that I was a good Catholic?

I turned off the sermon not only because it was in German, at which I was getting better, but because I knew enough German to know that it was pious tripe, the kind that I had often heard at St. Ursula when I was growing up, especially by "missionary" priests who had come around to stir up scruples in the people—as John Raven had bitterly informed me.

At Communion time, all three of the Wülfes went up to the rail as did about a quarter of the people in the relatively full church. What the hell! Didn't she know she was in the state of mortal sin because of what we had been doing? The good April had warned me that Europeans were "lax" in their morality. This was solid proof that she was right.

I was angry. How dare she not feel guilty when I did!

Well, maybe she'd made an act of Perfect Contrition.

Yeah, but that wouldn't do any good unless she had promised God to give me up and that was most unlikely.

I'm afraid that despite my (moderately) good intentions I didn't do much praying at mass.

After mass, when I had slipped away from a possible meeting, I realized that I was a hypocrite and that I would never dare ask her why she felt free to receive—not till after we were married anyway.

As John Raven would remark when I showed him my journal as part of my "general confession," maybe the woman understood God better than I did.

I guess she did. Heaven knows we'd need a lot of God's help in the next few days.

I spent the rest of the day in the PX darkroom working on shots that I would send home to the family on Monday with a letter telling how wonderful my summer life was here in friendly old Bamberg.

Nothing happened on Monday except that it started to rain and the temperature fell into the sixties, too much like autumn already. But next August I would be home, thanks be to God. I went over my plan repeatedly, picturing exactly what each move would look like. If only we had the papers now.

"Did it go well?" Brig asked me.

"I guess. He's an odd one."

"He is that. . . . Wasn't his room cute?"

"That's not the word I'd use."

"Be careful, Chuck. You are in grave danger."

"I don't really think so."

I also tried in my head to clear my friends the Nettletons from all suspicion. Couldn't do it.

I wrote the letter to my family.

Trudi phoned from the hotel saying she had to work nights that day and the next. So we could not meet each other. Possibly Wednesday too.

I finished up the few manuscripts that Captain Polly asked me to type—with her usual charming smile. How could I possibly suspect such an appealing woman?

I glanced over the schedule for the new course in American fiction and then picked up *Arrowsmith* and deepened my dislike for Sinclair Lewis. How could he ever have been so popular? Then I turned to Dante, which was much more to my taste though I figured I'd have to learn Italian to really enjoy it. It'd be much easier to pick up after four years of Latin than German was.

Fourteen-thirty passed and no Agent Clarke. However at sixteen hundred he finally showed up, weaving uncertainly across the floor of the old ballroom.

"Here's the stuff you been bugging me for, sport."

"Thank you, sir. I didn't mean to appear to bug you, but we need to have this material to focus our search properly."

"Well," he sneered, "now you'll be able to properly focus it."

"Split infinitive, sir."

I glanced over the documents. Not much in it that I had not already seen. I tapped my fingers on my desk. I could give the men just the material on Gunther Wülfe and hold back the descriptions of the others. But that might catch up with me. Better that I give them everything now. If we got the materials tomorrow from the elf with the cold eyes, we could move out on Tuesday night. So the men would have only part of Monday and Tuesday to search. Moreover the kids in the picture didn't look much like Trudi and Erika, and Magda had aged so much as to be hardly recognizable.

I told Captain Polly to inform the general, ma'am, that Agent Clarke had finally turned over the promised papers.

"Was that creep drunk, Chucky?"

"He sure was."

"Should I tell General Meade that?"

"Great idea."

Then I went downstairs to give the stuff to my "lads."

"Here are pictures of the family we're searching for and descriptions. Make copies and spread out in town and look for them."

"Sarge, how old is this picture?"

"Six, seven years maybe."

"Then the kids would be in their teens now?"

"Probably."

"Girls change in those years."

"Yeah, now that you mention it, I think I have noticed it too."

"So?"

"So you have to take that into account in your search."

Groans.

"We'll get in a lot of trouble if we ogle every blond adolescent in Bamberg."

"How will that differ from your ordinary behavior?"

Laughs.

"Is the guy still the important one?"

"So I'm told by the Bureau."

"Then maybe we should concentrate on looking for him."

"Good thinking, Ken."

"Do we have to start today?"

I glanced at my watch. "It's pretty late now."

"So we'll start tomorrow, eh, Sarge?"

"I imagine that will be all right. We received these materials too late to start today."

Tomorrow meant around noontime.

The conversation had gone better than I had hoped. Feeling more confident of what I was doing, I went back and made a note in the record I was keeping of the case.

"You may tell General Meade, Captain Polly, that my men have begun the search for our targets with the new material I have given them."

"It will begin tomorrow morning, you mean, Chucky?"

"That may be a correct interpretation, Captain, ma'am, but let the general make it for himself."

Polly chuckled at that. "Okay, Chuck. I'll let him use the intelligence that God gave him. . . . This is the case about people the Russkies want, isn't it? Who are they?"

"Alleged Nazis."

"Men?"

"A man and three women, his wife and two daughters."

"Are they really Nazis?"

"The man was a government functionary in Dresden so he had to belong to the party. So too apparently did the wife. The kids were in the Hitler Jugend."

"Any crimes charged?"

"Nothing specific."

"How old are the kids?"

"Middle teens."

"What will the Russians do to them?"

"Shoot the man, rape the three women to death. Turn them over to a battalion of sex-starved troops."

"My God, Chuck!" she gasped.

"That's the way they do things over there. And it's what we get into when we deal with them."

"Are we trying really hard to find them?" Captain Polly's usually bright face had turned pale.

I shrugged. "When do we try really hard at anything? Let's say that our main goal in this operation is to appear to have obeyed orders."

She nodded solemnly.

Maybe I had found an ally to whom I might turn in time of desperate need. Even if she and her husband were involved in the damn black market.

Obsession!

Then I did my journal for the day, in an obscure code that I had made up so no one would know what was going on. When I finished that, I gathered my books and left for the classroom and the darkroom. As I crossed the town-hall bridge, I noticed that a couple of Carpenter's gumshoes—a different pair this time—were dogging me. What was going on? Was Carpenter getting even with me because he imagined me standing between him and Brigitta?

When I left class, they had vanished. In the darkroom nothing worked the way it should. I gave up after a couple of hours.

My two roommates appeared for the first time in several days, harmless noncoms from Seventh Army whose only concerns were babes and beer. I suppose their intelligence level was a little higher than that of congenital morons, but sometimes it was hard to tell. I listened to them for a while and answered their questions about my own activities with polite caution. Then I sought solace in *Main Street*.

That night my dreams were filled with images of hundreds of Sam Houston Carpenters chasing me down the main street of Gopher Prairie.

— 21 —

"O'Malley, where the fuck are you?" General Meade emerged from his office shouting.

"The game's afoot, Brig," I said as my mouth went dry.

I had shown up at the *Residenz* at nine on Tuesday morning because I had hoped that Brigitta might have the papers for me.

"Not yet, Chuck." She shook her head as I was shedding my raincoat. "It's still too early. Maybe tomorrow or Thursday."

"I hope not any later."

"I hope so too."

"Where's Captain Nettleton this morning?" I had glanced up at that worthy's desk at the end of the ballroom. "She's almost as compulsive about work as you are."

"Out sick," Brigitta had replied with a complacent grin.

"Our Polly *sick?* That paragon of Irish New England sturdiness *sick?*"

I was pretty sure I knew what was coming.

"Morning sickness, Chuck. I'm so happy for them. They've been trying for some time. They will go home in December. We will all miss her. She is a wonderful woman."

Before I could agree, the general had emerged from his office, bellowing for me.

"Coming, sir."

But I did wonder if that might happen with Trudi. We had never spoken about it. Good Catholic that I was, I couldn't possibly practice birth control.

Fornication, not birth control.

"We've got another tip from Ninth Corps." The general waved me into his office. "A smuggling operation. Russian caviar coming across the border up in their sector."

"Up near Coburg?"

"East of there; place called Walldenburg."

I picked it up on General Meade's huge wall map before he did. "That's above the Lichtensteinerwald, sir. A peninsula surrounded by the Russian zone."

"Salient, son," he corrected me.

"Yes, sir. Of course, sir."

"How long to get up there?"

"It's about sixty kilometers, sir. Thirty-five miles or so. One could take Highway 279 up to 303 and turn right. Then we'd have to ride into the mountains. Those roads might be pretty muddy with this storm on our hands. At least an hour, maybe closer to two."

To emphasize my point a jagged burst of lightning cut the sky just outside the floor-to-ceiling windows of the throne room. The thunder came a second after, seeming right above the roof of the *Residenz*. General Meade, who had heard plenty of 88mm rounds coming in, winced.

"We have a border post up there," he said. "That's where the tip came from. They'll give us the location in which these exchanges usually occur."

"Yes, sir." Who was this "us"? I was afraid I knew. "Black-market operation?"

"I'm sure they're involved. The Russian soldiers can buy the caviar on their black market for the equivalent of fifty cents a pound. They sell it to our people for two dollars—three hundred percent profit and in American dollars, which are worth even more on their currency black market. Then our people turn around and sell it for ten dollars a pound. Profit for everyone."

"Nice markup, sir."

"What platoon is on duty today, son?"

"Second Platoon, C Company, sir."

I made it a point to keep track of the duty register. Prompt information on that subject could always be useful, especially since no one else in the HQ company was likely to know it.

"Hmm. How many men in three of their squads?"

"Theoretically thirty-six, but under the present circumstances, we'd be lucky to find twenty-five live ones."

He nodded grimly. "All right, O'Malley, you take those three squads up there and find out what the hell is happening."

"Yes, sir. Why three squads, if I may ask?"

"If I give you more, the CO of the platoon and probably the CO of the company will have to go along. I want you to be in charge."

"Yes, sir. But why, sir?"

The *Residenz* was crawling with captains, majors, and colonels with nothing to do. Why turn the operation over to an eighteen-year-old sergeant?

"Why what?" He frowned at me.

"Why me instead of one of the officers?"

"That should be obvious, son. You're smarter than they are, smarter than any two or three of them put together. Also sneakier, which is what a police unit needs in their leaders."

"No, sir."

"Pardon?" His face turned purple.

"With respect, sir, I may be sneakier than anyone in this outfit, sir. But I'm not smarter."

"Yes, you are. Sometimes I think I should urge you to go to the Point, but then I reason that you're too smart to make it in the Army. You're dangerously smart, O'Malley. I don't know what the hell shit is going on in your head most of the time. I'm not fooled by that polite respect you pretend to have. You're always thinking two steps ahead of me. But as long as you're under my command, I might as well make use of you."

"No, sir, that's not true. But, yes, sir, I will organize and take charge of the operation."

Dangerously smart! Ridiculous!

"Good. Here's a note to Lieutenant Martin, detaching three squads temporarily from his command. He won't like it but fuck him. . . . How long will it take before you're on the road?"

I glanced at my watch. "Ten-thirty, sir."

"All right, get it rolling."

"Yes, sir."

"And, Chuck . . ."

"Yes, sir."

"Be careful."

"Yes, sir."

As I left, he shouted after me, "Don't get too wet."

"No, sir," I muttered through clenched teeth.

We would all get very wet. Jeep covers always leak. It was a wild-goose chase. The sort of thing a good CO does when he's bored silly and nothing seems to work right. We'd come home with empty hands.

Nonetheless, my mouth was sandpaper dry. Moreover the whole operation was trivial—a few hundred dollars' worth of caviar, hardly enough to justify the cost of gasoline for our ride in the rain. A feint, a distraction, a piece of meat thrown to the hungry Constabulary animals.

It was not Lieutenant Martin's fault that we were able to leave the *Domplatz* at ten forty-five. A sawed-off (which is to say, shorter than me) recent graduate of the Point with a brush haircut and watery eyes, he absolutely refused to release his three squads to me.

"But, sir, this is an order from General Meade."

"The general must inform me personally of such a diminution of my command. It's regulations."

"May I use your phone to call the general."

"Absolutely not."

"Very well, sir."

I ran back to the *Residenz* in the driving rain and dashed by the young (but not unattractive) Wac second lieutenant who was Polly's temporary sub and into the general's office. "General Meade, sir," I said breathlessly, "Lieutenant Martin refuses to release the three squads without a personal order from you. He says it's regulations."

"You can't go in there," the Wac shouted as she rushed after me. A tiny woman, she had the audacity to try to shove me out. The terrible thing was that she could probably do it.

"Get the hell out of here, Lieutenant," the red-faced general bellowed.

Crushed, she withdrew quietly, but not without a venomous look at me.

"Martin, you fucking asshole," the general shouted into his phone. "If this operation is fucked up because of you, I'll hang your ass on the highest fucking flagpole in Germany. . . . Regulations? Look, jag-off, get out of my way or you're headed for a court-martial. Understand? . . . All right, O'Malley, move your ass."

Army foul language is not creative, though I am told it improved notably after racial integration. But in the mouth of an angry general officer it can be quite effective. Martin was nowhere to be seen when I returned to the duty room, and the three squads had already assembled. I had been overoptimistic. Only about twenty men were huddled outside the *Residenz*, all carrying weapons, though most of them awkwardly. Five jeeps with the covers on were lined up on the cobblestones of the *Domplatz*. The covers were white like the jeeps with elaborate blue trim and looked like some sort of tarted-up carnival vehicle. Well, it told people we were cops anyway.

"Men," I said, "we are assigned to intercept a smuggling operation up near the Russian zone. Russian soldiers are bringing contraband across the border to sell to our troops who are part of the black market. It is our job to stop them. There's an American border post near the site of the suspected exchange. They will direct us to that site. I will explain our tactics at that time. I want you to make sure that the safeties are on all your weapons. Do not take them off until I tell you to do so."

"Will we have to shoot at our own troops?" one soldier whined.

"Only if they shoot at us first or appear to be preparing to do so."

"How will we know that, Sarge?"

"If they aim their weapons at us, asshole!"

"How long is the ride," another asked.

"Maybe two hours, maybe longer. We'll know how long when we get there."

"Will we have to fight in the rain, Sarge?"

"I'll hold an umbrella over your head if you want, soldier!"

Laughter.

"Who drives the lead jeep?"

A kid raised his hand.

"Your name?"

"PFC Randolph, James, sir, three nine five—"

"I don't need your serial number, asshole. Let's move 'em out."

I hoped that I sounded like a commanding officer who knew what he was doing. Obviously I had no idea what I was doing, and standing there in the bitter rain, I was scared stiff. My bedraggled and unhappy force would be utterly useless in a fight.

As we rolled out of the Bishop's City, we encountered Colonel McQueen in his Chevy. He stopped and so did we.

"Off on another mission, Sergeant?"

"Yes, sir, Colonel, sir."

"Where?"

"North."

"God help the Russians!"

"Sir!"

"Don't shoot till you see the whites of their eyes."

"Even then I don't think we would hit them."

He laughed and drove on.

"Which way, Sarge?" Randolph asked.

"Across the river"—I studied the map—"and the canal, through Bamberg Nord to Hallstadt on Highway 4, continue on Highway 4 to Breitengrüssbach, then left on 279 up to the junction with 303. You go right on that and we're almost there. . . . Have you ever done any mountain driving, son?"

"No, sir, I'm from Fargo, North Dakota, and we don't have any mountains up there."

"Well," I said as we rumbled across the bridge over the Rhine-Main–Danube Canal, "it looks like you're going to learn how today."

Tough sarge, huh? Then why was he fingering the rosary beads in his pocket?

"Can we sleep on the way up, Sarge," one of the two men in the backseat asked.

"So long as you're in the state of grace."

The rain was terrible. Even with the windshield wipers swishing back and forth, we could see at the most fifty yards ahead of us. Fortunately, there was not much traffic.

I took fifty bucks out of the wallet I had replenished yesterday and put them in my raincoat pocket.

Private First Class Randolph turned out to be an excellent driver even in the mountains. Like me, he had joined the Army for veteran's benefits so he could enroll at North Dakota State. Like me, he wasn't sure it was worth it. Like me he had fired a weapon a couple times in basic training and never since. Unlike me he was sincerely and totally unafraid. "I put myself in the good Lord's hands when I came over here," he said. "He'll take care of me."

Sometimes maybe it's better to be a Protestant.

"What do they call the people at ND State, Jim?"

"You mean our football team?"

"Yeah."

"Fighting Coyotes, Sarge."

"Uh."

"You going to college when you get home, Sarge?"

"Sure. Another ND."

"Fighting Irish, huh, Sarge? Everyone knows that. Kind of appropriate for you, isn't it?"

"You'd better believe it, son!"

Lie! Lie! Lie! The Irish were not a fighting race. Contentious maybe, but not given to violence save under the influence of the drink taken. And I was the least fighting of all the Irish. I should tell him about my behavior on the football field that had somehow persuaded General Meade that I was the hero type. But, no, let the poor kid think that I was the toughest SOB in the Constabulary and that he therefore had a competent leader on this crazy venture.

General Meade had not used the hero argument earlier in the morning. Rather he had said that I was smart, dangerously smart. If I were so smart, how come I was out here? And how come I was plotting a clear violation of the military code either tomorrow or the next day? If I was indeed dangerous, I was dangerous mostly to myself.

And if I were truly smart, why was I being taken in by an operation that had little to do with taming the real black market?

I thought of my family. And of Rosemarie. What would they think if I was killed today or arrested later in the week?

I luxuriated in self-pity at the thought of my wake back home. They wouldn't make fun of me anymore.

Yeah, in fact, they probably would, damn them!

And if I was charged with trying to smuggle my mistress out of the American zone? They'd stand by me, arguing that I did the right thing.

Even Rosie?

Yeah, even Rosie. Maybe her most of all.

Jim Randolph was a damn good driver. He managed the Lichtensteinerwald just fine.

"These mountains are no problem at all, Sarge. They're not real mountains like the Rockies."

"That's for sure," I agreed, having never seen the Rockies.

We turned onto 303. I looked at my watch. Twelve-thirty. My two-hour estimate had not been all that bad. The knot in my stomach hardened. The Red Army, which had smashed the mighty *Wehrmacht* into little pieces and then chewed them up and spit them out, was about a mile and a half away.

"Next turn, I think, Jim."

We bumped down a rugged, muddy road that petered out into nothing. Two hundred yards away there was a wire fence, maybe twenty feet high.

"What's that fence, Sarge?" one of the guys in the back asked.

"Russia."

"Jeez!"

"Okay, Jim. You got us in here. Now get us out."

He laughed. "You got us in, Sarge. You said to take the turn."

"That's neither here nor there. How long you been in the Army? You know the guys with rank don't make mistakes. You drove the car. Now get us out of here."

He laughed more loudly. "You sure are funny, Sarge. You ought to be a clown or something after you go home."

"I am a clown already. Now turn us around and get us the hell out of here."

"That field sure is muddy."

"That's why we have four-wheel drive. Now move it out!"

The jeep had little trouble with the mud. We bumped, sloshed, and plowed by our four other jeeps and then hobbled back on the road—such as it was.

I poked my head out of our plastic window. "What the hell you fucking assholes waiting for? Let's go!"

After racial integration I would have shouted "motherfuckers" at them, a much more creative imprecation.

However reluctantly, they obeyed my orders. We redeployed back to 303.

"These jeeps sure are tough, Sarge."

"They're supposed to be tough, Jim. You don't always have good roads in combat."

Hardened old combat veteran knows all about it, right?

"It's gotta be this turn," I said when we came to the next dirt road.

"What if it isn't?" one of the guys in the back asked.

"Then we try every turn from here to Prague."

Fortunately for me, however, it was the right road. In five minutes we bumped up to a lonely border outpost—a hut, a bar gate, an American flag, and three GIs.

The rain had diminished to a drizzle. I jumped out of the jeep with as much poise as was possible and strode over to the hut. Even Constabulary raincoats are fancy, covered with white and blue doodads.

So the sergeant in charge, not able to see my stripes, saluted briskly, figuring I was some kind of big-deal officer.

"Good morning, Sarge." I saluted back. "Looks like you guys have done a fine job of holding back the Russkies."

He grinned. "Repulsed 'em so far, sir. Look, they're kind of excited about your arrival."

He handed me a first-rate pair of Bausch & Lomb field glasses, doubtless liberated at some point from the *Wehrmacht* and traded around by GIs who didn't want to bother taking them home.

I tried to focus them a couple of times and finally got them working. A hundred yards down the road was another hut, bigger than ours with tank traps in front of it and a gate that looked like a fence. About a dozen men were standing around in brown uniforms and funny, peaked caps, one of them with red trim all over.

Several of the men were pointing heavy machine guns right at us.

"Must be impressed by our fancy clothes and fancy jeeps."

"I guess so," the sergeant agreed. "Even if the jeeps are a little muddy."

"Constabulary jeeps, Sergeant, are never muddy. . . . Now, where do these deals go down?"

"Not far from here, sir. See that second hill out that way?" He pointed to the left of the road on which we had come in.

"Yeah."

"There's a little saucerlike depression over there. Our guys would normally deploy themselves and let the Russkies come in on the north side. The Russkies would dump their stuff, our guys would throw a bag of money, and the Russkies would run like hell."

"Why?"

"Our guys had automatic weapons aimed at them. Russkies figured they might blow them away. I wouldn't be surprised if they would one of these days."

"How many of our guys?"

"Four or five, a couple of jeeps."

"What time does it go down?"

"Our guys come up here"—he glanced at his watch—"about ten-thirty, give or take. They go out there and wait. You can't be sure when the Russkies show up, but our guys are usually out of there by fourteen hundred."

"Same day every week?"

"Not every week, sir. Every couple of weeks. Usually on Tuesday like today, but not always."

"You guys got it pretty well staked out, Sarge?"

He shrugged. "At first we figured it was none of our business. But these guys treated us like we were shit, stupid shit at that. So we figured it *was* our business."

"Are they up there now?" I waved toward the second hill.

"Nope."

I heaved a big sigh of relief. "So they didn't come today?"

"Nope. A tip-off, I suppose. One guy, the worst fucker of them all, said they'd never get caught because they had everything wired."

"We'll get them yet, Sarge."

"I sure hope so. If they figure we peached on them, they might come back here and get us."

"When they learn about our raid, they'll probably close this part of their operation down. It wouldn't make much sense for them to come back. Too big a risk. But I'll see that a recommendation goes to Seventh Army that you be reinforced."

"Thank you, sir. We appreciate it."

They were guys who were willing to go along on the great American principle that "it's no skin off my ass." But they had been pushed too hard. The black-market people didn't need a murder rap so they'd leave the border guards alone. Still I did recommend that they be reinforced and later discovered that it had been acted on.

"And thanks for the information, Sarge."

"Good luck, sir."

"We may need it. I don't want these young dolts of mine starting World War Three."

I lifted the glasses again. The Russkies were watching us still. I raised my hand and waved at them. The guy with red trim waved back. I saluted and he did too.

I gave the glasses back to the border guard. "I think we'll drive back over that rise in the road a hundred yards or so before we head for your saucer. We don't want our friends over there to know where we're going."

"Good thinking, sir. . . . Did they wave back?"

"Yeah."

"Never did that before. But then we never waved at them. Strange."

"Yeah. Well, keep holding back the Red horde, Sarge."

We both laughed and shook hands.

I gathered my men around behind the ring of jeeps.

"Now, get this straight. A hundred yards down that road there are a crowd of Russkies with automatic weapons aimed right at us. Their CO breathes heavy and we're dead."

A couple of my guys looked as if they were about to bolt.

"Before you try to bug out, you should realize that if we do anything abrupt, they'll certainly blow us away."

I don't think they would have. Their shavetail who had waved back was as much afraid of World War III as I was. But I wanted my guys to be careful.

"Now this is what we're going to do. We're going a hundred yards down the road behind that rise and then turn right and proceed across the fields to that second hill. When I stop, you guys stop too and dismount from your vehicles. Keep the safeties on your weapons unless and until I give the order. We are not about to start World War Three. Understand?

"Dismount from your vehicles." I was sure picking up the lingo of command.

"It's pretty muddy out there, Sarge."

"Really, I thought it was the Sahara Desert. Okay, let's move it."

Before I mounted my vehicle, I turned and waved good-bye to the Russians.

"God damn it," the border guard yelled. "Their officer waved good-bye."

"You were waving at their CO?" Jim Randolph asked with wide-open eyes. "Why?"

"I figure he doesn't want to start World War Three any more than I do. . . . Now, let's get this moving."

The mud in the field was worse than what we had encountered on our previous attempt. Some of the jeeps bogged down temporarily. I shouted curses I had never used before and I hardly realized I knew. The guys were afraid to use full power for fear they'd dig in deeper and maybe have to walk back to Bamberg. They didn't realize how good the jeep was.

We beat you on that one, I said to my friend Max Albrecht back in his camera shop. After all, we had invented Henry Ford.

Finally, we crunched to a stop at the foot of the hill.

"Now get this straight," I whispered to them as we crowded together at the foot of the hill. "A group of Russians are expected to deliver contraband in a depression over the top of that hill. I'm going up to the top to watch for them. I want you guys to deploy, first squad to the right, second squad to the left, third squad behind me. If they're not there, you stay down here. If they are or when they come, I'll raise my right hand, you scramble up the hill. *Quietly!* You keep your heads beneath the rim until I give the order. When I shout '*Polizei*,' which is Russkie for 'police,' you pop up and point your guns, ah, weapons at them—*with the safeties on, get it?* I don't think they're armed. If they are, I'll come back and modify the plan. Got it?"

They nodded solemnly.

"All right, fan out, *quietly.*"

I watched them fan out, stumbling and bumbling.

So I climbed the forty or fifty feet up the hill, slipping and sliding as I went and not exactly quietly either. Carefully I peered over the rim, expecting to see a squadron of T-34s.

The saucer, a small grassy meadow about five feet deep and maybe thirty feet wide, on a gentle slope beneath me, was empty.

I waited, glancing at my watch every couple of minutes. It was thirteen-fifteen (I was even thinking in military time!). How long would General Meade expect me to wait?

Till the Russians came.

If they didn't? Till about two hours before sunset. Sunset was at twenty-two hundred. Almost nine hours. I sighed and thought of all the women I loved—the good April, Jane, Peg, Rosie, Brigitta, Trudi. I would miss them all if I were dead.

Dumb thought.

Then I remembered that there was always the possibility that the black-market crowd would be late today. I began to watch the other direction too. What if their jeeps left the road and headed our way? I'd have to figure out an ambush in a hurry. Maybe when they turned the corner of the hill beneath us and bumped into our vehicles.

A lot of weird ideas floated around in my head while we waited. What if the Russkies were planning to ambush us? What if we had been set up by someone? Who could have set us up? What if Polly had planned it all and then used morning sickness as an excuse to be absent when the tip came so she would not be blamed for the leak?

There was something wrong with that idea, but I couldn't figure it out.

What about my planned run to Stuttgart tomorrow or the next night at the latest?

I couldn't force myself to think about it. Probably I shouldn't try. I ought to pay attention to the present situation. So, I swiveled my head back and forth between the road and the saucer. I had removed my helmet so that when I peeked, only the top of my head would appear. The red hair might make an appealing target.

And the rain began again. Our fancy Constabulary slickers helped, but they didn't cover everything. Soon my arms and legs were soaked with rainwater. I wondered how durable my slicker was. Beneath me, my men were also dripping wet and fidgety and uncomfortable. How long would they last?

I looked at the road again. Still no sign of our smugglers. That was good. There must have been a tip-off. Someone who knew that the tip from Ninth Corps had come to General Meade as soon or almost soon as the general knew.

Maybe the general himself. Maybe Dick McQueen. Maybe Sam Houston Carpenter. Maybe John Nettleton. Maybe all of them together.

My head was whirling. I couldn't think clearly. My body was growing stiff from clinging to the side of the hill. My back hurt more every minute. Then I peeked over the rim.

They were there, four bedraggled kids, soaking wet, in Russian fatigues. I mean kids. They all were younger than I was. Each was carrying a box, maybe weighing ten or twelve pounds. They appeared to have no weapons. They placed the boxes on the ground and, huddling against the now driving rain, looked anxiously around the lip of the saucer.

Again I checked to make sure there were no guns. A thought ran through my mind. Let's say there were fifty pounds of caviar. That would cost them twenty-five bucks. They were expecting to increase that threefold: one hundred Yankee dollars. Risk your lives for that? These guys must really be hungry. Okay. Our guys sell it for ten dollars a pound. Chicken feed. Would the fabulously wealthy ring bother with such trivial stuff? Or was this a small-time exercise in greed by some marginal guys?

Yep, a feint, a distraction.

I waved at my men and put my finger over my mouth. They made as much noise as a P-47. But the shivering and frightened Russians did not hear them. I waited till everyone was in position.

More comedy.

I rose unsteadily, almost slipped down the hill, steadied myself, and yelled, *"Polizei."*

My mouth was bone dry so the word came out as a croak. My men rose to the top of the hill—except those who slipped back down the slope. They pointed their guns in several directions, including at me. A few of them managed to aim at the Russians, who had fallen to their knees with their hands in the air.

Then there was a burst of automatic weapons fire on my right. The Russians fell on their faces.

"Who the hell fired that weapon?"

"I did, sir," said one of my guys. "I thought the safety was on and I squeezed the trigger too hard."

"You've started World War Three, asshole!"

"No, sir," he said miserably, "the ordnance went that way."

"Fucking asshole," I shouted at him.

I looked back at the Russians, who were kneeling again, surprised that they were still alive.

I sighed with relief. "Connors, Kean, Hoffman, Randolph, go down there and confiscate that contraband and put it in the back of my jeep. Hop to it."

The Russkies crawled away in terror as my guys slid and slipped down the inner lip of the saucer and began to collect the caviar, their weapons pointing in all sorts of dangerous directions.

Damn! I should have inspected the safeties before I left.

Comic-opera uniforms for a comic-opera bunch of clowns. It would make a funny movie. Was war always like this, except that people got killed?

"What's in those boxes, Sarge? Ammo?"

"No, soldier, caviar."

"What's caviar?"

"Fish eggs."

"What do you do with it?"

"Eat it."

"Who wants to eat fish eggs?" he asked in disbelief. The other guys laughed.

"People that want to get sick the next morning."

They laughed again.

"It's all in your jeep, Sarge," Jim Randolph told me. "What's the matter with those guys?"

The Russkies were begging for something, their lives no doubt.

"They think we're going to blow them away."

"Why do they think that?"

"Because that's what their officers would do to us if the same thing happened on the other side of that fence. Poor kids."

"Yes, Sarge. We're not going to blow them away, are we?"

"We're Americans, aren't we? Here, take this weapon"—I gave him mine—"and cover me while I go down and tell them to go home."

I palmed twenty-five bucks and tried to walk with some dignity down the hill. Naturally, I slipped and fell on my face; naturally, my men laughed; naturally, I turned on them and shouted, "Shut up, assholes, if you don't want to spend time in a disciplinary barracks."

They shut up. I struggled to my feet, gathered the remnants of my dignity together, and strode, or to be more precise, stumbled toward them. Their pleas for mercy became yelps like those from an injured dog.

I helped each of them to his feet and shook hands with them. I slipped the three bills into the hand of the guy who seemed to be in charge. Then I pointed toward the north. "Get the hell out of here!"

They bowed and scraped in gratitude and turned and ran quickly over the far rim of the saucer.

At least they had not lost their capital, poor guys. How long had they schemed and worked to assemble twenty-five Yankee dollars? I couldn't in good conscience take it away from them. More to the point, in a certain sense I could claim to be the owner of the caviar, bought at a fair-market price. The way I figured it, I had broken no American laws as I would have if I had bought it from American soldiers. Maybe I broke some Russian laws, but that was their problem. Moreover, I remembered a Latin dictum from Fenwick: *Res nullius fit primi occupantis.* Freely translated it meant "Finders keepers." If you come upon something that belongs to no one anymore, it's yours.

"Okay, guys, let's get the hell out of here."

"Why did you let them go, Sarge?"

"We were supposed to apprehend GI criminals, not Russkie criminals. They'll go back and tell their buddies that this place is closed. Besides, what are we supposed to do with them?"

There were murmurs of agreement.

We stopped at the border post. "Give me three of those things," I said to Randolph.

"Yes, Sarge. What you gonna do?"

"Watch."

I hid the caviar under my poncho and signaled the border guard to hide behind the hut where the Russkie field glasses could not pick him up.

I pulled out the three caviar containers.

"You guys send these home to your wives or mothers or sisters or girlfriends. And don't let the Russkies see you carrying them."

"Thank you, sir. . . . What about the smugglers?"

"I sent them home. They're more use to us alive. They'll tell the other jokers that this placed is closed down."

"Yeah, good thinking, sir."

"Thank you." I walked back into the open, saluted the Russians again, and got into my jeep and told Jimmy Randolph to get us the hell out of there. Let the Russkies try to figure out what we were doing.

"You know, Sarge," Jimmy said, "you're just a little crazy."

"I know what you mean, son."

I looked at my watch. Fifteen hundred. We'd be home by five o'clock.

It was a little bit before six when, weary and aching from our long drive, but happy to be alive, we bounced into the *Domplatz* and up to the entrance of the *Residenz*. I was sure my back would ache for the rest of my life. The rain had stopped, but the sky was still gray and the clouds almost over our heads. We were in for a lot of humidity tonight.

I dismounted from the jeep and tried to straighten my back. The men cheered and swarmed around me with congratulations for my brilliant tactics.

What they really meant was that they were happy I had brought them back alive. But I shook hands warmly with each of them. They'd have a story to tell their grandchildren that doubtless would grow in the telling and I'd be the hero.

Once again.

"Sorry about my weapon, Sarge," said the asshole who had fired his automatic pistol.

"Forget it, soldier. What counts is we're home."

"And haven't started World War Three!"

"Don't seem to have." I patted him on the back. And thought to myself that the whole event was a triumph for a slapstick comedy in which I was the biggest clown—either Larry or Curly or Moe.

"Okay, Randolph, Kean, Rubens, pick up these boxes of fish eggs and carry them to the general's office. Maybe he wants to start an aquarium!"

They howled at that. "He'll need something more, Sarge."

"That stuff is cheap. . . . The rest of you, *dismissed!*"

We carried the boxes up the vast staircase and marched the full length of the ballroom. The new Wac was still at the desk. She didn't try to stop us but favored me with a dirty look. I'd have to take care of that.

"General, sir, Sergeant O'Malley and team reporting with contraband. Excuse the interruption, sir, but our hands are filled."

"Any prisoners, Sergeant?"

"No, sir, it would appear there was another tip-off!"

"Damn," he exploded.

The other men, never having heard a general officer explode, jumped.

"Not your fault, Sergeant, nor your men. Who, I'm sure, performed brilliantly."

"Flawlessly, sir."

One of the guys sniggered softly.

"Thank you, men. Well done. Why don't you put the contraband here on this table by the window. O'Malley, you stay here and give a full report. The rest of you are dismissed and thanks again for your fine soldiering."

They left, half-persuaded that they were indeed fine soldiers.

"Well, Chuck?" The general waved me to a vast chair across the desk from his throne.

I told him the story, concisely enough and with no mention of the automatic weapon fire, but I did mention that I had fallen on my face. I also recommended more protection at the border post.

He nodded and jotted it down. "I'll take care of it, but I think you're right. The raid closed that exchange point down. Also you did the right thing with the Russkie kids. Their government would have accused us of kidnapping them."

"Thank you, sir. There's a couple of more things, sir."

"Shoot."

"First of all, doesn't it seem to you to be curious that the ring would go to so much trouble for a mere five-hundred-dollar profit? Much ado about nothing."

"How much caviar?" He paced up and down by the large windows of his office, staring grimly at the *Domplatz* and the gray sky above.

"Four boxes of twelve cases. Forty-eight pounds altogether."

"Odd." He rubbed his chin thoughtfully. "Damn odd."

Why hadn't he thought of that before? Or had he? Did he know that he was sending us not on a dangerous mission but a silly one?

"So this probably was some small fringe element in the ring, doing a little of its own on the side."

"Very likely." He nodded as if he had already figured it out.

"You may remember what the Outfit in Chicago does to people like that?"

"I've heard."

"So, sir, if the ring, the Bavarian Outfit, knew about this raid, why would they have tipped the punks off?"

"Maybe they were afraid they would talk."

"Wouldn't it be more likely they didn't know about it? Do you think the locals would want the Outfit to know?"

He turned around and stared at me. "So you think the link is local?"

"I'm not sure, sir, obviously. But that might be the case, might it not? When did the call from Ninth Corps come in?"

"Less than a half minute before I called you."

"Right."

That made it look good for Captain Polly, who had not been present to answer the phone. But not for John Nettleton.

"And I told no one in this office what was happening. They might have seen your jeeps pull away, but they'd have to guess where you were going."

"And make a quick call to their friends."

"Very quick." He sank as one exhausted into his throne. "Very quick. . . . Another dead end."

I wasn't so sure about that. A vague idea was forming in my head. Not clear yet. It would emerge eventually—once I got the idea of our escape, maybe tomorrow night, out of my head.

"What should we do with the contraband, sir?"

"Send it back to headquarters in Nürnberg, I suppose."

"It will never get there, sir."

"Someone will steal it."

"That would upset me, sir, because in a manner of speaking, it's my property."

"*Your* property!"

"In a manner of speaking, sir. You see, I gave the Russkie GIs twenty-five dollars to cover their expenses. They were so bedraggled and sad that I didn't want them to lose what was a hell of a lot of money to them."

"Encouraging them to more smuggling?" he asked skeptically.

"No fear of that, sir. They were too scared ever to try it again. Maybe I was only encouraging them not to give up completely on capitalism."

"You felt compassion for them, huh?"

"Yes, sir. Also, I figured that I could argue that the saucer was a marketplace and they were offering goods for sale and they offered them to me at a discount price. I could not be sure that they came by the goods illegally."

"You *are* dangerous. . . . Well, what do you intend to do with your property?"

"Our primary obligation is to see that it is used wisely and that no one profits from it. Therefore, I propose we give it away. I already gave three cans to the border guards—who, by the way, will be able to identify pictures of suspects, should we have any, and far more reliably than the Russian kids."

"Smart move."

"Then, sir, I'm giving you three cans." I lifted them out and put them on his desk. "One for you and one for your wife and one for your daughter; and I'm taking three cans, one for myself, one for my mom, and one for my girl."

"You have a girl, Chuck?" He looked surprised.

"Oh, yes, sir, indeed I do."

"You have her picture?"

"No, sir, we are both very young."

"She may be, but you sure as hell aren't. . . . What should we do with the rest?"

"I thought we might give them to herself, in honor of her good news."

"She'll certainly know how to use the stuff. Won't have to borrow it from the PX. And she'll need it as long as certain noncoms consume half a pound a sitting."

"Only a third, sir."

So everything had gone well.

I have never understood why I wanted to help those Russian kids.

We were not going to shoot them. It would have been crazy to bring them back, because their government would have shouted kidnapping just as the general had said. But why give them twenty-five bucks?

"Because you have a soft heart, damn it," John Raven would bellow at me when I went home.

I laughed at him again.

In the outer office, I set about repairing the damage done with the Wac lieutenant. "Staff Sgt. Charles Cronin O'Malley offers his apologies for rude behavior of this morning, ma'am. Military necessity compelled it, but I regret if I showed any disrespect."

My salute was one of the better that I have ever attempted.

She glared at me for a moment and then laughed. "Nan Wynn, Sergeant." She extended her hand. "You are the one they call Chucky, aren't you?"

She was really cute, a shapely little blond doll.

"Yes, ma'am. I prefer Chuck."

"They said that too. I'm sorry I didn't figure out this morning who you really were. But you were wearing your helmet liner."

"Who did they say I really was?"

"General Meade's smartest agent!" Her eyes widened in respect. "I hope we can be friends."

"I'm sure we can, Lieutenant, ma'am."

"Nan."

"Yes, Lieutenant Nan."

"Very good, *Sergeant* Chucky."

Her smile was bewitching. She was not wearing a ring. Probably too young to marry. My adolescent-male imagination began to indulge in lascivious fantasies. Still I hoped that Captain Polly would be back in the morning. If Brigitta brought me the papers in the morning, I'd need to requisition a car.

I returned to my desk. Nothing to type. I should go home and sleep, but I didn't like to miss the first couple of days of class. Besides, I was too keyed up from the day's adventures to sleep. Trudi phoned to say that she would be free at noon tomorrow and might we go for a ride in the country, if the weather improved? Why not?

Two new gumshoes followed me away from the *Residenz*, guys who were more professional than the previous two, but still easy to pick out in the crowd if you were looking for them. I glanced into the bar of the Bambergerhof, looking for Agent Clarke. He was slumped over a table, not only drunk but asleep. I also saw Sam Houston Carpenter and Brigitta at another table. She saw me and looked away.

None of my business.

The clouds had broken up when I came out of American Fiction with a stack of books by a new find, William Faulkner, a crazy Celt too.

I chose him and early sleep instead of the darkroom. I was going to do what I was going to do and no rabbinic arguments would make me hesitate.

I had delightful dreams about Nan Wynn; and worrisome dreams about whether Trudi was pregnant.

22

"I was only having a drink with him, Chucky," Brig said the next morning. She held an envelope in her hand. "I won't do it again. I promise."

"It's none of my business, Brigie. I'm not your father or your confessor."

"Of course, it is your business. I'm sorry." Brig laid the envelope solemnly on my desk like a priest putting a pall on the altar. "Here they are, Chuck. He finished them early because he liked you."

I picked up the envelope, old, thick, and brown at the edges, an old-fashioned, prewar, maybe pre-Depression, formal envelope.

"Have you looked at what's inside?"

"Of course not."

Glancing around to make sure that no one was watching, I opened the envelope. Papers for Maria, Anna, and Frieda Schultz, born in Hanover. Perfect in every detail. Tomorrow night we'd do the run to Stuttgart. My stomach turned over a couple of times and my throat turned dry. Driest yet.

"Perfect," I said hoarsely.

"I know you're tired of me saying it, but do be careful."

"I'm never tired of your concern, Brigitta."

"How long?"

"The operation will be over by the weekend."

She nodded. "I will pray."

"That will be a big help."

She turned to go to her desk. Then she turned back to me. "I love you, Chuck. I hope you know that. Not the way I love Kurt, but more than the way I loved my father. But not quite that way either. You *do* know that, don't you?"

Now what does an eighteen-year-old say to that, especially an eighteen-year-old who wished he could collapse into her (quasi) maternal arms so that all the bad things would go away?

"I know, Brig. I'm deeply honored. I'll treasure our friendship all my life—which by the way I plan on being a long one."

She laughed happily and left me. I have kept the promise, not that it was hard to keep.

"There are all kinds of loves in the world, Chuck O'Malley," John Raven would say. "God seems to have blessed you with quite a variety of them."

I would tell him that I wasn't sure it was a blessing.

"You wish you'd never known Brigitta?"

That would settle that.

Heart pounding fiercely, I approached Captain Polly.

"Staff Sergeant O'Malley's compliments, Captain, ma'am. And this time I really *mean* compliments."

I bent over and kissed her cheek. She hugged me with one arm.

Please don't be a crook, pretty Polly. But I'll love you even if you are.

"Oh, Chucky, thank you. Drat, I'm crying! I'm always crying these days!"

I stood up. She removed her arm.

"But we're *so* happy," she sniffled. "We've been trying for so long."

"I'm sure the kid will talk funny, the same way you and John do."

"At least he won't talk like he's from Capone's hometown . . . and thanks for the presents." She winked.

"Captain, ma'am," I got to the point, "I'm going to need a car till the weekend. Special operation."

"Sure." She reached for a stack of signed requisitions from the general. "Buick all right?"

"Why not?"

She filled in the details. "I'll tell them to fill the tank."

She had not asked why I needed the car or what I was going to do.

"Great."

She looked up at me, her dark blue eyes shrewd. She knew at least vaguely what I was going to do and did not disapprove. Later they would call it sisterhood, but loyalty to other women threatened with violation has transcended almost all other loyalties since the beginning of the species. Polly Nettleton did not want to know the details, but she was on my side.

"Be careful with it, Chuck." She gave me the requisition paper.

"You know me, Captain Polly, ma'am. Safest driver in the Army."

She sniffed her skepticism. "I hear you encountered my new assistant yesterday."

She waved at the cornflower blonde sitting at a smaller desk next to her.

"And naturally it was a pleasant encounter . . . Lieutenant Nan, ma'am."

"Sergeant Chucky." She was blushing.

"You certainly make your conquests in a hurry, Sergeant." Polly grinned impishly.

Nan's flush grew deeper.

"No, ma'am. I'm usually conquered almost immediately."

It was pleasant banter. I had no desire to become involved with Nan Wynn. Well, I had lots of desires to be honest about it. But other things had to be done and I did not need another woman thinking that she loved me.

Trudi called to ask, as always hesitantly as one who wrongly intrudes on an important person's time, if we were still to meet in the afternoon. It was, she said, such a beautiful day.

"I'll pick you up at your apartment at one?"

"Oh, how wonderful!"

No, I didn't need another one loving me.

Yet, as I gathered material off my desk, it occurred to me that I had not given quite the right answer to Brigitta. So I stopped by her desk.

"I want to add to what I said before, Brig."

She looked up from her typewriter, surprised. "There is no need for that."

"Yes, there is. I love you too, not like a husband, not like a father, not like a son." My face felt warm. "Rather like a combination of all three. That's what will never end."

She drew a sharp breath, emphasizing her lovely little breasts, and, with tears in her eyes, smiled softly.

"I'll never sleep with you," I rushed ahead madly, my face suddenly hot, "and I'll never stop thinking that it would be nice to do so."

Then she did weep, peacefully, happily.

I beat a hasty retreat.

The sergeant in charge didn't want to give it to me. It was not "fucking right" he informed me that he give a good car to a "fucking punk" like me. I warned him of the consequences of ignoring General Meade's signature and he backed off a little.

"Not fucking right you should have this, kid."

"You question General Meade's signature?"

"No, I question your ability to drive this beauty. If you mess it up, I'll cut off your balls."

"I'll note that observation in my report to General Meade. . . . Is there an extra key?"

"Fuck off, asshole."

"Where?"

"In the glove compartment, asshole."

I emptied my bank account—two thousand dollars of carefully saved money. Two gumshoes followed me to the Army bank. They might try to find out what I was doing, but they'd need to make charges before the tellers at the bank—as incorruptible as any Americans in Bamberg—would tell them. When I left the bank, they had disappeared.

Then I went back to my room and studied the maps I had gathered at the transport pool, despite the sergeant's protests that I had no right to them either. Some 460 kilometers round-trip, about 270 miles. Driving at sixty on the autobahn that was five hours, two and a half either way, if there were no delays. All right, since you are a cautious man, double it, ten hours. Leave at twenty hundred hours, be back in Bamberg at six hundred at the latest. Plenty of time to set up the playlet for the next morning. I would schedule that tentatively for eight hundred. I'd have to tell General Meade about it late tomorrow. That could be the trickiest part of the whole scheme.

I went over the maps again. I had driven to Nürnberg before and it was a piece of cake. I had never tried to drive farther. In fact I had never driven two and a half hours in all my life, especially at night. To say nothing of five hours. Well, there was always a first time.

Why not make our run tonight? I had reviewed that possibility several times and always came up with the same answer—on the lips of the good April: "Never forget, Chucky, that haste *always* makes waste." In fact, sometimes it doesn't. But in this case it would. There would not be enough time to prepare General Meade and Rednose Clarke. Nor enough time for the Schultzes, as I must now think of them, to organize their departure. They must not leave anything behind that would stir up Rednose's suspicions.

After lunch—four large sausages—I picked up Trudi in my shiny new Buick. She was appropriately impressed. "You have been made a general?" she asked with an impish grin.

"On special assignment from a general."

I drove into the country, proud of my car and proud of my woman. For a glorious couple of hours, I would forget that neither were mine by any rights and that in two days both would be gone.

We made love by our favorite rural bridge in the *Hauptsmoor*, plunged into the waters of the stream, chilly even in August, and then huddled under our GI blankets to warm up for another bout of love. I kissed every inch of her body, storing up memories of summer sweetness for the hard winter that would start in two more days. My love sighed contentedly, unaware of my own grim foreboding. She drew me into her mouth and I licked her loins. Our wanton love turned into reckless abandon. We groaned and screamed and moaned and shouted and then collapsed, spent and exhausted, on our blanket.

"You're fantastic, Karl," she sighed, "I want to do everything with you."

"I think we just about have."

She giggled and drew me close to her.

It was a bittersweet experience. It would be our last session of lovemaking for a month or two, maybe longer. I could not face the possibility lurking in the back of my head that it might be our last love ever.

Trudi did not seem to sense my unease. There was no point in telling her anything till tomorrow. I would not tell them about our escape until the last minute. I thought I could count on Trudi's nerves, but I wasn't sure about her mother and her sister.

We stopped at a little, old stone church near the bridge, named after St. Killian, the Irish monk who was the patron saint of Bavaria. (The Chicago Irish never did comprehend that the saints of the three great parishes of the South and West Sides in the 1930s—St. Mel, St. Killian, St. Columbanus—were patron saints in Germany. Needless to say, they did not want to comprehend that the Germans had appropriated three perfectly good micks.) The onion-dome roof, typical of many old churches, suggested Bavaria's onetime contact with the Orthodox world, not its religious dependency on Ireland.

"Let us pray again for our futures, Karl," Trudi said simply. I wasn't sure that I would be welcome in church twice in the same week. Nor could I understand why she thought God would welcome two sinners. Perhaps she didn't think what we were doing was a sin. Maybe she saw it as a necessity for survival and trusted that God would understand.

We knelt at the altar rail longer than I could usually manage without my knees protesting. In gloom, I saw her lips moving in rapid entreaty. For what? I wondered.

Help me save her, I asked the One in Charge. Give her a chance for life. You made me save one who didn't want to live. Assist me with this one who does want to live.

No one whispered reassurance into my ear. But I still left the little chapel feeling once more that I was one of the guys in the white hats.

When I dropped her off in front of the food store on the Untersandstrasse, I said casually, "Could you meet me for coffee tomorrow morning in the Grüner Markt? Ten o'clock? I'd like to talk over something with you."

She looked at me somberly, appraising my face as she had done the night I had pulled her out of the alley.

"Certainly."

There was even more affection and invitation than usual in her kiss. I drew her close, reached under her dress, and captured a breast, which I pushed against her ribs. She groaned in pleasure. Roughly I pulled the dress off her shoulders and played with her breasts and her nipples, licking, biting gently, sucking on them. She yielded herself completely. The dress fell to her hips and she clutched at it.

Why not make love here, on the Untersandstrasse under the stars? Would that not be a memory on which to cling in the lonely weeks ahead? She would not resist me.

Yet I could not do it. For all her wantonness with me, Trudi was a model of Catholic modesty in public. I had to respect that. So I released her and she dashed up the steps to their dingy apartment, pulling the dress up over her shoulders as she went.

There were no gumshoes watching at the Vinehaus when I returned.

Sometime during the night, the daimon crept into my head and took over. I was running for the end zone again, so scared that I could not eat breakfast when I awoke, but my mind was racing, leaping ahead, considering and rejecting alternatives, planning responses to contingencies, imagining answers to my friend Rednose if he violated the scenario I had prepared for him.

In my dreams I also engaged in violent sexual play with most of the women I knew and many I didn't know.

23

Inviting in her thin, white hotel maid's dress, despite her grim face, Trudi waited for me in a sidewalk café at the upper end of the Open Market. We had met there often before, indistinguishable I suppose from the scores of other young GIs with equally young, blond fräuleins. It was another glorious summer day. The market echoed and reechoed with young laughter. Winter and death had been put behind. Temporarily.

I kissed her lightly. "Sorry if I went too far in the Untersandstrasse last night."

"You understood and respected my modesty, Karl. You were wonderful."

The way she saw it, I was incapable of any wrong.

"Sit down, Trud, we have some serious work to do."

She nodded, waiting for my words.

"First of all, your friends in Stuttgart, they are close friends, you can trust them?"

"Of course."

"You know where they live?"

"Certainly."

"I'm afraid it will be necessary to bring you and your mother and sister to them tonight. Will your friends take you in on such short notice?"

"Naturally."

"Are you as confident as you sound in those answers?"

She touched my hand. "Yes, Karl. But you must not risk yourself."

"I don't intend to risk anyone." I picked up my coffee cup and then put it down again. My stomach was protesting that I was risking far too much. "There is some danger, I will not deny that, but much less danger than you have survived before. It is important that you and your mother and Erika obey all my instructions perfectly. Do you understand?"

"*Jawohl.*" She smiled.

"You are not to tell them our destination. Is that understood? . . . Good. Are they working tonight? . . . No? That helps. At eighteen hundred tell them that they must put on the best American clothes they have. They may bring one small bag each. Pack whatever is most valuable and anything American which might hint that you have a friend in the military. Understand? . . . Fine. Leave everything else. Don't worry about money, that will be arranged. I want the apartment to look like a German refugee room from which nothing has been removed, as if the three of you might return any minute. Got it?"

"*Ja.*" Her eyes bore into mine.

"Good. At twenty hundred proceed to the alley where we first met, beneath the *Oberpfarrekirche*. I'll be waiting in the Buick. Climb in and we leave. Any questions?"

"Papers?"

"They have been arranged."

"Truly?" Her youthful face exploded with joy. A passport to paradise.

"Truly. But you must tell no one, say good-bye to no one, talk to no one unless you have to. Insist that your mother and Erika do exactly what I have told you. Do not go back to the Bambergerhof for anything you might have left there. Do not leave your room between eighteen hundred and twenty hundred. Understand?"

"I think so."

"Any more questions?"

"I worry about you." She touched my hand again.

"Don't." I smiled like a cowboy hero—Randolph Scott or maybe Joel McCrea, a sturdy WASP this time. "It's going to work out all right. It'll be a few weeks before we can see each other, that'll be the hardest part for me."

"For me also."

"One more thing." I had a brilliant idea, or so I thought. "Do you have an extra picture of your mother and father and you two from maybe ten years ago that you could leave someplace?"

"Surely. Perhaps in the little box on the table."

"Great. . . . And, remember, do not tell your mother or sister where they are going. Do not mention the papers. Tell them that my orders are most strict. I will explain all in the car. Okay?"

"Okeydokey, Herr Yankee."

I didn't eat any lunch.

By now the reader of these pages, being wise and more experienced than was that callow lad playing Galahad or the Rider in the *Dom* in Bamberg, anno Domini 1947, has doubtless perceived the potentially catastrophic omission of which I was guilty.

In August the days are shortening rapidly in Europe, but there is still much more light than darkness. We would be driving in twilight or dusk most of the way to Stuttgart. I'd be returning in darkness, maybe in time to see the dawn. Even if I was delayed, there would still be time for the operation to be launched on schedule.

As long as I could sell the schedule to Clarke.

Then I walked over to the *Residenz* for a truly tricky part. It had been on my list of options and I had debated whether to try it. General Meade was not the kind of man whom you could easily fool, even if in this case he might not mind being fooled. I would not lie to him. I hope the reader notes that I rarely lie, but I certainly deceive—being skilled in Jesuit casuistry, albeit trained by the Dominicans.

Captain Polly had left some letters on my desk to type. I polished them off quickly and brought them and the carbons up to her. I noted with some relief that Lieutenant Nan was not around. I would hardly have made my next move if she was.

"Good morning, Captain Nettleton, ma'am. Staff Sgt. Charles C. O'Malley wonders if the captain persists in her request for personal information about Sergeant O'Malley?"

"What the hell are you talking about, Chucky?" Her face betrayed the look of your Irish woman when her patience with a recalcitrant male is about to reach its limit.

"You've forgotten?" I tried to sound as if I were devastated.

"I have forgotten what?"

"That you wanted to see the Clancy kid's picture. Well, that's all right." I turned to leave.

"You have it with you?"

"Well, yes."

"Gimme!"

She almost snatched the picture out of my hand. It was Rosie in her peach-colored prom dress, smiling and happy (pure fakery at the time).

"Gosh, Chuck," Polly said softly. "Is she really this gorgeous?"

I peered over her shoulder as if I were unfamiliar with the picture.

"Perhaps more so," I said judiciously.

"Are you in love with her?"

"There's some debate about that."

"No wonder you don't have any fräuleins on the line. . . . Do you plan to marry her someday?"

My stomach protested that question. "We're too young to think about that, Polly."

"I'd like to meet her."

"You can never tell what might happen." Not if I can help it.

"What's she like?"

"Typical Irish matriarch in the making—contentious, opinionated, outspoken, strong-willed."

"Ah?" Polly tilted her nose up in the air, ready to fight.

"Well, she's also smart and sensitive and generous and loyal and lots of fun." She drinks too much, but I was not going to say that.

"What more do you need? . . . What's her name?"

"Rosie, ah, Rosemarie."

"Fits her. She's lovely, Chuck." Polly handed the photo back to me. "Be good to her."

"I'll try. . . . Tell your man that I'm out here."

What was the purpose of that little skit? Damned if I know. Not all my sneaky games have purpose.

I was ushered into General Meade's promptly.

"What's up, Chuck?" He leaned back in his chair, hands behind his head, a sign that he was relaxed and thinking about golf.

"We have a pretty good lead on the Wülfe family, General, sir."

"Uhm." He leaned forward. "What is it?"

"There is a German family living over a bakery on the Untersandstrasse. A woman and two daughters. The father is apparently dead. They seem to fit the description pretty well."

The general's relaxation vanished. He leaned forward intently. "We'll have to confirm with the fingerprints."

The fingerprint records would always follow them. The Schultzes would have to avoid being fingerprinted for the next two years until the new German Republic (Federal Republic—Bundesstaat, it was being called) came into existence and its citizens were not subject to deportation at the whim of the occupying powers. But even now they'd be pretty safe. Despite Interpol, there was no central fingerprint file among the occupying powers, especially with the Russian zone.

"Yes, sir."

"What do you propose, Chuck?"

"To organize a team to apprehend them this evening, sir, with Agent Clarke's permission, of course."

"That seems reasonable," he sighed. "I can't say that I'm delighted at the prospect."

"No, sir."

"All right, son, carry on."

"Yes, sir." I saluted and left.

No lies. The general had not asked me why I was not planning to move on the Wülfes at once. I didn't think he would because as a good humanitarian he would not like the smell of what we were doing. But, if he had wanted an immediate search, it would have taken me several hours to find Agent Clarke. By the time I found him, it would be too late.

General Meade was a humane and intelligent man, sensitive to the needs of his troops, open to change, flexible enough to act on the unorthodox (but mistaken) notion that I was both a brave man and a brilliant investigator. But it would not have occurred to him to ask whether turning three women over to the Russians on the flimsiest of charges was as immoral as sending Jews to concentration camps—not as massive a cooperation in evil and surely not a cooperation in murder whose only justification was religion and ethnicity. Yet once you have crossed the border by sending one innocent person (or one person for whose guilt there is no evidence) to torture and death, you have joined the ranks of the guilty. The general would have been horrified if I had suggested that to him, and I was not about to do so. He thought of himself as a good man.

I wondered myself whether, if I had not been personally involved,

I would have refused to have anything to do with such a sin. I hope—and I still hope—that I would have refused.

In any case, instead of confrontation about moral issues and simple humanity we would evade the problem, maybe, by one of Chuck's slick schemes.

At lunchtime, I drove the Buick back to the Vinehaus and packed it with all the things I would need for the trip, especially the maps and some fruit and a couple of thermoses of water. In my mailbox I found a letter from Rosemarie.

Just what I needed now.

I stuffed it in my pocket. I would have to answer. Rosemarie needed my letters.

Before I drove back to the *Residenz*, I checked the bar at the Bambergerhof, to make sure that Rednose Clarke was not there. If he wasn't and General Meade asked me during the afternoon why I had not yet organized the raid, I could truthfully say that I had been unable to find Agent Clarke. If I could find him at noon, then I'd need another explanation. Perhaps I shouldn't risk a return to the *Residenz*, but it would help if I was seen by everyone there to be hard at work. Well, moderately hard since I was part, after all, of an army of occupation.

The plan was too clever by half, too many cute little tricks that were the result of too much time to plan. I was worrying about the gnats and ignoring the beams.

I inspected the bar carefully. No sign of Agent Clarke. Good.

No, perhaps not so good. I thought about it and had another of my bright ideas. I left a note in his box. "I will report to you in the bar at six, sir. I believe we might have located the people for whom you are looking."

Even if he didn't check his box, the note would serve as evidence that I had tried. I marked the fact of the note in the little black book in which I was jotting down the details of my search for the Wülfes.

Two gumshoes trailed me back to the *Residenz*. What the hell was eating them? Was Sam Houston Carpenter just harassing me for the fun of it?

The first thing I did at HQ was to type up my notes from the little black book in the form of a journal to be submitted at the end of the operation. It presented our efforts as a paragon of responsible investigation, hindered only by the bizarre behavior of Agent Clarke. There were, need I say, no lies in it.

I rose from my desk to bring the journal to General Meade. I stopped in my tracks. That was being too eager. Save the journal for tomorrow.

Then I turned to Rosie's letter.

Dear Chuck,

I'm writing from Lake Geneva where Peggy and I are staying for a week or two under the watchful eye of Mrs. Riordan. Not that there's all that much for her to watch. The boys up here are real drips. Peggy and I both agreed that it would be much better if you were here because we could at least fight with you and that's always fun.

So we swim and sail and play tennis and read. Peg is getting much better at tennis but I can still beat her. We'll have to teach you how to play when you come home.

Peg is reading Farrell now and loves it. She claims all the characters live in our parish too. I'm plowing through *Main Street*, which is dumb.

Your description of the party at Captain Polly's was wonderful. It did convince me that I will not try to come to Bamberg to see you. I'd be so out of place with those people. But you must be having a wonderful time showing off to them. Shame on you for eating so much caviar!

And the nerve of that Captain Polly! How dare she wonder what I look like! DON'T show her my picture—if you have one there, which I'm sure you don't.

Seriously, she sounds very sweet and someone has to take care of you since your mom and Peg and I are not there.

Whom should I read next?

I do miss you, Chucky, though when you get home, I know we'll keep on fighting.

Love,
Rosie

How do I answer as complex and intricate a letter as that—so much said indirectly and so much more implied. I had no time. I was about to go on a mission. I put the letter aside.

Then I knew I had to answer it.

Dear Rosemarie,

First of all, you would fit in all too well at one of Captain Polly's parties. They'd forget all about the punk with the wirebrush hair that brung you. I'm glad you decided not to come here mostly because it still isn't safe, but partly because you'd upstage me.

As for Captain Polly being my mother, I will have to contend with a sibling soon because, amidst universal rejoicing, she has announced that an heir or heiress to the Nettleton clan is forthcoming. They're leaving here before Christmas.

Alas, too late comes your (I suspect insincere) prohibition against showing your picture to happy Polly. She demanded that I show her one such and I had no choice but to obey because she is my superior officer. So I did show her one of the more dazzling exercises in my photographic skill from the prom night (about which I suppose the less said the better). She was most impressed as I knew she would be. The picture was easy enough to find because it has hung in an appropriate frame in my room at the Vinehaus Messerschmitt.

I don't claim you as my girl because I have no right to do so. But I'll admit that I do not deny the impression that some have that such is the case. I hung the picture for the same reason I showed it to Captain Polly. To have a picture of someone like you makes me look good—as a photographer of course but for other reasons too.

You should read Faulkner next. Then Graham Greene. The former is tough, but worth the effort. The latter is a convert who, mostly because he has never lived in a place like St. Ursula, doesn't quite understand Catholicism.

Shortly you will receive a pound of caviar from me—beluga, I'm told, the best. (Ask the good April, who is an expert on such matters.) I'll tell you the story of how I got it some other time.

It is, however, quite legal. Well, more or less. I'm enclosing a picture of the Biergarten Geyersworth (that's the Schloss Geyersworth in the background). Actually the place is far more degenerate than it seems.

I paused in my typing. I had to say something about fighting with her. I would probably survive the next eighteen hours without any trouble. But if I didn't, should I not say something more?

I thought of the letter I memorized up in the Bohemian Alps. It should be on the record, whatever my fears. I sighed. I didn't want to write it, but I should.

I sighed again and typed it in.

As for fighting, I don't want to fight with you anymore. It stopped being fun long ago. I'm sure we'll *argue*, but no more fights.

Maybe I've grown up a little here in Germany, not much, but perhaps just a little. So, I want to apologize to you for all the times I was rude or sarcastic to you. Maybe you know that it was just a silly little game that both of us played, but I was the one that kept the game going and I'm sorry. I hope we can be friends when I return.

I thought about writing those words up in the Bohemianwald and never did work up the courage to do so.

We've got an operation going now. It's not particularly dangerous, but I'm not very brave. By the time you receive this letter it will be over, and unless you have read bad news in the press, I'll be fine.

Love,
Chuck

I sealed it and threw it in the mailbox as I left. I wished a minute later I hadn't sent it. But then I was glad I did.

— 24 —

At eighteen hundred, when, I fervently hoped, the Wülfes, now Strausses, soon to be Schultzes, were packing, I walked to the Bambergerhof. Special Agent Clarke was, as I suspected, in the bar, reading *Stars and Stripes*. General Clay, the military governor, had testified that anti-Semitism was appearing again in Western Europe. (It had never disappeared as far as I could tell.) The English had imposed a curfew in Tel Aviv.

"Hiyah, sport, how's it holding up?"

"We have found two suspect families, sir, no male in either, I'm afraid. The male is reported to be dead in both cases."

"That may be State's problem when I report it back." He sipped at his drink. "It's no skin off my ass."

"Yes, sir. Do you want to arrange to investigate these two families tonight?"

"Any special reason, sport?" He glanced at his watch. "Think they're planning to fly the coop?"

"No, sir. Our informants are very discreet, you can count on that."

Well, at least Magda and Erika weren't planning on anything because they didn't know what was happening.

"Then why all the rush?"

"Entirely up to you, sir."

"You got a fräulein, sport?"

"No, sir."

"What about that blond kid I saw you with at the *Biergarten?* Great knockers."

"I wouldn't describe her as my fräulein, sir."

"Good-looking kid like you? I don't believe it, sport. Everyone in this asshole of the world has a fräulein. Anyway, go find yourself one and we'll hunt down these krauts in the morning. Okay?"

"Okeydokey, sir. What time?"

"Ten o'clock? That too early?"

"No, sir."

I thought about calling the general and informing him of the "delay." Indeed I picked up a phone in the lobby of the Bambergerhof and then tried to put it down, my hands so wet that the phone slipped off the hook, my body shuddering as if I had been stricken with the flu.

I commanded myself to put the phone carefully back on the hook and get the hell out of the Bambergerhof, slowly and calmly.

The general might have ordered that we pick up the Wülfes tonight. Then where would I be? I must restrain my sudden bright impulses.

The daimon, I would tell myself years later, is quick and resourceful as well as passionate; but he is reckless and imprudent and not to be trusted. Right?

Right.

I climbed into the Buick and, with a deep breath, launched on the great adventure, heart thumping, throat dry, bowels protesting.

And was immediately blocked by a jeep at the far side of the Schönleinsplatz—Sam Houston Carpenter and three of his bully boys.

"Who gave you the right to drive that car, punk?"

I fought to contain my temper. "Gen. Radford Meade, sir. Here is the authorization."

I showed the form that Captain Nettleton had filled out above the general's signature.

Carpenter made a lunge for it and I pulled it back.

"How come he gave you this beauty?"

"I'm afraid you'll have to ask him, sir."

"I'm asking you."

"Sir, I am on an operation to which General Meade assigned me. You are interfering with my carrying out that assignment. I must ask you, sir, with all due respect, to remove your vehicle from my path."

"Where you going?" He lifted his fist as if he were going to strike me.

"Sir, again with all due respect, I submit that it is not proper for you to ask me this question—unless you are prepared to make charges against me and General Meade."

"I've got a good notion to pull you in and beat it out of you."

"You do that, sir"—I was almost at the boiling point—"and I'll bring charges against you. That will mean a general court-martial and your career in the Army will be over."

I had gone too far.

"One more smart-ass comment from you, punk, and I'll break your front teeth."

I lost it, as my grandchildren would say.

"Look, you have been harassing me for a week, interfering with my work, hindering the missions General Meade has sent me on, following me with your incompetent gumshoes. You have done this in the absence of charges against me. Because of my concern about smooth relations between CID and Constabulary I have not complained about it. But now I'm fed up. Either you remove your vehicle from my path or I will ram into it. You, sir, will have to explain to General Meade why this happened."

I turned on the ignition.

"I'll get you, you Irish Catholic son of a bitch."

"I heard that too." I eased the shift into forward and began moving.

God or my guardian angel intervened to prevent me from calling him a fucking redneck bastard.

I shifted into second and picked up speed. The leprechaun was in a foul mood and he didn't care what happened.

"Get the vehicle out of his way, idiots," Sam Houston shouted at his flunkies.

They moved it just in time. I was not about to slow down.

Madness. He was harassing me. He had nothing against me. He was not in league with Agent Clarke or he would have let me ram his jeep. I had endangered everything in a temper tantrum. I was proud of myself for having called his bluff, not a good way to begin a difficult and dangerous caper.

The Wülfes arrived at the alley behind the parish church exactly on time. Thank God I was not dealing with American Irish women, who are genetically programmed to be tardy.

I said nothing until we were out of town and on the autobahn.

"You'd better translate for me, Trudi. There's an American FBI agent, obnoxiously incompetent, in Bamberg looking for you. Apparently the Russians have pushed someone in the State Department to find you and return you to their zone. I don't know why. You'll be safe in the French zone. There are papers in this envelope." My left hand on the wheel of the Buick, not as handsome as the Rider's horse in the *Dom*, I handed the large manila envelope to Trudi. "You are now Maria, Anna, and Frieda Schultz. Please God, you won't have to change your names again. I don't think the search is too serious. Once the American learns that your father is dead and you have escaped, he'll probably return to America. I will drop you at the *Bahnhof* in Stuttgart. I don't want to know who your friends are or where you will be. In a couple of weeks when this should have blown over, you can write me at the Vinehaus Messerschmitt and we can be in touch with one another again. You can begin your new life tomorrow morning."

She did not translate or respond to me for some moments. Sweating from the hot and humid August weather, we drove silently toward the setting sun.

"You are in danger?"

"Not really."

"I know that you are."

"Trudi," I said impatiently, "if I were, I would tell you. I'm trying to get this done, not to be a hero."

Two eighteen-year-olds trying to act like adults as they played what might be a deadly game.

"There is money here."

"Twenty-five hundred American dollars. It will help you not to be a burden on your friends and to begin your new life."

"It is your money, isn't it?"

"Never mind that, Trudi."

The noble knight must make sacrifices, must he not?

"I will not take it." Her voice had a hard, bitter edge. "I did not sell myself to you to escape."

"Did I say that you did?"

"No, but . . ."

"Act your age, Trudi; how are you three going to survive without money? Call it a loan."

"I will repay you, that I promise." Only a novice taking her first vows could have sounded more solemn.

"We'll worry about that later. Now translate for your mother and sister."

I had convinced myself that I would bring her back to America as my wife in a year. The money was not important save as a means to that goal.

Really convinced myself, so much that I could actually imagine her at the good April's supper table?

Hardly.

There were tears and protestations of gratitude in German from the backseat when Trudi had finished her translation.

"My mother and sister are very grateful," she said formally, "for your generosity and your bravery. Like me, they cannot understand why you are so generous to us. They express hope that you are not in any danger. All of us"—she choked—"would rather go to the Russian zone than endanger you."

"I appreciate that," I said with equal formality. "I'm in no danger."

"May I ask you a question, Karl?"

"I have to concentrate on driving the car, Trudi. Please don't bother me."

"But does the *E* on that gauge mean empty?"

"I'm afraid it does."

How big a fool can you be? You're leaving on a dangerous mission, you calculate all the details, but you don't look at the gas gauge. Polly's requisition had told them to fill it up. But in the occupying Army everything routinely went wrong. I had burned up much of what they had put in the tank on my extended tryst with Trudi. God was catching up with me.

I slowed the car. "Thank you, Trudi. When I do something dumb, please tell me."

"*Ja.*"

"We will turn around and go back to that fuel station a few miles up the road. I'm sure we have enough gas to make it."

"*Ja,*" she said with a little less confidence in me than I would have liked, more however than I deserved.

I drove across the thirty-foot median strip, an exercise that the elegant 1947 Buick did not like. It bumped and heaved and jolted.

What if I break an axle or the transmission?

The Buick lunged up on the pavement, shook once, and then proceeded on the highway back to Bamberg.

Only then did I realize that I should have used second for the trip across the median.

The car stalled a hundred meters short of the fuel depot. I eased it forward and limped into the station, where it died completely.

A yawning PFC ambled out of the station.

"What can I do for you, Sarge?" He yawned again.

"Fill 'er up." It was the first time in my life I had ever said that. I showed him the authorization from General Meade.

"Okay, fill out this requisition form." He glanced at the women in the car, smiled his approval, and started the pump.

I filled in the form with trembling fingers.

"Hey, Sarge, you damn near run this thing dry."

"I know."

"Nothing wrong with it. We all do it. Looks like you have some pretty good distractions."

"Yeah."

He put some numbers on the form, I signed it.

Then I glanced up at a car coming into the station from the west. John and Polly Nettleton were in the front seat. What were they doing out here at this time of night?

I turned over the ignition, shifted into first, and got the hell out of there. Fortunately there was pavement connecting both sides of the autobahn here, so I didn't have to put the Buick through another ordeal.

"Good," Trudi sighed in approval.

In the rearview mirror I watched the Nettletons' car. It crossed from the eastbound to the westbound lane. They too were heading for Nürnberg.

We had lost only twenty minutes, twenty minutes that could be very important before we were finished.

What would happen to me if I was caught? Would the general cover up for me? Perhaps a few months in a disciplinary barracks and then a general discharge without GI benefits? And disgrace to my family?

Or would someone higher up decide that it was necessary to make an example of me? Would they throw the book at me?

If they did, it would be a pretty heavy book.

Each kilometer reduced that possibility. Once I had delivered the Schultzes to Stuttgart, it would be impossible for a court-martial to connect me with their disappearance.

The headlights of another car turned on as sunset approached and continued steadily behind us. Was it still John and Polly? Were they trailing me? Or were they up to something else?

Then, about halfway to Nürnberg, we fell in behind a heavy convoy of Army trucks, rolling along at forty-five miles an hour.

Damn.

Then I recalled my trip to Nürnberg to pick up the Old Fitz for General Meade. That had been on a Thursday night too. It was about the same time that they had delayed me—and thus made it possible to rescue Trudi. I was in no hurry that night, but now I was. Damn them.

If I remembered correctly, they'd turn off in about ten minutes. I couldn't figure out what it all meant, but I thought I'd better measure the time.

Twelve minutes later they did exactly what they, or a similar convoy, had done in the winter.

Black market?

I would have to look at that next week if I was still a free man. I noticed I was shivering again. A bitter midwinter in August.

I tried to calm my nerves as we roared by Nürnberg where the real war criminals were on trial—theirs that is, not ours. Victors don't try their own criminals such as Winston Churchill.

I still had not thought of the trail I had left behind that would point right to me. There were no headlights behind us anymore. John and Polly—if it were they—must have turned into Nürnberg.

Stuttgart and safety suddenly receded into the distance. The Buick lurched and heaved, crunched into the other lane, and ground to a halt, despite my increased pressure on the gas pedal.

"The tire is kaput," said little Erika calmly as though we were on a Sunday-morning drive in the country.

"Do you know how to change a tire?" I looked helplessly at Trudi.

"*Nein.*"

"Neither do I."

Another noncom had taught me how to drive, but he had neglected to include tire changing in his lessons.

"The . . . machine for lifting the vehicle is, I think, in the boot."

"I know that much. It's called the jack. And in America it is not the *boot* but the *trunk.*"

"Thank you."

We pried the jack out of the trunk and tried to rig it under the car and pump on the handle.

It did not work.

We tried again and again. For the Schultzes it seemed amusing: Herr Yankee could not make his car work! Even Trudi, who perhaps sensed the dangers better than her mother and sister, laughed at my futile efforts.

I was humiliated, angry, and scared.

"Stop laughing at me, damn it!" So what if the knight can't shoe his steed?

"I am sorry, Karl, but it is better than crying, *nein?*"

Maybe.

We tried again; the chassis lifted an inch off the ground and then flopped noisily back on the shoulder of the autobahn.

The jack snapped in two, shooting parts in several directions.

Trudi did not laugh now. "We are in trouble, Karl, are we not?"

"Bad trouble."

This time I wanted to cry.

Then, as the sun edged toward the horizon, a jeep bounded by us, stopped, and backed up. Constabs? MPs?

No, just a corporal and a private from the Third Armored.

"Trouble, Sarge?"

"Flat tire and broken jack," I tried to sound cheery. "Guy taught me how to drive these things but not how to change tires."

"They don't make 'em like prewar anymore. Let's see if we can help."

Both GIs were younger, if such was possible, than I and glanced appreciatively at the Schultzes as they removed their "machine for lifting the vehicle" from the jeep.

They were a striking enough threesome, Erika now rapidly blossoming into a young woman, Magda in American clothes and makeup, looking like a mother in her late thirties again—too much like her picture in Clarke's documents.

"Three of them, Sarge," said the corporal as he pumped on the jack, "that's hoarding."

"I should be so lucky." I laughed. "I'm driving them to Mannheim for my CO."

"The one with the long hair is a real dish," he sighed. COs' women were strictly off-limits. And verboten too. "I wonder how good she would be in bed."

There was no particular malice in this talk, merely young-male conversation in a locker room.

"I tell myself that it's better not to think about it in a car at night . . . especially with her mother in the backseat."

We laughed innocently enough.

"The frau is not bad herself," the private sighed.

"You wanna drive me out of my mind with that idea?"

We laughed again, not so innocently.

But in ten minutes I was back on the autobahn, racing toward Stuttgart.

"Why did you laugh that way?" Trudi demanded.

"Want to guess?"

"They wondered why one soldier had three women?"

"I told them you were friends of my CO."

"Ah." Her voice was neutral.

"They also thought your mother looked very pretty."

"She does, Karl. You have brought life to all of us and some of her youth back to her. She loves you like she would love the son she did not have."

That was news to me. Scary news.

It was also not exactly what the GIs had in mind. But they were not the kind of boys who would have taken such fantasies seriously.

Not with a Constabulary trooper driving a general's car anyway. Probably not under any circumstances.

However, they'd implanted another fantasy in my head as we

drove, an hour behind schedule but still with lots of time to spare. It was a terrible and pleasurable fantasy—the total possession of three helpless women slaves to whom I could do anything I wanted. They were totally dependent on me. I could demand their three bodies for my amusement and they would have to comply. I would never act out such a daydream in the real world. The fact that it assaulted me and persisted in my imagination indicates how frightened I was and how severed from my moral roots.

My wet hands gripped the wheel of the Buick with grim determination.

We were all perspiring in the humid twilight now turned into darkness, unbearably hot for my companions in their expensive American dresses. The trip had become a surrealistic nightmare— unrelated sequences of strange lights, hideous shapes—a scary night in a film made by an angry drunk (and very like some of Fassbinder's later movies about postwar Germany).

At the checkpoint entering the French zone, the nightmare became terrifying.

The American guards took one look at my blue scarf and beret (worn even on a hot night if you want quick passage) and waved us through.

The African Zouave at the French end looked suspiciously at me and my passengers, glanced at our papers, and walked away without a word.

The three women gasped at the sight of the African. French black troops had a reputation in Germany after the war even worse than the Russians'. A mass rape by one of their regiments that went wild in Stuttgart was often cited by Germans as evidence that the Allies were not better than the Russians or the Nazis. It was said that the Africans had special amusements that made their rapes particularly degrading and cruel. Everyone in Germany knew the story and almost no one in America. How much basis in fact there was, I did not know.

And did not much care just then. I merely wanted our papers back.

A French corporal, a half-pint redhead, much like me, sauntered over to our car, the Zouave lurking behind him, fingering his automatic weapon.

I flipped open the holster on my .45 as my stomach did slow, lazy, and dangerous turns.

The corporal sneered at me in French that was too rapid to understand and gestured contemptuously at my ID. I shouted back at him in English, casting grave reflections on his ancestry and that of the entire French Army, Charles de Gaulle, Napoleon, and if I remember correctly, Joan of Arc, poor woman.

He backed down a little, shook his head dubiously, waved off the Zouave, and walked back to their guardhouse.

We waited five minutes, ten minutes, fifteen minutes, a half hour.

I knew I had to do something. If I delayed any longer, the Frogs would think I had a guilty conscience and keep us there all night.

The French were an occupying power by Allied courtesy. They hadn't done much to win the war; left to themselves they would have lost it and been part of the Thousand Year Reich till the very last day. "By rights," General Meade would mutter, "the Canadians ought to have a zone instead of the Frogs."

"Canucks, sir."

"That's right, Sergeant." He would laugh, not realizing that I was mocking his ethnic prejudice.

Well aware of our contempt for them, the French responded with bureaucratic harassment, a tactic at which they leave the rest of the world at the starting gate.

We in turn reacted by shouting them down, a ploy that usually worked.

Well, I had better start shouting.

I slipped out of the front seat, removed from my Ike jacket pocket the general's authorization to pick up the Wülfes, prayed that no one at the checkpoint could read English, and marched toward the guardhouse.

The African raised his rifle, not, I noted, releasing the safety. I placed my left hand on my .45 (I guess I haven't noted that among my other oddities I am a southpaw) and waved the general's letter in his face.

He backed down and stepped aside, whether impressed by my weapon or the general's letter, I wasn't sure. My knees quivering out of control I strode as best I could to the command post, shoved open the door, and screamed at the corporal, using language that was banned at the O'Malley house.

The red-haired corporal was snoozing, head on the desk in front of him, in the tiny room into which I pushed my way. Our papers were tossed casually on the edge of the desk.

"What the hell is the matter with you stupid sons of bitches? That goddamn African pointed his weapon at me. Do you guys want the fucking Third World War to start, between us and you? Do you know what this blue stands for? I'm Constabulary, are you too fucking dumb to recognize that? Do you want to see the orders from my general? Here they are, asshole, read them and get the hell out of our way or I'll nail your ass to the top of the Eiffel Tower."

I don't think he understood much except the vulgarities, which translate easily, but he was impressed with my document.

He shrugged his shoulders, a tactic at which the French also leave the rest of the world in the gate, and murmured, I think, that his commandant was asleep.

"Well, asshole, wake up the fucking commandant or I'll nail his ass right next to yours on the Eiffel Tower."

I picked up our papers and shoved open the door at the other side of the room. The trick with the French, the CO had often told me, was to be even more arrogant than they were. With dry throat and pounding heart, I sure hoped that he was right.

The commandant was an elderly lieutenant with a row of ribbons on his coat. He was sound asleep on a cot in the other room of the post.

I shook him by the shoulder, shouted pretty much the same line, and waved the CO's letter in front of him, pointing at the Constabulary letterhead.

His sleepy eyes twitched in fury at being awakened. He was about to chew me out when he noticed the fancy trimmings of my uniform. He reached for his glasses and snatched the general's letter away from me.

Please God, don't let him know any English.

He glanced at the paper, pretended to read it, and chewed out the corporal instead.

I didn't get much of his tirade, but I think he left out Joan of Arc.

Then he thrust the letter back into my waiting hand and rolled over on the cot, his face to the wall.

"Bonne nuit, mon commandant." I saluted and bowed.

He grumbled something unintelligible and probably scatological (we English speakers beat the rest of the world in that area). I strode out of the command post without a single backward look, jumped into the front seat of the Buick, turned over the ignition, and started to move toward the gate. The corporal waved us through, and the African kid, with a big, friendly grin, opened the gate.

He saluted me as if I were at least a field marshal. I returned the salute crisply.

Maybe I'd make a good field marshal. Too short?

What about Napoleon?

"What did you do, Karl?" Trudi asked anxiously.

"Pretended I was Gen. Omar Nelson Bradley." I laughed.

"Pardon?"

"Bluffed, darling, bluffed my fool head off. I could begin to enjoy this gumshoe business."

"Please don't," she begged.

Small danger. I was still shaking.

"Next stop Stuttgart," I said. "Lake Street Transfer, change for Douglas Park."

They knew, I guess, that I was a euphoric boy and did not ask what Lake Street Transfer was.

How would I have explained the Chicago el system of that time to them anyway?

My schedule had called for us to be in Stuttgart between ten-thirty and eleven. It was well after twelve when we finally pulled off the autobahn, climbed the ring of hills around the city, and drove down into the saucer in which Stuttgart lay like a rosary of faint yellow lights. It took another half hour to find our way into the center of town and to the *Bahnhof,* on which there was a lighted blue Mercedes-Benz symbol—which of course was the logo of the city before it became the logo of the auto. I helped them out of the car. With their small bags, they could easily pass as travelers waiting for an early-morning train in the quiet and empty platz in front of the ugly Gothic train station.

I was already more than two hours behind schedule, exhausted and drained. So, our leave-taking was brief and tense. All three women kissed me quickly, Trudi only a little less quickly than her mother and sister.

"Will you be all right?" I asked.

Trudi's thin face was pale and strained in the dim lights on the outside of the station. "Of course. We will wait in the *Bahnhof* till morning and take a taxi to our friends. We shall never forget—"

"Be sure to wait two or three weeks before writing." I cut her gratitude off with another quick kiss. "As soon as I find out your address from you, I'll drive over and tell you the whole story."

I noticed that the night air in Stuttgart was much chillier than it had been at the French checkpoint. We were not that high up in the Black Forest, were we?

"I love you, Karl." She embraced me gently. "I love you very much."

"I love you too, Trudi." I kissed her for the last time. "I have to rush to make it back to Bamberg. I'll see you soon."

"I want you to have this." She pushed something into my hand. "It represents me and my love."

I glanced down: her Leica.

"I can't, Trudi . . ."

"You must. I will be angry if you don't."

"It means so much to you." I was tempted, then ashamed of my greed.

"So does the money you saved mean much to you."

"Always be gracious when given a present," Mom had instructed us, "even if you don't deserve it."

"Thank you, Trudi." I hugged her again. "I will treasure it always. But in return you must accept the money as a gift, not a loan."

"I will *not*." She tried to pull away, then collapsed against me. "You are gracious and I am not, Herr Yankee. I thank you as you thanked me. God protect you."

"And you." The playlet ended with a benediction as solemn as that in any cathedral.

I still carry the Leica, a small, light, remarkably precise range-finder camera that, innocent of the gimmickry that would weigh down 35mm's in later days, fits in the palm of my hand. I can't say that I remember Trudi every time I use it. But I do often remember her and our terrible innocence on that dark August night in 1947.

As I drove out of town and over the rim of the saucer in which Stuttgart nestles, one part of me warned that the letter would never come and I would not see her again. I told that part of me to shut up.

Around me I could see dim hulks in the night, the new construction that was under way. Pre–Marshal Plan money was already at work, seeding the German "economic miracle" that was beginning.

I thought I saw Polly Nettleton in front of an old church halfway up the hill. Or was my imagination playing tricks on me?

I had little opportunity to reflect on either the construction or the three women I had left behind. When I reached the autobahn, I realized that the chilly air was not limited to Stuttgart. A weather front was moving into Middle Europe from the North Atlantic. Why had I not thought to check the weather? Another dumb move.

I was on the highway only a few minutes when I saw what the combination of hot landmass and cold weather front meant.

Fog!

Peering through the windshield with aching eyes, as though it were a massive curtain obscuring a movie screen, I calculated my chances. It was two o'clock. I had progressed forty kilometers since entering the autobahn outside of Stuttgart. A little better than twenty miles an hour. At that rate it would take between six and seven hours to return to Bamberg. I would arrive between nine and nine-thirty, barely in time for the phony "pickup" operation.

If nothing else went wrong.

But on the basis of what had already happened, something else was likely to go wrong. Therefore I had to drive faster, fog or no fog.

What if I had another flat tire? There was no spare in the boot, uh, trunk.

Chucky is kaput!

If, disregarding the fog, I increased the speed to thirty miles an hour, I would arrive in Bamberg about six or six-thirty, again if nothing else went wrong. That would be more like it.

What's the point in being an accountant in the making if you can't do a little elementary arithmetic?

Could I compromise at twenty-five miles per hour?

No, that would be cutting it too close. So it was thirty, no matter what might be ahead of me on the autobahn. It was night, wasn't it? And who else but a lunatic would be driving the autobahn at this hour in gooey fog?

So I pressed harder on the gas and leaned closer to the windshield. It would be a long night.

Maybe when the sun rose in another hour and a half or so, it would burn off the fog.

Wouldn't that be nice?

I had no idea what the visibility was. Moreover I had only been driving for a year and had no experience driving in fog and precious little practice in night driving on a highway. Would I see the red lights on a vehicle in front of me in time to swerve?

I had read an article in the *New York Times* about the time required to avoid an object ahead of you on the road. As best as I could remember the numbers, I would not have a chance.

Outside of Nürnberg, having relaxed a little and become confident of my ability at flying in visibility zero, ceiling zero (the name of a film I vaguely recalled), I inched up to thirty-five miles per hour. I soon learned how many seconds I had to swerve after seeing the first hint of red lights in front of me.

Two, maybe three at the most.

The vehicle was a big truck carrying a Sherman tank at maybe fifteen miles an hour.

At least the hulking monster that I raced by looked like a Sherman tank out of the corner of my eye. I didn't bother to look closely. A number of other such monsters were in front of the first one. I stayed in the passing lane until I was sure I had gone beyond them.

What sort of damn fools were moving a convoy of tanks at this hour in the fog?

The United States Army, that's what kind of damn fools!

Buy Russian war bonds, as we used to joke.

The second encounter was with an oil tanker, maybe fifteen minutes later.

It was an encounter in the full sense of the word: I banged into his rear bumper. And then saw his red lights, as it seemed, below my belt buckle.

It was a light enough bump, though probably enough to scare the hell out of him, even more than it scared me. He knew he was carrying some kind of combustible fuel and was probably terrified at the possibility of going up in a dirty-orange explosion at any moment even before I bumped him. I thought about the puff of orange only after I had swerved around him.

I literally vomited what little food there was in my stomach on the dashboard.

Dear God, what a rotten hero I was.

I pulled into Bamberg at six-forty and parked in front of the *Residenz* a little before seven hundred. Eleven hours for a five-hour trip. I was so tired and so spent from groping through the fog all night that I could hardly force myself out of the car. And the most intricate part of my scheme was still ahead of me.

God ought not to put such an incompetent into a situation such as this one, I complained.

I cleaned the vomit off the dashboard, staggered into the men's room, threw water in my face, brewed a cup of coffee, and tried to think what I was supposed to do next.

At ten hundred, Kelly and I and our team of eight men and two jeeps cautiously bumped up to the Bambergerhof. The fog was as thick as it had been on the autobahn, but now it was colored a faint purple instead of jet-black.

"You look tired, Sarge," Kelly said to make conversation. "Rough nights?"

"Too much school."

"Gotta do something to stay sane in this burg. Am I glad I'm getting the hell out next week."

I filed that bit of information. It might be useful. "Remember what I told you about this FBI jerk? We don't trust him."

"Sounds like a real asshole."

"That's putting it mildly."

Special Agent Clarke was late. We pulled away from the Bambergerhof at ten-thirty.

"Don't fret, sport." His eyes were bloodshot and his face unshaven. "What's the rush, our friends are not going anywhere, are they?"

"I certainly hope not, sir."

We went through the full routine in the narrow Untersandstrasse in front of the food store: two jeeps blocking the exits from the street; four men, automatic weapons ready (safeties on, I devoutly hoped), lined up in a semicircle on the street; the other four trudging noisily up the narrow, steep steps.

The Gestapo came in the middle of the night, didn't they?

Well, they still lost the war.

"Please stay behind my men, sir," I admonished Clarke, who did not seem disposed to be ahead of them.

"Sure thing, sport."

We knocked at the door, and there was, of course, no answer. I nodded at Kelly and Crawford. They tucked themselves into corners at either side of the minute landing. My .45 clutched firmly in my hand, I kicked at the door. It promptly popped open. More cooperative than the door out in the Bohemian Alps.

"Cover me, men," I ordered, repressing a terrible urge to laugh.

I sprang into the room, spun around, weapon in front of me, and surveyed the whole space.

"No one here, sir."

"Damn," Agent Clarke muttered. "I didn't think it would be this easy. Still, it looks like they'll be coming back, doesn't it?"

"Yes, sir, it does."

"Pretty cheap stuff." He fingered curtains on the single window. "Clean and neat place, isn't it? Goddamn krauts are compulsive, aren't they?"

"Yes, sir. Permission to search the quarters, sir?"

"Suit yourself, sport."

"Kelly, check with the store owner to see if you can learn where these women work and whether there is a father in the family."

"Sure, Sarge."

"Crawford, stand guard at the door. Cline, help me to search the quarters."

"Okay, Sarge."

Not much respect for their noncom, but Clarke didn't seem to notice.

While Cline went through the clothes in the closet, I opened the small paper file in which the Strausses had kept their personal effects.

My heart sank. At the very top were their old identity papers, good enough to get them a job in the American zone, but not good enough to get them out. I had not told Trudi to destroy the papers. So, obedient literalist that she was, she had left them.

If Clarke should see them, even such an incompetent gumshoe as he would wonder what they were doing for papers. That would mean that we—or CID—would raid the store of my ex-Luftwaffe friend, and he would, however regretfully, testify about the redheaded sergeant from the Constabulary who had tried to buy forged IDs for three women. Well, maybe he wouldn't. But I couldn't take the chance.

It was necessary to think of something. At once.

"Doesn't look like they've left, does it, sport?"

"No, sir. . . . Sir, look at this! Are these the people?"

I held out the picture Trudi had left, just under the old documentation. Magda and Gunther Wülfe and two kids, one of them an infant in her mother's arms. The young Magda did look enough like the woman I had said good-bye to a few hours ago to be immediately identified as the same person.

"Lemme see, sport? Hey, sure as hell looks like them."

He walked over to the window to study the picture in the thin sunlight the fog was permitting to shine on Bamberg that August morning so long ago.

As soon as he turned his back, I turned in the opposite direction, so Cline couldn't see me, and pocketed the three sets of documents.

"Hey, sport." Clarke whistled softly.

I turned back. He was still looking at the picture. I stuffed the papers deeper into my pocket.

"Sir?"

"Sure as hell looks like them, doesn't it?"

"If you would compare the picture with your documentation, sir."

I crossed my fingers.

He reached in his jacket pocket, patted his trousers, tried the jacket again, and shook his head. "Damn, must have left them at the hotel. Well, no harm done, eh, sport?"

"No, sir."

Not much.

Kelly returned.

"The guy talked up a storm, Sarge. Claims they talked with a Dresden accent, whatever the hell that is. I thought all krauts talked the same. Father died in a raid at the end of the war, he says. Work over at the Bambergerhof. He didn't notice them leaving this morning."

"Good work, Kelly. Send Mann up here and take the other three men and see if you can apprehend the three women—their name is Strauss—and report back here."

"Right, Sarge."

"Nice thinking, sport." Clarke heaved himself heavily onto the couch on which Trudi and I had first become lovers. "Damn, I bet I saw them in the corridors over there and didn't even recognize them."

"It's been a long time since that picture was taken, sir."

"Yeah, I suppose so." He closed his eyes contentedly.

Someone tapped on the door. Mann opened it. "Kelly would like a word with you, Sarge."

"Hasn't he left for the hotel?"

"He wants to talk to you first."

I walked out on the landing.

"I was waiting for you, Sarge. There's an odd thing . . ."

"Yeah?" My heart jumped again.

"The old guy down there said there was a GI who used to hang around here. One of ours."

"Constab?"

"Yeah, old guy says a blue-beret type."

"Wow! Any description?"

Kelly shrugged. "Old guy didn't know. Young Yankee in blue beret. I figured we didn't want that asshole in there going after one of ours, so I didn't tell you in there."

"If he doesn't ask, Kel, we don't tell him. Right?"

"Right, Sarge. See you later."

Kelly was an innocent; if he were covering for a redhead sergeant, he couldn't have kept a straight face. Just the same I'd breathe a sigh of relief when he went home next week.

The rest was easy.

An hour later Kelly was back.

He climbed up the stairs with a rattle that caused the sleeping Special Agent Clarke to open one of his bloodshot eyes.

"Bad news, Sarge," Kelly announced cheerfully. "I left the others over at the Bambergerhof, but I guess the fox has flown the coop."

I ignored his mixed imagery. "Details, Kelly."

"The three women work there all right. Mother and two daughters. Blond. The kids good-looking. Maids. They didn't show up for work this morning. . . ."

"What time were they due?"

"Zero six hundred, Sarge."

I looked at my watch, almost noon. "Hell, Kelly, they could be anywhere. Frankfurt, Stuttgart, Mannheim . . ."

"Must have known we were closing in, Sarge."

"How could they have found out?" Special Agent Clarke stirred himself enough to push off the couch. "Weak security, sport?"

"Might I make a suggestion, sir?"

"Why not, sport?"

"If they worked at the Bambergerhof, they might well have been in your room. . . ."

"So?"

"So, sir, is it possible that they might have seen your documentation and fled because they had learned you were here to apprehend them?"

"Don't be ridiculous, sport." He stuffed his hands into his pockets, an elaborate gesture of casualness. "That's pushing it too hard."

It also was a bear-trap closing.

The pickup operation fizzled out by the time the fog had lifted in late afternoon. Agent Clarke announced to us that the main goal of his trip had been achieved: Gunther Wülfe was dead.

"The woman and the kids don't matter, sport. Not at all."

He meant he could go home and tell his boss that there was no one to turn over to the Russians. "Husband dead, wife probably dead, kids vanished. Empty house."

All the bureaucracies—Justice, State, Russkies—would be happy.

I sent my team back to their quarters and walked over to the *Residenz*. I was so damn tired I could hardly move my feet.

In the ballroom, I smiled at Brigie and nodded, sat at my desk for a couple of moments to finish typing my journal of the operation with the appropriate notes, and walked down to the general's office.

"He said to go right in when you got here," Polly said, raising an eyebrow in a question.

I gave her a covert thumbs-up sign and she relaxed like a Notre Dame fan when they make the last, decisive conversion.

Maybe it was not her and John I had seen the night before.

"You look rotten, son. Operation blown?"

Without any pretense at military courtesy, I threw myself into the chair on the other side of his desk, a seat in the old days I had persuaded myself was for the bishop's fool.

"The son of a bitch left his papers lying around the hotel room, sir. The targets might have seen them and ran."

"Damn!" the general said. "One more failure."

"Yes, sir."

He relaxed a bit. "Well, we're not particularly unhappy about this one, are we?"

"No, sir. The people at the Bambergerhof said they were nice women."

He rubbed his hand across his face. "Tough times, son. Tough times. . . . You're not putting his carelessness about the papers in the report, are you, Sergeant?" He frowned heavily at me.

"Course not, sir. Should we put out a search order for them?"

"The husband, Gunther, uh, Wülfe, isn't it? You're sure he's dead."

"Yes, sir, all our information, even from CID, indicates that there were just the three women."

"And this FBI man is satisfied?"

"He's got a report that keeps him clean, sir."

"If we find them, we send the woman and the two girls back to the Russians. Would you want that to happen to your sisters—you do have sisters, don't you?"

"I see your point, sir."

"So, send out a low-priority notice, do me a report, and forget the whole thing until something else comes in, which I'll give you ten to one won't happen."

"Yes, *sir.*"

I handed him my journal. He glanced over it quickly.

"The idiot would not approve a pickup last night!"

"No, sir."

"You going to put that in your report?"

"In a low-key way, just in case we need it."

"Good thinking, son. Good thinking. . . . All right, you look dead tired. Take the rest of the weekend off and do your report on Monday."

"Thank you, sir."

Then, exhausted as I was, I saw a solution to the black-market mystery. I saw it clearly and in most of its details, at least as they affected us.

"One more thing, sir," I said at the door. "I think I know why all our attempts to get the black-market ring have failed."

"Oh?" The general seemed startled.

"With the general's permission, I'd like to work on it next week. I've got to think it through because it's complicated and potentially dangerous. I'll have to interview some people. I don't want to make charges till I can back them up. I'm afraid I'll need a car too."

General Meade considered me carefully. This was a change in our relationship for which he was not quite prepared: I was in effect telling him that I would not disclose my suspicions to him just yet, and he was not sure he liked that.

Then he must have decided. "What the hell, no harm done."

"No, sir."

"Have Polly arrange for the car."

"Yes, sir. Thank you, sir."

"I'll need the car next week," I told Captain Polly. "Don't worry, it's a completely different operation."

"Do you want it for the weekend?"

"Doesn't matter." I had no one to take for a ride in the country this weekend.

"Easier that way. How long? Indefinite?"

"You could spoil me, Captain Polly, ma'am."

She scribbled the required number on the form. "Just so long as I meet this Clancy kid someday."

"In the mysterious designs of Providence, as the nuns used to tell us, anything can happen. And the two of you will compare notes like all Irish biddies and I'll be in worse troubles than ever."

"It will serve you right." She smiled at me and gave me the form.

I picked up the stuff at my desk and stopped to talk to Brigie on the way out.

"It all worked out," I said. "Close at times, but we made it."

She nodded. "I am so glad."

"Thanks for the help."

"*Bitte.* Why don't you go home and have a long nap. You look exhausted."

"Yes, Mommy."

I walked outside into the clear sunlight of the *Domplatz.* It was a pleasant day. Despite the fog there was not as much heat or humidity as last night. So, it was all over.

I felt nothing at all, no elation, no satisfaction, only a kind of dull numbness, like the man who is told that he won't need surgery yet. They were safe despite all my mistakes.

I was lonely, however, terribly lonely; and I had not been separated from my beloved for more than a few hours. I would see her in a couple of weeks and all would be well. We could begin our preparations for marriage and America.

Even then, however, I wondered. I had deliberately not asked the names of their friends in Stuttgart. I didn't want to know those names if I should be asked. However, I would not be able to get in touch with them until Trudi contacted me.

Would she?

Crowds of people were pouring into the *Dom*. August 15. Mary's Day in Harvest time. Holy day of obligation. I might as well go over there and say thank-you. It never hurts when you're dealing with General Officers.

The Mary portal was banked with flowers. Inside the *Dom* flowers were everywhere. The congregation were wearing their best clothes, which were not necessarily all that good. The choir was singing a Palestrina kyrie. It was clearly a big feast in Bamberg. Probably some holdover from an ancient Teutonic harvest festival.

"Thanks for helping," I whispered to the one we were honoring. "Do you play the same role for Himself that Captain Polly plays for General Meade? If you do, that means you're the one who is *really* in charge. I guess Jewish mothers are not all that different from Irish mothers."

Several times during mass I found myself looking for Trudi and her family.

The ceremonies improved my morale. At the end of mass they sang the glorious Marian Easter hymn "Regina Coeli Laetare Alleluia." I joined in at the top of my voice, though my Italianate American Latin was pronounced differently from the Teutonic version. I sang loudly, but on key. Some of my neighbors in the pew looked at me with disapproval.

Fuck 'em all. I was happy again, at least for a few days.

I decided that, despite Jimmy Randolph's calm faith, I'd stay Catholic. Messy, confused, unpredictable, Catholicism still had the best images and stories.

My long nap, which lasted well into Saturday morning, was untroubled by dream terrors. When I finally did wake up, I felt as though a great burden had been lifted from my shoulders.

On Monday morning I refueled my Buick—never make the same mistake twice in a row—and drove up to the border post where we had "liberated" the beluga caviar. I took a chance that the same sergeant was on duty. I asked him some questions (once I had explained why a noncom like me had led the mission), showed him a picture, and asked him to fill out and sign an affidavit.

When I returned to HQ, I made a phone call to the hospital. The answer to my questions were what I had thought they would be.

On Thursday afternoon while it was still bright, I steered the car onto the autobahn and headed for Nürnberg. I timed the drive so that I would find the approximate place where the heavy convoy had turned off the road. It must have been where there was a crossover pavement because they had exited on the left side of the highway, and the big trucks and tankers would have a more difficult time than my Buick if they tried to cross the median strip. After a couple of misses I found the place, a forested area between Büttenheim and Forchheim, a little less than halfway to Nürnberg from Bamberg— the railroad and the Regens to the right of the highway. Sure enough, there was not only a crossover but also a graded dirt road coming out of the forest. The trees were so close to the autobahn in that spot that you would hardly notice the dirt road unless you were looking for it.

I crossed the median and headed down the dirt road. I was so despondent about the loss of Trudi, a temporary loss I kept telling myself, that I wasn't afraid of anything anymore.

About a quarter mile in I found a large meadow where the vegetation had been trampled by truck tracks. The Bavarian Outfit's trucks came here on Thursday night, one convoy from Bamberg, the other probably from Nürnberg, to exchange goodies, most likely around midnight, the goodies having been stolen from PX supplies, hospitals, and shipments from America arriving at the Rhine-Main airport up at Frankfurt. The thefts must be massive and brazen to require an exchange each week.

The rendezvous was also brazen: same place, same time every week. They must have felt confident that no one was looking for them or that no one cared. Most of the goodies belonged to the government one way or another. No one, they must have told themselves, objected to a little larceny if the victim was the government.

I would stay and watch the rendezvous tonight and get some pictures of it on Trudi's Leica. Where should I park my car?

I found a small dirt road, barely two tracks through the forest, which led out of the meadow in the opposite direction (east). Sorry, old girl, I said to my chariot and turned into the road. I was well into it before I realized that I would have to back up to get out. I had no skills at all in the difficult matter of driving in reverse.

About a half mile down the path, because that was all it was, I stopped the car and checked my map. The dirt road was not marked, but it seemed that a couple of hundred meters in the direction I had come there was a paved road leading to Büttenheim, where I could get back on the autobahn. When it was time for me to redeploy that night, I could poke my way down the dirt road, find the highway, and be home free. This route might also be useful when we came back to pick up the gang.

I would have to do my poking in the dark and without headlights. I sat and thought about that for a while. Then I realized that it would be at least an hour and a half before the convoy from Bamberg showed up. Probably the arrival times of both convoys would be synchronized; no point in wasting too much time in the exchange, even if you didn't feel in too much danger.

So in the dusk, I picked my way through the underbrush and the mud—forest floors are always muddy for some reason I could never understand—scared a few squirrels and a few quail, and bumbled down the path.

I was never a Boy Scout, never went to a marshmallow roast in Thatcher Woods, a Chicago forest preserve west of us, don't like hiking or (God save us all) camping, and deplore poking around in forests as if we are Neolithic hunter-gatherers (a line I use frequently on my children and grandchildren, some of whom fancy that the

Neolithic times might have been more "natural"). So, I did not enjoy my romp through the Bavarian woods. But finally I came upon a two-lane highway with a sign indicating that the next town was Büttenheim.

Proud of my performance as a woodsman, I struggled back to the Buick as darkness settled in. Clouds had drifted across the darkening sky. It would be a black, black night.

I waited until the blackness was total, reached for my flashlight, and flicked it on for a quick look at my watch.

The light didn't work. I tried it again; it still didn't work. The batteries were dead. A great Dick Tracy I was. First no gasoline in the car and then no batteries in the flashlight. So here I was on a dark night, in the middle of a German forest, and I would not be able to see two feet in front of me.

I'd make enough noise blundering through the forest to wake up Frederick Barbarossa from his grave. The smart thing to do would be to get back to the edge of the meadow before the Outfit guys arrived. So I fumbled for Trudi's Leica (which I had loaded before I left), the car keys, and a couple of more rolls of film, then climbed out of the car.

Should I bring my weapon?

What good would it do? If I was caught, I'd be outnumbered and I probably couldn't fire the thing right anyway. Besides, the safety catch could always slip off as I tried to get through the forest in the dark and I might literally shoot myself in the foot.

That would be typical of my behavior so far.

I can often cause great laughter among my descendants by describing how I lurched through the forest that night, often on my hands and knees, as I tried to find the road. It was so dark that I had actually entered the meadow before I knew I was there. The only way to tell it was the meadow was that it was a little less dark and no brambles were biting at my ankles. I felt my way back into the edge of the woods, groped for a safe place to sit, eased myself onto the ground, removed the cover from my Leica, and waited for them to come.

In those days we did not have wide enough lens apertures to do much night photography without a flash or a tripod, which would have permitted a long exposure. I was hoping that they would need a lot of lights to exchange their goodies. If they didn't, they'd have to work in the dark just like me. The best I could hope for were dim shapes. But that would be all I needed.

I waited forever, periodically shifting my weight in search of a more comfortable position. There weren't any.

Finally two headlights cut the dark and moved slowly into the meadow—toward me. The truck parked only a few feet from my hiding place and turned off its lights. Some ten others followed, including two tankers. So, black-market gasoline. I heard people complaining about the convoy from Nürnberg. So I had guessed that right.

This crowd was therefore from Bamberg. I strained for voices and heard the one I expected I would hear.

I thought about moving farther back into the trees, but was afraid to risk making noise. So I curled up and pretended that I was a woodchuck—one with a camera in his little front paws.

After a couple of eternities, another set of lights emerged from the forest and bumped across the meadow. The lights from the Bamberg crowd flicked on and off. The Nürnberg bunch moved slowly across the meadow until they had formed a tight semicircle. Then all the lights went on.

"Where were you guys?" someone shouted.

"Constabulary at our end was watching us."

Laughter. "We don't have that problem at our end. . . . Come on, let's get this shit moving."

The crowd worked efficiently, moving stuff back and forth. On the other end of the meadow they were transferring gas from one tanker to another—from Bamberg to Nürnberg it looked to me, but then that figured. There was enough light in the circle where they were working for some shots that would not be impossibly bad. They probably did not know each other very well since they always met in the dark. I was wearing fatigues just as they were.

So I canceled the woodchuck act and became one of them. I didn't move anything or talk to anybody but was just sort of there, walking around as if I knew what I was doing, and covertly shooting a roll of twenty shots. No one seemed to notice me. I was one more slightly dishonest GI wandering in the semidarkness.

Madness, absolute madness. I wasn't even scared—though heaven knows I should have been. The dice were falling my way and I'd keep playing them. Leaning against the side of a tanker, I got one first-rate shot of the suspect. I sort of edged away from them when the roll of film came to an end and slipped back into the woods to reload. I discovered that my hands were shaking so badly that I couldn't reload. The woodchuck returned and told me that I had more than enough shots.

A real photographer never has enough shots, right? Still, the woodchuck won that argument.

I waited till all the vehicles had returned to the autobahn, wished I were in bed with some woman's comforting arms around me, and generally felt cold and sorry for myself.

I forced myself to get up and struggle back through the forest to my Buick—which I discovered simply by banging into it, and hurting my knee. It was as if someone had attacked me with a baseball bat. Pain exploded from my scalp to my toes. I screamed loud enough to wake up not only Barbarossa, but also Arthur Pendragon and the combined forces of the Teutonic knights and the knights of the Round Table. I fell into the car and began to rub my knee. I'd have to find an ice pack as soon as I could. Fortunately I was less than a half hour from the Army Hospital in Bamberg.

I reached for the ignition key. It wasn't there. Of course not, I had put it in my pocket. I searched my left pocket and found the Leica case and nothing else. In my right pocket I found the Leica and nothing else. In my hip pocket were my wallet and some change. In my shirt pocket, more change, extra film, and rosary beads.

I panicked and went through everything again. I felt on the floor-board. I opened the door and grubbed around in the leaves. No keys. I was stuck here till the sun came out. Even then I would have to creep down the path and scour it on my hands and knees. Proverbial needle in a haystack.

I controlled the panic as best I could. I had to remember what had happened. I had certainly put the keys in my left pocket. Maybe when I stuffed the Leica case into my pocket up by the meadow, curled up in my woodchuck persona, I had accidentally jerked the keys out of my pocket. *Jerk* was the appropriate word.

So all I had to do in the morning was find my woodchuck hole and mess around among the worms and the molds looking for a

Buick car key. If I didn't find it, I would have to limp back to Büttenheim and call Captain Polly.

"Ma, it hurts!"

I didn't want anyone to know I was anywhere near Büttenheim, though it was not certain that the men in either convoy would know where Büttenheim was. They were creatures of the autobahn and probably never left it.

Still I had better find the key.

For lack of something better to do, I said the rosary. Despite my aching knee, I slipped into fitful sleep. Each time I woke up, I moved my knee, hoping it would feel better. Each time it felt worse. Finally, the sun awakened me—strong, bright, and already warm. I wondered where I was. Then I remembered where I was and groaned. I tried to move my leg and groaned again. Louder.

I had to find the key, absolutely had to.

Charles Cronin O'Malley, boy detective.

If only there were a spare key.

Wait a minute, what had shithead at the motor pool told me? *In the glove compartment?*

Desperately I groped through the glove compartment. Yep, there it was!

I threw back my head and laughed (maybe cried a little too). Perhaps I was the best operative in Bamberg, but that only proved how bad the others were!

I found my rosary on the floorboard, said a decade in quick gratitude, started the car, and headed for the two-lane highway, faster than I should have, but I knew that my white hat was deservedly white and nothing could go wrong.

I slowed down. That sounded like Jimmy Randolph and I had decided that it was better to be Catholic.

I limped into the hospital, though just barely, and immediately became the center of attention. Like most of the Seventh Army it wasn't very busy—babies, clap, and depression being its principal problems. A red-haired punk with a gimpy leg offered a little bit of variety.

"What happened, son?" the doctor asked.

"Bumped my knee."

"Been drinking?" He started to press the knee.

"No, sir. I don't drink. . . . Ouch!"

"Looks like nothing worse than a bad bruise. You should have put an ice pack on it."

"I know, sir. I played football in high school. But where I was there wasn't any ice."

"And where were you?"

"Classified, sir."

"What's your outfit?"

"Constabs, HQ company. I'm kind of an investigator, which means I gotta poke around in the dark at night."

The two nurses, both kind of pretty, giggled, which they did for the rest of my treatment.

"We'll take an X ray just to be sure."

So they took an X ray just to be sure and I was told that no serious harm had been done, that I should stay off my feet for a few days, and that by the end of the week I'd be fine. However, it would be necessary to drain some fluid away from the bruise.

"Fluid?" I erupted. "What kind of fluid?"

The giggles became louder.

"Blood of course, soldier."

"*My* blood!" I protested.

Even the doctor thought that was pretty funny.

So he gave me some kind of local anesthetic and then stuck a needle in my knee and drew off the "fluid," a grisly mix of dark brown stuff that looked like chocolate milk that had turned sour.

"That doesn't look like *my* blood."

"Some infection in there. We'll give you a shot of penicillin too."

That reminded me of Trudi and I was sad again. With the medical personnel, however, I must continue to play the clown.

"I'm sure it will make me sick."

"It will protect you from being sick," one of the nurses said.

"That's what people like you always say before they stick a needle into your rump."

More laughter.

So they gave me the shot and the pain pills, which I was not to use till I was finished with the car for the day, and I was to stay off my feet for three or four days.

"Will the medicine give me pretty dreams?" I demanded. "With people like you two in them?"

"More likely nightmares."

When the nurses departed temporarily to find me a cane, the doctor added, "Good act, son. That must hurt like hell."

"It reminds me of the time I fell two hundred feet off the *Jungfrau*."

"What happened?" he asked, actually believing me.

"I died."

The nurses, giggling still, outfitted me with a cane so elaborate with carvings and inlays that it must have belonged to Hermann Göring. They warned me again to stay off my feet. Maybe tomorrow. I had some things to do first.

I limped into the HQ, making as much as I could of my injury and my cane. Take the sympathy wherever you can get it.

"Chucky! What happened?" Captain Polly and General Meade were talking at the door of his office. She saw me first.

"What did you do to yourself, O'Malley?" the general demanded, as if my injury were somehow a violation of military discipline.

"It was done to me, sir. In the line of duty. I will accept any rewards that might be given. Purple Heart for example?"

Laughter.

"Who hit you?"

"A car, my car in fact. Or rather the Army's car which I'm driving."

"Where were you?" Polly demanded.

"Classified," I said ominously. This time it really was.

The general caught my eye and I nodded slightly.

"What did the medics do?"

"Robbed me of some of my blood, gave me some medicine, and said to stay off it for several days."

"You'll do that, naturally?"

"Of course, General, sir. Nothing I like more than staying off my feet."

"Where are you billeted, son?"

"Vinehaus Messerschmitt, sir. Named after the pilot and plane maker."

"I know who Messerschmitt was. . . . Captain Nettleton, we have some rooms available in the Bambergerhof, don't we?"

"Yes, sir."

"Let's transfer Sergeant O'Malley over there indefinitely. Get someone to move his things for him. He's obviously in no condition to carry anything. You might as well assign the car to him indefinitely too. No point in having it just sit in the car pool."

None of this had I counted on. I must have looked more pathetic than I thought. I was not, however, about to argue.

It was a shame, however, that they had moved me into the hotel where my girl had worked a few days after she had left.

"How soon, Chuck?" General Meade whispered when Captain Polly rushed off.

"If we're lucky, sir, a week from today. I want to have evidence that cannot be challenged before I make a charge."

"Good thinking. . . . Take care of that knee."

"I will, sir. Thank you, sir."

As soon as the GIs had moved my stuff to the luxury of the Bambergerhof (with suitable awe about the change in my status) and departed from the room, I shoved myself off my luxurious bed, removed the film from the Leica, and drove back to the *Residenz* and the darkroom in the basement.

The pictures were even better than I had expected.

Got 'em!

I drove back to the Bambergerhof, stumbled up to my new room, gobbled some of the painkiller medicine, and slept till the next morning. No dreams at all as far as I could remember when I made notes in my diary the next day.

The next Sunday morning, despite my still painful leg, I took a train to Stuttgart. I figured there would be more room to stretch out my leg in the train and I could finish my Faulkner books and maybe get into Hemingway.

In daylight the new construction was even more impressive than at night. Stuttgart was a great city struggling to be reborn—and succeeding.

All day I hobbled through the city and searched for a familiar beloved face. I realized that it would be pure luck if I found her. If I were in her position, I would have shaken the dust of the Mercedes-Benz city off my shoes as quickly as I could.

But, I told myself, I would keep in touch with the man who had saved my life.

Would I really? Or would I trust no one?

I was not so much hurt as numb. She was my love, my passionate partner, my whole life. And I had lost her.

Had I really ever had her?

Would I ever be able to answer that question?

When the numbness wore off, maybe the pain would start, just like my knee.

Was there a new life in Trudi's body when she kissed me good-bye? Somewhere in Germany was there a child in the making who would be my son or daughter?

I swallowed some painkillers and slept most of the way back to Bamberg.

Next week I would go back to the Outfit's rendezvous point and make sure they came every Thursday.

In the meantime, grace caved in on us.

27

Late Tuesday morning, Brigitta approached my desk. "Your knee is better?"

"Much better, thanks, Brig. I don't really need the cane, but it's fun to pretend that I'm a *Herr Feldmarschallgeneral.*"

"You look like one," she said, giggling. "But, Chucky, I need a favor."

"Good Chicago line. . . . Name it, you got it."

"Would you wait for the train this afternoon? I must do translation for Gen. Lucius Clay."

She handed me a tiny photograph of her husband, handsome and smiling in his *Wehrmacht* gray.

"I'm impressed. . . . Sure, I'll be glad to. Any special hunches about today?"

"I have special hunches about every day."

"What's Lulu doing here?"

"He and General Meade and the next chancellor will discuss police problems after the Federal Republic is established next year."

"I did not know they had chosen a chancellor."

"The people will vote for the Bundestag and they will choose the chancellor. Everyone knows it will be Konrad Adenauer."

"Good man?"

"He is of the Catholic Center Party like we are. He was the *Herr Oberbürgermeister* of Cologne. The Gestapo removed him because he was a democrat and because they couldn't intimidate him. The British reinstalled him and then removed him because they too could not intimidate him. Recently because of pressure from General Clay and President Truman, they restored him to office."

"Tough man. How old?"

"He was born in 1876."

"Seventy-one years old! He won't last very long."

"He is a very strong man. He was chairman of our Senate during the 1920s and resisted Hitler to the end. They were always afraid to kill him. He knows what German democracy should be like."

"That is?"

"Much like yours. Our states will be called *Lands* or *Länder* and they will have much power. In a truly federated country, nothing like the Nazis could ever happen again."

Her eyes shone brightly. She had something political to believe in again. I was skeptical about this old man. Were there enough people in the country who would really believe in a kind of United States of Germany?

"I hope it works," I said cautiously.

"It will be a great pleasure for me to meet him again. That would not be enough to keep me away from the *Bahnhof*. But they need me here and I cannot refuse after all that has been done for me."

"I'll be glad to wait for the train."

I wondered as I stood under an umbrella at the *Bahnhof* how long Brigitta's faith would last or even should last. Stalin was still sending a few prisoners home occasionally for no particular reason, save perhaps to torment those who were still waiting. Kapitän Kurt Richter was probably dead. Surely the odds were heavily against his surviving. Her confidence that he was alive was rock solid. But how much should one credit a wife's confidence?

I shivered again. Still a bitter winter. The sky was gray and the wind was biting. The rainstorm had ended in a drizzle. We'd have some nice weather for another month and then it would be rain every day, and soon after that winter would arrive. However, next spring I'd be on my way home.

The train from the border beneath Leipzig chugged into the station only a couple of minutes late. They said that Mussolini made the trains run on time in Italy. Hitler didn't do that in Germany. Here the trains *always* ran on time.

A few German civilians climbed off and a couple of our military personnel. No one else.

Another disappointment for poor Brigie.

I folded my umbrella and walked back to the Buick—now *my* Buick. I opened the door and paused to think a minute.

On other days she had not come up here—not many but a few.

This was the first time she had asked me to fill in for her. She must have had some sort of hunch that was different from the usual one.

So I turned to look back at the station, still a pile of ruins from one of the few air raids to hit the city. (It would be rebuilt by the time I left for home.) Walking slowly in front of the station was a man in a ragged *Wehrmacht* uniform and peaked fatigue cap. I drifted back to the station to get a good look at him.

He was obviously sick and weak. His cheeks were unshaven, his face was hollow from hunger, he was dirty and terribly thin. Yet, despite his hesitant gait, he had a certain jaunty air, a defiance of sickness and death.

I removed the photo Brigie had given me from the pocket of my Ike jacket. Up close he did look like he might be Kurt Richter. Only one way to find out.

"Herr Kapitän Kurt Richter?"

He was startled by the words and perhaps even more so by the comic-opera uniform.

"*Ja* . . ."

"Staff Sgt. Charles C. O'Malley, sir. Headquarters Company, First Constabulary Regiment, Army of the United States." I saluted. "Welcome home to Bamberg. Frau Richter sends her compliments, sir, and regrets that urgent duty as a translator for the next chancellor makes it impossible for her to be here, but she has sent me to represent her."

The man swayed as if he were about to collapse. But he spoke to me in good, Chicago English.

"My Brigie is still alive!"

"Very much so, sir, as are your children Heinrich and Cunnegunda. Lovely children, sir. Now, if you'll accompany me to the car"—I raised the umbrella and steadied him by taking his arm—"we will drive to the *Residenz* where the Constabulary is headquartered and then find you some medical assistance."

"Chancellor," he mumbled as we approached the car. "Who?"

"Well, I guess there will have to be some elections, but he is what we call the winter-book favorite."

"Ah? But who is he?"

"I understand that he is the *Herr Oberbürgermeister* of Cologne."

"Adenauer!" he exclaimed.

"That's it."

I eased him into the front seat and closed the door.

"I am confused, Sergeant," he whispered as I turned on the ignition. "How did my wonderful Brigitta know that I would be here today?"

"She didn't, sir. She has waited here every day for two years."

He moved his thin lips in what might have been a smile. "That would be my Brigitta."

"Mulier fortis," I quoted the Bible.

"Yes, *fortissima*. . . . You're from Chicago?"

"Absolutely, sir."

"You have taken care of my Brigitta?"

"Not exactly, sir. I'm kind of a photographer. I was taking pictures up here one day and she upbraided me for exploiting German misery. I told her that my picture was of fidelity, not misery. We spoke for a bit and I realized that she had studied in Chicago. We needed a really good translator and I felt that Chicagoans ought to stand together."

"Your family is in politics?"

"Kind of . . . like most Chicago Irish."

"I thought so. . . . Thank you for what you have done for my wonderful Brigie."

"She deserves the best, sir."

"What is your unit again, Sergeant?"

"Constabulary, sir. Kind of a national police force in the transition to the new German government. We wear these musical-comedy uniforms to persuade people, including ourselves, that we are an elite group, though to be perfectly candid, we're not, but neither is anyone else."

He smiled again and then drifted off into half-consciousness.

He opened his eyes and looked at me. "I am very tired and very weak, Sergeant, but also very happy, and"—he rested the claw that was his right hand on my arm—"very grateful to you."

Classy guy.

"Thank you, sir. But there are others more deserving of your gratitude."

We pulled up to the *Residenz* just as an array of brass, military and civilian, came out of the building. It was easy to pick out the next chancellor. He may have been a democrat politically, but this tall, dignified, aloof old man was a patrician to his fingertips.

I pulled up behind the string of black limos that were waiting to take them away and helped Kurt out of the car.

Konrad Adenauer was only a few feet away from me, chatting with General Clay and General Meade. I figured I ought to get his attention so he would see Kurt.

"Guten Tag, Herr Oberbürgermeister."

He looked up, startled. Then he gave me a slight, frosty smile. *"Guten Tag, Herr Roter."*

It could have meant Mr. Socialist, but in the context it meant only Mr. Redhead.

Generals Clay and Meade frowned. Then Adenauer recognized Kurt.

"Kurt?" he said hesitantly.

"Ja, Herr Oberbürgermeister." He saluted weakly.

The two men embraced. I think there was a tear in the corner of the eye of Der Alte (The Old One) as he would come to be called.

The exchange in German was too fast for me to understand in detail. Adenauer said that he had just seen Frau Doktor Doktor Richter and she was as lovely as ever. Kurt said he could hardly wait to see her and praised me for taking good care of her. Adenauer said that both of them were needed to build a new and democratic Germany and that he was more optimistic now that *"unser Kurt"* (our Kurt) was home.

I had the feeling that I was seeing here a hint of the new Germany, not a perfect Germany perhaps—no country is ever perfect—but a much better one than the German people had known for a long time.

Kurt and Adenauer disengaged. I held Kurt's arm again. I was introduced to General Clay, who returned my dubious salute with a crisp smile. "Good work, soldier."

"Thank you, sir. Now with your permission I'll bring Kapitän Richter to a reunion with his wife."

As we hobbled through the doorway, the *Oberbürgermeister* called, *"Herr Roter!"*

"Ja, Herr Oberbürgermeister?"

He saluted me and said, *"Danke schön, Herr Roter."*

"Bitte schön, Herr Oberbürgermeister." I saluted back.

I hoped that I would meet him again. As it turned out, I would.

Generals Clay and Meade were whispering, doubtless about me.

Clay was undoubtedly wondering where the hell Meade had found me.

Well, as the Chicago Irish in imitation of their Irish cousins would say, "Fuck 'em all."

We rested halfway up the steps while Kurt recovered his breath.

"Never fear, *Herr Roter.* I will survive."

"You damn well better, sir."

He made a sound that could have been a laugh.

There might have been better ways to arrange the reunion between these two married lovers that would have given them more privacy. Yet no one in the ballroom of the *Residenz* on the late afternoon of that gloomy day would ever forget what he saw.

Her back to the door, Brigie was pounding away furiously at her typewriter, oblivious to everything else in the room. Minutes of the meeting probably. When I came in with Kurt, everyone in the room stopped moving, stopped talking. In front of the general's office, Captain Polly was frozen into a statue. Softly and implacably, Kurt and I approached his wife.

He drew a breath when we stood behind her. Then, slipping out of my supporting arm, he placed both his hands on her shoulders.

"Brigie," he said gently. *"Liebe Brigie."*

Shocked, she looked up and then screamed, "Kurt!"

They did not so much embrace as collapse into each other's arms, both weeping softly.

The whole room applauded.

Kurt turned his face away from his frau and looked at me. "Why do they applaud, *Herr Roter?"*

"For your wife's fidelity, *Herr Kapitän.*"

He raised his arm in a feeble salute.

They cheered and applauded again.

Then Captain Polly and the general took charge. Kurt, leaning on his wife now, was promptly and efficiently spirited away to the American hospital, to whose services he was entitled since his wife worked for the American government.

"They're pumping antibiotics and nourishment into him," pretty Polly told me later. "He's close to starvation and has all kinds of infections, but he's going to be all right. They'll take care of him for a week or ten days and then send him home. Brigie and the kids are with him now."

"He damn well better be all right," I repeated my warning.

Polly tilted her head, as she usually did when trying to figure someone out, especially me.

"You're not just kidding," she agreed.

On Thursday afternoon I drove down to Büttenheim again and checked the place out. It was a pretty little town built on a couple of hills, with low mountains in the background, kind of like the pictures of towns in the Swiss Alps we had seen in our geography books. Men and women were working in the fields, raking in the last hay of the harvest. Cattle were contentedly grazing on meadows. An old Catholic church with an onion dome looked as if it had been repainted recently. A town that would have been perfect for a Disney film about the good princess and the wicked dwarf. I found it hard to believe when I was in Germany that so many pretty towns, too unimportant to be destroyed in the war, could exist in a country where there was so much ugliness.

I found the places in the town that would be perfect for my purposes. We would park the jeeps and the trucks and the buses for removing the prisoners (should there be any) off the main street. We would set up a command post behind the church, with communications back to the *Residenz* in the unlikely event we would need reinforcements, and a medic station nearby should there be any wounded, theirs or ours. We could set up in such a way that, once we deployed our combat platoons in the forest, someone driving down the two-lane highway would not know that there was a Constab any closer than Bamberg.

I remained pretty sure that our crooks were autobahn people and that they rarely if ever traveled the back roads. But there was no point in taking chances.

I checked carefully each spot on the aerial map I had liberated from the Seventh Army. The scheme looked good so far.

Would the Outfit fight back? Not very likely. They had probably made lots of money already, and a few years in a disciplinary barracks or even at Fort Leavenworth was a lot better than being dead. Still, they might.

Satisfied with Büttenheim, I returned to my Buick and searched for the two tracks that were the dirt road to the back door of the meadow. I thought I had a good idea where it was. Still it was hard to find, almost invisible. I backed into the trail and perhaps ten yards along its length, got out, and from the highway determined that the Buick was totally invisible.

All right, what we'd do is deploy our men and weapons at this point and send the vehicles and the required personnel back to Büttenheim. Then, preferably while it was still light, we'd march down the path and deploy ourselves around the edge of the meadow on three sides, far enough into the forest so that at night no one would see us, not even if a stray headlight should come close to where we were hiding.

Then we would wait; and I would pray that the rendezvous was not scheduled for three Thursdays out of four. I timed the walk from the two-lane road to the meadow. Between ten and fifteen minutes, say fifteen.

We would wait till the work had actually begun and crates of goodies were moving back and forth. Then General Meade would make his announcement on the portable public address system we would bring along, and hopefully the crooks would surrender. All very neat.

So I found my woodchuck position and curled up to wait for the two convoys to arrive. As soon as I was certain that it was another scheduled night, I would slip away back into the forest, pick my way through the trees to my car—more than fifteen minutes in the dark—and drive back to Bamberg. Again all very neat.

And much safer than the last time, if I didn't foul up one way or another. I had brought my flashlight, with new batteries and a spare set in the car, along with me to be used only in the direst situation as I crept back to the Buick. But the stars, which were dense in the sky above me, would probably provide enough light.

My knee was hurting again. A pain pill would help, but now was no time for deep sleep.

No camera this time. I had all the pictures necessary to make my case the next morning to the general. Camera in hand, I might take some new damn foolish chances.

Just as dusk was turning into night, as I rearranged my body in a foolish search for comfort, I felt something metal under my hand. The key, naturally. Now I had another spare. Damn fool.

About twenty-one thirty (I was wearing a luminous wristwatch this time), the first headlights broke the dark in the meadow. Approximately the same number of vehicles as the last time.

Nine-thirty was about the time I had noticed them on the occasions when I was on the autobahn and probably the same time as a week ago when my watch was of no help. So they were pretty punctual; they had reason to be. Get in, get it done, and get out. No communication necessary except if there was a cancellation. The other bunch should be here soon.

They were. At nine thirty-five they rolled into the meadow. This was the way it was supposed to have been a week ago. No wonder the Bamberg guys were upset about the delay. Probably they had to meet scheduled distributions when they returned to Bamberg. A clockwork system. Time for me to get out.

I waited a few more minutes, however, because I was fascinated by the scene. Twenty trucks and about forty men jammed into a couple of acres of meadow. The men were unloading and reloading government property as if they were preparing for the Normandy landing while bantering obscenely as GIs always do. Some of them probably were involved in Normandy, but hardly in the front lines. They didn't act like criminals and they probably didn't think they were criminals. They were just good Americans trying to make a little profit for themselves during dull duty in what used to be Germany. Stealing from the government was perhaps a crime technically but certainly not a *real* crime, was it?

Not quite innocents abroad, but not malicious either. In the Occupation, all were on the take, weren't they?

Their mental attitude was not my problem. I thought of the assault on Trudi. That was what the black market was about: preying on the hungry and the sick. Worse than rum-running for Capone during prohibition. I recognized the orderlies who had attacked her. I had expected they'd be part of the Bamberg convoy.

Definitely time for me to go. Unfortunately, as I struggled out of my woodchuck mode, I bumped against a dead branch on a small tree—that's what I thought it was anyway—and sent the branch crashing into the forest.

How could a single branch make so much noise?

I jumped as quietly as I could behind a big tree.

"What the fuck was that?" someone in the unloading circle said.

"I didn't hear anything."

"Someone out in the forest."

"Animal?"

"It didn't sound like no fucking animal."

"One of our guys taking a leak."

"I'm going to have a look."

A flashlight beam swept the area around me, brushing against the tree behind which I was hiding.

"See anything?"

"Nah."

Did he know that a primitive road led away from the meadow? Maybe he had never noticed it because at night it would not catch anyone's attention.

He kept swinging the light back and forth.

"Hey, there's a road here."

"So what?"

"I didn't know there was a fucking road here."

"What difference does it make?"

"People could come down the road. They could be spying on us."

"Hey, the bosses must know that. They're not worried."

"Maybe you're fucking right."

He walked a few feet down the road and stood next to the tree where I was hiding. Time stopped. I held my breath. I listened to the GI's breath and smelled his body odor. I willed for him to leave.

All right, wise guy, what do you do now? He isn't armed; why don't you knock him out or choke him or do something like the commandos do in the movies? Maybe shoot him with a bow and arrow, except you don't have a bow and arrow.

He swept the road with his light.

"Not much of a road. Doesn't look like you could get any of our vehicles down it."

Wrong, asshole. You can drive a Buick on this road. I know. I did it. A jeep could do it easily.

I could stab him in such a way that he would die silently. I didn't have a knife; I would not know how to use one if I did; and I couldn't plunge a knife into another human being's body, anyway.

He fanned the forest on the other side of the road with his light and then, beginning at the far reach of his beam, began to search my side, slowly moving the light in my direction.

Maybe, I prayed, he'll miss me.

A sharp noise erupted on the other side of the road, a creature of the night bolting through the forest. The GI fanned the forest in that direction with his light.

"A fucking deer!" He laughed. "Nothing but a fucking deer!"

"Let's get back to work. The bosses will say we're dogging it and dock some of our pay."

I was unwilling to start breathing until he and his buddy had returned to the work circle.

Wage slaves, was that all they were? But the courts-martial would give them the big sentences and let the officers off with a slap on the wrist.

I warned myself to be careful and crept back toward the highway. It was easier this time because of the starlight and because I knew the path a little better. It was probably safe to use my flashlight after the first hundred meters. But I wasn't going to take any more chances. I limped the last hundred meters to the car, climbed in, turned on the ignition with my rediscovered keys, and redeployed out of there in a hurry.

A letter from Rosie awaited me at the hotel. I read it as I swallowed a couple of pain pills.

Dear Chuck,

Thanks for the picture of the lovely beer garden. I'd like to sit in it with you some evening and drink beer (in very moderate amounts because that's the most I dare) and eat sausage and listen to the band playing polkas.

That's what they do in beer gardens, isn't it?

Do you drink beer in them? I bet you don't.

I'm still not sure that I'm no longer the obnoxious little Rosie who plagued your childhood. I have changed a lot, Chuck. Or sometimes I think I haven't changed at all. And then I think that maybe both are true. But I accept your offer of a truce and maybe even permanent peace. I can't promise that I'll always keep my bitchy little mouth shut, but I'll sure try.

Peg says that sometimes she thinks I'm too bright for my own good. I see too much and think too much. She says that's why we're a perfect match: we both think too much and worry too much. But the difference is that your worries are superficial and mine aren't.

I don't mean to insult you, Chuck, or your precious worries. I think that they're cute. But, because you're an O'Malley and have been loved intensely all your life, you don't have any deep down uncertainties. You are not ambitious enough, maybe, but, like Peg says, you're going to be a great man someday despite yourself. (She adds that will happen only if you marry the right woman, which I'm sure you will.)

Your worries don't go to the bottom of your soul like mine do. You are not afraid that you'll mess up and ruin your life. I am. If I amount to anything at all, it's because the wonderful O'Malleys have always loved me.

That's more than I want to say, but I've written it and I won't tear it up.

I'd better stop now. I've said too much already.

All my love,
Rosemarie

PS. Your last letter arrived just as I finished this one. There was nothing in the papers, so I guess you're all right. Please let me know for sure.

I would write a reply tomorrow. Now it was time to sleep.

In my dreams I was chased through a forest but not by GIs. Rosemarie and Trudi and Peg and maybe my mom ran after me, shouting GI curses.

The next morning, my knee dormant again, I sat across from General Meade at a conference table beneath the windows of his office. He would not like what I was about to say. I'd better do it right.

"Well, son, shoot!" he began with a skeptical frown.

"Sir, you told me several weeks ago that you told no one else in the office about our raid on the caviar smugglers. But did you tell anyone outside the office?"

"Certainly not," he bristled. "Are you accusing me of being the leak?"

At one time I was pretty sure that he was. Now I doubted it, but I had to be certain.

"Hardly, sir. I'm merely asking whether as a matter of routine policy you may have informed someone who was not in this office."

"I don't like the way this is going, son. I said I told no one and I meant no one."

I then told him who else might know.

"I can't believe it."

"A week ago Monday, sir, I took the liberty of driving back to the border post. I interviewed Sergeant Lane, who was in charge of the post. I showed him a number of pictures of officers and enlisted men and asked him if any of them had been a routine part of the smuggling operation. He identified this man as the leader.

"Here, sir, is an affidavit from Sergeant Lane, testifying to the identification."

General Meade shook his head sadly. "Well, I guess you've found the leak all right," he admitted grudgingly. "I almost wish you hadn't."

"Yes, sir."

"No way we can give him a pass, is there?"

"It's your call, sir."

The general nodded, still not quite willing to accept what my narrative implied.

"You remember, sir, the night last winter when I brought a shipment to you from Nürnberg?"

"I do. That wasn't black market, at least I don't know that it was."

"Do you remember anything else about that night?"

"Something about three hospital orderlies who had stolen penicillin and tried to rape a fräulein?"

"Yes, sir, a young German woman. You will also remember that I reported the crime to CID. They found the names of the men, but no action against them was ever taken."

He nodded glumly. "It all begins to fit together, doesn't it, Chuck?"

"There was something else that night. I did not mention it to you because it didn't seem important. I was delayed for about ten minutes between here and Nürnberg behind a heavy convoy that was occupying both lanes."

"They're not supposed to do that."

"So I understand, sir. I drove out there again on a recent Thursday evening and encountered the same convoy. They turned off the road at approximately the same point. I discovered that it was in this general area around Büttenheim." I showed him the large-scale aerial map I had liberated from Seventh Army. "The changes took place in this meadow."

I described their modus operandi.

"How do you know about this, son?"

"I was there, sir."

"You were there?"

"Yes, sir. I secreted myself in the woods and watched them."

"That was very dangerous."

"I don't believe it was, sir. Except to my knee when I stumbled into my car as I was redeploying down this road."

"I see. . . . Chuck, I don't doubt any of this, but do you have any proof that what you claimed to have observed was actually happening?"

"Of course, sir."

I removed my five best prints and spread them on the table, including the close-up of the leader of the Bamberg Outfit.

"How did you get these pictures?"

"I joined them, sir. I was wearing fatigues as they were. I assumed that they didn't know all their counterparts from the other end—whichever end it was. I reasoned that if I drifted in like I belonged there, no one would notice me. I did so and managed to take a few covert pictures."

"That was very, very risky."

I shrugged indifferently. "As you probably have guessed, sir, I was there again last night. So were they." I smiled slightly. "I didn't think more photography was necessary."

"No, it wasn't," the general sighed. He paused a moment to ponder. "Why, son?"

"Why did I conduct this investigation?"

"Oh, no. I understand that. You take your oath to protect the laws of the United States of America seriously . . . as I do, as much as it will pain me to do so in this matter."

Moreover, the general was well aware that if someone else discovered the black-market links when he was in command, he himself would be suspected and held responsible. That would be the end of his career. He realized, or would shortly, that I had saved his ass.

"You mean why this officer . . . For the money I suppose. It was there to take. No matter what happened to his career in future years, he would never be poor. He did not expect to be caught."

"And he was responsible for the attempted rape on the young woman you rescued?"

"Indirectly, yes, sir."

The general nodded grimly. "I'm sure you have a plan, son. I presume it is brilliant. I hope it isn't too dangerous."

"It's not dangerous at all, sir. We will have to move on it in the utmost secrecy."

I outlined the plan I had developed in Büttenheim yesterday.

He nodded. "I see you've thought it all through."

"Yes, sir."

"Three platoons? B Company?"

"Yes, sir. We brief the officers on Thursday morning and forbid them to discuss it with anyone. We gather the troops at sixteen hundred and take the two-lane highway to Büttenheim. Only when we've mobilized the troops there do we explain the mission to them."

He studied the maps and then studied me. "What are you going to be, Chuck?"

"You mean when I grow up, sir?"

"All right, young man, what are you going to be when you grow up?"

"An accountant, sir."

His laughter at that filled the whole episcopal throne room.

I didn't see what was so funny.

So, it was all set.

Now to respond to Rosemarie.

Dear Rosemarie,

I'm fine. Everything went well. Someday I'll be able to give you all the details.

It's kind of interesting here now, all kinds of other things going on about which I can't write, but I can explain later. General Meade has moved me from the Vinehaus to the Bambergerhof across the street, a real hotel, even a luxury hotel I imagine. I have never lived so well in all my life and don't expect that I ever will again. Also he has assigned a brand-new Buick to me *indefinitely*. I guess they think I'm making a useful contribution, though I'm not sure why. Maybe because I've been limping around here for the last week with a banged-up knee I won in a football game!

No, it wasn't football. I bumped into my car during a night operation. Typical Chuck O'Malley gaffe. It's mostly better now and I can walk without a limp most of the time, but I kind of like limping a little and carrying my cane, which must have belonged once to a *Feldmarschallgeneral*. The Germans have a way of running words together, don't they?

Speaking of Germans, you remember Brigitta, the woman who has waited at the *Bahnhof* every day for her husband? Well, he finally came home, half-dead but only half. They're very happy, for which I don't blame them. He's recovering in the Army hospital. And I met a man the other day who they say will be the next chancellor here when they get a government organized. His name is Konrad Adenauer, though I suspect you'll never read about him in an American paper. He is a democrat (and Catholic) and has a long record as an anti-Nazi. He seems one tough, patrician son of a bitch. But I kind of liked him.

Now as to Rosemarie (née Rosie), you are too hard on your- self—which is what you say to me. Let's both agree that the charges are true on both sides and take it from there. You're going to be a great woman. And as for love, you'll always have the crazy O'Malleys around to protect you and care for you and support you and love you.

With them in your corner, you can't possibly lose—unless they drive you crazy first!

I'm looking forward to seeing you again soon.

Love,
Chuck

On the following Monday, General Meade, Colonel Nettleton, and I went over to the hospital to see Kurt Richter—but only after we were sternly warned by Captain Polly that, although he was *much* better, we should under no circumstance wear him out.

To which I replied that I wouldn't, but I couldn't testify for the general or a certain Boston Irishman.

I lugged along, schlepped as Dr. Berman would have said, a thin package.

Actually Kurt looked like a different man. He was still weak and thin, but the food and the medicine fed into him by the needles sticking out of his arm had transformed him. His skin was clear and bright, his voice strong, his eyes lively. He reminded me a little of John Nettleton, not as tall and not as wide and a lot more handsome in chiseled Teutonic fashion; but he displayed the same kind of facile expressions—mobile, shrewd, witty. His eyes twinkled and his lips twitched mischievously, and his smile and laughter were quick and sincere.

Not what one would expect of a man who had led a squadron of Tiger tanks. Nor for that matter of a man who had led a squad of Shermans. Kurt and John hit it off right away, as one might have expected they would.

"I don't know what you people put in these bottles." Kurt gestured at the one over his head. "They certainly work. I never expected to feel alive again."

"We made a lot of progress during the war in developing medicines," the general said.

"Thank God something good came out of it. . . . I still don't quite understand," Kurt added, "why you are salvaging me."

"You're a dependent of an American employee," General Meade responded.

"Dependent?"

"The general means relative," I interjected.

"I don't mind being a dependent or a relative or anything else." Kurt smiled. "I am always astonished by American generosity."

"Soothes our consciences," I offered.

Both Kurt and General Meade looked at me as though I had said something odd. In fact, I had spoken the truth—which may be odd.

"You were in the battle of Kursk," I said, changing the subject, "weren't you? The biggest tank battle in history?"

"Is that what they are calling it? It was a stupid mistake in a stupid campaign in a stupid war. Anybody who thought about it knew we had already lost. The Russians were making more tanks than we were and better ones too. Our Tigers were no match for their T-34s. Our eighty-eight shells couldn't penetrate their armor except if we hit the vents in the back of them. Most of our gunners weren't that good. The generals wanted to pull back to Poland and resist there. That damn fool wouldn't let them. He couldn't admit that invading Russia was a disastrous mistake. I haven't caught up yet on what happened after Kursk, but the end result is pretty clear, isn't it?"

"You think the war was lost at Kursk?" John Nettleton asked. Typical American, he thought it was lost at Normandy. How could the war have been lost without us?

"It was lost when we began it," Kurt snapped bitterly. "It was lost when we invaded Russia. It was all folly . . . and I worry about my part in it. I thought it necessary to defeat Communism. Now I realize that we were as bad, maybe worse. Losing was bad, but winning would have been worse."

"The war is over," General Meade said softly.

"It is over." Kurt shook his head sadly. "Yet for some of us it will never be over."

Changing the subject again, I said, "Tell us about the battle of Kursk."

"Well, in their winter offensive in the Ukraine in 1942–1943— after they had destroyed our Sixth Army at Stalingrad—the Russians had pushed a deep salient into our lines." He drew a large, imaginary U on the bedsheet. "They had recaptured Kharkov for the second time—what was left of it—right here and were hoping to push on to Kiev, which was here. But they bogged down in the mud and ran out of gasoline and supplies. Our generals had the wonderful idea of snipping off that salient and doing to the Russians, who were building up their forces, what they had done to us at Stalingrad. The sensible thing would have been to attack here and here"—he gestured with his fingers, at the base of the salient—"but they decided to confront the Russians up here at the apex so they could take on and destroy the Russian tank forces. That was one stupid decision we can't blame on Hitler. We had three thousand tanks, including many of our new Panthers. I don't know what General Hoth, the commander of our Fourth Panzer Army, thought, but in the field we knew that we had all those tanks and eighteen hundred planes. Most of us were convinced that we were better than the Russians. I had my doubts. They had more tanks and I had seen one of the T-34s we had captured and I knew it was better than ours. Still, I was convinced we were more skillful."

He paused for breath. If Captain Polly had been there, we would have been banished from the room.

"So"—he shrugged—"they were at least as good if not better. It was a hot, sultry summer morning, and we charged into them with formations of two hundred tanks, like Tennyson's light brigade. They counterattacked with even more tanks. It was a nightmare after that. We were fighting in clouds of dust that turned day into night. Often we were shooting point-blank range at each other. Airplanes screamed out of the sky, Stukas dive-bombed the Russians, but they still kept coming. Most of us were temporarily deaf because of the sound of the machines and the artillery and the rockets. It became almost hand-to-hand combat. We would discover a T-34 coming out of the mists, just as they had discovered us. We would fire at each other, not twenty-five yards away sometimes. Even if we got off the first shot, it would often bounce off their armor. In that four- or five-hour nightmare the battle was lost. Then a big summer rainstorm hit us, lightning and thunder even louder than the guns. The dust cleared away, but it was impossible to see through the heavy rain. Still we shot at everything that moved. We bumped into abandoned tanks and crunched over hundreds of dead bodies. I remember wondering whether hell could be any worse."

Kurt sighed deeply. The general and I said nothing.

"I've been there, Kurt," John Nettleton said in almost a whisper. "A place called Saint-Lô. Nothing like Kursk, but I'll not forget it either."

"You won?"

"Just barely."

Silence pervaded the room. The war in the west was over after Saint-Lô, but there was no point just then in adding that information to the conversation.

With another sigh, Kurt went on.

"We held them. A standoff. Except that we were the attackers and our attack had failed. The next morning when the sun rose, they had another thousand machines lined up against us. That's when our generals decided to withdraw. My panzer was hit as we were covering the retreat. Our ammunition exploded. Everyone else was killed. I thought about charging the T-34 that killed my men with my bare hands. Then I thought of my beautiful Brigitta and wanted to live. Someone took care of that T-34 anyway, a direct hit on the ammunition. The shock knocked me over. When the Russian infantry captured me later, I was wandering around in a daze. They weren't bad men. Before we were turned over to the prison camps, they treated me much better than we would have treated one of theirs, though"—he grinned—"not as well as you Americans have. It was only the picture in my head of my wonderful Brigitta which kept me alive."

"Any man with a wife like Brigie would want to stay alive."

"Perhaps. Even now I think I'm selfish. All my men are dead; all my friends are dead. And I am home with my wife and"—he waved a hand weakly—"in the luxury of an American hospital."

"As my mother would say, God must have something special for you to do."

He closed his eyes.

General Meade looked at me as if to say, "Should we leave now?" You bet.

"Chuck, if I may call you that, *Herr Roter*, do you have that picture of my Brigitta at the *Bahnhof*?"

"Sure. I thought you might want to see it." I opened the package I had brought along and presented him with an eleven-by-fourteen print on the best paper I could find, mounted on a sturdy backing. Brigie did not look as healthy and vital as she was now, but the shot showed a haunting and appealing—and determined—woman, whose allure no one could escape.

"I call it 'Fidelity.' "

"It is my Brigitta," he said as he admired the print. "This will appear in a book? It should be in a book."

"I just take snapshots," I said.

"A man that sensitive ought not to be a tank commander," General Meade said to me as we left the hospital.

"No one, sir, should be a tank commander," John commented.

"He will have a hard time," I said. "So will she."

The general merely nodded.

Would they make it? I wondered. They damn well better.

On Thursday morning, we briefed the officers of B Company in their barracks over in Bamberg Nord. A major, two captains, and three lieutenants. They did not much like the idea of a sergeant outlining tactics on a large aerial map—with a pointer no less.

"How the hell do we know they'll be there tonight?" the major demanded in a surly tone.

"We don't, sir. They have been in the same meadow on the last three Thursdays, but we cannot be sure that they don't omit one operation a month. It would seem, however, that the exchange of goods is a routine matter for them."

"What do we have besides your word," one of the captains growled, "that any of this has happened?"

I placed my prints on the briefing table, not including the close-up of our suspect.

"How did you get these, kid?" Lieutenant Lowry, a young shave-tail, just out of the Point and not two years older than me, demanded.

"I merely walked among them, Lieutenant Lowry, sir. In the dark they all assumed I was from the other convoy."

"Very risky," said the major with a hint of respect in his voice.

Very crazy too, I thought, but did not say. "Photographers will risk anything, sir, to get a good shot."

They didn't laugh. Dullards!

So we left Bamberg Nord late in the afternoon, under a clear

blue sky. It was a pleasant day, but it might be a chill evening. Everyone was dressed in combat fatigues instead of fancy uniforms and
with helmets over helmet liners. The troops were silent for most of
the ride on the two-lane road down to Büttenheim. Most of them
had not been in combat and clearly did not relish the prospect of
going into battle against fellow Americans. They were not supposed
to know what the operation was about, but they had doubtless heard
rumors.

There were the usual snafus—flat tires on some of the vehicles,
mechanical failures on others, wrong turns by those trying to catch
up. We had been a half hour late leaving Bamberg Nord. After the
general had completed his detailed briefing behind the onion dome
in Büttenheim, we were almost an hour behind schedule. It was already getting dark. We gotta hurry up.

I was the only one who knew what that trail was like, and I didn't
want to lead two hundred men down it in the dark.

"Now, remember this," General Meade continued to babble.
"Most of these men are not armed. They may be criminals but they
are Americans just the same. We will try to avoid violence. After I
order them to put up their hands, you emerge from the forest with
your weapons at the ready. I will then order them to drop such
weapons as they may have. Then we will move in and take them into
custody. Keep your safeties on until I give the order to open fire. Is
this clear?"

The men nodded solemnly. This was not the cushy garrison duty
that they had come to take for granted.

"All right! Let's move out." The general sounded a little bit like
John Wayne in later films.

The thought of these kids (most of them my age) flicking their
safeties off and opening fire terrified me. They would kill a lot of
unarmed men and maybe some of their own men too. I resolved to
stay out of the line of fire.

We found the trail on the first effort, thank heaven. It was already
dusk when they had all dismounted from their trucks and the general
and I began to lead them down the trail. I had slung my weapon
over my shoulder and secured my Leica and extra rolls of film in one
thigh pocket of my fatigues and Rosie's Kodak in the other. I made
sure a dozen times that my safety was on.

As we blundered through the forest and night quickly spread over the sky, I felt for a moment or two that I was Dan'l Boone leading the settlers out of the village and into the forest to repulse a marauding band. I figured then that it was probably the most exciting thing that would ever happen in my life (I was wrong), so I might just as well enjoy it. Thus far, I felt no fear, no tight knot in my stomach, no dry throat, no rapidly beating heart.

Routine. Piece of cake. Right?

The men complained about everything, as GIs will do—the dark, the rough trail, the underbrush, the cold.

"Quiet back there," the general yelled.

That shut them up for a few minutes.

"It is absolutely essential that when we get into the perimeter around the meadow, they be quiet," I told him.

"Don't worry, they'll be quiet."

Only a few traces of light were still in the sky, rose and gold stains from the sunset, when we finally deployed around the meadow. The general supervised the deployment and made sure that we were far enough into the trees so that the headlights of the trucks would not pick us up when the two convoys bumped into the meadow.

"How long, son?"

"Half hour maybe an hour."

I fixed a small (for those days) flash attachment, purchased the day before at the PX, on my camera. I would use it on both cameras, so there would be no time wasted in changing films. I had practiced the night before switching the flash from one camera to the other. I had finally got the hang of it.

The cameras were my idea, another nutty one that almost got me killed.

As we waited, I was still not afraid.

Dummy.

An hour and a half later, neither convoy had arrived.

"They're late tonight, son."

"Yes, sir."

Maybe somehow they had got wind of our operation. Or maybe it was just a night off.

A half hour later, the general whispered, "How much longer should we wait? The men are pretty restless."

We would not be able to keep this operation a secret. By to-morrow evening, everyone in Germany would know about it. Our suspect would simply suspend operations.

"Fuck 'em," I snapped. "We should wait till the convoys arrive."

Then I added belatedly, "Sir."

What the hell, the Army wasn't going to be my career.

I thought about Trudi. She had exploded with joy when I told her that I had new papers. Was that what she wanted all along? Was I played for a sucker so she and her mother and sister could get the documents they needed?

The more I thought about it, the more I became convinced that this is what had happened. But the painful emptiness inside me did not diminish.

Finally, two and a half hours after we had settled in and all of us were shivering with the cold, just after the general had shouted an order for silence, the first headlights poked through the woods. They pulled up to our side of the meadow and turned off their lights. It was the Bamberg convoy. Sam Houston Carpenter's voice was louder than those of the others as the men stretched their legs outside the trucks.

He had hassled me throughout the summer not because he wanted Brigitta, not because he was in league with Agent Clarke, but because he was worried I might go after the three hospital orderlies he had not arrested and they would talk. Dummy.

Then the second convoy appeared and the unloading and reload-ing began, a smooth, efficient, and practiced routine. As before, twenty trucks, including the two tankers and forty or so men. We watched them for a couple of minutes. I heard the general fiddle with the mike on the portable PA we had brought along.

"All right, you men, listen to me. I am General Radford T. Meade. You are surrounded by my Constabulary troopers and are under arrest. Put your hands behind your heads *now* or you will be charged with resisting arrest. Anyone who reaches for a weapon will be shot. Now *move!*"

As they did, the PA whined loudly.

The black-market guys hesitated, paralyzed by the sudden voice out of the dark forest and the ominous screech from the PA. Then blinking against the lights of their trucks, they saw our men slipping out of the forest with their weapons ready, ghosts in the night from some long-forgotten army.

"Last warning." The general sounded mad. "Hands over your heads or we open fire."

They complied quickly after that.

Where was Staff Sgt. Charles C. O'Malley at that point? Cowering behind the general where he belonged? No, he was out in front of everyone else, shooting away with his two cameras and right in the line of fire.

Asshole.

Dick McQueen's hand moved slowly toward the huge Colt .45 he was lugging in a massive holster. Then he lost his nerve. I caught him in the act with the Leica.

"That's better," General Meade said calmly. "Now those who are carrying side arms step one pace forward."

A dozen men, probably officers, stepped forward hesitantly. Sam Houston was the last to move, Dick McQueen the first. A brave man, if a crook. I felt sorry for him.

Our men slowly closed in, a noose tightening around the crooks' necks.

"Now unfasten your gun belts and drop them, real carefully."

The fight was gone out of the guys on the other side. They did exactly what they were told, even Carpenter.

I switched to the Kodak, changed the flash, put the Leica in my pocket, and continued to shoot, still a good five yards ahead of the rest of the Constabs.

"All right, men," the general ordered, "take these criminals into custody."

Our guys moved into the circle of light and began fastening handcuffs on our prisoners, despite loud protestations of innocence from the latter.

McQueen, in a last desperate ploy, rushed up to the general. "What the hell are you doing? I've had this crowd staked out for months! You're ruining it all!"

"Yes, sir!" Sam Houston joined him. "We just about had them! This is a big mistake!"

I got a couple of marvelous shots of him, the sort of thing that in some future election campaign would be useful to his opponents.

"Too late, Sam," the general said sadly. "We know now what game you've been playing."

I had run out of film in the Kodak and tried to reload the Leica with hands that, I noticed for the first time, were trembling. So maybe I was a little afraid after all. I finally got the film in and tried to switch the flash.

McQueen continued to argue with the general. He was not one of these criminals. He was preparing a major operation to seize the leaders of the gang. Why in the hell was the general ruining it?

The general lost his patience. "Shut up, Dick. You're lying through your teeth. . . . Cuff these two men!"

I heard the noise of a brief tussle and a warning cry of "Look out!" My Leica finally in operation, I looked up and saw Sam Houston Carpenter pointing a small pistol at my head.

"Die, you sneaky little bastard!"

For want of something better to do, I pointed the camera at him and flicked the release. Rosemarie's face appeared in my imagination. I think I may have said a quick Act of Contrition.

The exploding flash disturbed Sam Houston. He fired and missed. The small-caliber bullet, like a crazed mosquito, hissed by my head. I shot again.

And managed to catch in the picture Tim Lowry, the young second looey from the Point, twisting the weapon away from Sam Houston. Lowry hit him in the jaw just once, and Sam collapsed into the grass. The shavetail leaned over him and pointed the weapon at the middle of Sam's forehead. A couple of our guys ran up and cuffed him and held him on the ground.

That made an excellent shot too.

"O'Malley," Lowry said in an awed voice, "you're plain crazy. Why didn't you run?"

"It's the iron bars that were tied around my feet."

The lieutenant laughed. "Good work anyway."

"The same to you and many more."

We shook hands and grinned at each other. "Thanks," I said, "you're pretty quick."

"So are you."

"What the fuck were you doing?" General Meade bellowed at me.

"Getting evidence, sir. It will be hard for the courts-martial to ignore photographic evidence."

I was wrong. In some of the cases, the courts-martial ignored my pictures.

I continued to shoot away at the scene until I ran out of film.

The rest was routine. The prisoners were herded into buses. Some of our men were detailed to drive the vehicles back to the *Residenz*. I sat in the Buick and waited for the general. My knee was hurting again. I was numb emotionally. I objectively considered the image of the pistol pointed at my head and listened with similar detachment to the whisking noise of the bullet—a .25 it turned out— as it buzzed past my ear. I was still alive, so why worry? Except that I was a damn fool.

"Good thinking, son," the general said as he motioned me out of the driver's seat. "Those pictures of yours will be indispensable as evidence."

"Yes, sir," I said glumly. I was perfectly capable of driving myself, I thought. So what if my hands were quivering?

General Meade was quiet for most of the ride back.

"Would you consider accepting a field commission, son?" he asked me as we pulled into Bamberg Nord.

"Thank you, sir, but no thank you."

"I thought so. I'm sorry but I understand."

"Thank you, sir."

No way I wanted to stay in the service for a couple of more years. Good thing I turned him down or I would have ended up in Korea.

It was four-thirty when I sank into my bed at the Bambergerhof. I figured I would sleep soundly till noon. Instead I started to shiver. Uncontrollably. For the next three hours. I still shiver when I have dreams of that small muzzle pointing at my head. Sometimes I practice saying the Act of Contrition in a hurry. Just in case.

There was no word from Trudi that day and no letter from Rosemarie. I felt abandoned. On Saturday as usual I boarded the train for Stuttgart. My knee was in good enough condition for me to roam the streets all day. I thought I saw her a couple of times in the stores, but it was always someone else.

Most of the enlisted men we picked up at Büttenheim got two

years (which would mean a little more than one year with time off for good behavior). A few officers got a year (nine months) and were dishonorably discharged. The other officers were acquitted or fined. Sam Houston Carpenter got six months and a discharge "without honor." Dick McQueen, the brains of it all, was permitted to resign without charges being brought. General Meade got another star on his shoulder. The kid from West Point who had saved my life was soon wearing a silver bar. I got another stripe on my arm and a medal.

That was that.

"He tried to kill me," I protested to the general when he told me of the court's verdict on Carpenter.

"I know, I know. He was very cooperative in testifying against the others. The judge instructed the jurors to consider the possibility that he really was spying on the ring and the possibility that he was under severe strain when he shot at you."

"Not as much as I would have been if he hadn't missed."

"Sam has lots of good friends," the general murmured.

"He sure does."

"And he acted every inch the soldier during his trial."

"Yeah."

"He'll never dare run for political office anyway."

"Yeah?"

"Someone sent those pictures of him to the newspaper in the capital of his state. Seems that the paper is on the opposite side of Sam's family. They spread same all over the front page."

"Can you imagine that?"

We did haul in some of the big fish in the operation, but only one did time in a disciplinary barracks. In a few months a new operation was hard at work. New faces maybe, but the same old crimes.

On Monday the week after our roll-up of the black-market gang, Kurt Richter went home from the hospital, not completely better but much improved. Brigie was fretful and nervous that afternoon, but radiant the next morning.

Good for them, I thought.

Now all the adventures were over and I could settle down to my class work.

28

There was one more small matter to clear up.

Brigitta was not happy. Each morning she showed up at her typewriter sad and distracted.

You get what you've been praying for and it turns out to have a bitter taste.

"What's the matter with herself?" I asked Captain Polly.

"Kurt is acting like a bastard," she said with the contempt that outraged women of our ethnic background muster when men are not "acting the way they should."

"What's he doing?"

"Well, he's not beating up on her. But he's nervous and irritable and shouts at the kids and won't talk to her."

"Needs to see a shrink."

"Refuses. Absolutely. He can take care of his problems himself, if only his family would give him a little support. Someone ought to talk to him."

"Okay. I'll go over tomorrow morning."

"You?" She opened her mouth in surprise. "What do you know about marriage?"

"Nothing, but I do know an asshole when I see one."

"And you will take Nan out on Friday night."

"Huh?"

"Nan Wynn on a date—D-A-T-E. We've been talking about it for days and you finally agreed."

"Against regulations."

"We've been through that, Chucky. She's not going to wear her bars."

"No money."

"Come on, how much money did you make selling those pictures of the operation to *Life*?"

"Classified. Besides, when the courts-martial decided they didn't need the pictures, I couldn't let them go to waste. It was my film."

I had made enough and a lot more than enough to fill the void in my bank account from the Trudi operation.

"So you will take her out? She is a sweet little thing and very vulnerable and very lonely. She's afraid of most of the men around here."

"But not of me?"

"You're dangerous, Chucky, very dangerous, but you'd never hurt a woman."

"Yeah?"

"Will you take her out?"

"Sure," I said as if I couldn't understand what all the discussion was about.

Actually, the date was fun. As soon as she felt relaxed and secure, Nan was a delightful young woman. So we dated for a while and both of us enjoyed it and became fond of one another. I had never dated before and I discovered that I liked it (brilliant discovery, Charles C.). The protocols of a date, the flirting and the restraints, the careful exploration of each other's personality, the advances and the retreats, were a fascinating experience, especially after the high intensity of Trudi.

Early on, the two of us decided implicitly that while we enjoyed each other's company, we had no future together. That was all right, our relationship was in the present.

It was all chaste, well, moderately chaste. Sweet but hardly passionate kisses and only featherlight petting.

I forgot about Trudi when I was with Nan, which was a sign of something, I told myself, but I wasn't sure of what.

When it was time for me to leave for home (and Captain Polly had long since left), I figured that I was responsible for finding another date for Nan. A young banker named Ben Harding was working with currency-control people at figuring out how the new German currency system would work when the Federal Republic came into existence. A good-looking guy, he was from the same part of the world as Nan, shy like her, and the scion of a wealthy banking family.

Why not?

The morning after their first date, she stood next to my desk, hugging herself as if she were standing in a snowstorm. "He is so sweet, Chucky, so sweet."

A half hour later Ben called me.

"That was quite a tractor that ran over me last night, fella. I didn't even see it coming."

"I told you that you'd have a good time."

"That doesn't even come close to describing it."

"Good luck."

"I figure I have that already after last night."

"Then congratulations."

He did not try to persuade me that I was being premature.

The morning after Captain Polly had informed me about the problems with the Richters and sandbagged me into taking Nan out, I waited till Brigie was in the office and then ducked out and dashed over to the Seventh Army Hospital.

"I need a favor," I told Jack Berman.

"Always the Chicagoan!"

"I'm going to bring a patient over to you in an hour or so. Panzer commander, dependent of a Constab employee. I want you to cure him."

"We don't cure," he said, laughing, "we help people to become a little better. Tell me about him."

I told him the whole story.

"You are just a little mad yourself, Chuck. You do know that, don't you?"

"Regardless. You will help him, won't you?"

"Naturally."

Yes, naturally.

I then stormed over to the Richter apartment.

"Good morning, Chuck," Kurt said genially, a book in his hand, finger marking the place. He was wearing a new brown suit with a light sweater—clothes that Brigitta had doubtless bought for him. He seemed healthy again, contented and happy.

"Kurt Richter," I began mildly, "you're a fucking asshole."

"Pardon me?" He seemed genuinely surprised.

"Any man who has a wife like Brigitta and hurts her is a moron; such a man ought to be sent back to the prison camp for the rest of his life."

He sat down in his rocking chair, put his book on the floor, and tried, all too casually, to light his pipe.

"I do not hit her," he said uneasily.

"Damn good thing for you that you don't."

"She has spoken to you." He glared at me suspiciously.

"Don't give me that fucking Prussian look, shitface. Of course she didn't talk to me. For some stupid reason, she's still loyal to you. Sure, you don't hit her, you only break her heart."

He put the pipe down and hunched forward. "I don't want to do that. But they don't understand what it was like."

"And you don't understand what it was like for them."

"It was much worse for me."

"So an intelligent man like you is going to go through life comparing pains?"

He shut his eyes and thought about it. "That would be very foolish, wouldn't it?"

"Fucking foolish."

"You think I should talk to a psychiatrist at the Army hospital?"

"You mean you aren't seeing one every day?"

"No . . . ," he admitted.

"Then you really are an asshole. You don't deserve Brigitta."

"I certainly do not deserve her."

"Well?" I demanded.

"Now? Today?" He smiled ruefully at me.

"Why not?"

"No reason," he sighed. "You will of course accompany me to make sure I do not turn away?"

"You bet your life I will."

So we walked over to the hospital on the other side of the canal.

"That is not your normal language, is it, Chuck?"

"You're fucking right, it's not my normal language."

We laughed together, male conspirators against what John Knox had called the "monstrous regiment of women."

The next day Brigie seemed more happy and relaxed, but hardly what you would call serene. It was a slow process, but as the months went on, they seemed to be working it out.

Kurt had extravagant words of praise for the wonderful Dr. Berman.

"He is Jewish, Chuck. Did you know that?"

"No kidding."

"I do not understand, why is he so concerned about me?"

"Ask him sometime."

I don't know whether Kurt ever did.

I celebrated St. Nicholas's day with them. The two kids were ecstatic about their presents. The parents kept their arms around each other through the evening, save when I was being served food. They told me that Brigitta was pregnant, an announcement at which I pretended to be surprised.

There were two big farewell parties that December—one for the Nettletons, who were returning to civilian life and politics in Boston, and one for General Meade, who was assuming command of an armored division at Fort Knox. The parties were sad for me. I was losing another family. Everyone else treated the events like a celebration.

The new commander of the Constabulary in our part of Bavaria was a quieter and more formal man than General Meade and ran a much less relaxed operation. While he didn't particularly enjoy my style of wit or mode of dealing with superior officers, he had been told by General Meade that I was valuable and used my help on an occasional project. He didn't mess with my Buick or my room at the Bambergerhof. I don't think he ever found out that I was dating his adjutant. He surely would not have approved. He even considered getting rid of Brigitta, but was talked out of that by a phone call from General Clay.

I forget who talked to General Clay.

So my time was virtually all my own during the last five months in Bamberg. I did a lot of studying and reading. Rosemarie and I continued to write to one another, but we were afraid of what we had said in previous letters. So, our correspondence was less intense and self-revelatory and eventually less frequent.

I took the extra money remaining from my sale to *Life* and paid a visit to my old friend Max Albrecht.

"Max, I want twenty of your best prints of German warplanes. Thirty dollars a print."

He stiffened. "You're joking!"

"No, I want to see the prints first."

So we haggled over photography for an hour or so. The prints still hang in the office of my house in the dune—Heinkels, Junkers, Focke-Wulfs, Messerschmitts—and are probably worth a hundred thousand dollars now. At least.

I gave him the twelve fifty-dollar bills I had brought along. He put them in his pocket.

"You should count them."

"*Nein.*" He rolled his eyes.

"What are you going to do with the money?"

None of my business, but I was curious as to what kind of camera equipment he might buy.

That was not what was on his mind.

"A wife." He lowered his eyes shyly. "I now have enough money to marry. You wonder who she is? A young woman from Bamberg of course. Husband killed in the war. A small child. Girl. Very lovely, the mother I mean. Daughter too. We will be happy."

"I'm sure you will." I shook his hand. "Congratulations!"

And despite the pleasure of my dates with Nan, I continued to mourn for the lost Trudi.

I spent my Christmas leave in Rome that year, after another of my by then routine searches through Stuttgart. It was a disaster. Christmas is not the same, I would learn to my dismay, in the Mediterranean countries as it is in Northern Europe: not like the kind of warm, noisy family festival that it had become in the countries where winters are cold and hearts are distraught in the darkness of night. I learned also that Rome is one of the least religious cities in the world and that beneath the splendor and pomp of papal ceremonies there is hypocrisy and unbelief. I would remember that later when I went to Rome for other purposes.

"An empty place," I said to my priest recently after doing a book on the pope and the Vatican.

"Indeed." His nearsighted eyes blinked rapidly. "As to intelligence, sensitivity, and Christianity."

"I hope it shows in my pictures."

"Those who have eyes to see, as Himself put it, let them see."

"Do they realize how bad they look to the rest of the world?"

"Consider that Rome"—he tapped me on my chest—"is a proof that God protects Catholicism with Her special love."

"What do you mean by that?"

He beamed happily, as he always does when he makes a point. "We have been able to survive the corruption and the idiocy of the Romans."

Not an original argument with the good bishop, but still valid.

However, for a nineteen-year-old boy, sitting in a sidewalk café on the Via della Conciliazione on a warm and sunny Christmas morning and dreaming of Christmas at home, such wisdom was not available. The dirty, scruffy Vatican clergy with their haughty eyes and thin lips did not seem to have the Christmas spirit. Nor did the crowds of Romans who were able to celebrate the holiday without the need of going to mass—or when they went to mass without the need to remain silent during its most sacred moments.

I tried to read one of the English-language newspapers: Italy had a new republican constitution, the Greeks were driving back Communist rebels, a new political "third force" was emerging in France. Sugar Ray Robinson had defeated Chuck Taylor and retained his welterweight boxing title.

I crumpled the paper in disgust. Who cares?

Tears of homesickness stinging my eyes, I recalled our family carol sings—Peg with her incredible violin, Mom on the harp and singing soprano with Rosie, Jane and Michael doing the alto, Dad a solid if pedestrian bass, and me carrying, with considerable protest, the tenor line.

By the time I came back, Mike would probably be a bass too. Tall people are basses, short people tenors, right?

"Mom, it isn't fair that Chucky has a voice like that!"

"Hush, Peg dear, God gives each of us what we need. Besides he and Rosie blend so nicely, don't they?"

That Christmas in Rome I would not have minded being kidded about how well Rosie and I blended with each other.

I had found a priest hearing confessions in English in St. Peter's on Christmas Eve and made my peace finally with God in the matter of Trudi Wülfe.

"I committed sins of action with a woman, Father, scores of times."

"Scores? How many scores?"

"Six, seven."

"The same woman?" He did not seem angry, but then why should he be? If anyone had reason to be angry, it might be God.

"Yes, Father."

"Are you still seeing her?"

"No, Father. It's over. Irrevocably."

"She is dead?"

"No, Father, but . . . well, gone."

"I see."

"Yes, Father."

"You intend to avoid the occasions of these sins in the future?" He sounded young, perhaps ordained only a year or two.

"As best I can, Father."

"That's all God expects of us."

"Yes, Father."

He probably had me perfectly pegged. A GI with a German mistress. There were other details, but he would not care about them and they would not make any difference anyway.

"How old are you, my son?"

"Nineteen, Father."

"You have your whole life ahead of you—marriage, family, children, grandchildren. You don't want to endanger that, do you?"

"No, Father."

"I'm sure you know the risk of disease in these kind of relationships."

Disease? With Trudi?

Well, why not? There had been men before me, had there not?

"I don't think that would have been a problem in this case, Father."

"You cannot be sure of that. And you must be aware of the dangers of pregnancy and a marriage you don't want."

What about a marriage that I did want? Or thought I wanted?

"Yes, Father."

So I was assigned a rosary and adjured to go and sin no more.

I felt that God understood, more or less. I only wished that I could understand.

"God is quite ruthless," my little bishop sighs. "He pursues us in all relationships, even those of which his servants the moral theologians and the Church leaders disapprove."

"It was a ménage à trois?"

"I wouldn't put it past God."

If he is right—and his boss, Cardinal Sean Cronin (a distant cousin of the good April's), says that he always is—then I can make some sense out of the triad of Trudi and God and me.

But that is now. Long ago, sitting at the sidewalk café, nursing my cup of cappuccino and feeling utterly isolated from the rest of the human race, I saw for the first time how disgraceful my behavior in Bamberg had been. I had used a frightened young woman. I was complacent with my conquest, even though I had confessed it as a sin and promised I would not do it again.

I might indeed not do it again, but until that moment I had felt little remorse. I had soothed my conscience with the consolation that I had after all saved her life—probably anyway.

What would my mother or my sisters think of me if they knew what I had done?

They would be ashamed of me. And I ought to be ashamed of myself.

What would Rosie think of me?

It was none of Rosie's business.

And in feeling that I should be ashamed, I was ashamed. Bitter waves of remorse swept over me like a rising tide in a storm. I did not weep, but I wanted to weep.

I drained my cappuccino cup and hurried back to the little hotel off the Piazza della Repubblica that catered to American GIs. Since I could neither cry nor drink myself out of my loneliness and remorse, I did the next best thing.

I escaped from reality by sleeping through the rest of Christmas.

I awoke at three the next morning, still lonely, still remorseful, still disgusted with myself, still incredulous at how badly I had let my family down.

Please, God, don't let them find out.

I was still preoccupied with my guilt and had little time for thought about the evolving cold war and the Berlin airlift, which saved our former enemies from hunger, cold, and the Russians that winter. The Russians had closed all the ground routes to Berlin, thus violating the agreement about access to that city. So Allied planes flew supplies—five thousand tons a day—into the small Tempelhof airport in the center of the city for eleven months. The Russians finally backed down. When John Kennedy gave his famous "Ich bin ein Berliner" speech, it was in praise of the bravery of the people of Berlin during this siege. So quickly do enemies become allies!

I continued to dream about Trudi and my family, vague, horrible dreams in which Mom and Jane and Peg and Rosie became confused with Trudi and denounced me, together with her, for my sins.

—ᴈ 30 ᴈ—

What happened to the people who had been my family while I was in Bamberg?

The Constabulary was rolled up in 1949 when the new Federal Republic took over police duties. Loyal to the end, *Time* and *Life* both celebrated its great accomplishments in "bringing order to chaotic, postwar Germany."

We had not done all that badly at a job that was not all that difficult. Still, if a stumblebum such as me had become one of its folk heroes, the Constabs were not all that hot a unit.

In January of 1948, Kurt began teaching again at the university, as had his father before him. They named their new son Karl, which I thought was excessive. Eventually Brigie also began to teach. She won an American prize for her major book on how European historiographers had viewed American history—a fairly acerbic book for the gentle Brigitta. Her husband served as a member of the Bundestag (the federal parliament in Bonn) and became rector of the university in Bamberg.

General Radford Meade became Army chief of staff.

The Nettletons went back to Boston and became involved in local and national politics and raising a large family. John was a staff member of the Kennedy White House. The son who was conceived in Germany died twenty years later in Vietnam. A younger daughter did time in prison as part of the Berrigan crowd. She later returned to the family. The Nettletons nonetheless continued to be happy despite the sufferings. I see them at least once a year.

Der Alte, Konrad Adenauer, did indeed become the first chancellor of the German Federal Republic. Despite my predictions, he continued in office for fourteen years, resigning his office in 1963 at the age of eighty-seven. He continued in the Bundestag until his death four years later. He was truly one of the great men of the twentieth century. He and I would meet again. I was always *Herr Roter* to him and he *Herr Oberbürgermeister* to me, even when the proper title was *Herr Reichskanzler.*

Sam Houston Carpenter disappeared. He never ran for public office. Dick McQueen made a fortune in real estate development in California and was a political ally of Ronald Reagan's.

I don't know what happened to Rednose Clarke and I don't care. Someday maybe I'll ask some people I know at the Bureau about him.

Nan married her Ben Harding. They returned to Kansas and his family bank, which was very successful during the fifties and sixties. They had three children. Nan died of cancer in her early forties. She told me as I held her hand on her deathbed that she didn't mind dying young because she had enjoyed such a happy life.

Jack Berman is a distinguished psychoanalyst in New York and has written two books on survivors of the holocaust. We have lunch occasionally when I venture to Manhattan.

Max Albrecht became a world-famous photographer of airplanes. I bump into him and his wife occasionally, the latter as pleasant and happy a woman as I have ever met. Not one of your intense and neurotic Irish-matriarch types.

Trudi and Rosemarie? That's another story. Maybe a couple of other stories.

Most men of my generation look back on the late forties with what I consider shallow nostalgia. They had great times, they tell me, they grew up in those years, they became men, they found out who they were. Those were the good old days.

That was not my experience at all. I still shiver when I think of that bitter wintertime of my life. I didn't grow up. I didn't find out who I was. Those were not the good old days.

Mom would say when I came home that I had grown up. Dad would say that the Army had made a man out of me.

All of this is nonsense. I had not grown up. Perhaps I never grew up. The Army had not done anything positive for me. The notion that it turns a boy into a man is nostalgic rubbish. The "service" has never really helped anyone. I didn't learn much during those two years, a little about myself maybe and a little about humankind. But not very much about either. I had met some interesting people, taken some reasonably good pictures, and seen a few marvelous works of art. I had grown in years perhaps but neither in wisdom nor grace.

Or so I thought for most of my life. Now I'm not so sure. Maybe I did grow up a little, but not in the expected direction for someone who really wants to grow up.

John Raven and I fought it out after I returned home.

Trudi?

Of course she loved you, Chuck.

I would have married her.

I think she disappeared because she knew you would and that it would not work. She loved you too much to marry you.

I did a lot of damn fool things.

Chuck, you are the most brilliant and eccentric child of a brilliant and eccentric family. You've got to make your peace with the fact that you're a whimsical genius, dazzling but a little unusual.

I don't want to be brilliant. I don't want to be a genius, I don't want to be dazzling, and I especially don't want to be defined as unusual. I just want to be an accountant and live a normal, quiet life. I'm just an ordinary person.

You can look back on the last ten years and say that?

Why not?

Also you have a compassionate heart so large that it could embrace the whole world.

I do *not*. I'm a nasty, mean son of a bitch. And a heartless cynic too!

John laughed at me and we agreed to disagree. I'm still not sure after all these years which of us was right. Maybe I wrote this book to try to work it out in my head.

—ₑ*31*ₛ—

I did not recognize my parents on the day I was honorably discharged from the Army of the United States.

Somewhere in the Quonset-hut barracks a radio was playing "Buttons and Bows," a description of the kind of old-fashioned woman who was not waiting for me. I sighed and shoved Evelyn Waugh's novel *The Loved One* into my khaki duffel bag, on top of *The Heart of the Matter*. I began to zip the bag, tugged at the last obstacle, shoved the books down deeper, and quickly, before something else could pop up, pulled the zipper to the end.

I sighed again and walked out into the crystal sunlight of Fort Sheridan. Master sergeant or not, I did not like the Army. My two years of service in postwar Germany had earned the money for my college education and corrupted my morals. I was happy to leave the service, happy to be almost home in Chicago, happy that I would see my parents again. I was even happy that I had come home without any romantic entanglements—no German wife following me, no American girlfriend waiting eagerly for me.

It was the sort of postcard June day in which Chicago specializes, a day that not even the down-at-the-heels Fort could ruin: clear blue sky, light breeze, temperature in the low eighties, almost no humidity. The lake was a darker blue, color coordinated with the sky. On a Sunday like this, when you're coming home, you should be happy to be alive. The golf courses and the beaches would be jammed. Kids would be running and screaming. Softball games would be about to begin. Young lovers everywhere in the city would be holding hands against the coming of winter.

I didn't play softball or golf; I wasn't a young lover; and almost twenty, I wasn't a kid anymore.

Maybe that was the reason I was depressed.

I was to meet Mom and Dad in the lobby of the officers' club, a dilapidated red-brick building constructed before the First World War. Although he had left the Guard in 1945, Dad maintained some kind of vague relationship with the Army that gave him club privileges. I hoped we were not going to eat dinner here. I'd had enough Army food.

They were not in the lobby when I entered. A younger couple were staring at the lake through the window at the end. No one else around. I glanced at my (inexpensive) Swiss watch. Mom and Dad were never on time; so there was no reason to expect them to be waiting for me, even if they had not seen me in twenty months.

The orderly at the door considered me suspiciously. "This is the officers' club, Sarge."

"Discharged sarge," I said, spoiling for a fight. "I'm waiting for a member."

I glanced around the lobby. Where were they?

"Maybe you'd better wait outside—"

"Chucky." The young woman from the window embraced me, tears pouring out of her brown eyes. "You're so grown up, I didn't recognize you."

Mom's voice and Mom's eyes, so it must be Mom. And the red-bearded man pumping my hand must be Dad. What the hell! I hadn't changed, they had.

"Same weight," I said, "same height, still a skinny little runt with wire-brush red hair."

Mom held me by my shoulders at arm's length. "Same sense of humor too, but you have changed. Oh, Chucky, we've missed you so!"

The tears, embraces, and exclamations continued. I was forced to conclude that these were indeed my parents.

But why hadn't I recognized them?

Because they had changed, obviously. I was the same old pint-size cynic. They had become younger. And more affluent. Much more affluent.

Mom was wearing a fluffy and frilly light blue dress, buttons and bows I suppose, with a tight waist and a long skirt. Chic New Look. Her shoes and her hat were off-white, as were her purse and the rims of her sunglasses. She smelled of a cautious and expensive scent— hints of rare flowers—and her makeup was perfect. When I was growing up, she had almost never worn makeup. And there were a lot more curves than I remembered: she had put on some more weight since I left for Germany and no longer looked like a skinny if vaguely pretty refugee countess.

"Dear God, woman"—I patted her back—"have you become a fashion model or something? You're gorgeous!"

"That's the girl I married." Dad beamed proudly.

"Now I understand why!"

"Chucky!" she protested, blushing happily. "Both of you are very wicked, flattering an old woman's vanity."

"We'd better get her out of here, Dad." I took his right arm. "This kind of American woman could drive the troops to desperate action."

"Chucky!" The blush deepened as I hugged her again. "You stop this minute!"

God help me if I had.

Dad was still bald, so there was no reason for me to think that he was too young. No reason except the navy blue blazer, the white flannel slacks, the trim waist, and the trim red beard.

"Why the disguise?" I asked.

"Isn't it simply divine, Chucky? It makes him look so artistic."

"What the promising young architect wears? Kind of looks like a villain in a German opera, not that I saw any. Or maybe a pirate in Gilbert and Sullivan!"

I began to hum a patter song about pirates from Penzance. Mom and Dad joined in.

"We'd better get out of here," I suggested, "before they summon the MPs."

"You do look, well"—my father hesitated—"more mature."

"Maybe I've grown up a little in the last two years. But don't bet on it."

"What's that ribbon you're wearing?"

"Legion of Merit," I whispered because I still felt guilty about it.

"For extraordinary service in a position of grave responsibility?" The poor man was as excited as if he had won it. All he had done in the service was to come close to being buried alive in the flu epidemic of 1918.

"Something like that."

"You didn't tell us about that," Mom said.

"Nothing much to tell. Someday soon I'll tell you the story."

I had of course worn the ribbon to impress them.

I had grown older and they had grown younger. The chemistry between the two of them, once barely hidden, was now completely out in the open. He's a teenage lover with a beard and a woman in buttons and bows, and I'm an old man without any kind of woman.

Somehow, this is all wrong.

"You don't want to eat here, do you?"

"No thanks, Dad. Not another Army meal, not even an officer's meal."

"Then let's go, you two." Mom grabbed one of us with each arm and marched us toward the door. "We have a real surprise for dinner. And a serious problem to settle. Then we'll go home for a party with the rest of the family. They're dying to see you, especially poor little Rosemarie, but we said we had first claim."

"Suits me."

Under the cloudless sky again, I was still disoriented. This attractive twosome were clearly my parents, but what had happened to them?

Mom wore her sunglasses inside. Prescription lens? The new solution to nearsightedness—stylish bifocals?

How much had it cost? All of it, the clothes, the makeup, the scent, the food, the exercise, the fancy sunglasses? All right, we weren't poor anymore. The Depression (not yet called the Great Depression) was over, though I assumed that it would return. But Dad wasn't making that kind of money, was he?

"You want to drive it?" Dad gestured at the long, sleek, black Buick parked in front of the club. "You said you learned to drive in Germany."

"That's our car?"

"Your father's car," Mom said. "I have a cute little white Studebaker convertible."

"Matches the frames on your glasses? No thanks, Dad. I wouldn't want to celebrate my return by banging up this black beauty Buick."

They both laughed, as though banging up cars was no longer a problem.

Two cars? The only car the family had possessed when I left for Germany in late 1946 was a decrepit, old, secondhand 1936 Chevy

that Mom had bought for a hundred dollars to drive up to the Douglas plant where she slapped paint on B-24s.

"We can get you a car"—Dad hesitated as he opened the door
of the Buick—"if you want one for school."

"A cute little Ford, maybe; or a Dodge?"

What did my mother know about cars?

"They don't let students drive cars at Notre Dame." I climbed
in the backseat. Three-car family? Good God!

"The vets can drive them," Mom insisted.

"Only if they're married and live off campus."

"Maybe you should get married." Dad chuckled as he turned the
ignition.

"I'd rather walk."

I was still dazed as we pulled out of the Fort and turned south
on Green Bay Road.

"I thought I'd take Half Day Road west to Waukegan Road and
then down that till it becomes Harlem?"

He was asking for my approval of the route?

"You're the chauffeur."

"You'll just love the new house in Oak Park, dear." Mom turned
in the front seat to look at me, still not sure that I was really hers.
"You'll have a room all to yourself."

For the first time in my life.

Well, there was the room at the Bambergerhof.

"And a darkroom in the basement," Dad added. "All the latest
equipment."

"Great. I can hardly wait."

I told myself sternly that there was nothing tasteless in their display of wealth. Well, maybe two cars and the thought of a third was
a little tasteless.

"Is the airlift to Berlin going to work?" Dad asked, breaking the
silence and interrupting the thought that these two strangers might
look a little like my parents and sound a lot like them, but they were
not my parents.

"You bet," I said. "It finally gives the military something to do
besides hunting for an imaginary Nazi underground."

"Neither of you," Mom sighed, "have any respect for our leaders."

"The lucky thing for us, Mom, is that the Russian leaders are even more stupid. Give Americans a technical challenge and they are certain to rise to the occasion. Which reminds me, what's with the election? *Time* says it's Dewey in a walk."

"There's a little bias there." Dad turned onto Half Day Road, concrete where there had been gravel before the war. "Did you hear the Democratic convention on the radio?"

"No. They were jamming us into a C-54 for the trip home."

"I think Harry is going to give them so much hell that he'll win. People don't like Thomas E. Dewey. He's able enough, but they don't like his mustache and they don't like the impression he's giving that he's got it all wrapped up. Americans love the underdog; heaven knows Harry is the underdog."

"Everyone says the poor Mr. Dewey looks like a statue on a wedding cake." Mom laughed. "And really, he does."

"And my mother looks like a model." I leaned forward in the car and brushed her cheek with my lips.

"Don't exaggerate, Chucky," she warned with a complete lack of sincerity.

"You've improved at the art of compliment giving," Dad observed. "Of course no man ever is good enough at it!"

"The rest of the kids," he continued, "said that we should meet you and they'd wait at home."

Peg had said it and everyone had agreed. So, what else is new?

"Rosie will be over later on."

"So, what else is new!"

I would definitely not let her kiss me. On second thought, I would kiss her first, more vigorously than she would expect; and I'd play Nelson Eddy and sing Victor Herbert's "Rose of the World" to her. That would stop them all.

I would, in fact, kiss her twice.

Maybe three times.

"She's becoming a very lovely young woman, Chuck," my mother insisted. "Be nice to her."

"Maybe."

As we drove through Deerfield, Northbrook, Glenview, and Northfield, my eyes bulged at the new construction. Homes and businesses had appeared in places that I remembered only as vacant prairie.

"Is all the expansion here in the north suburbs?"

Dad chuckled. "I have a hard time remembering that when you left, we had shortages and price control. The answer to your question is that the growth is even more dramatic on the west and the south sides. It's the biggest building boom in American history. And, if one is to judge by the birth rate, it will continue for a long time."

"It's so different from Germany, even from England," I said slowly, remembering the pinched faces, the dull eyes, the hopeless slouch of shoulders.

"Are those poor people really so terribly poor?"

"Some of them just a notch above starvation, Mom. The Marshall Plan money is supposed to take care of that. Here we seem to have a head start. I suppose we'll arrive at the next depression before they do."

"There are some people," Dad spoke judiciously, weighing the evidence, "who think it won't happen for a while, maybe not so bad ever again. There were a lot of things people couldn't buy during the thirties—homes, cars, radios, fridges, boats, washers—because they didn't have the money. During the war they couldn't buy them because the products weren't being made. So now there's a big buildup of demand."

"And a lot more babies."

I tried to digest it. The economics courses I had taken in Bamberg admitted such a possibility. But no depression? Hadn't there always been one?

"Interesting thing about the word *depression*," Dad mused. "Hoover used it as an alternative to *recession*, which was supposed to be much worse. Now the words have the opposite meanings."

Not so long ago, the Depression was a reality that had blighted their lives, not a term to be pondered academically. The doctor's daughter and the politician's son had lost their home, their summer home, their parents, and almost everything they owned. They were forced to live with their four children in a small, crowded, drafty third-floor apartment. Mom had to carry dirty clothes down to the laundry tub in the basement. Dad earned twenty-two hundred dollars a year as an "assistant architect" at the Sanitary District. They had bought new clothes for themselves only every couple of years. They rode the el and the streetcars. Sometimes I had been sent to the store to buy twenty-seven cents worth of beef stew ground for supper. They never stopped laughing or singing, but lines of poverty and worry had been etched on their faces.

Now they owned two cars and a house in Oak Park and dressed like men and women in a fashion magazine.

Wonderful, but . . .

But what?

"I suppose the country has changed a lot since you went away to Europe?" Mom considered me anxiously, perhaps sensing my confusion.

"It sure has. For better or for worse?"

"Both, I think." She paused to consider. "More better than worse."

"It is no fun to be poor," Dad agreed.

I'd known we were poor. No one had told me, exactly, that we weren't poor anymore.

"A lot of people are making a lot of money," Mom continued. "Some of them think it's because they deserve to."

"Do we?"

"Deserve to?" Dad snorted. "Hell no, Chucky. Like most of the rest of them, we were lucky enough to come out of the Depression with our health and our skills. There's a lot of building, which means they need a lot of architects. Pure luck."

"The ship came in?" I asked.

They both laughed at the old promise from the Depression, as in "We'll buy a new bike for you, Chucky, when our ship comes in."

I ought to be happy about the ship, I told myself. And I suppose I am. But I can't quite believe any of this.

"The point is, Chucky," Dad went on, "we can afford to pay your Notre Dame tuition now."

"You won't have to. The GI Bill takes care of all my expenses."

I'd joined the Army to earn a college education. I could have saved myself the effort.

(And, though obviously I didn't know it then, I would have been drafted for Korea.)

"We'd like to help," Mom said softly.

"I appreciate that." I searched for the words. "You'll have to educate the other kids too."

"That's all taken care of."

"Buy war bonds then."

All of us laughed, more than a little nervously.

At Harlem and North we turned west. I hardly recognized North Avenue, too many new buildings, too many stores. Would I gawk at the new America for the rest of my life?

"Where are we going?"

"A surprise," they said in chorus.

We turned north on Thatcher. There were new homes everywhere in Elmwood Park and River Grove.

"A lot of these houses don't look like much," I observed.

"They're not. Thrown up in a hurry by developers who are making millions." Dad shook his head. "Everyone wants a home of their own."

"They're a lot nicer than the places in which these poor people used to live," Mom added.

"Some of the people in these homes didn't have indoor bathrooms in the old neighborhood." Dad turned off Thatcher to the right. "They think they're in paradise. And, mark my words, they'll keep up these homes like they're priceless treasure. Which maybe they are."

We passed under an arch of oak trees and through a wide green lawn. A big, elegant Tudor building awaited us.

"What's this?"

"Oak Park Country Club."

"*Wow!*"

"We thought you might like to eat your first civilian dinner here, dear."

"Whose membership are we using?"

As far as I could remember, we didn't have any friends who belonged to the club.

"Our own."

"What! They don't admit Catholics!"

"They do now." Dad beamed as we pulled up to the awning leading to the entrance.

"They wanted your father to design a renovation." Mom waited for the doorman to open the car. "And then they asked him to join."

"Good afternoon, Mrs. O'Malley . . . Colonel."

"Good afternoon, Mike. This is our son, uh, Charles. He's just returned from Germany."

The man bowed and smiled. "Good afternoon, Charles."

"Chuck." I winked at him and he winked back. We two members of the working class against the gentry.

"He plans to attend Notre Dame." Mom smiled proudly.

"Wonderful. My daughter will be going to Marquette next year."

Working-class kids don't go to Marquette. Or do they now?

Maybe I should return to Germany and start over again.

"Why didn't you join Butterfield, if you had to join a club?" I asked in a whisper as we entered the solemn sanctuary of the club. "Didn't we Catholics start that because they wouldn't let us in here?"

"Oh, we belong to Butterfield too."

"Your father thought it was important to break the religion barrier here." Mom removed her sunglasses and replaced them with clear glasses, also with white frames. "He plays golf at Butterfield most of the time."

"*Golf!*"

"Sure." Dad motioned for the maître d'. "I used to play before the Crash. Too busy with work now to play as much as I'd like."

"But his handicap is down to eight. Mine is fourteen."

"*Eight!*"

"This way, Colonel O'Malley. We have a table by the window for you. Lovely view of the sunset these days."

"*Colonel!*"

"You don't have to salute."

We were poor people. How dare we belong to two country clubs?

"The usual wine, Colonel?"

"No, Steven. Let's try some Château Lafitte tonight. We're celebrating our son's return from the service."

"*Rothschild!*"

There was nothing extravagant about the behavior of my parents, I reassured myself. They were not showing off. They were not recent new rich. I could have lived with that, I suppose. What troubled me was that they casually took it all for granted.

I ordered a fillet and disposed of it in perhaps two minutes.

"They're not going out of style, Chucky."

"Will they throw me out, Dad, if I ask for another?"

"Certainly not. More wine?"

"You bet." I remembered that I didn't drink. Well, it was a special day.

"There's something we want to discuss." Dad shifted uneasily.

"Your reaction is very important." Mom nodded.

I put down the wineglass. "Bad news?"

Peg, my beloved sibling, in trouble?

"Not at all."

"Good news really."

"We're thinking of building a summer home, Chuck."

"Huh?"

"Your father and I both think Grand Beach over in Michigan would be nice. For us and for the children and for the grandchildren too."

"Grandchildren?"

"Jane is getting a ring at Christmas."

"And someday not too far away, you and Peg will have kids too."

"Not me!"

We all laughed. My laugh was phony.

"But we know how much you like Lake Geneva. Maybe you'd like to raise your children there?"

"Me?"

"Grand Beach has a better future." Dad began to tick off reasons. "Not as crowded, better scenery, closer to Chicago, I've already designed some houses there, and over in Dune Acres and Beverly Shores—"

"But you can play golf here!"

"Do you want to play tomorrow, say four o'clock?"

"No . . . yes . . . maybe . . . I don't know!"

"If we build the house down at the lake"—Mom, who had spent her girlhood summers in the Indiana dunes, moved a fork nervously on the tablecloth—"we could always join Long Beach Country Club if you wanted to play golf down there."

Three clubs!

"The other kids"—Dad frowned uneasily—"say it's up to you. They know how much Lake Geneva means in your life."

Since when?

My mom and dad were asking my permission to build a summer home in the dunes.

"I don't care. Build it wherever you want."

I hadn't said that properly.

"We'd really like Lake Geneva just as much."

I took a deep breath. "Dad, don't you think it's dangerous to mix with the South Siders down there?"

"Dangerous?" He was puzzled.

"Sure, what if I fell in love with a girl from the South Side?"

"No point"—Dad grinned wickedly—"in repeating the same mistake in another generation, eh?"

"Precisely." I emptied my wineglass and held it out for a refill. Technically, I was still underage. Oh, well, the law did not apply inside the Oak Park Country Club.

"I think you're both terrible!"

So I kissed her again.

I had begun to understand. My parents were gentry. They'd grown up with money, not as much as they had now perhaps, but enough. In their thirties they suffered through the agonies of the Depression. Now it was over and they could revert to the values and the behaviors of their youth. For them the Depression was over.

I was a Depression baby. It would be with me for a long time, maybe all my life.

I had an honorable discharge from the Army of the United States. Mom and Dad had earned their honorable discharge from the Depression. Would I ever earn mine?